D1417338

193849

A Different Plain

Contemporary Nebraska Fiction Writers

Edited by Ladette Randolph

Introduction by Mary Pipher

University of Nebraska Press

LINCOLN & LONDON

Publication of this book was assisted by a grant from the Nebraska Arts Council

Acknowledgments for the use of previously published material appear on pages 391–92, which constitute an extension of the copyright page

Typeset in 10pt Adobe Minion by Kim Essman at the University of Nebraska Press. Book design by Richard Eckersley

♾

Library of Congress Cataloging-in-Publication Data
A different plain : contemporary Nebraska fiction writers / edited by Ladette Randolph; introduction by Mary Pipher.
p. cm.
ISBN 0-8032-3958-0 (cloth : alkaline paper) –
ISBN 0-8032-9002-0 (paper : alkaline paper)
1. American fiction – Nebraska.   2. Nebraska – Social life and customs – Fiction.
PS571.N2D54 2004 813.008'09782–dc22 2004000603

906-A
c.2

For the young writers of Nebraska

Contents

Editor's Note

LADETTE RANDOLPH

The writers gathered here are an impressive group by any definition. What comes as a surprise is that they are all associated with the state of Nebraska. These writers have all met the first requirement for inclusion in *A Different Plain*: they have published at least one book of fiction. The second requirement for inclusion is that the writers have either spent a significant period of their childhood or a formative time as a publishing writer in the state of Nebraska, or that they currently live and write there.

I am well aware of the many excellent contemporary fiction writers associated with Nebraska who are not included in this volume because they have not yet published their first book. Nor does space allow us to include fiction writers from previous generations, although their work continues to be important to the writers who carry on their legacy. By its nature such an anthology is one of omission as much as it is of inclusion. I am forced to omit the many talented nonfiction writers and poets associated with Nebraska as well. Their good work suggests future volumes.

The support and hard work of many people made this anthology possible. Thanks to Terence Smyre and Chad Ellsworth for being good sleuths and cheerful assistants from the beginning; to Kelly Grey, who spent hours in the library and even more hours reading and narrowing selections; and to Jeremy Hall, who made a potential permissions nightmare a dream, and who made much of the hard work of final preparation seem easy. Thanks as well to Gary Dunham for always being supportive, to Elizabeth Demers for her brilliance and her generosity, and to Margie Rine, for her enthusiasm about this project and her insights as a reader. Without them this would not have happened at all. Particular thanks to Hilda Raz, Mary Clearman Blew, and Mary Pipher, who saw what I wanted to do and helped me do it more completely. And finally, thanks to the generosity, the spirit of cooperation, and the kindness of all the contributors to this volume who always responded patiently to my queries and requests for help.

I am a fifth generation Nebraskan. I spent my childhood in the same section of rural Custer County where my great-grandfather was born and lived out his life. Despite these deep ties to the state, I did not read a single Nebraska writer until I was an undergraduate at the University of Nebraska, and then it was Willa Cather and only her Nebraska novels. I had spent all of my years growing up believing that no stories had ever sprung out of the place where I lived. It was not until years later, as a graduate student, that I discovered Cather's other novels. I then found other Nebraska fiction writers of note: Wright Morris, Tillie Olsen, Weldon Kees, Mari Sandoz, Jim Thompson, Bess Streeter Aldrich, and Dorothy Johnson.

In the process of reading Nebraska's past writers, I also found its contemporary writers. While some of these writers have spent their entire lives in the state, others spent only their youth in Nebraska before moving on. Others came for jobs or graduate school and then left again. Still others came and remained. Of these "transplants," some continue to write stories set exclusively in the place of their formative years – writers, in other words, who live in Nebraska but have not written a story set in the state. Does this mean they have not been influenced by the place in which they spend their days? Does it imply that there are no characteristics of their stories that have not been changed by a changed space? I like to believe, along with some literary theorists, that stories grow out of places and that we are affected, in ways we cannot always identify, by the spaces in which we live our lives.

Although over half of the stories collected here are set in Nebraska, it is not a Nebraska immediately identifiable by landscape or cityscape. Some stories are set just across the border in neighboring Wyoming or South Dakota. Other stories reflect the influence upon the writer of another place: Oregon, New York, Tucson, Texas. What these stories most share in common is not Nebraska's specific setting, but rather the sense of mobility that has characterized this country since its beginning, and mobility – perhaps more than anything – defines our life on the Great Plains. As if to underscore this fact, many of the stories in this collection involve cars, buses, and airplanes. Someone, it seems, is always going to or returning from somewhere. There is restlessness evident here, but not rootlessness. The sense of place is everywhere. It is as subtle as the landscape itself.

In addition, these are stories that reflect contemporary life in all its complexity: alternative lifestyles, murder, divorce, significant encounters with strangers, violence against women, adultery, responsibility for both aging parents and growing children, immigration, AIDS, car accidents, medical advances that outstrip our ethics, and radical life changes of all sorts. But these are also stories with enduring themes of love and betrayal, the search for meaning and happiness, the joys and troubles of families, the awkwardness of growing up, the complications of class identity, angst about life in a changing world, confusion over gender roles, complicated sexual identities, fear, and jealousy.

So, is there such a thing as a Nebraska voice? Is there something transformative about living on the plains beneath the great vault of the sky? Does the imaginative vision of these writers reflect the expansive horizons of Nebraska? Can you hear the relentless prairie wind in their voices? I could try to make a case that there is and that you can, but I will leave it to the reader to draw his or her own conclusions. Whatever else they are – and they are many things – these are Nebraska writers.

Introduction

MARY PIPHER

I am honored to introduce this collection of stories by writers I have long admired. The publication of this anthology is an important milestone in building Nebraska's literary community and sharing the fruits of that community with the world.

Editor Ladette Randolph has assembled this cornucopia of authors and stories. The pieces are fresh and sophisticated. Many have won critical acclaim and prestigious awards. The stories are not necessarily set in Nebraska or even in the Midwest. Nor is there uniformity of style. Rather the stories show the flowering of Nebraska writers with many points of view on the universe and diverse manners of self-expression. What unites the stories is their readability and high quality. Nebraska has produced many great writers – Willa Cather, Mari Sandoz, Wright Morris, and John Neihardt. This volume demonstrates that the literary legacy continues.

In Karen Shoemaker's "Playing Horses," the narrator, a girl from a street called Goat Alley says, "We weren't much and we knew it." This story exemplifies the power of this collection. On the surface it is a simple, albeit beautifully written, story of a young girl who be-friends another girl who shares her love of horses. But the narration is laced with revelations about growing up, time, friendship, and loss. The breathtaking closing lines of the story weave all of these themes together.

Dan Chaon's "I Demand To Know Where You Are Taking Me" also pyramids to an amazing ending. Set in Wyoming, the story tells of a woman's increasing frustration with the brutish and coarse men in her husband's family. It captures a woman's point of view in a world where tender, vulnerable things are crushed.

In "Dancing," by Kent Haruf, a man says, "I got tired of standing in front of the picture window, looking out at the wind blow dirt across the yard." The man leaves his wife and small town, but returns a year later. He sits in a bar, talks to a divorced woman and watches his ex-wife dance with other men. The elegantly simple plot explores the loneliness of marriage and the serial nature of coupling in modern times.

Jonis Agee's "Binding the Devil" is earthy and offbeat, full of surprises. Anna Monardo's, "Our Passion," a story about a nontraditional family, shimmers with humor and profundity. Marly Swick's "Crete" conveys a sense of place so strongly that, as I read it, I could envision the elevators and smell the cereal aroma of the Crete mills. Ron Block's "St. Anthony and the Fish," tells of a Pennsylvania nun who moves in with a bachelor farmer. Block manages to be hilarious and poignant at the same time. Of the farmer, he writes, "Nothing-to-do was like room temperature to him."

"Watermelon Days," by Tom McNeal, is an account of one day in the life of a young mother who, like most of us, feels both contentment and sorrow with her lot. Her ordinary summer day is sanctified by the quality of McNeal's attention. Brent Spencer's modern story, "The Last of the Nice," nails a certain kind of Midwestern man, one uneducated in, and almost morally opposed to, understanding his own feelings. At one point, the narrator thinks to himself plaintively, "I only wanted to be left alone. One day I got my wish."

Gerry Shapiro's brilliant story, "Bad Jews," reveals a man who learns little, even with the death of his father. Ron Hansen's story, "My Communist," Lisa Sandlin's, " 'Orita on the Road to Chamayo" and Richard Dooling's "Diary of an Immortal Man" offer us stylized, idiosyncratic voices. Judy Slater's "The Glass House" is an edgy, urban story about sophisticated people.

The diversity of places and topics makes this collection sparkle. Nebraska voices are not just rural, white, Christian or heterosexual. These authors give us postmodern slices of life and reports about moments and small turnings. They write of the pain of being misunderstood, the difficulties in finding a place, the loss of partners, and the weirdness of adult relationships. A surprising number of the stories explore men struggling to understand a world that overwhelms them with its complexity and nuance. Many of the stories involve pilgrimages, leaving on a quest, or searching for something that's been lost.

These stories resonate with each other in their depth of analysis about emotional, social, and moral issues. This is a volume of serious writers engaged in serious work. All of the weighty issues of the world are tackled by this group – love, choices, work, and forgiveness. The stories are provocative in their intelligence and energy. They unfurl with all the beauty of spring leaves. They manage to be both cutting edge and deeply familiar, as if written by one's closest friends. I invite you to delight in this blossoming of world-class writers from Nebraska.

A Different Plain

I Demand to Know Where You're Taking Me

DAN CHAON

Cheryl woke in the middle of the night and she could hear the macaw talking to himself – or laughing, rather, as if he had just heard a good joke. "Haw haw haw!" he went. "Haw haw haw": A perfect imitation of her brother-in-law, Wendell, that forced, ironic guffaw.

She sat up in bed and the sound stopped. Perhaps she had imagined it? Her husband, Tobe, was still soundly asleep next to her, but this didn't mean anything. He had always been an abnormally heavy sleeper, a snorer, and lately he had been drinking more before bed – he'd been upset ever since Wendell had gone to prison.

And she, too, was upset, anxious. She sat there, silent, her heart quickened, listening. Had the children been awakened by it? She waited, in the way she did when they were infants. Back then, her brain would jump awake. Was that a baby crying?

No, there was nothing. The house was quiet.

The bird, the macaw, was named Wild Bill. She had never especially liked animals, had never wanted one in her home, but what could be done? Wild Bill had arrived on the same day that Tobe and his other brothers, Carlin and Randy, had pulled into the driveway with a moving van full of Wendell's possessions. She'd stood there, watching as item after item was carried into the house, where it would remain, in temporary but indefinite storage. In the basement, shrouded in tarps, was Wendell's furniture: couch, kitchen set, bed, piano. There were his boxes of books and miscellaneous items, she didn't know what. She hadn't asked. The only things that she wouldn't allow were Wendell's shotguns. These were being kept at Carlin's place.

It might not have bothered her so much if it had not been for Wild Bill, who remained a constant reminder of Wendell's presence in her home. As she suspected, the bird's day-to-day care had fallen to her. It was she who made sure that Wild Bill had food and water, and it was she who cleaned away the excrement-splashed newspaper at the bottom of his cage.

But despite the fact that she was his primary caretaker, Wild Bill didn't seem to like her very much. Mostly, he ignored her – as if she were some kind of *wife*, a negligible figure whom he expected to serve him. He seemed to like the children best, and of course they were very attached to him as well. They liked to show him off to their friends, and to repeat his funny sayings. He liked to ride on their shoulders, edging sideways, lifting his wings lightly, for balance. Occasionally, as they walked around with him, he would laugh in that horrible way. "Haw, haw, haw!" he would squawk, and the children loved it.

But she herself was often uncomfortable with the things Wild Bill said. For example, he frequently said, "Hello, Sexy," to their eight-year-old daughter, Jodie. There was something lewd in the macaw's voice, Cheryl felt, a suggestiveness she found troubling. She didn't think it was appropriate for a child to hear herself called "sexy," especially since Jodie seemed to respond, blushing – flattered.

"Hello, Sexy," was, of course, one of Wendell's sayings, along with "Good God, Baby!" and "Smell my feet!" both of which were also part of Wild Bill's main repertoire. They had subsequently become catch phrases for her children. She'd hear Evan, their six-year-old, out in the yard, shouting "Good God, Baby!" and then mimicking that laugh. And even Tobe had picked up on the sophomoric retort "Smell my feet!" It bothered her more than she could explain. It was silly, but it sickened her, conjuring up a morbid fascination with human stink, something vulgar and tiring. They repeated it and repeated it until finally, one night at dinner, she'd actually slammed her hand down on the table. "Stop it!" she cried. "I can't stand it anymore. It's ruining my appetite!"

And they sat there, suppressing guilty grins. Looking down at their plates.

How delicate she was! How ladylike! How prudish!

But there was something else about the phrase, something she couldn't mention. It was a detail from the series of rapes that had occurred in their part of the state. The assaulted women had been attacked in their homes, blindfolded, a knife pressed against their skin. The first thing the attacker did was to force the women to kneel down and lick his bare feet. Then he moved on to more brutal things.

These were the crimes that Wendell had been convicted of, three months before. He had been convicted of only three of the six rapes he was accused of, but it was generally assumed that they had all been perpetrated by the same person. He was serving a sentence of no less than twenty-five years in prison, though his case was now beginning the process of appeals. He swore that he was innocent.

And they believed him – his family, all of them. They were all determined that Wendell would be exonerated, but it was especially important to Tobe, for Tobe had been Wendell's lawyer. Wendell had insisted upon it – "Who else could defend me better than my brother?" he'd said – and Tobe had finally given in, had defended Wendell in court, despite the fact that he was a specialist in family law, despite the fact that he had no experience as a criminal attorney. It was a "no-brainer" Tobe had said at the time. "No jury would believe it for a second." She had listened, nodding, as Tobe called the case flimsy, "a travesty," he said, "a bumbled investigation." And so it was a blow when the jury, after deliberating for over a week, returned a guilty verdict. Tobe had actually let out a small cry, had put his hands over his face, and he was still in a kind of dizzied state. He believed now that if he had only recused himself, Wendell would have been acquitted. It had affected him, it had made him strange and moody and distant. It frightened her – this new, filmy look in his eyes, the drinking, the way he would wander around the house, muttering to himself.

She felt a sort of hitch in her throat, a hitch in her brain. Here he was, laughing with Jodie and Evan, his eyes bright with amusement as she slammed her hand down. She didn't understand it. When the bird croaked, "Smell my feet," didn't Tobe make the same associations that she did? Didn't he cringe? Didn't he have the same doubts?

Apparently not. She tried to make eye contact with him, to plead her case in an exchange of gazes, but he would have none of it. He smirked into his hand, as if he was one of the children.

And maybe she was overreacting. A parrot! It was such a minor thing, wasn't it? Perhaps not worth bringing up, not worth its potential for argument. He stretched out in bed beside her and she continued to read her book, aware of the heaviness emanating from him, aware that his mind was going over and over some detail once again, retracing it, pacing around its circumference. In the past few months, it had become increasingly difficult to read him – his mood shifts, his reactions, his silences.

Once, shortly after the trial had concluded, she had tried to talk to him about it. "It's not your fault," she had told him. "You did the best you could."

She had been surprised at the way his eyes had narrowed, by the flare of anger, of pure scorn, which had never before been directed at her. "Oh, really?" he said acidly. "Whose fault is it, then? That an innocent man went to prison?" He glared at her, witheringly, and she took a step back. "Listen, Cheryl," he'd said. "You might not understand this, but this is my brother we're talking about. My little brother. Greeting card sentiments are not a fucking comfort to me." And he'd turned and walked away from her.

He'd later apologized, of course. "Don't ever talk to me that way again," she'd said, "I won't stand for it." And he agreed, nodding vigorously, he had been out of line, he was under a lot of stress and had taken it out on her. But in truth, an unspoken rift had remained between them in the months since. There was something about him, she thought, that she didn't recognize, something she hadn't seen before.

Cheryl had always tried to avoid the subject of Tobe's brothers. He was close to them, and she respected that. Both of Tobe's parents had died before Cheryl met him – the mother of breast cancer when Tobe was sixteen, the father a little more than a decade later, of cirrhosis – and this had knit them together. They were close in an old-fashioned way, like brothers in westerns or gangster films, touching in a way, though when she had first met them she never imagined what it would be like once they became fixtures in her life.

In the beginning, she had liked the idea of moving back to Cheyenne, Wyoming, where Tobe had grown up. The state, and the way Tobe had described it, had seemed romantic to her. He had come back to set up a small law office, with his specialty in family court. She had a degree in educational administration, and was able, without much trouble, to find a job as a guidance counselor at a local high school.

It had seemed like a good plan at the time. Her own family was scattered: a sister in Vancouver; a half-sister in Chicago, where Cheryl had grown up; her father, in Florida, was remarried to a woman about Cheryl's age, and had a four-year-old son, whom she could hardly think of as a brother; her mother, now divorced for a third time, lived alone on a houseboat near San Diego. She rarely saw or spoke to any of them, and the truth was that when they'd first moved to Cheyenne she had been captivated by the notion of a kind of homely happiness – family and neighbors and garden, all the mundane middle-class clichés, she knew, but it had secretly thrilled her. They had been happy for quite a while. It was true that she found Tobe's family a little backward. But at the time, they had seemed like mere curiosities, who made sweet, smart Tobe even sweeter and smarter, to have grown up in such an environment.

She thought of this again as the usual Friday night family gathering convened at their house, now sans Wendell, now weighed with gloom and concern, but still willing to drink beer and play cards or Monopoly and talk drunkenly into the night. She thought back because almost ten years had now passed, and she still felt like a stranger among them. When the children had been younger, it was easier to ignore, but now it seemed more and more obvious. She didn't belong.

She had never had any major disagreements with Tobe's family, but there had developed, she felt, a kind of unspoken animosity, perhaps simple indifference. To Carlin, the second oldest, Cheryl was, and would always remain, merely his brother's wife. Carlin was a policeman, crew-cutted, ruddy, with the face of a bully, and Cheryl couldn't ever remember having much of a conversation with him. To Carlin, she imagined, she was just another of the womenfolk, like his wife, Karissa, with whom she was often left alone. Karissa was a horrid little mouse of a woman with small, judgmental eyes. She hovered over the brothers as they ate and didn't sit down until she was certain everyone was served; then she hopped up quickly to offer a second helping or clear a soiled plate. There were times, when Karissa was performing her duties, that she regarded Cheryl with a glare of pure, self-righteous hatred. Though of course, Karissa was always "nice" – they would talk about children, or food, and Karissa would sometimes offer compliments. "I see you've lost weight," she'd say, or: "Your hair looks much better, now that you've got it cut!"

Cheryl might have liked Tobe's next brother, Randy – he was a gentle soul, she thought, but he was also a rather heavy drinker, probably an alcoholic. She'd had several conversations with Randy that had ended with him weeping, brushing his hand "accidentally" across the small of her back or her thigh; wanting to hug. She had long ago stopped participating in the Friday night card games, but Randy still sought her out, wherever she was trying to be unobtrusive. "Hey, Cheryl," he said, earnestly pressing his shoulder against the door frame. "Why don't you come and drink a beer with us?" He gave her his sad grin. "Are you being antisocial again?"

"I'm just enjoying my book," she said. She lifted it so he could see the cover, and he read aloud in a kind of dramatized way.

"*The House of Mirth*," he pronounced. "What is it? Jokes?" he said hopefully.

"Not really," she said. "It's about society life in old turn-of-the-century New York."

"Ah," he said. "You and Wendell could probably have a conversation about that. He always hated New York!"

She nodded. No doubt Wendell would have read *House of Mirth*, and would have an opinion of it that he would offer to her in his squinting, lopsided way. He had surprised her, at first, with his intelligence, which he masked behind a kind of exaggerated folksiness and that haw-hawing laugh. But the truth was, Wendell read widely, and he could talk seriously about any number of subjects if he wanted. She and Wendell had shared a love of books and music – he had once stunned her by sitting down at his piano and playing Debussy, then Gershwin, then an old Hank Williams song, which he sang along with in a modest, reedy tenor. There were times when it had seemed as if they could have been friends – and then, without warning, he would turn on her. He would tell her a racist joke, just to offend her; he would call her "politically correct" and would goad her with his far-right opinions, the usual stuff – gun control, feminism, welfare. He would get a certain look in his eyes, sometimes right in the middle of talking, a calculating, shuttered expression would flicker across his face. It gave her the creeps, perhaps even more now than before, and she put her hand to her mouth as Randy stood, still wavering, briefly unsteady, in the doorway. In the living room, Tobe and Carlin suddenly burst into laughter, and Randy's eyes shifted.

"I miss him," Randy said, after they had both been silently thoughtful for what seemed like a long while; he looked at her softly, as if she too had been having fond memories of Wendell. "I really miss him bad. I mean, it's like this family is cursed or something. You know?"

"No," she said, but not so gently that Randy would want to be patted or otherwise physically comforted. "It will be all right," she said firmly. "I honestly believe everything will turn out for the best."

She gave Randy a hopeful smile, but she couldn't help but think of the way Wendell would roll his eyes when Randy left the room to get another beer. "He's pathetic, isn't he?" Wendell had said, a few weeks before he was arrested. And he'd lowered his eyes, giving her that look. "I'll bet you didn't know you were marrying into white trash, did you?" he said, grinning in a way that made her uncomfortable. "Poor Cheryl!" he said. "Tobe fakes it really well, but he's still a stinky-footed redneck at heart. You know that, don't you?"

What was there to say? She was not, as Wendell seemed to think, from a background of privilege – her father had owned a dry-cleaning store. But at the same time, she had been comfortably sheltered. None of her relatives lived in squalor, or went to prison, or drank themselves daily into oblivion. She'd never known a man who got into fistfights at bars, as Tobe's father apparently had. She had never been inside a home as filthy as the one in which Randy lived.

But it struck her now that the trial was over, now that Randy stood, teary and boozy in her bedroom doorway. These men had been her husband's childhood companions – his brothers. He loved them. He *loved* them, more deeply than she could imagine. When they were to-gether, laughing and drinking, she could feel an ache opening inside her. If he had to make a choice, whom would he pick? Them or her?

In private, Tobe used to laugh about them. They were "characters," he said. He said, "You're so patient, putting up with all of their bullshit." And he kissed her, thankfully.

At the same time, he told her other stories. He spoke of a time when he was being abused by a group of high school bullies. Randy and Carlin had caught the boys after school, one by one, and "beat the living shit out of them." They had never bothered Tobe again.

He talked about Randy throwing himself into their mother's grave, as the casket was lowered, screaming "Mommy! Mommy!" and how the other brothers had to haul him out of the ground. He talked about how, at eleven or twelve, he was feeding the infant Wendell out of baby-food jars, changing his diapers. "After Mom got cancer, I practically raised Wendell," he told her once, proudly. "She was so depressed – I just remember her laying on the couch and telling me what to do. She wanted to do it herself, but she couldn't. It wasn't easy, you know. I was in high school, and I wanted to be out partying with the other kids, but I had to watch out for Wendell. He was a sickly kid. That's what I remember most. Taking care of him. He was only six when Mom finally died. It's weird. I probably wouldn't have even gone to college if I hadn't had to spend all that time at home. I didn't have anything to do but study."

The story had touched her, when they'd first started dating. Tobe was not – had never been – a very emotional or forthcoming person, and she felt she'd discovered a secret part of him.

Was it vain to feel a kind of claim over these feelings of Tobe's? To take a proprietary interest in his inner life, to think: "I am the only one he can really talk to?" Perhaps it was, but they'd had what she thought of as a rather successful marriage, up until the time of Wendell's conviction. There had been an easy, friendly camaraderie between them; they made love often enough; they both loved their children. They were normally happy.

But now – what? What was it? She didn't know. She couldn't tell what was going on in his head.

Winter was coming. It was late October, and all the forecasts predicted cold, months of ice and darkness. Having grown up in Chicago, she knew that this shouldn't bother her, but it did. She dreaded it, for it always brought her into a constant state of predepressive gloom, something Scandinavian and lugubrious, which she had never liked about herself. Already, she could feel the edges of it. She sat in her office, in the high school, and she could see the distant mountains out the window, growing paler and less majestic until they looked almost translucent, like oddly shaped thunderheads fading into the colorless sky. A haze settled over the city. College Placement Exam scores were lower than usual. A heavy snow was expected.

And Tobe was gone more than usual now, working late at night, preparing for Wendell's appeal. They had hired a new lawyer, one more experienced as a defense attorney, but there were still things Tobe needed to do. He would come home very late at night.

She hoped that he wasn't drinking too much but she suspected that he was. She had been trying not to pay attention, but she smelled alcohol on him nearly every night he came to bed; she saw the progress of the cases of beer in the refrigerator, the way they were depleted and replaced. "What's wrong?" she thought, waiting up for him, waiting for the sound of his car in the driveway. She was alone in the kitchen, making herself some tea, thinking, when Wild Bill spoke from his cage.

"Stupid cunt," he said.

She turned abruptly. She was certain that she heard the words distinctly. She froze, with the kettle in her hand over the burner, and when she faced him, Wild Bill cocked his head at her, fixing her with his bird eye. The skin around his eye was bare, whitish wrinkled flesh, which reminded her of an old alcoholic. He watched her warily, clicking his claws along the perch. Then he said, thoughtfully: "Hello, Sexy."

She reached into the cage and extracted Wild Bill's food bowl. He was watching, and she very slowly walked to the trash can. "Bad bird!" she said. She dumped it out – the peanuts and pumpkinseeds and bits of fruit that she'd prepared for him. "Bad!" she said again. Then she put the empty food bowl back into the cage. "There," she said. "See how you like that!" And she closed the cage with a snap, aware that she was trembly with anger.

It was Wendell's voice, of course: his words. The bird was merely mimicking, merely a conduit. It was Wendell, she thought, and she thought of telling Tobe; she was wide awake when he finally came home and slid into bed, her heart was beating heavily, but she just lay there as he slipped under the covers – he smelled of liquor, whiskey, she thought. He was already asleep when she touched him.

Maybe it didn't mean anything: Filthy words didn't make someone a rapist. After all, Tobe was a lawyer, and he believed that Wendell was innocent. Carlin was a policeman, and he believed it too. Were they so blinded by love that they couldn't see it?

Or was she jumping to conclusions? She had always felt that there was something immoral about criticizing someone's relatives, dividing them from those they loved, asking them to take sides. Such a person was her father's second wife, a woman of infinite nastiness and suspicion, full of mean, insidious comments about her stepdaughters. Cheryl had seen the evil in this, the damage it could do.

And so she had chosen to say nothing as Wendell's possessions were loaded into her house, she had chosen to say nothing about the macaw, even as she grew to loathe it. How would it look, demanding that they get rid of Wendell's beloved pet, suggesting that the bird somehow implicated Wendell's guilt? No one else seemed to have heard Wild Bill's foul sayings, and perhaps the bird wouldn't repeat them, now that she'd punished him. She had a sense of her own tenuous standing as a member of the family. They were still cautious of her. In a few brief moves, she could easily isolate herself – the bitchy city girl, the snob, the troublemaker. Even if Tobe didn't think this, his family would. She could imagine the way Karissa would use such stuff against her, that perky martyr smile as Wild Bill was remanded to her care, even though she was allergic to bird feathers. "I'll make do," Karissa would say. And she would cough, pointedly, daintily, into her hand.

Cheryl could see clearly where that road would lead.

But she couldn't help thinking about it. Wendell was everywhere – not only in the sayings of Wild Bill, but in the notes and papers Tobe brought home with him from the office, in the broody melancholy he trailed behind him when he was up late, pacing the house. In the various duties she found herself performing for Wendell's sake – reviewing her own brief testimony at the trial, at Tobe's request; going with Tobe to the new lawyer's office on a Saturday morning.

Sitting in the office, she didn't know why she had agreed to come along. The lawyer Tobe had chosen to replace him, Jerry Wasserman, was a transplanted Chicagoan who seemed even more out of place in Cheyenne than she did, despite the fact that he wore cowboy boots. He had a lilting, iambic voice, and was ready to discuss detail after detail. She frowned, touching her finger to her mouth as Tobe and his brothers leaned forward intently. What was she doing here?

"I'm extremely pleased by the way the appeal is shaping up," Wasserman was saying. "It's clear that the case had some setbacks, but to my mind the evidence is stronger than ever in your brother's favor." He cleared his throat. "I'd like to outline three main points for the judge, which I think will be quite – quite! – convincing."

Cheryl looked over at Karissa, who was sitting very upright in her chair, with her hands folded and her eyes wide, as if she were about to be interrogated. Carlin shifted irritably.

"I know we've talked about this before," Carlin said gruffly. "But I still can't get over the fact that the jury that convicted him was seventy-five percent female. I mean, that's something we ought to be talking about. It's just – it's just wrong, that's my feeling."

"Well," said Wasserman. "The jury selection is something we need to discuss, but it's not at the forefront of the agenda. We have to get through the appeals process first." He shuffled some papers in front of him, guiltily. "Let me turn your attention to the first page of the document I've given you, here . . ."

How dull he was, Cheryl thought, looking down at the first page, which had been photocopied from a law book. How could he possibly be more passionate or convincing than Tobe had been, in the first trial? Tobe had been so fervent, she thought, so certain of Wendell's innocence. But perhaps that had not been the best thing.

Maybe his confidence had worked against him. She remembered the way he had declared himself to the jury, folding his arms. "This is a case without evidence," he said. "Without *any* physical evidence!" And he had said it with such certainty that it had seemed true. The crime scenes had yielded nothing that had connected Wendell to the crimes; the attacker, whoever he was, had been extremely careful. There was no hair, no blood, no semen. The victims had been made to kneel in the bathtub as the attacker forced them to perform various degrading acts, and afterwards, the attacker had left them there, turning the shower on them as he dusted and vacuumed. There wasn't a single fingerprint.

But there was this: In three of the cases, witnesses claimed to have seen Wendell's pickup parked on a street nearby. A man matching Wendell's description had been seen hurrying down the fire escape behind the apartment of one of the women.

And this: The final victim, Jenni Martinez, had been a former girlfriend of Wendell. Once, after they'd broken up, Wendell got drunk and sang loud love songs beneath her window. He'd left peaceably when the police came.

"Peaceably!" Tobe noted. These were the actions of a romantic, not a rapist! Besides which, Wendell had an alibi for the night the Martinez girl was raped. He'd been at Cheryl and Tobe's house, playing cards, and he'd slept that night on their sofa. In order for him to have committed the crime, he'd have had to feign sleep, sneaking out from under the bedding Cheryl had arranged for him on the living room sofa, without being noticed. Then, he'd have had to sneak back into the house, returning in the early morning so that Cheryl would discover him when she woke up. She had testified: He was on the couch, the blankets twisted around him, snoring softly. She was easily awakened; she felt sure that she would have heard if he'd left in the middle of the night. It was, Tobe told the jury, "a highly improbable, almost fantastical version of events."

But the jury had believed Jenni Martinez, who was certain that she'd recognized his voice. His laugh. They had believed the prosecutor, who had pointed out that there had been no more such rapes since Jenni Martinez had identified Wendell. After Wendell's arrest, the string of assaults had ceased.

After a moment, she tried to tune back in to what Wasserman was saying. She ought to be paying attention. For Tobe's sake, she ought to be trying to examine the possibility of Wendell's innocence more rationally, without bias. She read the words carefully, one by one. But what she saw was Wendell's face, the way he'd looked as one of the assaulted women had testified: bored, passive, even vaguely amused as the woman had tremulously, with great emotion, recounted her tale.

Whatever.

That night, Tobe was once again in his study, working as she sat on the couch, watching television. He came out a couple of times, waving to her vaguely as he walked through the living room, toward the kitchen, toward the refrigerator, another beer.

She waited up. But when he finally came into the bedroom he seemed annoyed that she was still awake, and he took off his clothes silently, turning off the light before he slipped into bed, a distance emanating from him. She pressed her breasts against his back, her arms wrapped around him, but he was still. She rubbed her feet against his, and he let out a slow, uninterested breath.

"What are you thinking about," she said, and he shifted his legs.

"I don't know," he said. "Thinking about Wendell again, I suppose."

"It will be all right," she said, though she felt the weight of her own dishonesty settle over her. "I know it." She smoothed her hand across his hair.

"You're not a lawyer," he said. "You don't know how badly flawed the legal system is."

"Well," she said.

"It's a joke," he said. "I mean, the prosecutor didn't prove his case. All he did was parade a bunch of victims across the stage. How can you compete with that? It's all drama."

"Yes," she said. She kissed the back of his neck, but he was already drifting into sleep, or pretending to. He shrugged against her arms, nuzzling into his pillow.

One of the things that had always secretly bothered her about Wendell was his resemblance to Tobe. He was a younger, and – yes, admit it – sexier version of her husband. The shoulders, the legs; the small hardness of her husband's mouth that she had loved was even better on Wendell's face, that sly shift of his gray eyes, which Wendell knew was attractive, while Tobe did not. Tobe tended toward pudginess, while Wendell was lean, while Wendell worked on mail-order machines, which brought out the muscles of his stomach. In the summer, coming in from playing basketball with Tobe in the driveway, Wendell had almost stunned her, and she recalled her high school infatuation with a certain athletic shape of the male body. She watched as he bent his naked torso toward the open refrigerator, looking for something to drink. He looked up at her, his eyes slanted cautiously as he lifted a can of grape soda to his lips.

Stupid Cunt. It gave her a nasty jolt, because that was what his look said – a brief but steady look that was so full of leering scorn that her shy fascination with his muscled stomach seemed suddenly dirty, even dangerous. She had felt herself blushing with embarrassment.

She had not said anything to Tobe about it. There was nothing to say, really. Wendell hadn't *done* anything, and in fact he was always polite when he spoke to her, even when he was confronting her with his "beliefs." He would go into some tirade about some issue that he held dear – gun control, or affirmative action, etcetera, and then he would turn to Cheryl, smiling: "Of course, I suppose there are differences of opinion," he would say, almost courtly. She remembered him looking at her once, during one of these discussions, his eyes glinting with some withheld emotion. "I wish I could think like you, Cheryl," he said. "I guess I'm just a cynic, but I don't believe that people are good, deep down. Maybe that's my problem." Later, Tobe told her not to take him seriously. "He's young," Tobe would say, rolling his eyes. "I don't know where he comes up with this asinine stuff. But he's got a good heart, you know."

Could she disagree? Could she say, no, he's actually a deeply hateful person?

But the feeling didn't go away. Instead, as the first snow came in early November, she was aware of a growing unease. With daylight-saving time, she woke in darkness, and when she went downstairs to make coffee, she could sense Wild Bill's silent, malevolent presence. He ruffled his feathers when she turned on the light, cocking his head so he could stare at her with the dark bead of his eye. By that time, she and Tobe had visited Wendell in prison, once, and Tobe was making regular, weekly phone calls to him. On Jodie's birthday, Wendell had sent a handmade card, a striking, pen-and-ink drawing of a spotted leopard in a jungle, the twisted vines above him spelling out, "Happy Birthday, Sweet Jodie." It was, she had to admit, quite beautiful, and must have taken him a long time. But why a leopard? Why was it crouched as if hunting, its tail a snakelike whip? There was a moment, going through the mail, when she'd seen Jodie's name written in Wendell's careful, spiked cursive, that she'd almost thrown the letter away.

There was another small incident that week. They were sitting at dinner. She had just finished serving up a casserole she'd made, which reminded her, nostalgically, of her childhood. She set Evan's plate in front of him and he sniffed at the steam that rose from it.

"Mmmm," he said. "Smells like pussy."

"Evan!" she said. Her heart shrank, and she flinched again when she glanced at Tobe, who had his hand over his mouth, trying to hold back a laugh. He widened his eyes at her.

"Evan, where on earth did you hear something like that?" she said, and she knew that her voice was too confrontational, because the boy looked around guiltily.

"That's what Wild Bill says, when I give him his food," Evan said. He shrugged, uncertainly. "Wild Bill says it."

"Well, son," Tobe said. He had recovered his composure, and gave Evan a serious face. "That's not a nice thing to say. That's not something that Wild Bill should be saying, either."

"Why not?" Evan said. And Cheryl had opened her mouth to speak, but then thought better of it. She would do more damage than good, she thought.

"It's just something that sounds rude," she said at last.

"Dad," Evan said. "What does 'pussy' mean?"

Cheryl and Tobe exchanged glances.

"It means a cat," Tobe said, and Evan's face creased with puzzlement for a moment.

"Oh," Evan said at last. Tobe looked over at her, and shrugged.

Later, after the children were asleep, Tobe said, "I'm really sorry, Honey."

"Yes," she said. She was in bed, trying hard to read a novel, though she felt too unsettled. She watched as he chuckled, shaking his head. "Good God!" He said with amused exasperation. "Wendell can be such an asshole. I thought I would die when Evan said that." After a moment, he sat down on the bed and put his fingers through his hair. "That stupid Playboy stuff," he said. "We're lucky the bird didn't testify."

He meant this as a joke, and so she smiled. Oh, Tobe, she thought, for she could feel, even then, his affection for his younger brother. He was already making an anecdote to tell to Carlin and Randy, who would find it hilarious. She closed her eyes as Tobe put the back of his fingers to her earlobe, stroking.

"Poor baby," he said. "What's wrong? You seem really depressed lately."

After a moment, she shrugged. "I don't know," she said. "I guess I am."

"I'm sorry," he said. "I know I've been really distracted, with Wendell and everything."

She watched as he sipped thoughtfully from the glass of beer he'd brought with him. Soon, he would disappear into his office, with the papers he had to prepare for tomorrow.

"It's not you," she said, after a moment. "Maybe it's the weather," she said.

"Yeah," Tobe said. He gave her a puzzled look. For he knew that there was a time when she would have told him, she would have plunged ahead, carefully but deliberately, until she had made her points. That was what he had expected.

But now she didn't elaborate. Something – she couldn't say what – made her withdraw, and instead she smiled for him. "It's okay," she said.

Wild Bill had begun to molt. He would pull out his own feathers, distractedly, and soon his gray, naked flesh was prominently visible in patches. His body was similar to the Cornish game hens she occasionally prepared, only different in that he was alive, and not fully plucked. The molting, or something else, made him cranky, and as Thanksgiving approached, he was sullen and almost wholly silent, at least to her. There were times, alone with him in the kitchen, that she would try to make believe that he was just a bird, that nothing was wrong. She would turn on the television, to distract her, and Wild Bill would listen, absorbing every line of dialogue.

They were alone again together, she and Wild Bill, when Wendell called. It was the second day in less than two weeks that she'd called in sick to work, that she'd stayed in bed, dozing, until well past eleven. She was sitting at the kitchen table, brooding over a cup of tea, a little guilty because she was not really ill. Wild Bill had been peaceful, half-asleep, but he ruffled his feathers and clicked his beak as she answered the phone.

At first, when he spoke, there was simply an unnerving sense of dislocation. He used to call her, from time to time, especially when she and Tobe were first married. "Hey," he'd say, "How's it going?" and then a long silence would unravel after she said, "Fine," the sound of Wendell thinking, moistening his lips, shaping unspoken words with his tongue. He was young back then, barely twenty when she was pregnant with Jodie, and she used to expect his calls, even look forward to them, listening as he hesitantly began to tell her about a book he'd read, or asking her to listen as he played the piano, the tiny sound blurred through the phone line.

This was what she thought of at first, this long ago time when he was still just a kid, a boy with, she suspected, a kind of crush on her. This was what she thought of when he said, "Cheryl?" hesitantly, and it took her a moment to calibrate her mind, to span the time and events of the last eight years and realize that here he was now, a convicted rapist, calling her from prison. "Cheryl?" he said, and she stood over the dirty dishes in the sink, a single Lucky Charm stuck to the side of one of the children's cereal bowls.

"Wendell?" she said, and she was aware of a kind of watery dread filling her up – her mouth, her nose, her eyes. "Where are you?" she said, and he let out a short laugh.

"I'm in jail," he said. "Where did you think?"

"Oh," she said, and she heard his breath through the phone line, could picture the booth where he was sitting, the little room that they'd sat in when they'd visited, the elementary school colors, the mural of a rearing mustang with mountains and lightning behind it.

"So," he said. "How's it going?"

"It's going fine," she said – perhaps a bit too stiffly. "Are you calling for Tobe? Because he's at his office . . ."

"No," Wendell said, and he was silent for a moment, maybe offended at her tone. She could sense his expression tightening, and when he spoke again there was something hooded in his voice. "Actually," he said, "I was calling for you."

"For me?" she said, and her insides contracted. She couldn't imagine how this would be allowed – that he'd have such freedom with the phone – and it alarmed her. "Why would you want to talk to me?" she said, and her voice was both artificially breezy and strained. "I . . . I can't do anything for you."

Silence again. She put her hand into the soapy water of the sink and began to rub the silverware with her sponge, her hands working as his presence descended into her kitchen.

"I've just been thinking about you," he said, in the same hooded, almost sinuous way. "I was . . . thinking about how we used to talk, you know, when you and Tobe first moved back to Cheyenne. I used to think that you knew me better than anybody else. Did you know that? Because you're smart. You're a lot smarter than Tobe, you know, and the rest of them – Randy, Carlin, that stupid . . . moron, Karissa. Jesus! I used to think *What is she doing here? What is she doing in this family?* I guess that's why I've always felt weirdly close to you. You were the one person – " he said, and she waited for him to finish his sentence, but he didn't. He seemed to loom close, a voice from nearby, floating above her, and she could feel her throat constricting. What? she thought, and she had an image of Jenni Martinez, her wrists bound, tears leaking from her blindfold. He would have spoken to her this way, soft, insidious, as if he were regretfully blaming her for his own emotions.

"Wendell," she said, and tried to think of what to say. "I think . . . it must be very hard for you right now. But I don't know that . . . I'm really the person. I certainly don't think that I'm the *one* person, as you say. Maybe you should talk to Tobe?"

"*No*," he said, suddenly and insistently. "You just don't understand, Cheryl. You don't know what it's like – in a place like this. It doesn't take you long to sort out what's real and what's not, and to know – the right person to talk to. Good God!" he said, and it made her stiffen because he sounded so much like Wild Bill. "I remember so much," he said. "I keep thinking about how I used to give you shit all the time, teasing you, and you were just so . . . calm, you know. Beautiful and calm. I remember you said once that you thought the difference between us was that you really believed that people were good at heart, and I didn't. Do you remember? And I think about that. It was something I needed to listen to, and I didn't listen."

She drew breath – because she *did* remember – and she saw now clearly the way he had paused, the stern, shuttered stare as he looked at her, the way he would seek her out on those Friday party nights, watching and grinning, hoping to get her angry. Her hands clenched as she thought of the long, intense way he would listen when she argued with him. She worked with high school boys who behaved this way all the time – why hadn't she seen? "Wendell," she said. "I'm sorry, but . . ." And she thought of the way she used to gently turn away certain boys – *I don't like you in that way. I just want to be friends* . . . It was ridiculous, she thought, and wondered if she should just hang up the phone. How was it possible that they could let him call her like this, unmonitored? She was free to hang up, of course, that's what the authorities assumed. But she didn't. "I'm sorry," she said again. "Wendell, I think . . . I think . . ."

"No," he said. "Don't say anything. I know I shouldn't say this stuff to you. Because Tobe's my brother, and I *do* love him, even if he's a shitty lawyer. But I just wanted to hear your voice. I mean, I never would have said anything to you if it wasn't for being here and thinking – I can't help it – thinking that things would be different for me if we'd . . . if something had happened, and you weren't married. It could have been really different for me."

"No," she said, and felt a vaguely nauseous, surreal wavering passing through the room. A bank of clouds uncovered the sun for a moment, and the light altered. Wild Bill edged his clawed toes along his perch. "Listen, Wendell. You shouldn't do this. You were right to keep this to yourself, these feelings. People think these things all the time, it's natural. But we don't act on them, do you see? We don't – "

She paused, pursing her lips, and he let out another short laugh. There was a raggedness that sent a shudder across her.

"Act!" he said. "Jesus Christ, Cheryl, there's no *acting* on anything. You don't think I'm fooling myself into thinking this appeal is going to amount to anything, do you? I'm stuck here, you know that. For all intents and purposes, I'm not going to see you again for twenty years – if I even live that long. I just – I wanted to talk to you. I guess I was wondering if, considering the situation, if I called you sometimes. Just to talk. We can set . . . boundaries, you know, if you want. But I just wanted to hear your voice. I think about you all the time," he said. "Day and night."

She had been silent for a long time while he spoke, recoiling in her mind from the urgency of his voice and yet listening steadily. Now that he had paused she knew that she should say something. She could summon up the part of herself that was like a guidance counselor at school, quick and steady, explaining to students that they had been expelled, that their behavior was inappropriate, that their SAT scores did not recommend college, that thoughts of suicide were often a natural part of adolescence but should not be dwelled upon. She opened her mouth, but this calm voice did not come to her, and instead she merely held the phone, limp and damp against her ear.

"I'll call you again," he said. "I love you," he said, and she heard him hang up.

In the silence of her kitchen, she could hear the sound of her pulse in her ears. It was surreal, she thought, and she crossed her hands over her breasts, holding herself. For a moment, she considered picking up the phone and calling Tobe at his office. But she didn't. She had to get her thoughts together.

She gazed out the window uncertainly. It was snowing hard now; thick white flakes drifted along with the last leaves of the trees. Something about Wendell's voice, she thought restlessly, and the fuzzy lights of distant cars seemed to shudder in the blur of steady snow. Her hands were shaking, and after a time, she got up and turned on the television, flicking through some channels: a game show, a talk show; an old black-and-white movie.

She could see him now very clearly, as a young man, the years after they'd first moved back to Wyoming – the way he would come over to their house, lolling around on the couch in his stocking feet, entertaining the infant Jodie as Cheryl made dinner, his eyes following her. And the stupid debates they used to have, the calculated nastiness of his attacks on her, the way his gaze would settle on her when he would play piano and sing to them. Wasn't that the way boys acted when they were trying not to be in love? Could she really have been so unaware, and yet have still played into it? *What is she doing in this family?* Wendell had said. She tried to think again, but something hard and knuckled had settled itself in her stomach. "My God," she said. "What am I going to do?" Wild Bill turned his head from the television, cocking his head thoughtfully, his eyes sharp and observant.

"Well?" she said to him. "What *am* I going to do?"

He said nothing. He looked at her for a little longer, then lifted his pathetic, molting wings, giving them a shake. "What a world, what a world," he said, mournfully.

This made her smile. It was not something she'd heard him say before, but she recognized it as a quote from *The Wizard of Oz*, which Wendell used to recite sometimes. It was what the Wicked Witch of the West said when she melted away, and a heaviness settled over her as she remembered him reciting it, clowning around during one of the times when they were just making conversation – when he wasn't trying to goad her. There were those times, she thought. Times when they might have been friends. "Yes," she said to Wild Bill. "What a world."

"Whatever," Wild Bill said; but he seemed to respond to her voice, or to the words that she spoke, because he gave a sudden flutter and dropped from his perch onto the table – which he would sometimes do for the children, but never for her, not even when she was eating fruit. She watched as he waddled cautiously toward her, his claws clicking lightly. She would have scolded the children: *Don't let that bird on the table, don't feed him from the table,* but she held out a bit of toast crust, and he edged forward.

"It's not going to work," she told Wild Bill, as he nipped the piece of toast from her fingers. "It's not," she said, and Wild Bill observed her sternly, swallowing her bread. He opened his beak, his small black tongue working.

"What?" she said, as if he could advise her, but he merely cocked his head.

"Stupid cunt," he said gently, decisively, and her hand froze over her piece of toast, recoiling from the bit of crust that she'd been breaking off from him. She watched the bird's mouth open again, the black tongue, and a shudder ran through her.

"No!" she said. "No! Bad!" She felt her heart contract, the weight hanging over her suddenly breaking, and she caught Wild Bill in her hands. She meant to put him back in his cage, to throw him in, without food or water, but when her hands closed over his body he bit her, hard. His beak closed over the flesh of her finger and he held on when she screamed; he clutched at her forearm with his claws when she tried to pull back, and she struck at him as he flapped his wings, her finger still clutched hard in his beak.

"You piece of filth!" she cried. Tears came to her eyes as she tried to shake loose, but he kept his beak clenched, and his claws raked her arm. He was squawking angrily, small feathers flying off him, still molting as he beat his wings against her, the soundtrack of some old movie swelling melodramatically from the television. She slapped his body against the frame of the kitchen door, and he let loose for a moment before biting down again on her other hand. "Bastard!" she screamed, and she didn't even remember opening the door until the cold air hit her. She struck him hard with the flat of her hand, flailing at him, and he fell to the snow-dusted cement of the back porch, fluttering. "Smell my feet!" he rasped, and she watched as he stumbled through the air, wavering upward until he lit upon the bare branch of an elm tree in their back yard. His bright colors stood out against the gray sky, and he looked down on her vindictively. He lifted his back feathers and let a dollop of shit fall to the ground. After a moment, she closed the back door on him.

It took a long time for him to die. She didn't know what she was thinking as she sat there at the kitchen table, her hands tightened against one another. She couldn't hear what he was saying, but he flew repeatedly against the window, his wings beating thickly against the glass. She could hear his body thump softly, like a snowball, the tap of his beak. She didn't know how many times. It became simply a kind of emphasis to the rattle of the wind, to the sound of television that she was trying to stare at.

She was trying to think, and even as Wild Bill tapped against the glass, she felt that some decision was coming to her – that some firm resolve was closing its grip over her even as Wild Bill grew quiet. He tapped his beak against the glass, and when she looked she could see him cocking his eye at her, a blank black bead peering in at her – she couldn't tell whether he was pleading or filled with hatred. He said nothing, just stared as she folded her arms tightly in front of her, pressing her forearms against her breasts. She was trying to think, trying to imagine Tobe's face as he came home from work, the way he would smile at her and she would of course smile back, the way he would look into her eyes, long and hard, inscrutably, the way Wild Bill was staring at her now. Are you okay, he would say, and he wouldn't notice that Wild Bill was gone, not until later. I don't know, she would say. I don't know what happened to him.

The rich lady on television was being kidnapped, as Wild Bill slapped his wings once more, weakly, against the window. Cheryl watched intently, though the action on the screen seemed meaningless. "How dare you!" the rich lady cried, as she was hustled along a corridor. Cheryl stared at the screen as a thuggish actor pushed the elegant woman forward.

"I demand to know where you're taking me," the elegant woman said desperately, and when Cheryl looked up Wild Bill had fallen away from his grip on the windowsill.

"You'll know soon enough, Lady," the thug said. "You'll know soon enough."

Playing Horses

KAREN SHOEMAKER

The first time Bobbi came back for a visit, my mother warned me she might have outgrown me. "She might have matured faster than you did," were her exact words. I was helping her hang the wash on the line that stretched across the back yard when she told me this. As always, I was in charge of clothespins. I straddled a little red wagon and scootched along behind her, imagining the wagon a prairie schooner and the wet clothes around me canyon walls. I didn't answer her. I just handed her another clothespin and thought about Bobbi's visit.

In her last letter she had told me she was going to bring pictures of the horses in the field across from her house.

"I wake up every morning and first thing I do is look out and see them in the field. I always pretend that the palomino is mine and the big black one is yours because I know how much you like black horses," she had written. She didn't sound any different than when she left. Even though my mom said she probably was a whole lot more grown up than I was, I went on planning her visit as if she was still my best friend. Just like she had been when she moved away.

The neighborhood where Bobbi and I had been friends was full of kids but few friends. My family lived in a rundown house with big yard that wrapped around the last house on the block like the cookie that's left after the bite. On one side we looked toward a trailer court, on the other toward rentals in varying degrees of disrepair. Both of those views were superior to what adjoined us on the north. On that side, across a narrow alley, was our little town's little slum. Nine or ten houses on one block that we all called, for reasons that still escape me, "Goat Alley." We were better than *anybody* on that street, and on the other streets most people moved in and out so fast we hardly had time to get to know them.

Only three families stayed in our neighborhood for any length of time and we had something like sixteen or seventeen kids between us. The neighborhood felt full and we all felt we belonged to something bigger than ourselves. We weren't much. We didn't love each other intensely or even like each other all that much all the time. But we were familiar to one another and that seemed to count for something. When the chill wind of winter blew into town we knew we could count on one another to show up next summer for the next baseball season. We could trust one another to remember who hit a home run and who had to climb over Old Man Ogden's fence to retrieve the lucky ball.

On the other hand, rental people came and went in no discernible pattern, and you couldn't be sure they would be there next week much less next season, so what was the point of them? You might play hide and seek with them some evening, or let them in on neighborhood games just to even up sides when necessary, but if push came to shove, it was us against them. We were a team and no rental kid was going to get in on that solid front. We even made up a rule just so they would know their place. We said, loudly and often, that you couldn't be a *real* neighbor until you had lived in your house for five years.

Okay, so we weren't much and we knew it. There's an ugliness that comes with that kind of knowing. It wasn't that we had a leader we followed into trouble, it was that we didn't and so we sometimes followed a base instinct to be better than something. If it hadn't been rental kids it would have been something else. Each other maybe. Probably.

All our parents worked during the day. In the early days of the neighborhood there may have been some kind of day care arrangements, but by the time I came along the authority figure in most households was an older brother or sister. If we were alive at the end of the day they had lived up to their responsibility. Once, on one of those long unsupervised days, my brother and one of the neighbor boys decided they didn't want us girls playing in the same yard they were in. They told us to "Get out or die."

Mary and Lucy yelled a few names at them, used words they shouldn't have even known, but they did it over their shoulders on their way to another yard. I don't know if I was being stupid that day or rebellious or what, but I said no, I wasn't going anywhere. We were there first.

"Anyway, it's my yard and you can't make me leave," I said. I sat down on the grass to prove my point.

The boys just looked at each other and laughed. They didn't say anything to each other. They just knew what to do.

My brother grabbed one ankle and the neighbor boy grabbed the other.

"You're gonna wish you left when you had the chance," one of them said. Then they took off running.

I wasn't much more than nine at the time and my little girl body wasn't much weight for two teenage boys. They ran through the garden where last year's cornstalks stuck up from the ground like spikes. They didn't slow down until they got to the gravel driveway and then only because they were laughing so hard they couldn't run anymore. I screamed the whole time and that seemed to make it funnier.

When I rolled over to stand up the sight of my bloody back scared them into silence.

"Oh shit, we're dead," one of them said finally and then the neighbor boy took off as if there was someplace to hide in this neighborhood.

My brother knew there was no where to go and at first he just stood there staring at me, saying, "Oh shit oh shit oh shit oh shit."

I know it was fear of the punishment in store for him that made him help me into the house, but I also know there was remorse, kindness even, in his touch when he washed my back, carefully wiping away the mud, cleaning the cuts with peroxide. He kept saying, "I'm sorry. I'm sorry." And I kept crying. "It hurts. It hurts."

Maybe I would have forgiven him. He looked so sorry standing there with that bloody wash cloth in his hand and his touch on my back was so soft it felt like love. But when I turned around and gingerly pulled my shirt down he said, "Don't tell Dad." Just because it feels like love doesn't mean it is.

I did tell Dad, and when my brother got the belt that night I plugged my ears and didn't cry. My dad couldn't do anything about the neighbor boy, but the boy didn't know that. He stayed away from our house for a month after that.

Like I said, we weren't much, and we knew it. But we weren't rental kids either, so we had something to stand on. Looking back at all this, at the run-down state of all our houses and the little secrets we hid behind closed doors, it is downright shocking that we had the gall to affect snobbishness.

But affect it we did, and that's the world Bobbi dropped into when her mom and dad dropped their double wide in the corner of what was supposed to be our baseball field. No one in the neighborhood was going to ever forgive the Kellers for messing up a perfectly good baseball field, and until that summer I didn't know I could do anything different than what the neighborhood did. For three whole weeks after they moved in, Mary, Lucy, and I made a point of not playing with Bobbi. We played right in front of her house just so she would know we weren't playing with her. We would take sticks out of her yard to draw hopscotch squares in the dirt road in front of her house. When suppertime came we threw our stones into her yard like so much trash. I can still see her small white face peering out the window at us. Watching while we pretended she didn't exist.

It would be easy to paint Bobbi as some kind of savior in this scene, some kind of second – better – part of me, but that wouldn't be completely honest. She was just a girl my age that lived near me for awhile. In the way of proximity we became friends, in the way of young girls we became Best Friends.

I'm not sure where Mary and Lucy were that day I first talked to Bobbi. I just remember that I was alone and I was doing what I always did when no one was around – I was pretending to be a wild horse.

After all these years I can still recall how *real* my imagination made this game. Words just aren't enough to explain it and saying it now makes me laugh, but back then it was serious business. Our yard, the biggest in the neighborhood and with the most trees, was big enough to hold a tropical island, a mountain range, and high plains so wide you couldn't walk from one side to the other in a day's time. I didn't need Mary or Lucy. I didn't need anybody. I was a wild stallion, the fastest, strongest, wildest, most beautiful wild stallion that ever walked the earth. As a little girl I was timid and clumsy, but when I became a horse I became everything I ever knew about power and freedom.

Sometimes even now, when the late afternoon light is slanting just so across green space or through trees I can remember just exactly what it felt like to take on that magic. I can close my eyes, breathe deeply and feel my velvety nostrils flare, picking up the scent of danger, freedom.

That day, alone in my yard, in the small part between the house on the corner and the alley, I was running from wolves when suddenly I saw Bobbi across the street. She was leaping across fallen trees and dodging branches. She stopped and at first I thought she was looking at me, but then I realized she didn't see anything that was around her. She tossed her hair back and lifted her nose to the wind. I knew that movement like I knew the beating of my own heart. She was pretending to be a horse! I swear my ears pricked up, flickered in an attempt to hear her. Somehow or another I found myself across the street in her yard, and then we were in mine. We didn't talk that first day. Instead, we just raced and jumped and dodged, not needing to explain what we were running from or jumping over or dodging around. Like horses, we just *knew*. Isn't that what friendship is supposed to be?

That's what I thought, and more importantly, I believed it could stay that way. When Bobbi's anxiously awaited visit came I was standing on the porch waiting. As soon as I saw them pull up I raced out to the car to meet her. My mom frowned at my obviously childish behavior when I jumped off the porch, but I went right ahead and galloped toward the car. For her part, the allegedly more mature Bobbi came out of the car like a bronco out of a chute. We met at the end of the sidewalk and grabbed each other in a bear hug. Then we remembered how dumb we thought hugging was so we backed up and laughed.

Bobbi's mom got out of the car then and walked up the walk to the house. My mom met her halfway. I knew she didn't want her to come in because it was wash day and she didn't like anyone to come in on wash day. I was also aware that Mom had never, not once, invited Mrs. Keller into our house in the two years that they lived across the street. As far as I knew Mom had never been in the Keller's house, either.

Mrs. Keller stood there in front of my mom, lighting up a cigarette and blowing smoke out the corner of her mouth. I knew Mom was not going to invite her in then. A smoking father was one thing, but a smoking mother? They stood together in that weird stiff way grownups do when they don't like each other but don't want to admit it. Finally, Mrs. Keller said, "Well, I'll come back for Bobbi around four o'clock."

She looked at us and said it again, as if we couldn't hear or understand the language she used when she talked to Mom. "I'll come back for you around four, okay?"

"Okay!" Bobbi answered, and then she grabbed my hand and started to run. We were off like startled colts and suddenly it was as if she had never left.

Our play that day was as much like it had been the day we met as any two days could be. We raced and jumped and raced some more. I thought I was in heaven. No one else knew quite how to do this with such abandon as Bobbi did. The fabric of our imagination wore thin only once when I asked if she had remembered to bring the picture of the two horses that lived across the street from her house. She said there were no horses across the street from her house.

"God," she said, "I live in a *city*. It's not like this at all." Then she shook her head like a horse shaking off a fly and took off running again.

There have been moments in my life where everything becomes suddenly clear to me. Where one piece of information settles into place and completes the whole picture. This was not one of those times. In fact, it made no sense to me at all, so I chose to ignore it. Even later, when I went back over everything Bobbi said to me, looking for clues of what eventually occurred, I still couldn't make sense of this. When she left me, she left me, and that may be all I'm ever going to know.

The world Bobbi left behind was no city. At night through our open windows we could hear crickets and frogs and freight trains that sounded their whistles but didn't slow down when they passed through on the south edge of town. Car traffic on the main street, two blocks away, settled down to almost nothing by about ten most evenings, though it picked up a little on Friday and Saturday nights when the bars closed. Trucks were the constant. Day or night you could always hear an eighteen-wheeler gearing up somewhere.

My dad drove a truck and so did about half the fathers and older brothers of everybody I knew. The sound of that rising shifting whine can still get to me, especially at night. I hear it and think somebody's leaving home. Somewhere there's a little girl at a window, watching taillights.

Every time before my dad left I would beg him to bring home a horse for me. He hauled cattle so he had all the right equipment and went right up into the heart of cowboy country almost every week so how hard could it be to put just one horse in with the cows and bring it home? I explained how easy it would be for him to get the horse here and once it was here I could keep the horse in the playhouse out back. I would take care of it, I told him, honest I would.

This routine went on for years. Me begging, him ignoring. It got to be such a habit I forgot to stop when I realized I didn't really want a horse anymore. I came to that realization right before Christmas the year after Bobbi's first visit. I was writing a letter to her the moment it hit me. I remember writing, "Tonight, I'm going to tell my dad he HAS to bring me a horse or I will die. I will. I know I'll die if I don't get a horse soon." As I re-read what I had written I realized it wasn't true. I wouldn't die if I didn't get a horse, I wouldn't even be all that upset.

Something about it scared me, I mean, who was I if I wasn't the lover of horses? I knew I was too tall to be racing around the yard kicking up my heels and pawing at the air with my forehooves, but I still loved horses. Didn't I?

I was writing this letter to Bobbi when my Dad came home. As he sat at one end of the table pulling off his work boots I sat at the other writing my heart's desire as if by rote. I kept re-reading those words, "I'll die if I don't get a horse soon," and I couldn't even remember what it felt like to believe it. I felt older than I had ever felt before. My Dad sat across from me eating fried potatoes and chopped steak, oblivious to the change taking place across the table from him. The rest of the family had eaten hours ago, before Dad came home, so it was just he and I at the table. Mom was moving around the kitchen doing something that didn't interest me. Between bites he told her about his week. As was often the case, he would only be home long enough to eat, shower and refill his suitcase. This was the time I always made my plea. I let him leave the table and I put my letter in an envelope, licked it closed, and sat looking at it for a long time.

He was pulling on his coveralls before I said anything. He had the look of somebody already gone and I just wanted to say something to him to make this new feeling in me go away. I don't remember exactly what I said because it all came out in a rush, but my mom heard the last part of it and the look on her face stopped me dead in my tracks.

"Don't ever say anything like that ever again!" she said. Dad didn't seem to hear either of us. He just kept leaving.

"I didn't mean I didn't want him to ever come home again," I whined. "I just want a horse really really bad."

"You! Go and think about what you just said." She turned her back on me and walked with Dad to the door. Good-byes were the only time I ever saw them kiss. This time she held on to his arm a little longer than usual, but other than that I figured it was just another night watching taillights.

When he didn't come home the night he was supposed to I knew it was my fault. I could hear my last words to him in my head, a refrain running over and under the memory of everything I had ever thought or done in my entire life.

"If you don't bring me a horse don't come home at all."

And he didn't come home. Mom was gone when I got up for school that day so I took care of myself. I poured a bowl of cereal, but I didn't eat it. My little sister and I walked to school together. She didn't know anything was wrong and I didn't know what was wrong so we walked in silence.

When you learn something like this from a stranger you remember odd things about the moment. Bob Johnson wasn't really a stranger, but until that day he had never spoken to me or me to him. That morning I wasn't all the way in the classroom door before he was in front of me. He was wearing a green plaid button-down shirt and the top button was loose. Threads stuck out like little antennae.

"Hey," he said up close to my face. I could smell the peanut butter on his breath. "I hear your old man killed somebody."

"What?" I said.

"Yeah, it came over the police scanner this morning. My dad always turns it on first thing in the morning. Your dad killed somebody with his truck." He looked almost puffed up with this information. "Deader'n a doornail."

Fear feels icy when it first comes but then it turns to fire and I could feel it creeping up my neck, onto my face. I can remember lifting up first one foot and then the other, as if walking was a newly learned skill. I walked to my desk and put my books down. A yellow No. 2 pencil with my teeth marks on it rolled out of the pencil slot and onto the floor. When I bent down to pick it up I felt my breath leave me and I couldn't remember how to get it back. I just kept going, slowly, until my whole body was on the floor beside the pencil. I didn't black out, I just forgot how to move.

They let me go home after that. They let me walk by myself the way they did in small towns in those days, and I found my way by staring straight ahead and letting my feet walk the familiar path. When I was about a block away from home I saw a glint of red in front of our house. I felt again the icy tingle up the back of my neck but this time it stayed icy until I got close enough to see my dad's truck parked in front of the house. It looked naked somehow, without the trailer behind it, but it was there.

When I got home my dad was sitting at the table, eating sausage and eggs and talking to my mom. I could hear the low growl of his voice as I stepped onto the porch and somehow I knew when I stepped through the door his voice would stop. Like the war stories he never told, whatever had happened to him that night would join the silence of what looked like adulthood to me. I stood outside the kitchen door, my back pressed up against the cool stucco and listened to him tell my mom what it felt like to be the instrument of what he called another man's suicide. "He came up behind me and drove under the trailer. I never even saw him." I heard him tell the whole story three times, each time he said, "I never even saw him," as if he couldn't quite believe his sense of sight had failed him so completely. When I opened the screen door and walked in they both looked at me with stricken faces. Where did I come from, they seemed to say, how did I get here? I didn't remember how to talk yet, and even if I did I wouldn't have known what to say. I felt closer to them than I ever had, but they didn't know that, so I just went into my bedroom and cried. For what, I didn't know.

The second time Bobbi came back for a visit I didn't need my mom to warn me that Bobbi might be a little more mature than I was. Two years had passed since that first visit and I had changed some. I had started my period, had my first crush on a boy, and learned to live without horses. All that had happened to Bobbi too, but she was way beyond me.

Bobbi, who had written only about five letters in those two years, wasn't coming back alone. She was bringing a husband. I never did learn the whole story and trying to fit all the mismatched pieces of our letters and conversations didn't help. She didn't *have to* get married – I know because I had tactlessly blurted that question out when she called and arranged a time for a visit and gave me the big news.

Married? We were only fifteen. I hadn't even gone out on a date yet and she was married. What could I do with that kind of information? My mother wasn't much help. She remained as silent about this mystery as she did about her dislike for Bobbi's mother. She didn't seem all that surprised though. Her lips got tight when I told her and she didn't say anything at first, but when I kept talking about it, about how I just couldn't believe it, she said that the Keller family was "different." That's as far as she would go.

My new best friend, Janelle, was the one who first got me thinking about the possibility of this being a "Love Match."

"Maybe she just loves him so much that she can't live without him," she said when we were walking to school one morning. Janelle had never known Bobbi so her view of her could be anything she wanted it to be. I, on the other hand, had to work with my image of Bobbi as a wild horse in a young girl's body. Horses don't fall in love. They love their freedom, they love the wind, they love open spaces and green grass. But to fall in love, get married, be a wife. Who would have thought such a thing? Not me, I can assure you.

But I didn't have anything else to explain it, so along with Janelle I began to see Bobbi as some kind of romantic heroine. She was the first of my friends to fall under that deep mysterious spell of love and as such she became a romantic mystery herself. In the days before her visit I began to imagine her husband with the same kind of detailed, exacting daydreams I had formerly limited to dreams of horses. Though any psychologist worth her salt would point out here that the leap from fantasizing about wild horses to imagining a friend's husband is a small and deeply related leap, I didn't see it that way. I didn't try to imagine their sexual life together. In fact, I spent most of the time thinking about them riding horses together, usually across some misty moor or along a deserted beach. That he would love horses was never in question for me. Of course he would. Bobbi hadn't changed *that* much I was sure.

The day she came was as cloudy and dreary as the first visit had been sunny and warm. This time Bobbi and her husband came for me. I wasn't waiting on the porch and when they pulled up Bobbi's husband honked the horn. They both stayed in the car and waited until I came out. I got in the back seat; Bobbi talked about almost everything under the sun from the minute I got in the car until the minute we got to the ranch where the Keller family was staying. I say she talked about *almost* everything: she didn't talk about her husband, she didn't talk to her husband, and she didn't tell me his name. When we got to the ranch she got out of the car and said to me, "Come on, I want you to see the horse we get to ride today." Her husband walked over to the fence, lit up a cigarette and watched us walk away.

It wasn't until we were on the horse, riding double, that I got up the courage to ask his name.

"Vincent," she said. "But I call him Vinnie." She touched her heels to the horse's flank and started off at a trot. "Man, this nag sure has a rough ride."

It was rough enough to keep me from asking any more questions, and, I guess that was the point.

When we got back to the corral Vinnie was still waiting by the fence.

"My turn," he said, and took the reins before we answered him. He jumped up onto the saddle without using the stirrup, sort of a Roy Rogers move that would have been cool when we were twelve. I didn't look at Bobbi though so I don't know what she thought of it. I still thought he must be good with horses or Bobbi wouldn't have married him. I kept thinking that even when I saw him grab a switch from the willow tree at the edge of the corral. Surely he wouldn't use that on a horse, I thought. But he did. He started whipping the horse right in front of us and he was still whipping it when they disappeared from sight over the hill.

I looked at Bobbi, but she was studying something on her finger and didn't meet my eyes. Finally she said, "I'll show you where we're sleeping this week. It's kind of a cool little cabin."

We walked in silence toward a small building that must have at one time been a milk house. An old-fashioned separator still stood outside the door. Bobbi opened the door and pointed inside. I started to walk in but when I saw that all there was inside the building was a mattress on the floor covered with twisted up sheets and blankets I stopped in my tracks.

"Cool," I said, and backed away from the door. I don't know how many years it would take for me to figure out why that scene made me feel uncomfortable. I was, as my mom recognized long ago, immature for my age. Truth be told, I think I still am. I seem to be walking through life one or two steps behind my peers. I have this feeling hanging over me that everyone else knows something I don't, has discovered the next stage before I'm completely finished with the one we're in. That's what it was about playing horses that I loved so much, that all my senses were so acute nothing got past me. I could see, hear, and smell the future and I knew what to do about it. When I raised my nose to the wind and whinnied the whole herd would follow me, and I always knew where to go. Oh, the thrill of knowing.

I honestly don't remember how long it was before Vinnie came back, and I don't remember what Bobbi and I did or what we talked about while we waited. All I really remember about the rest of the day was the sight of Vinnie racing toward us, still whipping that horse. He must have been only a few yards in front of us when he jerked up on the reins and stopped that poor horse. Mud shot up from its hooves and pink-tinged foam flew from its mouth. Vinnie leapt off the horse before it came to a complete stop. Bobbi and I just stood there; we didn't get out of the way or move to protect one another, our human senses so poor at preparing us for action. We weren't playing horses anymore.

I never saw Bobbi again after that day. The awkwardness in the car when they took me home hardened into a silence neither of us was able to break. Some how or another I learned that the Keller family had moved again, that Bobbi had moved with them, without Vinnie, but I never learned her new address.

The summer we turned eighteen, the summer before my last year of high school and the last year I lived in that little town, the Kellers came back for a visit. Bobbi didn't come that time. I learned of their visit when her mother came in to buy cigarettes in the store where I worked. I had already rung up her purchase and was handing back her change before we recognized each other.

"You're that girl who loved horses," she said.

I smiled my best customer service smile and asked her about Bobbi. She nodded and started walking away before she answered.

"Oh, Bobbi. She and her husband Dan moved up to Phoenix," she said over her shoulder. "They got jobs up there. I'll tell her I ran into you." The door swished shut behind her.

I watched her open a pack of cigarettes before getting into her car. The clear cellophane flittered across the parking lot, almost invisible. I pictured Vinnie, how he stopped that horse in front of us that day, the bit pulled tight against the softness of its mouth. When I played horses I knew how to take that bit in my teeth and though I had never seen a real horse do it I still believed it was possible. Bobbi's remarried, I thought. Man, I didn't see that coming, again.

It wasn't until Mrs. Keller's car pulled out of the parking lot that I remembered what she had said about me and horses. I watched her receding taillights until they were out of sight and thought about the time when that was true, when I was the girl who loved horses. "No," I finally said to myself. "I didn't just love horses." The slowness of my response bringing back the ache of something long since lost. "I didn't just love them."

Watermelon Days

TOM MCNEAL

Early one August evening in Philadelphia in 1926, Doreen Sullivan paid her fifteen-cent admission to the Aldine at Nineteenth and Chestnut. The attraction was *Beau Geste* with Ronald Colman. Doreen was early. She lingered over the encased posters in the downstairs lobby (for a long moment she stared frankly into the eyes of Ramon Novarro), then took one of the curving marble staircases to the upper lobby and sat down in a brocaded armchair. No one else was there. Doreen lit her own cigarette, something she was rarely required to do in a public place, and from her handbag unfolded a letter she'd already read three or four times. It was a funny and disturbing letter from Lulu Schmidt, her sometimes best friend who almost two years before had run off to New Orleans with Clarence Nottingham and had not been heard from since.

It began, *Dear Dory – if you receive this you must be at the same old address living with Aggie and still wasting away in Phil-a-delph-eye-aye! I got disentangled thank you from Clarence Nottingham (a big drip and how!) and you'll never guess where I am now Yankton South Dakota – Ha! This town is full of hoot and holler – you've got bridge builders and train men and best of all cowboys and even a few Indians but now they dress just like us. Here's the good part though – the males outnumber the girls three to one! which means they walk up to you and tell you how you look like Lillian Gish only more so! Ha!* The letter went on for three skittering pages. It ended with, *Come see for yourself Dory, there's jobs and men galore who if they think I'm Lillian Gish will think you're Greta Garbo Ha!* She'd signed, *Your everlasting friend Lulu Schmidt.*

People had begun to mass in the upper lobby, their talk light and expectant. Beyond the auditorium doors the pipe organ was playing. A boy materialized beside Doreen and said, "How 'bout I escort you in?"

He was hatless with his hair slicked back and parted down the middle. He was neither good-looking nor bad-. He looked in fact more or less like all the other boys Doreen saw everyday. Coolly she said, "No, thank you, I'm waiting for someone," which was true in only the most abstract sense, but she didn't give the boy another look.

Thirty minutes into the movie, Doreen went out to the lobby for popcorn. When she got to the counter she was surprised to find not only that she didn't want popcorn, but didn't want to return to the movie. She drifted outside. Normally Doreen came out of the movie house refreshed, and the lights and voices and laughter of the street would slip into her bloodstream like alcohol, but tonight everything seemed worn out by familiarity. The warm night air smelled faintly sour. She wore a thin, sleeveless dress over a light camisole, but the stares of men, which she usually craved, had no effect on her. There were places to go – there were always places to go – but she felt only like returning home, where Aggie would likely be entertaining one of what she called her gents.

Doreen had grown up believing her mother to be dead and Aggie to be her older sister, but one day when Doreen was fourteen she came upon a box of documents that included her own birth certificate. The space for the father's name was blank. Agnes Lee Sullivan was listed as the mother. When confronted with the document, Aggie didn't blush or stammer. She said, "Why you little snoop!" And then, "Well, now you know." And finally, "It's kind of funny, this morning you didn't have a mother and, presto, tonight you do!" (In truth, little had changed – Doreen still called Aggie Aggie.)

When Doreen stepped into the flat tonight, there was a man's hat on the center table. It was a snap-brim fedora with a nicely creased crown. Doreen picked it up and did what Aggie always did when handed a coat or hat to hang. She ran her fingers over the material – soft felt – and checked the label – *Lord & Taylor*. Not *Saks Fifth Avenue*, Aggie would've said, but not bad.

Doreen glanced at Aggie's door. It was closed. If she waited for it, she would hear a laugh. In men, Aggie looked for what she called the three *m*'s – married, moneyed and merry – and she gazed upon the boys Doreen brought home with a frozen smile of disapproval. Aggie had produced the same smile a few weeks before when Doreen told her she'd taken a new job at Kresge. "Managed by a man and staffed by girls?" Aggie asked. Doreen's cheeks pinkened and Aggie pressed her advantage. "Twenty cents an hour?" she said, and Doreen, glancing away, had murmured, "Fifteen."

Doreen used the bathroom and went to her room. She double-bolted the door from within (surprisingly often the merry men returning from the bathroom would try the wrong door). The room felt close. Doreen shed everything but her camisole, switched on a black table fan, and opened wide the room's two windows. She pulled back the bed cover and lay atop the sheets with three pillows plumped behind her bare back. She lit a cigarette, drew the smoke deep into her lungs and held it for a moment before exhaling, reaching for her handbag and again unfolding Lulu Schmidt's funny letter.

When Doreen Sullivan started work at WBDY in downtown Yankton three weeks later, she brought with her from Philadelphia an attunement to fashion that the citizens of Yankton had rarely seen outside of magazines – her bobbed hair was marcelled into deep horizontal waves, she wore a wide ribbon in her felt cloche, and she sported a scarf with a King Tut motif. She also used a scarlet lipstick to form her lips into a fresh cupid's bow that both her male and female co-workers, privately and for different reasons, found unsettling. Shortly after Doreen arrived, a station employee named Monty Longbaugh came in early one morning and very slightly repositioned his desk so he would have an unobstructed view of her as she worked.

In the early twenties, Monty Longbaugh had not quite made a name for himself as a cowboy balladeer and then had looked around for stabler employment. For the past two years he'd been reading the WBDY weather and farm reports in a consoling voice perfectly suited to solemn stories. In 1925, when he started at the station, Yankton was a river town of just under six thousand, set out on tableland that gently sloped down to the Missouri, the town's uncertain southern boundary. Monty liked the town. He liked living in one of its neat, white-fenced neighborhoods and he liked working in one of the stout red-stone buildings that dotted its commercial district.

The Stapleton Building had housed the Birney Seed & Nursery Company since 1913, and it was Henry Birney, the founder's son, who had grasped the happy commercial implications of radio transmission and quickly purchased the license and frequency designation for WBDY, built its facilities on the Stapleton Building's third floor and, when the station's transmitters were fortified to five hundred watts, had himself hit upon its first slogan: WBDY, *Your Big Buddy on the Great Plains*.

Weekday mornings, the station aired a show called "Neighbor Macy, the Farmwife's Companion," hosted by an exaggeratedly amiable woman who dispensed budget-stretching recipes and practical domestic tips. She also sold a number of household products available only by mail order from WBDY. For the past four months, and with growing boredom, Doreen Sullivan had been processing these orders. One day she noticed a red envelope among the shifting sackful of white. It was addressed to *Neighbor Macy, Mail Order*, but off to the side of the address, neatly printed, were the words *Attention Doreen*. Doreen slid her letter knife under the sealed flap. On the enclosed sheet of paper – also red – were the words, *I must talk to you before another sun sets. Signed, Monty Longbaugh*. When Doreen looked up and searched out Monty Longbaugh sitting at the far reach of two dozen desks, he was staring back with an expression that somehow seemed both hopeful and forlorn. Doreen had seen the look before. Nothing important had ever come of it, but it had been the source of some nice presents.

They walked down the street to Wilkemeyer's Drugs. It was cold. In the street, wheel tracks ridged the frozen mud. He ordered coffee and she sipped lemon coke from a glass that was soon printed with lipstick. In a tight voice he asked her about the weather and why she'd come to Yankton and how she liked living there and what her relations thought of it. Doreen kept her responses breezy. She told him if it got any muddier she thought the whole town would slip into the Missouri and she'd only come to Yankton because her friend Lulu Schmidt had written letters singing its praises but then two weeks after she got here Lulu Schmidt went back to a man in New Orleans named Clarence Nottingham, who, it turned out, was Lulu's husband! She said her sister Aggie in Philadelphia was her only living relative and that her sister Aggie thought Yankton was just across the crusty bog from Timbuktu. After the last of these answers Doreen gave Monty Longbaugh a saucy smile and said, "Was that the reason you needed to talk to me before another sun sets?"

Finally Monty Longbaugh shoved his coffee away. He spread his hands and ironed them along his thighs, twice, which made Doreen think of a comic movie where a rural type was about to go after the greased pig at a state fair. Monty cleared his voice and lowered his eyes. "Well," he said in a low voice, "it's like all my life up until now I've been sleepwalking, and now I'm wide awake."

Monty Longbaugh lifted his eyes and allowed them to rest fully on hers. They were black brown and their wet glisten made her think of a staring deer. None of the three *m*'s applied to him and the *m* for money never would. Aggie would've said, "Would you excuse me half a half a minute?" and left without looking back. Doreen said, "What was it that woke you up?"

His gaze broke from hers and shifted to the plate glass window that gave onto the street. To Doreen, his long smooth pure white face seemed suddenly and shockingly handsome. "Why, you are, of course," he said. "What woke me up was you."

The sauciness slipped from Doreen's smile. She didn't know what to say. She said, "I never expected to be anybody's Prince Charming before."

He turned and gave her an open smile. "Well, I never knew I'd been asleep," he said. He'd reclaimed his normal voice. It was a nice voice, low and assuring, his radio voice.

She leaned forward. She spoke in a whisper. She said, "Wait till I kiss you. Then you'll know what waking up is."

When Monty proposed marriage five weeks later, Doreen thought I don't know and said yes. "Next Sunday?" Monty said. Doreen nodded. The union was witnessed only by the officiating judge's wife. Monty made the informal public announcements, often with Doreen standing uneasily nearby. She kept the news from Aggie – she knew the kind of judgments her return questions would contain – and was relieved when their already haphazard correspondence ceased completely.

To Doreen, the marital state seemed different, but not unpleasant, and she did her best to do exactly what Aggie had never done. She made curtains for their rented house (crooked, though she hemmed them twice) and painted its dingy rooms (in the morning she noticed that drips had hardened on walls and trim boards alike). In the spring she spaded a garden, but the carrots bent as if they'd hit metal and slugs tattered the lettuce. Winter nights, she tried to teach herself knitting, then began weaving rag rugs, which were homely but at least freed her from the reading of unfathomable directions. Doreen began to realize that she missed going to work. She missed going to dances. She missed putting on her camisoles and beaded chiffon dresses and feeling goose bumps in the cold. She began to hate housework and laundry and cooking horrid meals her husband indiscriminately praised. In the first weeks of their courtship, she had loved sitting naked inside Monty's old wool robe and listening to him sing his cowboy tales – Little Joe the Wrangler, The Strawberry Roan – but he had proven a heedless, exuberant lover, one who, even when he chanced upon some happy ministration, seemed never to remember it on later occasions, and over time Doreen had grown first indifferent and then secretly hostile to the sentimental stories his ballads contained.

Two winters passed, one longer than the next. The stock market crash meant little to most citizens of Yankton (few had had money to invest), but it was the latest in a long line of bad news stretching back almost ten years, the cumulative effect of which Monty reported in his daily farm report. He might try a joke or anecdote afterwards, but when he reported Chicago wheat at ninety-seven cents a bushel or feeder calves at a nickel a pound, his voice was low and somber.

In the third summer of their marriage a record drought hit the northern plains. The wind blew. Dust settled over fields and houses. Gardens, lawns, and pastures browned. Temperatures shot up and seemed not to fall. At night families laid out blankets on Ohlman Hill hoping for some refreshment. One night when Monty and Doreen both lay awake in their screened sleeping porch, he rose to look at the thermometer and then went to the kitchen. When he came back he said, "It's 2:40 AM and 86 degrees." After that they didn't speak. He'd wrapped some chipped ice in a wetted washcloth. He lifted her gown and began damping her ankles and legs with the cool cloth. The pleasantness of this surprised her. She closed her eyes and lifted her buttocks so he could push the nightgown past and made murmuring sounds of a type Monty had never before heard. The hot spell continued and several other nights Doreen without opening her eyes would in a whisper ask him to go fetch his iced cloth and he as if in a dream would begin moving about.

Doreen became pregnant. She told no one, and didn't quite believe it herself until the fact became undeniable. When finally she announced the news to Monty, he was so pleased that his expression collapsed, his eyes moistened and he had to turn away in embarrassment. This had a strange effect on Doreen. "I'll need to slow down," she said. "I'll need to do less around the house."

"I can cook," Monty said. The sudden expansion of his spirits seemed nearly visible. "I know a couple of pretty good camp meals."

Doreen almost felt Aggie's presence in the room. She seated herself carefully. "And the cleaning," she said. "Someone will have to clean."

The town's two baby doctors were Dr. Carlton Johnston, a genial but clumsy man, and Dr. Jennie Murphy, whose custom of presenting herself in men's suits made some citizens standoffish, but Doreen preferred the gynecological intrusions of an eccentric woman to a butterfingered man, so it was Dr. Jennie Murphy who delivered the baby in the early morning hours of April 5, 1931. Toward the end, between coaxings to push, Dr. Murphy repeatedly muttered, "That's the stuff!" and "Now we're cooking!" When finally the baby was expelled, it was taken quickly away by the nurse while Dr. Murphy did some stitching and daubing, then took away the soiled bedding. A minute or two later she returned, adjusted her suspenders, buttoned her sleeves, and slipped into her suitcoat. She laid a hand on Doreen's forehead to check for temperature. Then, making to go, she looked down at her patient and said, "You did splendidly, Doreen," which for no reason whatsoever made Doreen want to cry. Monty returned with the baby swaddled and pinkly clean. "Girl," he announced, beaming. "A dandy little girl." Doreen looked at the baby's squinchy face, wept hopefully and fell into a hard sleep. Some indeterminate time later, she awakened confused. The room was dark and the windows were rattling gently. In a faraway room a baby was crying. The clock said one fifteen, but the dark was not the darkness of night. Doreen called suddenly for Monty and after a time a nurse appeared. She closed the door quickly behind her to muffle the sound of the baby's crying. "Where's Monty?" Doreen asked.

"He's gone to the station on account of the storm," the nurse said. She was stout, middle-aged, veiny in the cheeks and nose. "It's terrible dust. Middle of an afternoon and the autos outside are passing with their lights on. Mr. Longbaugh on the radio called it a black blizzard and I thought, Well that's close enough." The window glass shuddered. A moment later, Doreen became again aware of the dim, stretched-out cries of a baby. The nurse said, "It's a funny storm. Edna Arlene don't like it."

"Edna Arlene?"

"Your baby. Mr. Longbaugh said that was her name, after his deceased mother." She waited a second. "Should I bring the baby in now?"

The nurse thought Doreen would say yes, and so did Doreen, but when she opened her mouth she heard herself say, "Not for a bit yet."

"You just rest then," the nurse said, and when she came close to arrange Doreen's bedcovers she brought with her the faint smell of liquor. Doreen closed her eyes. Outside, behind the wind, there was a steady drone that became a kind of silence.

Doreen had no experience whatever with babies, and to the degree she'd thought of them at all, she'd sketched them in as sleepy, genial creatures, pleasing to dress up and roll about in buggies, but Edna Arlene was none of these things. She was drooly, colicky and overly covetous of her mother's touch. At night she would not sleep alone – Doreen would rock her to sleep, but the moment she set her down in the cradle and let go, Edna Arlene awakened screaming, so Doreen finally brought the baby to bed, where she slept between her and Monty. During the day, the baby cried when awake and napped only when held. Doreen's exhaustion was complete.

She hadn't exchanged a word with Aggie for over two years, but now dashed off a penny postcard. *Did I mention I was a missus and a momma? Edna Arlene is my baby girl, cute as a button but a demon for ceaseless screaming. Advice? Love, D.* The return card read, *Dear Yoked Up in Yankton, Must be in the bloodlines – you were a Banshee yourself and saved from sacrifice only by use of earplugs! Love, A.*

One day when Monty was off at the station and Edna Arlene's shrill cries were like a strafing, Doreen wanted more than anything to clamp her hand over the baby's mouth and face but instead laid her down screaming among pillows on the floor. She went out on the front porch and closed the door, but the cries pierced the walls. She began to walk. When she reached the corner of Fifth and Mulberry, she stood for a full minute meaning to go back, but didn't. Instead she walked the five blocks more to Wilkemeyer's Drugs and bought a package of Lucky Strikes. When she thought the girl at the register was staring at her, she said, "The neighbor's watching my baby." Doreen made a little laugh. "That baby's a handful. It's awful nice to be out for a minute or two." She hurried back to the house, uphill, breathless, and was at first terrified when she heard nothing at all from the room where she'd left the baby. But Edna Arlene was nestled among pillows sleeping so calmly she seemed hardly to breathe. Doreen lay down on the floor beside the girl and on an impulse leaned close to lightly kiss her smooth forehead, which snapped Edna Arlene awake and started a fresh course of screaming.

By the second year the crying had somewhat abated. Edna Arlene would play quietly as long as Doreen or Monty were within eyeshot. And though the girl made syllablelike sounds, they didn't evolve into intelligible words. If she were hungry or otherwise needed something, she made a series of urgent guttural squeals that Doreen couldn't help but think of as piggish. When Doreen raised the subject with Monty, he was unalarmed. He said that he himself hadn't spoken until his fourth year and that big tongues ran in his family. "Big tongues?" Doreen said. She'd never heard of tongues hereditarily big. She considered writing Aggie about it, but instead took the girl to Dr. Murphy, who peered into Edna's mouth and, pinching the tip of the suspect tongue, waggled it side to side. Then she released it and said, "Well, it's good-sized all right." She smiled at the girl and turned to Doreen. "Your daughter will talk when she's ready. She might lisp and she might not, but in any case it's nothing to worry about." In all other ways, Dr. Murphy said, Edna Arlene was perfectly normal.

When Edna Arlene began to talk shortly before her fourth birthday, she did in fact lisp, which her father found endearing. He began to use it on the radio. After reporting, for instance, that the WPA boys were in town cleaning Marne Creek and widening Main Street, he said, "Well, as my baby daughter likes to say, 'Thank goodneth for Mitha Woothevelt.'" Listeners responded favorably, and the observations Monty Longbaugh passed as his lisping daughter's soon became the standard closing element in his news summaries.

Edna Arlene liked hearing her father's voice on the radio, and enjoyed it when he talked in the funny lisping voice. One morning, at the end of the eleven-thirty market, weather, and news, Monty Longbaugh said, "Well as my baby girl said just the other night, 'God muth not've been payin attenthin when he made up gwathhoppeth.'" Doreen, sitting smoking a cigarette, didn't laugh, but Edna Arlene did. Then she asked her mother why papa didn't bring that baby girl home to visit.

Doreen asked what baby girl she was talking about and Edna Arlene said the one on the radio that talks like that.

Doreen stared for a moment at Edna Arlene, then began to laugh. It had become a husky, hollow laugh, rattly, as if there were in her throat tiny dry leaves she couldn't expel. Edna Arlene's first five years had corresponded with drought and other assorted maladies. Hopper swarms defoliated fields and formed horny encrustments on the walls and porches of lighted houses. Whole herds of anthrax-infected cattle were shot and bulldozed into mass graves. Civic-minded hunters brought to the Red Cross bloodstained flour sacks weighted with rabbits for the hungry. Barbers gave free haircuts to those who couldn't pay, and the town's two banks consolidated. At night, tramps congregated around cookfires along the riverbank south of Burleigh Street. It was a life as distant from Philadelphia as Doreen could imagine. She said, "Edna Arlene, the girl your papa's imitating on the radio is you." She wanted to stop, but couldn't. "It's you everybody's laughing at."

Edna Arlene's body stiffened. Her face contorted and her lower lip doubled downward. She was about to cry, but instead she did something surprising. She turned stoic. Her eyes settled. Her face became itself again. "No," she said, "thath not twue."

Doreen's voice softened. "The world's full of hard truths, little miss, and the sooner you learn it the better."

Edna Arlene went to the sewing room and slipped into the kneewell of her mother's Singer. From there she could see what her mother couldn't. It was true that Monty Longbaugh on the radio was her father, but not exactly, because Monty Longbaugh on the radio was always someplace different, where he was somebody different and where he had his own radio family that was different, too. That baby girl her father talked about on the radio couldn't be herself, Edna Arlene, because she didn't sound like that girl her father talked about, not one bit, and, besides, she never said the things the radio girl said. She'd never said anything about God not paying attention when he made grasshoppers, for example.

To a surprising degree Edna Arlene was able to believe what she told herself that day. Still, she began to talk more quietly and less often, so people wouldn't make the same mistake her mother had.

One Sunday afternoon in mid-August, while Monty was at work, Doreen sat on the front porch with Edna Arlene. It was hot and dry and gritty. Doreen had damp-ragged the dust from the porch chair before she sat in it. Edna Arlene played with a miniature car, painted orange, except where the metal showed through. She ran the car slowly along the top porch rail, one end to the other and back again, something she could do for an hour, trancelike, without uttering a word.

In the center of town a watermelon festival was in progress, and its distant music pulled at Doreen. "Let's go to the festivities," she said, and Edna Arlene stopped her car and turned around to stare. Doreen said, "There'll be music and carnival acts and a pyramid of melon."

Edna Arlene quickly tucked her car into her pocket to indicate she was ready to go.

Doreen took the girl's hand and walked toward the music. In the park there were sack races, seed-spitting contests and free melon, all of which interested Edna Arlene, but Doreen was drawn to the pavement dance. It was the accordion player and his Honolulu Fruit Gum Orchestra. Doreen positioned herself among the encircling fringe of onlookers and after a while stepped onto the pavement and pulled Edna Arlene out with her, trying by her own example to coax the girl into dancing, but Edna Arlene stood miserably with her eyes down until Doreen gave up and slipped back among the nonparticipants.

Doreen bent down and said in a tight whisper, "Little miss is a horrible lump."

Edna Arlene held tightly to her mother's print skirt with one hand and her orange car with the other, and peered straight ahead.

They'd watched perhaps three dances when a man in a cowboy hat broke free from the opposite fringe and started working his way through the dancers toward Doreen. He was a complete stranger, a tall loose-jointed man, pleasing to look at as he moved easily through the dancers, smiling and apologizing politely, nodding and touching the brim of his dress Stetson, but all the while keeping his gaze fixedly in Doreen's direction. Doreen thought, Oh, Lord, and didn't know whether she was hoping he was going to ask her to dance or hoping he wouldn't. He was handsome. He was handsome, and how. As he moved nearer, Edna Arlene's grip on Doreen's leg began to tighten and Doreen herself was suddenly overcome with something that seemed equal parts panic and exhilaration. He wore a neatly pressed pearl-buttoned green shirt. His smile seemed playful. But his eyes, which had seemed fixed on Doreen's face, seemed to shift just to her side. He was looking beyond her. His shirtsleeve grazed Doreen's bare arm as he slipped past her. Behind her, she heard him say, "Well, if it ain't Gordy McAllister! And here I thought you musta succumbed ages ago."

A big laugh issued forth, presumably from Gordy McAllister.

Doreen took Edna Arlene to the free-watermelon line and found herself a bench in the shade. She waved when Edna Arlene turned to wave from line, and again when the girl turned happily as she neared the men handing out slices. Doreen felt all-overish. She closed her eyes and opened them again when a woman passing by hummed a tune vaguely familiar to Doreen. *I'm Billy Jones, I'm . . .* something something *. . . and we're a – .* Doreen couldn't remember it.

Across the square Edna Arlene was eating her melon with another girl, who then led her off to a small group of girls playing a game Doreen couldn't fathom. The girls sat stock-still in a circle for a time and then out of the blue two of them would suddenly stand, race to touch a nearby tree trunk and return shrieking to the circle. The one who lost was consigned to run again against someone else. It was plain that Edna Arlene, slow and clumsy, would be doing a lot of running.

The girls grew silent as they noticed Doreen drawing close. "It's okay," Doreen said, "don't stop your game. I just wanted to tell Edna Arlene that I'm running a tiny errand and will be back in a little bit."

Doreen had thought she might go home for something to settle her stomach, but gravitated instead to Wilkemeyer's, away from the hubbub. There were a few other customers, but Doreen met no one's eyes. She seated herself in the same booth she'd shared long ago when Monty Longbaugh had to speak to her before the next sun set. She ordered a Seltzer and Saltines. While she waited she took a pen from her purse. She printed her maiden name on a napkin – Doreen Sullivan – and stared at it in hopes of remembering what it meant to be that person with that name, but all she saw now were oddly familiar letters – the feelings that defined the name had slipped away completely. Doreen was crying before she knew it, and when a waitress she knew came over and in a kindly voice said, "You all right, darlin'?" Doreen had snufflingly nodded and said, "Oh, you know, it's just one of those days."

The waitress waited a second or two. "Monty was in a little bit ago, beaming like a bride. He said if you came in to tell you he had some news that might interest you."

Doreen snufflingly laughed. Well, I've got a little news for him, too, she thought, but what she said was, "Well, I'll be looking forward to his news flash."

The waitress said, "He probably spent the morning dreaming up some new way for you to make him money. That's what my Donald does."

A few minutes later, while Doreen was sipping her water, the waitress came to the table with a rolled magazine, which she presented to Doreen. It was the new *Photoplay*, with a sultry James Stewart staring out from the cover. In a circle superimposed on his shoulder were the words, *Born to Dance!* Doreen looked at the waitress.

"Keep it," the waitress said. "I've already read it."

The elusive tune streamed again through Doreen's mind – *I'm Ernie Jones, I'm blankety-blank* – and she gave her head a quick shake to dispel it. It was a novelty song, she was pretty sure, and she didn't like novelty songs. She paid her bill in change, then stood for a moment outside the pharmacy wondering if Edna Arlene was still playing with those girls. She decided to walk up to the station to hear Monty's news, but when she got there she walked by and kept walking until she found herself in Foerster's Park, strangely quiet with the citizenry drawn to the festivities in town. She seated herself at a shady table near the rock amphitheater and pretended not to see three tramps standing and drinking some distance away, also in the shade. She read her magazine for a minute or two, then lay her arms on the table and her head in her arms. She closed her eyes. Even when she heard a crack of twigs and the definite tamp of footsteps, she kept her head down and eyes closed.

"Everything all right, Miss?"

A male voice, a little high in pitch.

Doreen didn't speak.

"You sick or something?"

As Doreen raised her head, the tramp removed his cap. He was surprisingly young, a boy in fact. His cheeks were pink and smooth. "What do you want?" she said.

He shrugged. "You looked like something might be wrong."

"There's not though."

The boy stood where he was.

Doreen said, "Aren't you awful young for a tramp?"

The boy with some spine in his voice said, "I'm full sixteen." Doreen doubted this, but didn't say so. The boy said, "And I just think of myself as an unfunded traveler." Then he said, "I used to have a job in Omaha killing chickens but that ran out." He said, "A lot of the old guys ride up in the boxcars but I ride underneath, on the connecting rods. You never get caught riding down there."

Doreen gave the boy her first full and direct look. "What're you and your unfunded traveler buddies over there drinking?"

"I'm not drinking nothing," the boy said. "I made a promise I wouldn't till I was eighteen."

Doreen said, "Who was that promise to?"

The boy for the first time looked down.

From town a rousing cheer carried.

The boy lifted his head and said cheerfully, "Guess the prize fighting's started."

They were both quiet, as if listening, but no other cheers followed. Abruptly Edna Arlene came to Doreen's mind, but then she thought, Edna Arlene is fine. To the boy she said, "One day from our front window I watched a tramp working his way down our street. He stopped and knocked at some houses and others he left alone. Why do you think he did that?"

The boy's eyes moved to Doreen's as if pulled. "Did he come up to your house?"

He had, but Doreen said he hadn't.

"Oh," the boy said. The news seemed to disappoint him.

She suddenly wanted a cigarette, but knew that lighting one in the presence of this tramp would seem to an onlooker familiar. Yankton was a good-sized town, but it was small at heart. She said, "You hungry?"

"I could go for something to eat, sure."

"I don't cook," Doreen said. She opened her purse, found her package of cigarettes and tapped one out. She made a wry face and said, "Reach for a Lucky instead of a sweet." She was searching for her matchbook when the boy said, "I got it." He held a lighted match in his cupped hands. She leaned close, took the smoke into her lungs and leaned away. She exhaled and stared forward. She said, "My husband does all the cooking, every bit of it, and the clean-up, too." She inhaled again, and this time released the smoke through her nose. "He made me promise I'd never tell that to a soul – " here she fixed the boy with her eyes – "and now I have."

The boy said, "I'm good at keeping secrets." He said this so smoothly Doreen tried to look behind his eyes to see if he meant something by it, but all she found was more earnestness. She said, "What other sins did you forswear until age eighteen?"

"Tobacco."

"That all?"

The color rose in the boy's pink cheeks.

Doreen said, "So I guess there's one other thing."

The boy said, "Yes, ma'am."

Doreen laughed. "And it's not snuff."

The boy shook his head and said blandly, "Snuff's included with tobacco."

The boy's simpleness was both an annoyance and an enticement to Doreen, and in the past few seconds she'd experienced a strange effusion of feeling that while unshaped she knew at bottom to be illicit. Without looking at the boy she said, "In my coin purse there's maybe seventy-five cents. It's all I've got. Go ahead and take it."

The boy didn't move. "I'd rather you handed it to me, if it's all the same to you. So I wouldn't be removing it from your purse."

She poured the coins into his cupped hands. The boy said, "Thank you, lady." The term had a deflating effect. Doreen smoked for a few seconds, then she said, "So how'd that tramp know? How'd he know to go to just the nice houses?"

The boy shrugged. "There's probably marks on the gatepost or under the letterbox or something. A circle means good for a handout and a circle with rising squiggles means good cook." The boy made an odd, crooked grin. "A circle with a crosshatch means a cranky lady or bad dog."

As the boy was leaving, Doreen said, "It was your mother who made you promise those things, wasn't it?"

The boy stopped. He took a quick glance at his companions as if to judge whether they might overhear. He returned a few steps and kept his voice low. "It wasn't my mother. It was the mother of a pal of mine. In Omaha. This was two years ago just before him and me were going off to Oklahoma to start up with a harvesting crew. She made us both promise." The boy had a sheepish smile, like he was trying to explain something unexplainable. "She was just my pal's mother so I didn't think it would matter but then I found it did."

The sun was low in the sky when Doreen returned to the Watermelon Days. Almost everyone was gone, but there were more flies than Doreen had ever before seen in one place. Edna Arlene was alone, slowly walking among picnic tables eating pink remnants from discarded rinds. When she looked up and saw her mother, she dropped the rind at hand and ran over crying. Her chin was pink and dripping with juice and her cheeks were dirty with tears. "Momma," she said and Doreen leaned down to take her into her arms. The girl held on as if for dear life. Doreen held and soothed her until she felt the dampness of her sleeve beneath Edna Arlene's buttocks, then she set her down at once. "You've wetted yourself," she said. She took her to the water fountain and while the girl cried in humiliation took off her clothes and bathed her. The girl bawled and trembled uncontrollably. "Wheah wuh you?" she said, "Wheah wuh you?" and for a flashing instant Doreen wanted to say in a mimicking whisper, *Wheah wuh you? Wheah wuh you?* but by this time there were onlookers, two women, not close by but within possible earshot. "I wasn't far," Doreen said. "I wasn't far at all. I was right over there all the time."

When they got home and opened the front door, the air was rich with frying meat. Monty stood at the stove tending wienerwurst and onion slices in a black skillet. Doreen in a flat voice said, "I thought Sundays were meatless." This referred to a belt-tightening strategy Monty himself had initiated.

"Well, we're celebrating," Monty said, turning. He was wearing an apron over his faded street clothes. "I've got some good news."

"Me, too," Doreen said, "but you first."

But Monty Longbaugh's eyes were now fixed on his daughter, who stood whimpering in her damp blue dress. She held her wet underdrawers in front of her, pinched between two fingers. Her face was contorted from efforts not to weep. He said, "What happened to Edna?"

Doreen shrugged. "That's part of my good news. She ate too much melon and wetted herself so completely I had to clean her up in a public water fountain."

Monty Longbaugh looked at the girl and said, "Oh, Sweetie."

Edna Arlene said, "Some boyth took Tootie." Her orange metal car.

Monty said, "I know where we can get another Tootie. I know just where." He turned off the stove and took her hand. "But right now let's find you some fresh clothes," he said, sweetly, almost crooning. "Then we can come back and all of us have a wienerwurst sandwich." In her smallest voice, Edna Arlene asked if she could have a puddle of ketchup in the middle of the plate, and her father said, "Sure you can, Sweetie. Smack dab in the middle."

In their absence, Doreen forked a sausage and several coils of fried onion onto a slab of bread, folded it, and ate it quickly over the sink, washed down with a room-temperature Schlitz. Then she went to the front porch and smoked. It was early evening, but still hot. She sat back in the shadows, watching boys pass by on bicycles, the occasional automobile, citizens on constitutional walks. From somewhere a man yelled, "Cyrus, where are you?" Doreen recrossed her legs and waited, for what she had no idea. She thought about going in for another Schlitz but didn't. The man called again for Cyrus.

Eventually Monty stepped onto the porch and quietly set the screen door closed behind him, which meant Edna Arlene was asleep. He settled into the chair beside Doreen. After a time, he said, "She seemed kind of shaky."

Doreen didn't speak until she'd finished her cigarette and flicked the stubbed butt over the porch rail. She said, "Somebody whose voice I don't recognize keeps calling for somebody named Cyrus. Who do you suppose he is, this Cyrus?"

Monty wasn't interested in Cyrus. "Edna Arlene said you left and told her you'd be back in a little bit but you didn't come back."

Doreen hadn't looked at Monty since he'd come out, and she didn't now. In a flat recitative voice, she said, "After I left Edna Arlene at the little melonfest, I thought I was going to come home but instead I went to Wilkemeyer's for a lemon coke and a magazine. Then I was going to come see you at the station but instead walked on to Forester's Park to sit in the shade. While I was there I talked to a tramp who was sixteen and had taken an oath against all sin. After that I came home and read my Photoplay in the bathtub until I remembered Edna Arlene. I'd just added hot water and I wanted to finish reading the magazine, so I did, and then I went and got her." For Doreen, telling her husband these things in this voice provided a kind of repudiative satisfaction – it made her think of the childhood pleasure of carving a swear word into a park bench.

Monty Longbaugh said, "You went alone to Forester's and talked to a tramp?"

Doreen had to laugh. "Why? Did the town council write up a rule against that?"

Sullenly Monty said, "They didn't have to." He waited a few seconds. "So how long was Edna Arlene alone at the watermelon festival?"

Doreen hadn't thought of it that way, and gave it a quick computation. Two hours, and then some. "A while," she said. "I wasn't keeping a logbook." Then she said, "Look, if what you're trying to point out is that I'm not the tip-toppest mother, don't bother. I can see my shortcomings." Another silence developed. Finally Doreen in a quieter voice said, "Which brings us to my own bit of news." She made an unhappy smile and kept her eyes forward. "It turns out I'm just a little bit pregnant."

She felt him staring at her, but she still didn't turn. "And that's not all the good news," she said. "It also turns out that our good citizens have run out of town the only abortionist who kept her kitchen clean."

A second or two passed, then he said, "Abortionist? What in God's name are you talking about, Doreen?"

She said, "I'm talking about the present situation as I see it."

Someone was again calling for Cyrus.

Monty said in a small voice, "Well, whose – " but Doreen cut him off. "It's yours, Monty. Don't worry your pretty little head about that."

"Then – " His voice trailed off.

She said, "I'm bad with one child, Monty. I'll be worse with two. And these aren't exactly halcyon days, if you've been paying attention. There's not a lot of loose change laying around."

Monty Longbaugh had turned from her and was staring out toward the street. "We'll be all right," he said, almost more to himself than to her.

A full minute of black silence passed. Then Doreen said, "Okay, so what's your big news then?"

Monty seemed jerked back from some distant place. "What?"

"When we came home you said you had some big news. You never said what."

In a low voice he said, "I didn't say it was big news, Doreen."

"I just figured it must be, what with your breaking out the wienies and all." *Wienies*, she knew, was a term her husband didn't like.

He said, "It seemed like bigger news at the time."

"Well, either you tell me your news or I'm going to walk down to the river to cool off." When he didn't speak, Doreen stood up.

"I won the new-slogan contest for the station," he said, flat-voiced. "*WBDY, your midwest address for CBS*. Mr. Birney said the vote was almost unanimous. He said there was over five hundred entries."

Doreen said, "What did you win?"

"A treasury bond," he said. "Just a small one." Then he said, "It's for five dollars."

Doreen stepped around him and walked toward the street. At the sidewalk she stopped to look back. Their house faced west. The last slanting light turned the white fence and gateposts a buttery yellow. She looked at one gatepost and then the other. There, a few inches above the ground, was some penciling. She bent close. A circle with vapors rising. She looked up at Monty sitting perfectly still on the porch beyond the light, a hobo's idea of a good cook.

She began to walk.

He called after her. Take a coat, Doreen.

She pretended not to hear. It wasn't cold and she didn't look pregnant. She took a meandering route to the river, waiting for dark. She felt the grip within her loosen. It was what she used to feel long ago after evenings in the Aldine, the unencumbering conversion of light to darkness, of known to unknown. She liked the river best when everything slipped up from darkness, the heavy rush of the water, its murmurings and shiftings, the wood smoke from the cookfires attended by tramps standing in half light, laughter without cheer, songs she knew were bawdy but could not quite hear. To the side of the pilings a landing overlooked the river. A lamp fixed to the underside of the bridge's truss beam shone down on the overlook. When she paused a few moments to stand in that illumination with her hands folded below the waist and her back straight, she could sense a stillness coming over the camps, and feel herself pulling imaginations up out of darkness.

An hour or so after setting out, Doreen returned to the house. Monty sat waiting in the same place. He'd known she'd be back. She often walked; she always came home, usually with her spirits improved. She unlatched the gate. She seated herself on the porch next to him and after perhaps a minute had gone by, she said, "Pretty down there tonight." Meaning the river.

He didn't speak. As they sat, the voice again called out for Cyrus.

Doreen in a low voice said, "I think maybe it's time Cyrus should get his little hindquarters home."

Monty's laugh was sudden and caught him by surprise. It changed his mood slightly, caused some mysterious ignition of hope. He said, "Maybe Cyrus is doing something *real* important," and was glad when Doreen threw in with a little laugh of her own.

"Real important like what?" she said.

In a low, loose voice Monty said, "Well, maybe Cyrus and somebody are conjugating a certain verb."

Doreen laughed easily and slid down just a bit in her chair. The tune came again to mind, and she hummed it for Monty, breaking in with the words she knew. "Yeah," he said when she was done, "It's that song from the Happiness Boys."

> *How do you do? How do you do?*
> *Gee, it's great to see all of you*
> *I'm Billy Jones*
> *I'm Ernie Hare*
> *And we're a silly-looking pair,*
> *How do you doodle doodle do?*

He sang it slow tempo in his low pleasant voice, his radio voice. It was a novelty song all right, but the way he sang it, it didn't sound like one. "One more time," she said. Doreen blinked closed her eyes and had a hard time opening them again. There was a handbill from Monty's singing cowboy days. It presented his long, smooth, almost equine face framed top and bottom by a dark kerchief and a black Stetson, and that's who, turning toward him in the dark, he seemed now to be.

The Marijuana Tree

TRUDY LEWIS

Denise got the inspiration at her local Trust & Loan. She was off work for the afternoon, due to an untimely trip to the gynecologist, and when she dropped by to make another deposit toward retirement, she noticed the unusual Christmas display they'd set up in the foyer. Bells and bobsleds she could stomach, and yes, even a few sly-faced elves who looked like they might be contemplating a career hike to upper management. But there was no tree, or none to mention, only three fat dollops of tree shrub, no trunk in sight, as if the Republican's famous trickle-down policy had finally dripped into the heart of Christmas and eroded it into pint-sized portions. The treelets looked attractive enough in their white flocking and tasteful bulbs and bows, but she didn't see a lot of evergreen underneath. In fact, she realized, scraping off some of the flocking with a Kleenex, the trees were downright brown, not even needled, but shriveled into the ropelike texture of an ivy vine in winter. She slipped the Kleenex back into the pocket of her beige wool cape – the centerpiece of her new gracefully aging lady wardrobe – and twirled around the display slowly, the way she would at an art gallery if she couldn't quite make a piece out.

A man in a gray striped vest and yellow power tie nodded in her direction. "Afternoon, Miz Crane," he said. Only in Wheeler would this be an abbreviation of "Mrs." rather than an out-and-out concession to the changing times. Denise bit her tongue and smiled.

"Afternoon, Larry. Management down-scaling? Holding a Christmas benefit for dwarves?"

The banker blushed in a delicate filigree around his male balding pattern. How maudlin, Denise thought, when she noticed herself waxing sentimental about some receding hairline in a crowd. Carl, her husband, had a lovely one, a curling blond flame over each ear, and a pink cervical cap of scalp at the top. More and more, it was this bit of exposed flesh that she called up when she felt obligated to remind herself of her love for him.

"This is your new ecological style Christmas ensemble, ma'am. No harm to the environment, no shedding pine needles, minimal cleanup." He laughed into his handkerchief. "We just roll them away."

"Artificial?" she said, raising an eyebrow. She'd staved off her craving for artificial greenery for years, regarding it as an embarrassing half measure. When she finally gave in, it would be for a wooden crèche, a pinecone wreath, and a gallon carton of unspiked eggnog.

"No, ma'am," Larry paused, dramatically, for a banker. "Tumble-weed."

Tumbleweed. They didn't stock them at the supermarket, or heap them up in bundles on the uneven asphalt lot of the volunteer fire station. But you could go chasing them out on Highway 66, as they went rolling out from under your tires like wild turkeys. Which is exactly what Denise did, since she'd lost the afternoon anyway, and had some considerable thinking to do.

She pulled off the road at an observation point and just watched them run for a while, pretending to be a state policeman clocking their speeding violations: seventy-five, sixty-nine, a whopping ninety-seven. What wonderful power men must feel, rushing through the world at car-chase velocities. Denise never speeded. It was bad for her heart, which murmured at any disorderly conduct. She had a number of minor health conditions: heart murmur, insomnia, dysmenorrhea, with which Carl was unsympathetic. He hated any mention of her fragility, and would turn to some pressing project and hum a country ballad every time she had any new development to report.

Not that Denise was frail. She'd raised three children, saved two businesses, jogged through the fitness craze, and mellowed into aerobic walking. But she needed to pace herself. Carl, on the other hand, was a sprinter. He'd work himself into a frenzy with every major law case, discarding first social engagements, then formal meals, sleep, and any unnecessary contact hours with herself and the children. Afterwards, he'd simmer off at a slow boil, sleeping ten hours at a stretch, preparing extravagant meals, family outings, and demanding athletic sex at all hours. Denise regarded it as a sign of health, a hunter-and-gatherer instinct. She loved feeling the fever break at each one of these pressure points, his body too hot to touch all night, then, in the morning, magically cooled by a fresh sweat smelling of lemon and newly mown grass.

But it was hard on her. There was no denying it was hard to keep up, she thought, as she changed into her tennis shoes, slammed the car door, and went after her Christmas tumbleweed.

By the time she got the thing home she was more enthusiastic At some point in the quarter-mile chase, her adrenaline had kicked in and infused her with the Christmas spirit. Or maybe it was just Christmas panic. Since her children left home, she'd been leaving preparations later and later, until she was practically buying her gear on the very eve of the blessed event, just in time for their annual bed-and-breakfast in the country. Carl didn't notice anyway, and the kids wouldn't show up until late afternoon on Christmas Day.

At least there was no struggle up the stairs, no mechanical difficulty with the tree stand, no chopping and hacking to the proportions of the room. Denise pushed up her sleeve and shook the can of flocking spray, then delivered the blasts with all the energy of the street vandal, her own winter storm. As she worked, she fantasized about being pricked with a pine needle and falling asleep for a hundred years. When she woke up, she'd be a truly old woman, past all the quandaries and embarrassments of transition. Her lawn would be overgrown with mysterious vines, her great-grandchildren would be hosting their golden anniversaries, her retirement fund would have blossomed with interest.

The tumbleweed looked delicious now, like a huge ball of Christmas candy rolled in powdered sugar. Denise went to the kitchen, poured herself a vermouth and dumped in some candied fruit, for color, then climbed up onto a kitchen chair and went digging for ornaments in the cabinet above the refrigerator. Over the years, they'd collected every kind of decoration: glazed gingerbread, Styrofoam snowballs, stuffed and embroidered rocking horses and Santas, pipe-cleaner sugar plum fairies with glitter matted in the pink netting of their skirts. At some point, Denise got in the habit of buying each child an ornament every Christmas, and there was a fuss if everyone's favorites didn't make the tree. Then the children started earning their own incomes and bought her ornaments in return. As her collection got bigger, her trees got smaller. And now that she was reduced to this tree nublet, she didn't know how she'd manage.

She pulled out a snaky strand of red glitter, some glass bulbs, and selected one novelty ornament for each member of the family, including a baby in swaddling clothes for Sally's newborn, her first grandchild. Denise had always wanted to simplify, to plan a color-coordinated Christmas, but the children panicked at any mention of restraint, preferring the usual jumble of unmatched wrapping paper, family memorabilia, and clashing motifs. Maybe she could get to like this new era, she thought, pouring herself another drink, garnished with a sprig of mint this time.

When Carl came in at six thirty, his camel coat half unbuttoned and his scarf tangled over his arm, Denise knew he'd started another one of his manic jags. He sat down to beef stew and Caesar salad without even loosening his tie. Denise pleated her napkin in her lap. If she didn't make her move soon, she would lose the advantage of attacking while his mouth was full. She forced herself to eat a carrot or two, but she didn't have much of an appetite for what would follow. Then, with his last sip of iced tea, Carl began a long explanation of his latest frustration: the plaintiff in a libel suit wouldn't settle out of court because he was so interested in the glamour of courtroom procedure. He wanted to edit all the briefs. He wanted to choose Carl's tie for the court date.

"This would never happen in Chicago. I can't believe I'm out here in the provinces doing nickel-and-dime melodrama. We didn't need to raise the legal consciousness of your average small-town citizen. We need to lower it. Take the goddamn soap operas off the air."

Denise turned her wrist over and looked at her watch under the table. This could go on twenty minutes without interruption. She knew. She'd timed it before. Carl's favorite subject these days was the inadvisability of his move to Wheeler, three years ago, to take over his father's law practice. Anything could lead to his long-running, fast-moving disquisition on the woes of small-town life.

"The choice of health care providers in Wheeler isn't too tempting either," she said, throwing her napkin onto her plate.

Carl looked down at his salad hopefully, searching for any bits of roughage that he'd missed.

"You've been home for half an hour and you still haven't asked about my day."

He slapped his hands on his knees and pushed away from the table. "My God, what's that?" he said.

He was staring into the living room, at the tumbleweed balanced among the throw pillows on the window seat.

It did look strange, Denise thought, like some kind of alien space pod masquerading as an igloo. Well, it would do him good to try and figure it out, look at the holidays from a different angle.

He was already at it with his key chain by the time she cleared the plates.

"Don't scrape off all the flocking. I spent all afternoon decorating."

"But decorating what? Where'd you get this thing, Denny? Do you know what it is?"

Denise brushed some hairs off the back of his suit coat and resisted the impulse to tell him it was a plant from the Pentagon, a New Age herb remedy, a bonsai tree imported for Western converts to the Buddhist faith.

"I'm serious, Den. Do you know what it is?"

"Why, you must remember Christmas trees. Very popular among Christians and nonpracticing atheists in the late twentieth century."

"Jesus Christ. Where do you get this stuff? Some guy's going to come in here and sell you a rainbow some day and charge you extra for the fucking cloud cover. Come here. Come here, you."

He cut off a sprig with the nail clipper on his key chain and held it up to her nose. Denise was smelling very little but vermouth at this point.

"Mistletoe?" she said.

"Well, there won't be any at my office party. It's cannabis, sweetheart. Herb, hemp, weed."

Denise's nose itched. She was going to laugh, and there wasn't a thing she could do about it. "Where do you get that from, a *Dragnet* rerun?"

"Very funny, Den. Do you remember that I'm a representative of the law? How do you think it looks for me to have illegal substances displayed in my picture window? Not to mention fines and penalties. The real possibility of being disbarred."

"For what? Illegal importation of holiday cheer? Hunting down shrubbery without a license?"

"Possession. That's a lot of reefer, love. Ignorance is no excuse in the mind of the law. It doesn't matter if I'm blindfolded in the bedroom and you're out here passing out quarter baggies. I'm still responsible."

"So, now you suspect me of dealing weed? Sure, that's what I'm planning on giving as Christmas gifts. Little bags of marijuana dolled up as party favors. I hide them in the Christmas ornaments. Want to see?"

"Never mind. I'll take care of it for you. Just let me get on my work clothes."

"This is not a marijuana plant. This is a tumbleweed I picked up out on the highway."

"So you just picked it up somewhere. How do you know what it is? You're not a botanist."

"No, but believe me, I recognize our friend Mary Jane. I'm the veteran of three teenagers, remember?"

Carl pushed her arm away and gave her his wrinkled forehead glare. The man was all concern, and the waves broke further and further up his forehead as he aged. "Just what are you trying to tell me?" he said.

"Oh nothing that you'll pay any attention to, dear. Why don't you run upstairs and put on your play clothes. Then you can go putter in your study."

"I'm not the one who's going senile."

"Humor me," she said. "Or if you can't do that, muster a little fear. You're not going to ruin Christmas again for me."

Carl touched the oversized art brooch on her blouse. "You want to come upstairs and help me change?"

Marijuana, the kids used to sing. L-S-D. *All the teachers have it. Why can't we?* This before they had any idea what they were talking about. *Marriage-you-wanna? Meet me in Tijuana. You can bring your own iguana. Where the air is like a sauna. And the honeymoon is sweet.* A jump-rope chant she'd heard Sally and Darla yelling in the street, before she got them in their father's study and explained. Tim was worse. At fifteen, he used to come home with his pupils dilated like chocolate chips expanding in the oven and sit down to eat all the cereal in the house. When she brought her magazines and her cup of tea into the kitchen and tried to engage him in conversation, he'd laugh at all the wrong spots, as if he was listening to the seedy underside of what she said. She was afraid for him, but she was also embarrassed for herself, trapped in a frame of mind where she couldn't understand her own son.

So when she found a couple of joints in his jeans pocket, she looked around the laundry room and decided to give it a try. She turned into a suffragette out there sneaking a smoke. At first, she didn't feel anything, just a prickly irritation in her throat. The stuff sure smelled good, like the tea shop in Marshall Field's. She certainly preferred it to beer. Then, when she was ironing one of the girls' church dresses, it dawned on her: the peachy glow of illumination. Her fingertips were transparent on the handle of the iron. The knot on the back of her neck unwound, nerve by nerve, until she worried it was the only thing holding her together. The more she ironed one side of the frilly dress, the more wrinkled the other one became. And this suggested some kind of truth to her, as if the smooth, well-tailored self she'd made up over the years of her marriage was just one half of the garment: the fresh face she put on all the irregularities of body and soul. If I were standing on the other side of the ironing board, she wondered, would I be the same person? The light bulb stuttered and a strobe kept beating a consistent rhythm in her head. Who am I? Who am I? Who am I? it said, like one of the riddles they told to the children.

A three-legged stool. A teapot. Twenty white horses stomping on a red hill.

I'm just Timmy's mother, and I'm here to take him home.

That's when Tim barged in the laundry room, looked toward the washer, and spotted the joint in a canning lid on the end of the ironing board. He gave a small, embarrassed smile and held up his hands, arrested. Denise will always remember the rip under the arm of his blue work shirt, the sparse blond hairs poking out underneath, and the change that started somewhere behind his eyes and swept up toward his father's forehead when she began to giggle.

"You thought I was going to be mad, didn't you?"

"What are you doing with this stuff?"

"Oh, I ran across it in your dirty clothes and I thought it was some kind of tip. I didn't want to look a gift horse in the mouth."

"Geez, Mom. You're stoned as a fish."

"Oh, is that what this is? Hmm, it's pretty zippy, huh?"

"Oh, yeah, it's real bebop material."

"So I'm stoned. You've been stoned for the last six months now, haven't you? You've been stonewalling me."

"Well, off and on. You know, that's what kids do now." He leaned back against the dryer, prepared to settle for a while.

"So, how do you like it?"

"What?"

"Being stoned as a fish?"

"It's okay. Okay, Mom, could you just go ahead and ground me or something?"

"Here, why don't you come over here and smoke a peace pipe so we can make it up."

He edged up to the ironing board, reached over and rubbed the back of her neck with a deep, muscle-drenching kindness, the way he'd done when he was small. But by now, he was so strong that the force reconnected her bone by bone. "Hey, I'm sorry. It doesn't mean I'm going to turn out to be an axe murderer or anything."

He still smelled of baking soda, something she remembered from his first days of life. As if he was always meant to grow up this sweet and expansive, extended beyond her kin. Denise felt her tear glands squeeze open. She figured the drug made her more susceptible, and dismissed it as an allergic reaction. She pushed the half-smoked joint toward Tim. "Shut up and take your medicine, boy."

Tim inhaled in an audible and expert manner that made her heart complain. But in the middle of the second drag, his handsome face turned red and he started choking. "We're not going to tell the D.A.D. about this, are we?"

Lying in bed with her leg crossed over Carl's, she realized that her loyalties must have shifted long before that point. Once she's completed her family, what use does a woman have for a man? she asked herself, reversing the doctor's rhetorical question. Even money wasn't a consideration, since she'd been nourishing her own nest egg at the Trust & Loan. But tonight, just as she'd almost given up on him, she felt a physical twinge toward her husband, as if someone was wringing out a dishtowel in the general location of her womb. Her legs were still good, but when he lifted and twisted them in lovemaking, she noticed new licks of cellulite at the tops of her thighs. In certain lights, her breasts looked similar. And now fibroids were proliferating in her uterus.

Carl touched her eyes and closed them as if she were dead already. "Relax," he said. "If you could have anything you want for Christmas, what would it be?"

Possibly, her life wasn't even two-thirds over yet. She might need all her remaining organs for the long nights ahead.

"Anything?"

"Carte blanche for a white Christmas."

Denise ran her hand over his chest, and felt the hairs springing up under her fingers, thicker than she remembered. When she married him, there was just a trickle of gold running down in a gully toward his groin, but now it looked like he'd be a hairy man, before he was done. "A marijuana tree," she said.

Later, when Carl wandered off to his study as she'd predicted, she went down to the kitchen and called Tim in Chicago. They let it ring four times before picking up. Then Miranda answered. The two of them weren't formally married, but they had both voices on the answering machine in a kind of electronic prose poem, and Denise assumed that amounted to almost the same thing, these days. She wondered if she'd interrupted something.

"Hi, Mother Crane. He's just coming in from the lab. It's your mom, Mr. T."

Denise supposed Miranda was a good choice: a girl with a crisp mind and farmer's market beauty, the kind that would wear well. Tim was too wise, even at twenty-five, to be running after the flashier models. But Denise worried about the proprietary note in her voice, as if she had to cajole the boy into talking to his own mother. Denise would never take that maternal tone with her son. But maybe that's what Tim was looking for. Maybe he'd been missing it all along.

"Hey, Mom. Did you get my message?"

"Seven o'clock Christmas Day? I guess that gives me time to come across with the goodies."

"We'll bring the wine. There's something I want you to try."

"Tim, I have to tell you that this Christmas might be different."

"Did you forget the mistletoe again?"

"Worse, the tree."

"Well, we'll bring Miranda's rhododendron. That ought to do her."

"And I went to the doctor's today, and got, not really bad news. But he's trying to convince me to yank out the spare room."

Tim paused. "Hysterectomy?"

"What do you think?"

"Just a minute," he said. "Let me switch to the other phone."

While she waited, Denise scraped at the coagulated stewage stuck to the counter. It was Carl's night for the dishes, though he hadn't gotten around to it yet. Perhaps he thought the sex would act, miraculously, as a substitute. When the children were home and he was in an amorous mood, he'd say: "Your mother and I are going upstairs now . . ." and the kids groaned, knowing he was about to put half an hour of soapy water between them and their evening's play. Denise sometimes pretended they were still down there, little blonde elves clattering away at the china and cutlery while he did the inventory of her body. Who would ever notice if a cup or plate turned up missing some day?

"Did you get a second opinion?" Tim said. "Is there any particular reason the guy's harping on it now?"

" 'Tis the season, like they say. No, I've been having some pains, nothing serious. But he thinks it'll improve family existence for your father and me. His wife did it last year and he's never been happier."

"I'll bet. You've got to come up here and talk to someone else, someone who's read a little literature in the past twenty years."

"Well, the good doctor is quite the bedside companion. 'Think of it as an orange,' he says. 'Once you eat the fruit, you can throw the peel away.' "

"Mom, he didn't say that."

"I wish I'd had a tape recorder."

"Why don't you fly up here and see your old doctor, then we'll take you back for Christmas?"

"Well, that might not be a bad idea. You're always the practical one. You know, I suppose it would make more sense to call your sisters, but Sally's so taken up with the baby and Darla is just discovering her sexuality and all. I don't want to put a damper on the process."

"What about Dad?"

"Lost in space. He's more worried about my drug consumption."

"You've got to tell him sometime."

Denise heard a creak on the stairs. "There's the old Claus now. I'll get back to you. Thanks a lot, Timmy."

"At least give the guy a chance to screw up first," he said, and Denise wondered if his loyalties weren't shifting too.

Every morning for almost a week, Carl offered to throw the Christmas tree out on his way to the garage, and every night, Denise talked him down again, took him upstairs for consultation. She pulled out gowns and camisoles she hadn't worn in years, brought dessert to bed, lit scented candles all around the room, narrated him through the erotic scenarios of a lifetime. By now, she knew all the springs and catches to his libido and she built her stories accordingly, with the levers and false leads of a mousetrap: her imaginary love affair with the schoolgirl vampire haunting the old hotel in Charleston, the commuter train ride where she'd put his hand up her skirt, then carry on a conversation about the shocking stuff they were showing on television with the woman next to her. The time they'd pretended to be brother and sister on a trip to Spain, not touching until their shadows tickled on one another's skin.

Carl started leaving his shoes at the door, his tie draped over the mantle of the fireplace.

Denise stopped spending her usual half-hour in the bathroom each morning and put her makeup on in the car instead, the way she'd done in her twenties, rushing from bed to board and back again.

Her flesh hummed as she drove. Her breasts responded when she lifted a coffee cup or picked up the phone. It was like the desire to have a child, only in reverse. She craved everything burnt and bitter: coffee grounds, popcorn kernels from the bottom of the pan, rhubarb crisp. She walked around in a fever of feeling, her skin worn thin as an old Victorian gown, so all the light came through.

She didn't tell him about the doctor.

He didn't insist about the tumbleweed.

They arranged their usual Christmas Eve outing to a little Swedish town devoted to tourism – the closest thing to a resort within a hundred-mile radius of Wheeler. There, they'd stay at a bed-and-breakfast with hand-carved furniture, eat cinnamon rolls served to them by air-brushed blondes in embroidered aprons, and shop for handcrafts and more extraneous Christmas decorations, then hear the *Messiah* sung by a choir of Lutherans who descended like mayflies from all over the country. It was usually a treat, but this year, Denise was reluctant to go, nervous that any alien element would upset their rare equilibrium.

Carl, who took his leisure seriously, packed a cooler full of champagne and told her she was faking.

"You know you'll be fine once we're there. You did this with New Orleans and Europe too. The minute we're up in the air you think you left something burning in the oven."

"I left the coffee pot on that once."

"And who called the Delaharts to come in and turn it off? When will you learn that details are just details? Whatever it is, I can expedite it, Den."

Denise untied the scarf around her throat and rearranged it over her head. She was practicing posing as an old peasant woman. She only hoped he could get to like that too. "You think everything's just logistics. Some situations are real, well, situations. You can't just write a memo and make it go away."

Carl shifted behind the wheel, his long legs jammed up against the steering column. "What are we talking about here?"

She set her purse in her lap and started going through the contents: Kleenex, Tampax, nasal spray. "Famine, for one thing. And then there are plagues, like AIDS. World wars. The greenhouse effect. Old age."

"Oh, not that again. I thought we already did the middle-age crisis routine."

Denise snapped the purse shut: you could tell the old lady models because they made a more resounding cackle as they closed. "Excuse me. You went through the middle-age crisis routine. I sat home waiting with bated breath for you to renounce your racquetball partner."

Carl blushed, then blanched, so that she could see the long, double-branched vein standing out in his temple and then glanced back to check his blind spot, pretending that he wanted to change lanes. "I kept my marriage vows, that's something not many men can say."

"I kept my mouth shut, but then a whole gaggle of women have that to brag about."

"Let's continue the trend, shall we?" Carl turned into the left lane, a little recklessly.

"Well, you sure wanted to go on about it at the time."

"I was being open and honest, like all your self-help books are always preaching."

"You were trying to negotiate your position."

"Maybe you really don't want to take this trip?"

"What about you? Do you want to go back to Chicago? You can drop me off at the nearest rest home."

He put his hand on her knee and her nerves flinched all the way up to her armpits. "Denny, it's been three years. Have some mercy. Haven't I been a good husband to you?"

She untied the scarf again and wiped at her eyes with one corner, then unwadded the silk to see how much damage her mascara had done. She had no idea what it meant anymore, to be a good husband. Someone who tilled the womb well, didn't overgraze or sow wild seed, grafted his ragtaggle genetic material into sturdier stock? At this point, she'd rather have a houseplant.

"Don't worry," she said. "No one can ever tell you that you haven't done your job."

The hotel wasn't as crowded this year, and as Carl unwound his butter twist, Denise sipped the strong, fennel-scented coffee and surveyed the other patrons: a young couple with identical sweatshirts and tawny collar-length hair who couldn't afford a more exotic honeymoon, a pudgy man and wife badgered by two preteenagers playing war games across the tablecloth, a thirtyish grade-school-teacher type with an older woman, perhaps her mother, in tow. The mother woman kept going on in a squeaky leather voice, like bare skin peeling off a car seat: "They're clean, they're decent, they're trustworthy, but they like their coffee breaks, these Swedish folk. From ten to eleven, then from two to three in the afternoon. Makes you wonder how they find time for lunch in between. Could be we'd have a lighter skin population right now if the Vikings weren't always off on some mead-fest killing time."

The younger woman held her coffee cup in both hands and looked into its depths. Then she tipped the cup toward her, spilling it, deliberately, Denise thought, from the tick flickering in the dimple of her pretty cheek.

"Goodness, Lucy. Your table manners haven't improved much since the harvest banquet in seventh grade. What do you ever do when men take you out for dinner? Or is that still happening much these days?"

Carl wiped his fingers on his napkin and touched his knee to Denise's. She strained to catch Lucy's reply.

"No, nowadays we usually cut straight to the cappuccino," Lucy said. "That's actually more difficult for them, since they have the extra added problem of keeping the cream off their mustaches."

Denise made an effort not to laugh and felt the caffeine hit her capillaries in grand style, producing more space in her head than she thought possible. She hoped she wasn't this way with her daughters, especially Darla, who was so sensitive she'd turn white and start pinching the backs of her calves when anything remotely squirmy turned up in conversation. Denise gave Carl's knee a nudge. The skin behind her ears burned, and there was a little preliminary gnawing in her personal forest of fibroid tumors. The doctor told her that coffee only exacerbated her condition, but she couldn't give up the feeling of expansion, her consciousness doubled and trebled.

"Don't you ever hear chords?" she asked Carl.

"Only when I'm with you."

"I mean, do you think it's possible to read someone's mind?"

He looked right into her eyes, the way he'd done when they were dating and they held long staring contests in her dorm room, in his Plymouth, in the First Methodist parking lot, where the first one to look away had to give in and say what they were thinking. His milk-blue irises iced over and the sunburst wrinkles around his eyes flexed. "After all this time, why would you want to?" he said.

During the afternoon of Christmas Eve, Carl bought an antique end table and a pipe stand; Denise found a pair of hand-carved candlesticks and a brooch made out of pheasant feathers. No more Christmas ornaments, to her relief, though the little town seemed to be on permanent Yule time with its festive blue-and-yellow tiles, potted pines, and the red Swedish rocking horses painted on every possible surface. This was even odder, Carl pointed out, because the snows here were so sparse. The early settlers must have missed their native climate, and built this town as an island of winter on the plains. Denise liked the idea. She'd just as soon live here as in Wheeler, as long as they were off in semi-retirement repenting of their sins.

They came back to the hotel room and took off their clothes for a nap before dinner; just as Denise suspected, now that they were on actual vacation, Carl wasn't interested anymore. He lay on top of the bedspread with his hands crossed over his stomach. Denise listened to his wispy breath deepening into a long, uncanny snore. She had the covers stripped off her side of the bed and had to keep adjusting them to the changes in her body temperature: the whole bedspread combination, twisted-back blanket, bare cotton sheet. Her torso was a low-lying plain subject to the slightest atmospheric shift, with cold fronts coming in from the north, unexpected heat waves flashing up from the stippled mountains of her thighs. She smelled of green tornadoes and thunderstorms. She rolled over and bit the corner of one pillow, pulled another down between her legs.

When she finally fell asleep, she heard Carl rustling on the other side of the bed, getting up and running the shower. In her dream, this was the noise of the locker room behind her. A woman in a white shorts set came out of the steam, her sandy hair frizzed up in a halo around her face, her low-cut sweater revealing freckles sifted deep into the snowdrift of her cleavage. She took a balloon out of her pocket and proceeded to fill it at the sink. As she did, her breasts wobbled, and her lips moved. Denise's abdomen pulsated in response, its walls pushed and polished to the texture of chewing gum. Then the woman held the balloon up to the fluorescent light, a warm red water bottle, with a round belly and a long turkey's neck stretched out with the water's weight.

"Do you know the ceremony?" she said.

"I'm not paying for anything," Denise told her. "Just remember that."

"Hold out your hands."

The woman let the bottom of the balloon rest on Denise's cupped hands, and Denise felt suddenly dirty, as if she was touching herself in a way she hadn't done since she was twelve, and spent all those hours in the bathtub letting the water run between her legs, opening the secret panels of her labia to find the second belly button inside.

"Tell the truth, do you really want to go?"

In those days, the nursery song about Alice kept running through her head, and she was convinced that she'd be another one to go slipping down the drain if she didn't stop just in time, before she fell into a trance and forgot her milk money, before her mother called out for her to stop primping and come set the table, before she turned into a grown woman who had to cross her knees in public, even in slacks, and sleep on her back to avoid squashing her bosoms.

"I want to stay," Denise said. "It's not even dinnertime yet."

The woman lifted the balloon above her head and swallowed it, like a circus seal swallowing a fish. Then she followed it with a steak knife, a thermometer, a syringe.

Denise felt herself getting warmer. "Why are you punishing me? You're the one going around stealing husbands. You're the one who has to go."

The woman pointed to her full cheek, and Denise saw the dimple winking in its hollow.

"Okay, just this once, you can talk with your mouth full."

Then the racquetball partner pulled something off her tongue, like a hair that had gotten caught there during lovemaking. She held it out to Denise.

It was a whole branch of evergreen, a shred of shriveled red balloon caught in its needles.

"One for the road," she said.

Denise woke with a strain in her belly, as if she was in labor again and a fourth child had set about unraveling her intestines like a pretty strand of glitter. She was marinated in sweat, and the sheets were wet underneath her. Everything smelled acidic, like her urine in asparagus season, and she was convinced she was going to die.

Carl sat at the foot of the bed fiddling with his cufflinks. When he saw her eyes open, he gave the springs a couple of bounces and grabbed her around the ankle.

"My God, Den. You're soaked. What, did you have a little private work-out session without me?"

"I think I'm having a miscarriage," she said. "You better take me home."

In the car, Denise lay in the back seat and grasped onto her purse. She felt the pain build and burst in fever blisters underneath her. At the moment of the fiercest pressure, she bore down hard, knowing she was about to get the payoff of a couple seconds of relief. It took all her concentration just to ride the contractions, which she imagined as a series of men far too young for her. If she let down her guard, they would notice her gray roots and kill her off right away. But Carl kept calling to her over the seat, wanting reassurance that she was still conscious. She couldn't really talk, but she managed the single syllable: "Hi." Even at this late date, he was getting her signals crossed.

"Do you want me to turn the heat up? Are you okay back there?"

"No."

"Denny, we've got this thing under control. The hospital's only three miles away. Den, you just hold on there. Remember, you can do this. You've done it before."

"No." Denise knew there was something else, outside the rhythm of her pain that she had to think about. Did she want to die without having it out with Carl, letting him off the hook for eternity?

"There's something," she said.

"Something important?"

"Something to say."

"Denny, love, you should just maintain back there."

"Got a bank account."

"Money's not a problem. We don't need to talk about money now."

Denise lifted her head off the seat so she could speak louder. "Saving up to leave."

"Leave where?"

"Back to Chicago." She waited for the downbeat of the contraction to make sure, then added: "I'm not dead yet."

"What? What are you talking about?"

"Give it to Darla. She'll need it now."

"Denny, don't you know how much I love you? How much I need you to stay?"

Denise dropped back down to the seat. She didn't doubt him, but it seemed too late, and beside the point somehow. He couldn't help her now, she was riding out beyond his reach, where she was probably headed all along. The highway was spun glass beneath her, and she felt herself hydroplaning up off the surface of her pain. It was like the moment when the aircraft tipped up off the runway, her Darvon kicked in, and the question of elevation didn't matter anymore. She was finally speeding, tumbling faster than any spin cycle or rambling weed, and she didn't want to stop.

They did the operation on an outpatient basis, so Denise was scheduled to be home for Christmas after all. Her doctor wasn't too enthusiastic about being consulted at ten o'clock on Christmas Eve.

"This is going to keep haunting you until you have the surgery," he said. "You need more R & R after every D & C."

"Thanks for the tip. Don't call me, I'll call you."

"You really can't take care of it soon enough. What does your husband say?"

"If you don't mind, I'm in pain. Merry Xmas, doctor."

"Suit yourself, but I'm going on the record recommending surgery."

"And I'm bloody exhibit one."

The nurse took the phone away from her and handed it back to the intern-on-call.

"All over, Miz Crane." she said, "We can get you ready to go home now."

Denise looked into the nurse's unlined face and grimaced. Was she going to have to go through the rest of her life hating younger women for an ignorance they couldn't conceal? Her breath curdled in her mouth, and she remembered a year when her mother wouldn't go shopping for clothes with her anymore, when she stayed in her bedroom wearing a mottled green housecoat and transferring photos from one album to another, sorting out items for Goodwill. Was that the year it had happened to her? Did she have to separate herself from Denise to make the change? And then – Denise felt her heart burn thinking of it – she met Carl and started confiding her problems with Mother in him. Her sadness shaded into a deep, warm melancholy where some new feeling could begin.

The nurse touched Denise's forehead and looked at her chart. "Now, we need you to take it easy for a while. Let that cute husband of yours baste the turkey for a change."

When Denise woke up, it wasn't morning anymore, and she was lying on the couch staring at the daguerreotypes of the three children on the wall: a cowlick, a headband, a ponytail. They were period pieces by now, with no particular resemblance to anyone in the family. But she kept them on because they reminded her of a black-and-white segment of her life when she was too busy to bother much with the color details. Strange smells were coming from the kitchen. She got up and dragged the grate away from the fireplace, poked around the fire until she felt a stitch in her gut. Then she went over to the marijuana tree. Lucky it was so light, she told herself, not much to weigh her down here.

The tumbleweed bristled against her robe, and a couple of ornaments rolled off onto the floor, knocking against the furniture and tinkling like icicles breaking on the pavement. It was difficult to get a handle on the thing. It had no shape, no stem, no bottom and no top. Denise ended up holding it in her arms as if it were a fat baby, picking stars and ballerinas out of its hair. She gave it a final dusting, tweaked one of its branches, and rolled it into the fire. The flame flapped against her face, lighting up her whole nervous system with the hot pipes and blown fuses it was specializing in lately. But the weed didn't catch fire right away. It rolled toward the flue, resettled, crackled and crinkled. There was an industrial smell from the flocking that wafted up and stung her eyes.

Then a spark jumped from a yule log to one spiny strand of the tumbleweed and followed it all the way around the maze of curves. Another licked up next to it, lit out on a second circuit of branches. A different scent rose from the fireplace now, something spicy and woodsy and too close to the earth for perfume, like a black-eyed cow flower, or Denise's own sour sweat. She stood back and admired the tree. She could see the whole thing now, its broad girth and delicate filigree of embers. She could remember what had mattered in her life.

She sat back down on the sofa to enjoy the show, and as she did, Carl came running into the living room, the tail of his work shirt flapping behind him, and the curls over his ears flying like a winged Mercury.

"Don't panic. Don't panic. I'll get it," he said. He reached into the fireplace and lifted the tree by its top branches, those that hadn't been touched yet. The sparks shot into the living room, blind fireflies nose-diving into the carpet and the drapes. And just for once, as he stood there holding the burning bush up over the hearth, unable to admit he couldn't save anything, Denise was glad of his speed.

The New Year

JOHN MCNALLY

At midnight, party horns blow obscenely, strangers kiss with tongues, and champagne corks fire perilously across the smoky room like a barrage of SCUD missiles. No one here has ever heard of "Auld Lang Syne," so what they do instead to celebrate the New Year is blast the first few tracks off Ozzy Osbourne's *Blizzard of Ozz*.

Two hours later, half the people have gone home, fearing the approaching snowstorm. The remaining half have coupled, staking out for themselves every bedroom, hallway, and closet in the house. Here and there, men and women copulate – some, discreetly; others as if auditioning for the victim role in a slasher film: lots of panting, then moans, then a high-pitched squeal followed by a howl or scream, then nothing at all.

Dead, Gary thinks.

This is how he entertains himself: absorbing the reality around him and turning it into something other than what it is, something menacing. Only he and Linda remain among the flotsam of the party – cigarette butts rising like crooked tombstones out of bowls of salsa; a slice of pizza dangling like a limp hand over the edge of the coffee table – and Gary, lost in his own private world of the macabre, is listening for the next rising moan, the next victim, when Linda, joint in one hand, vodka tonic in the other, tells Gary that she's pregnant.

"I'm keeping it, too," she says, meeting Gary's eyes and smiling wildly, as if announcing an extravagant purchase she cannot afford, like alligator shoes or a raccoon coat, challenging Gary to tell her *No, you'll have to take it back*.

Gary dips his hand into the ice bucket, scoops out the last pitiful shards of ice, and deposits them into a tall glass. With the assortment of leftover liquor, he mixes himself what he thinks is in a Harvey Wall-

81

banger, a name his father uses freely for all occasions, exclamations of surprise and scathing insults alike, the way another man might say *Great Scott!* or *Son of a bitch!* Gary sips the drink tentatively, squinting at Linda while he does so. The first concert he ever took her to was Megadeth in Omaha, and he wants to ask her if that had been the night, in a dark and cavernous loading dock at Rosenblatt Stadium, that he'd unceremoniously knocked her up, but he is having a difficult time summoning the proper words, let alone stringing them into a meaningful sentence.

"Do you mind?" he asks and picks up the four-foot bong he had packed earlier in the night but had somehow forgotten about. He holds it to his mouth as if it were a saxophone, and while Linda leans over to light the bowl, Gary sucks hard on the tube. He inhales for what seems an impossibly long time, and when he finally exhales, he tilts his head back so as not to blow smoke in the face of his girlfriend who is carrying his child.

Over their heads and scattered about the room float swollen clouds of marijuana smoke, thick as doom, and though Gary has long since run out of breath, smoke continues to leak from his nose and mouth. He's been working out daily at the gym, and he's amazed at how much his lung capacity has improved in just two short weeks.

"Wow," he says, amazed at *everything* – the pending baby, his new lungs – and it's the word *wow*, this last puff of smoke streaming from his mouth when he speaks, that triggers the smoke alarm. The alarm is deafening, piercing Gary's consciousness, one steady shriek after another, like a knife thrust repeatedly into his head, and though Gary wants nothing more than to stop the noise, he has no idea where to start looking.

Four men instantly appear from each corner of the house. They arrive like Romans, bedsheets draped around hips and torsos. One man stands on a chair, disappearing into a head of smoke, and when he rips open the smoke alarm's casing and yanks free the battery, along with the two wires the battery had been connected to, the noise mercifully stops.

The man steps off the chair, looks Gary in the eyes, and says, "What the fuck?"

Gary shrugs. He's still holding the bong, resting it against his shoulder as if it were a rifle. Then he tips the bong toward Linda, points the smoking barrel at her stomach, and says, "She's pregnant."

At this news, women emerge one by one from the darkest chambers and alcoves of the house. Some are barely dressed, wearing only underthings. Others wear long hockey jerseys or concert T-shirts that belong to the men they have chosen for the night. They surround Linda and gently prod her belly. *How far along are you?* they ask. *Is it a boy or a girl?* They move in closer and closer, confiscating her vodka tonic, relieving her of the roach pinched between her thumb and forefinger, until Linda becomes the nucleus, the Queen Bee of the party, pleasantly crushed by a circle of women who "ooooo" and "ahhhh" against her stomach and buzz with spurious tips on prenatal care.

Gary backs away from the chatter and smoke. As soon as he is outside, he bolts for his car. His coat, he realizes, is somewhere in the house, but it's too late now. If he returns, Linda will see him and want to leave as well, and what he wants now is to be alone. What he *needs* is to think.

Inside the Swinger, where everything is ice-cold to the touch, Gary starts the engine, then rubs his hands together, blowing frequently into the cave of his cupped palms. "Harvey *Wallbanger!*" he yells. "It's friggin' *cold.*" He yanks the gearshift into drive and pulls quickly away from the party, heading for the unmarked road that will take him home.

Only after putting a safe distance between himself and the party does Gary allow himself to entertain the otherwise unthinkable, that Linda is pregnant. He says it aloud, trying out the feel of it. "So," he says. "You're pregnant." Then he laughs. He laughs until his throat burns and the windows fog up all around him. "Pregnant," he says, clearing a swatch of windshield. "Yow!"

Other girls he's known have called it *prego*, like the spaghetti sauce, or *preggers*, which sounds to Gary like something made by Nabisco, a new brand of snack cracker. He can't stop shivering, and the convulsions come stronger each time he thinks of Linda walking around with a smaller, mucousy version of himself inside her. *Inside her.* The very idea! A person inside of a person! Now that he really thinks about it, pregnancy makes no sense whatsoever, a horror movie where a living organism grows and grows, until, finally, it bursts through an innocent victim's stomach, a terrible surprise for everyone.

Truth is, Gary knows less than squat about the finer points of the subject. He'd slacked off in Sex Ed, unable to stop himself from laughing out loud at words like *fallopian tube* and *mons glans*. And the textbook, with its floating orbs and scary cross-sections, was like some kind of underground Science Fiction comic book, where body parts looked extraterrestrial, and their corresponding names, like *vas deferens*, were obviously chosen for haunting effect. The one time he ever even remotely touched on the subject of pregnancy was with a kid he knew named Jim Davis.

It had been a peculiar friendship from the start, one that had materialized between seventh and eighth grade because all of Jim's real friends had gone away for the summer, and because Gary seemed the least harmful of prospects. The subject had come up in regard to Jim's mother, who was much younger than Gary's mother, and who doted on her son in ways that Gary's mother had never doted on him. Jim and his mother played this game, acting as if Gary were not among them: mother and son whispering, pinching each other, always telling the other one how cute they were. Gary never knew where to look, what to do, so he would stand off to the side, rearranging the fruit-shaped magnets and family photos on the refrigerator: a pineapple in lieu of a toddler's head, a giant banana sprouting from their schnauzer's butt.

One day, after a game of eightball in their basement, Jim Davis made a confession that he had once tasted an eighteen-year-old girl.

Gary imagined a fork and knife, a dash of salt. "When was this?" he asked.

"Birth," Jim said.

Gary leaned his head sideways, scratched the inside of his ear with the tip of the pool cue. What Jim Davis was claiming was that when he was born, he kept his tongue out the whole time, and even now, twelve years later, he remembered how it tasted.

"You want to know what it's like?" he said. "Go home and lick two hot slices of liver. I'm telling you, man, that's it. I shit you not, my friend."

Gary is on the unmarked road now, and since he is driving into the storm, it's significantly worse here than it had been on the highway. Visibility is zip. The wind has picked up, and snow swirls about the highway like smoke from a fog machine, not at all unlike the opening of that Megadeth concert three months ago. *Liver*, Gary thinks. He never touches the stuff. Gary squints for better vision. For stretches as long as fifteen seconds he can see one or two car-lengths ahead, whips of snow wiggling snakelike from one side of the road to the other, but soon they dissolve into dense sheets of white that repeatedly slap the windshield, and Gary cannot see more than a foot beyond his headlights. He doesn't want a child. Earlier that evening, in fact, he was devising a strategy for breaking up with Linda. Strategy is everything when it comes to breaking up, and what he always strives for is to find a way to make it look like his girlfriend's idea, and not his. You have to flip-flop the argument, twist words, drag the murky past for minor infractions. It's an ugly way to conduct business, but sometimes you have to jumpstart the end of a relationship, otherwise it'll just rot and stink up the rest of your life.

He knows he should ask for advice on this one, but he doesn't know who to turn to. Gary's father has his own problems right now: the man hasn't spoken a word to anyone in two weeks. And besides, Gary was cured years ago of asking his father anything about sex after the day his father pulled him aside to warn him about transmittable diseases.

"In the old days," his father began, "when I was your age, if you had the clap, the doctor would make you set your thing onto a stainless-steel table. You know what I'm talking about, right? Your thing. Your Howard Johnson. So you'd do what the man said. You'd slap it down for him to look at, and after you told him what was wrong, he'd reach into a drawer and pull out a giant rubber mallet, and then he'd take that mallet and hit your thing as hard as he could with it, and that would be that. Believe you me, son, you'd be *damn* particular from that point on where you went sticking man's best friend."

Gary is imagining his own thing getting whacked with a rubber hammer when someone or something steps out in front of his car. He is doing sixty or seventy miles per hour, the road is slick, and he touches his foot to the brake only after he has hit whatever it is that crossed his path. People claim that these moments always occur in slow motion, but Gary is so stoned, the opposite is true: everything speeds up. One second he is thinking about his thing getting whacked; the next, he is lying with his head on the horn of his car. He has no idea how much time passes before he lifts his head and steps outside, but it's still dark when he does so, and the falling snow, sharp as pins, has thickened.

Gary hugs his arms and limps to the front of what's left of the Swinger. What he hit was the largest deer he's ever seen: a twelve-point buck. A gem of a kill if he were a hunter, which he's not – the only nonhunter, in fact, in a long line of men who prefer oiling their rifles and shitting in the woods to smoking dope and listening to Ratt. The deer, apparently, had slid all the way up onto his hood, smashed the windshield, then slid back down after Gary, either semi- or unconscious, brought the car to a stop. It lay now in front of the Swinger, its black eyes eternally fixed on something far, far away. Clots of fur sprout from the tip of the crumpled hood, as if the car itself is in the first stages of metamorphosis.

Gary licks his lips and tastes blood. No telling the damage he did to his face when his head hit the steering wheel. For all Gary knows, his forehead is split wide open and his nose, through which he can no longer breathe, is permanently flattened. He may have a concussion, too, his brain puffy, slowly inflating with blood. But far more pressing than any physical damage is the sub-zero temperature. His entire body is starting to stiffen. He shuffles from foot to foot to keep warm. He rubs his bare arms and yells *Fuck* over and over. "Fuck, fuck, fuck."

Years ago he read a wilderness story in which a man stuck out in the freezing cold sliced open the carcass of a dead animal and crawled inside to keep warm. It was a bear, Gary remembers, and the man stayed inside of the bear until someone discovered him in there. Gary craves warmth, he's willing to make deals with a higher power, but he'll be goddamned if he's going to hang around inside of a dead deer and wait for his worthless friends and neighbors to find him. Besides, it's a small town, word travels fast, and he can't imagine any girl ever wanting to date him after hearing where he'd been. The girls he knows, they'll overlook the fact that you've slept with the town hosebag, but there is always a line, and sleeping inside of anything dead is clearly on the other side of it. Gary's about five miles from home – walking distance, really – close enough, he decides, to make a go of it, even without a coat.

Gary starts to jog, but his legs aren't working quite right. It's as if he's running on stumps instead of feet. He suspects a bone somewhere has snapped in two, so he works on the basics of walking instead, just keeping one foot in front of the other. He hugs himself the whole way, hands secured under his armpits. He'll have to wake his father when he gets home so they can tow the car before sunrise and avoid getting a ticket. He'd prefer not bothering him at all, but he sees no way around it. Gary's mother left home a year ago, and for a while Gary thought that this was the worst thing that could possibly happen to his father. Then, two weeks ago, his mother surprised everyone and married his father's best friend, a man named Chuck Linkletter. And that's when his father quit talking. He quit going to work at the gas station he owns, and he has quit taking calls. He has, it seems to Gary, quit altogether, like an old lawnmower.

Gary's ears and fingertips throb, and the snow pelting his face temporarily blinds him. His eyebrows are starting to ice over and sag, as are the few sad whiskers on his upper lip, a mustache Gary's been closely monitoring these past few months. He wishes he had taken the bong from the party. He'd be standing in the middle of the road right now, his back to the storm, lighting a fresh bowl. And then everything wouldn't seem so bad – Linda's news, his car, the pain.

When he finally reaches his house, shivering his way inside, he collapses next to the sofa.

"Oh. My. God," he says. "*I made it.*" His voice, a croak in the dark, sounds like the voice of nobody he knows. Now that he's home and out of the cold, he's thinking maybe he won't wake his father after all – towing the car no longer seems so dire – but then the light in his father's bedroom comes on, the door swings open, and his father appears as if from one of his own nightmares: sleepy but crazed, thin hair crooked atop his head like bad electrical wiring. This is how the man has looked ever since learning the news of the marriage, and though Gary is starting to wonder if he should seek professional help for his father, they live in a town of two hundred, and the only people around who claim to be professionals of anything either strip and refinish wood work or groom dogs.

Gary himself holds no grudge against his mother. As far as he's concerned, she's been a good mom. When Gary was in the third grade and his father refused to bring him a cat from the pound, his mother took Gary outside with several spools of thread. "You have to use your imagination," she'd told him. It was summer, and while Gary captured a few dozen grasshoppers, holding them captive inside of a Hills Brothers coffee can with holes punched in the plastic lid, his mother made several dozen miniature nooses with the thread. "Here," she said. "Let's see one of them." Gary gently pinched a grasshopper and held it up for his mother while she slid a noose over the insect's torso, then tightened it.

"What's his name?" she asked.

"Fred Astaire," Gary said.

Later, while Gary walked thirty or so of his grasshoppers down the street, Old Man Wickersham stepped down from his front stoop, stopped Gary, and asked him what he was doing.

"I'm taking my pets for a walk."

"Oh," the old man said.

Near the end of summer Gary had caught several hundred bumblebees, and over the next month, using his mother's tweezers and suffering through one painful sting after another, Gary managed to tie each surviving bee to one of his mother's nooses, and when he finished, he took all of them out for a stroll. The bees, droning overhead, followed him like a dark cloud. Old Man Wickersham burst out of his house, yelling, "My God, son, they're after you," and Gary, not realizing the old man meant the bees, let go of the strings and took off running. For days after that, people in town – and as far away as North Platte – reported getting tickled by mysterious airborne threads.

"Dad," Gary says now. "I totaled the car. We should probably tow it home before the police find it." Then Gary tells his father the story, omitting the pregnant girlfriend, the endless kegs of Old Style, and the four-foot bong. What he focuses on is the deer.

"You should see this thing," he said. "It's gargantuan. A twelve-pointer. Swear to God, I thought I slammed into a bulldozer."

His father puts on a coat and disappears through a door in the kitchen that leads into the garage, reappearing seconds later carrying an ax.

Gary, unable to stop quivering, the night's deep freeze still trapped in his bones, slips on leather gloves, zips himself into his father's wool trench coat, and pulls on a ski mask that covers his entire head except for his eyes and mouth. They take the new pickup, Gary's father skillfully navigating the vehicle at high speeds through miles of virgin snow. Amazingly, they cover in less than ten minutes the distance it took Gary an hour and a half to travel on foot.

His father parks in front of the dead deer and the demolished car, illuminating the scene with the pickup's high beams. The deer is already dusted with snow. Outside, towering over the carcass, Gary's father reaches down, takes hold of the base of the rack, and lifts the deer's head. He jiggles the head a few times, then crouches to get a better look.

"What do you think?" Gary asks through the ski mask. "Should we drag it by the horns or just back it ass-first into the ditch?"

His father doesn't answer. He walks to the pickup. He returns with the ax, lifting it over his head and taking aim.

"Dad," Gary says. "What are you doing?"

The blade comes down hard, slamming into the deer's neck. The deer's head rises off the ground, as if looking up to Gary for help, but it's the force of the blow causing it to do this, and the head falls quickly back into the snow. His father swings a second time, then a third, each time hitting a different part of the animal, though keeping within the general vicinity of the neck. It slowly creeps up on Gary that what it is his father is trying to do is chop off the deer's head. "The car," Gary says. "Maybe we should, like, shift our focus?" He points at the Swinger, but his father plants his foot onto the deer's ribs, jerks free the ax, then lifts it again. Each time his father lands a blow, Gary's fingertips and ears throb, a jolt of pain pulsing through the thousands of miles of nerves that twist and wind throughout his own body. In a few weeks, when Doctor Magnabosco asks Gary why he waited until the frostbite had progressed to this point before seeking help – this *critical* point, he'll add for effect – Gary will have no idea where to begin, nor will he know how to tell the story of this night in such a way that his father won't end up looking like a madman, and so Gary will simply shrug.

Gary watches his father through the tiny slits of the ski mask, and still unable to breathe through his nose, he starts gasping for air. His father is crying. He keeps slamming the ax into the deer, each strike harder than the last, and Gary realizes that he, too, is crying. He chokes out one breath after another, large plumes of air, ghostly in the truck's headlights, spewing from his mouth. He's about to say something to his father, a word or two of consolation, when a car approaches, slowing at the sight of them. The car hits its own high beams to see what's the matter, and what they see is a wrecked car, a dead deer, a weeping man holding an ax, and another man wearing a ski mask and a trench coat, glaring back into the eyes of the driver. In this moment, seemingly frozen in time, Gary spots Linda in the backseat, mittened hands cupped over her mouth. He starts walking toward the car, but the high beams blink off and the car speeds away, disappearing into thick swirls of snow, the red glow of taillights dissolving into two pinpoints, then nothing.

When Gary turns back to his father, he sees that the deer's head has finally come detached. His father lifts the head by the rack and carries it to the pickup where he heaves it up and over, into the bed. As for the other carnage – the headless deer, the wrecked car – they leave it all behind.

Once they are inside the truck's cab and on their way home, Gary experiences a surge of adrenaline, a genuine rush, and he can't wait to call Linda. He wishes he could hug his father, he wishes he could say, *Shit, man, what the hell just happened back there?* but his father is driving more cautiously now, both hands on the steering wheel, and any impulsive move on Gary's part may cause his father to drive them into a snowdrift.

Why another man's misery – his dad's, in particular – inspires Gary to want to call Linda and make amends, he's not sure, but he feels suddenly pumped, as though he has just had a great workout at the gym, his best workout ever. He feels almost *possessed*, but possessed by *what* he doesn't know. He's still too messed up to put his finger on it, to understand how one thing in his life could possibly be connected to another, but after he gets some sleep, he's going to call Linda and tell her that he has come to a decision. He, too, wants to keep the child.

"Fuckin' Aye, Dad," Gary says. "We took the bull by the horns, didn't we? And now we're bringing home the head to prove it."

His father laughs. His mood has taken a dramatic turn for the better. He is chipper, even. "We'll mount it," his father says. "We'll mount it and we'll send it to your mother and that son of a bitch she married for a wedding present. What do you say? You want to give me a hand with it tonight?"

"Tonight?" Gary asks. The sun is about to rise. Tonight, as far as Gary can tell, is over. It's already tomorrow. "Don't we have to get it taxidermied first?"

"Oh no," his father says, smiling. "Not this one. They'll get it just like this, nailed to a sheet of plywood. And I want to ship it off, lickety-split. I want to FedEx this baby right to their front porch. I'll show those two Harvey Motherfucking Wallbangers I mean business."

Gary removes his ski mask and touches his face experimentally. His flesh is disconcertingly spongy, and each time he presses down on his cheek or forehead, he leaves behind the soft imprint of his fingertip. "I think I'll pass," he says. "I'm sort of beat."

"Suit yourself," his father says. "But mark my words, this is going to be the highlight of the year. You can bet your ass on that."

Gary nods. He reassures himself that all of this is a good sign. At least his dad's talking again. Surely that's a step in the right direction.

They drive the rest of the way home in silence, the deer's head rolling around behind them, antlers clawing the truck's bed. Though the storm has ended and the sun is peeking over the tree line, the wind is still fierce, and Gary stares blankly at the snow whirling across the highway. His surge of adrenaline is on the wane now, the rush of exhilaration over. He's falling asleep, slipping into that precarious crack between consciousness and unconsciousness, but for a moment, before he drifts completely away, Gary pretends that he and his father have been in a fatal collision, and that although dead, they are still puttering along in the pickup, maneuvering it through swirling clouds instead of snow, and they are having the best time they've ever had together, father and son floating high above the rural roads and farms, two men no longer of this Earth.

Binding the Devil

JONIS AGEE

Eddie Falconer closed the front door of the Golden Rule Realty and took a long, hard look at the '72 Olds Cutlass at the curb. The black paint had a couple of dings in it these days, more farms on dirt roads for sale now that the tire factory had been bought by the plastic replica company and that Computer Camp, that's what they called it, had opened its doors to every sort of person from around the world. They even had a Bosnian restaurant-billiard hall in town now. Main Street had been dying on its feet, staggering into the next century when all this business hit like it was blown in by a good Kansas wind.

The Hirsh engine roared alive, and the twenty-eight rounds on the odometer stared accusingly as he shifted into reverse. "I know," he muttered. It was a good car – no, a great car – but it belonged in a collector's garage, not on dirt roads with the sound of gravel pinging against the paint. He needed to get something more practical that could take a beating.

Two blocks up Main, Eddie parked in front of Frock's Clean Center.

"Thank God, I gave my heart to Jesus thirty-eight years ago," Frock Walz said. Raising his coffee cup in a toast to the car out the window. "I'm tempted, I really am." Frock was the dry cleaning–laundry specialist in Bellefontaine, with a bank of washers and dryers churning out dollars twenty-four seven, and a daughter, Ivo, with nobody-home eyes to run them. His wife had up and died when the girl hit high school, which was just as well as it turned out. Even Frock didn't begrudge her that.

Ivo drifted to the coffeepot on the counter and stared out at the car too. Her flat gray-green eyes as vacant as the store windows on Main used to be. She poured a cup of coffee to the brim and let it spill over some, almost as if on purpose, then she swiped at the strands of dirty blond hair sticking to her hot face and spooned sugar into the overfull cup so it spilled some more. Black ants began to collect along the edges of the spill. Ivo dumped some of the coffee back in the pot and took a sip, then added more sugar, stirring with a finger that seemed oblivious to the heat. Eddie could understand how lucky Frock was to have Jesus in his heart.

"I'll buy that car," Ivo said to the air in the room.

Eddie's heart chunked. Later, he would tell his ex-wife, "You know how I used to say there's some things worse than death? Well, I really think that now."

Ivo was wearing a pair of men's red plaid undershorts, so large the elastic waistband clung to her naked hip bones as if it were going down for the third time, and the too-white thighs sticking out of the holes were so skinny they looked like a man's hand would crush them. On top she wore a red tee shirt cropped just short of her bra, the edges still bearing the violent scissor slashes as if she'd just cut it up this morning. Eddie remembered seeing Ivo running along the blacktop outside town at dawn and dusk, her long pale arms and legs churning awkwardly. She always looked like she was about to trip and tumble, her body made up of spare parts that couldn't be expected to move gracefully – tiny feet stolen from some child, big hands grabbing the air, boy hips and flat butt and then those breasts she must've inherited from her mother, high full saucers that bounced painfully on her chest.

"Honey, I don't think – " Frock said.

"I don't know, my mind's not right," Eddie said.

She drank some of the coffee, then poured in another tablespoon of sugar, spilling enough to make the ants swarm drunkenly. Setting the cup down, she said, "I'll get my purse so we can go for a test drive."

"At the light there's always a tunnel," Frock said, and Eddie could see the apology in his eyes. "She's got the money."

Eddie shook his head, refusing to look at the car again. This place smelled of hot bleach and soap bound up with cottony dryer lint, plus the stream of dry-cleaning chemicals that flowed in from the next room, but generally stuck to themselves in the hot, humid air. One of the reasons he'd never joined the Jesus boys was the Wednesday night Bible meetings here. But he was getting desperate about selling the car, his black beauty, his baby.

"Ready." Ivo appeared with sandals on her feet and a huge black leather shoulder bag that looked heavy enough to split her arm off. Then she'd need more spare parts. Eddie followed her to the car, intending to drive around town, show her how things worked before she drove, but she beat him to the driver's side, climbed in, and began adjusting the seat. Nobody ever touched the seat. He'd had it in the same place for twenty-five years, and when she pushed it back, there was a rim of brighter beige carpet beneath her legs. Even his ex had known not to touch that seat.

She started slowly, running the gears like she knew something and Eddie nodded as if consenting. He looked in Dub's Barber Shop to see if the usual characters had collected, but it was empty. They coasted by the Gem Theater, closed now.

"That's closed now," Eddie jerked a thumb toward the empty marquee and padlocked doors before he could stop himself.

"I do get out of the house, you know." Ivo pressed on the gas.

"Place was coming apart," Eddie continued as if she hadn't answered. "Just trying to find a seat was a trial, so many of them busted. Screen had holes in it, roof leaked, bugs and mice having a field day."

Ivo gave the big engine a real shove and the car leaped forward. She gripped the wheel tighter and grinned crookedly. The last of Belle-fontaine zipped by with Eddie half hoping the deputy was lurking behind the Quick Sack and Gas, which took over when Ideal Motors closed its doors. Now he had to go all the way to Useful to get his cars worked on.

They were rolling along at eighty mph, the big engine stroking smoothly when she used her knee to hold the steering wheel and started digging in the bag. He reached over to hold the car steady, brushing her leg in the process and she jerked back like she was snake bit, glared, and pulled out a pack of cigarettes. She put one to her lips and pushed in the lighter, then retook the wheel.

"No smoking in the car," he said in a small voice. He was losing control of the situation.

She acted like she hadn't heard him and held the glowing lighter to the tip of her cigarette, drawing deeply and filling the car with plumes of smoke. He cracked his window, which only drew more smoke toward him. She smoked hungrily, as if she couldn't get enough fast enough. He wondered how she could smoke and run.

Glancing over at him, she unrolled her window and let the smoke pour out over her. For the first time she grinned. "It's the kind of car makes you have to smoke in." She held up what was left of the cigarette, which was burning away quickly. "Organic. Had to give them up though." She pulled out the pristine ashtray, looked at him and quickly stubbed the cigarette on the cuff of her shorts instead, then tossed the butt out the window. She wet her thumb and rubbed the blackened cloth.

They rose up a hill, the engine never changing tempo, and coasted down the other side. Woods began to surround the road, and the air in the car cooled and sweetened. Last time he'd been this way was to show a little bitty place in Useful. Converted garage. But he'd made five hundred dollars and given it to his ex to catch up on the alimony. Twenty-five years of marriage and now he was paying for the privilege. The car was their last bone of contention. He'd rather sell it than hand it over and watch her drive it up and down Main Street, the engine dragging in first, until she ground into second. And she'd drive it out to see her folks on that gravel road and pretty soon she'd crack the windshield with a rock like always happened and let it go because it'd just get another one if she fixed the glass. Before long the special order beige leather seats would be cracked and split too because he wouldn't be around to rub them with the imported cream to keep them soft and pliable.

Ivo slowed and looked around. "Road should be – there – " The car coasted onto the dirt road and Eddie's heart thumped again.

"Go slow!"

This time she listened, downshifting, and the car immediately filled with a bobolink whistling and a woodpecker's persistent thumping on a tree overhanging the road. Red, black, and yellow butterflies flitted in front of the car and bounced off the windshield. A pair of cardinals chased each other in the limbs of trees just ahead of them. Somewhere in the shadows a blue jay squalled like a baby. The damp spice smell grew denser and filled the car, a heavy, heady scent that made him drowsy. He could almost hear the noise of their wings as the butterflies swam the air around them, dipping, curving back, coupling and releasing.

"My boyfriend's been UC-NR," Ivo said. "Unemployed on the couch, no revenue. Dad won't let me use the car to see him. On the weekends I can run out here, but it's too far during the week."

"Why didn't you just buy a car?"

Ivo thought about it. "I don't actually have a license, number one. And number two, I didn't want to – until I saw yours was for sale." Her voice softened and he felt it reach out for him in some obscure way, like a tendril, a hand.

"Here we are – " She pulled up and stopped in front of an ancient shack built of raw split pine logs that must have once been used as someone's hunting cabin. To the right, set a couple of feet off, was a tilting outhouse, the door tied shut with a red bungee cord.

Ivo honked the horn twice, filling the little clearing with the loud noise as she got out with the keys in her hand. She stood beside the car for a moment, then looked back inside. "Come on."

Eddie thought about the spare key he kept in his wallet. He should probably just go on back to town. Somewhere behind the shack, a dog howled and shut up abruptly. Yeah, he should just slide over and peel out of there. Ivo could run back to town, even if it was a weekday. He looked around for the boyfriend's vehicle. There was a rusted-out Jeep with its doors lying tangled in vines that had taken over the interior, walling the windows with green shadows.

"Les?" Ivo tapped her flat palms on the top of the car-door frame and scanned the shack and woods around it. "It's just me, Les – " she called and glanced over at him. "And Mr. Falconer. I got his car, come on – " She looked worried now and stepping out from behind the car door, she called again in a higher, more childlike voice, "Les? Les, honey? Are you in there, Les?"

"We should go on back," Eddie said. "I got an appointment." He hoped Les wasn't home. He hated the insides of these hillbilly shacks and just wanted to get back in the car with the too-skinny girl and drift on down the road to Useful, stop and have a burger maybe, talk the way two people can. Now that they'd stopped, he realized it felt good to have someone else drive, someone who had a real gift for it, and Ivo was a natural. Not the kind of woman he'd ever – she was just a girl, his friend's daughter, and come to find out she was hooked up with some out-of-work, no-good hillbilly –

They waited in the silence that had gradually settled around them, as if everything was waiting to see if they stayed or went away again.

Ivo made a sound like hiccuped whimper. "We have to go see – "

Eddie shook his head, looking down at his black dress shoes and tan trousers. He was at the end of his clean clothes and patience. Frock Walz would owe him dry cleaning for a month, but then Frock would probably blame him for being sucked into a deal like this with another man's daughter. The nearest dry cleaner outside Bellefontaine was twenty miles away.

On the porch, Ivo hesitated, then pushed the door open with her foot, standing to the side like a cop on TV before she could bring herself to look inside. Her boyfriend wasn't on the couch.

"Maybe he got a job," Eddie offered to avoid going further into the dark house belonging to a stranger in the Ozarks woods. They were officially trespassing in shotgun territory.

"He's here, I can feel it." Ivo lifted the surprisingly clean pink chenille bedspread on the couch as if he could be lying underneath.

The house was tidy, even the raw pine floor was swept up, and fresh field flowers dripping yellow pollen sat in a pickle jar on the homemade pine plank table. The cheese on the lunch plate had started to sweat and the edges of crackers were falling in the damp heat. Eddie hoped Ivo wouldn't notice, but she was already heading down the narrow hallway. The bedroom and kitchen would be strung in a line behind the first room in this layout. He hesitated before following her back there. She was stopped outside the door, her head leaning against the warped knotty pine that bulged at the top of the frame. Even before she pried the door open, Eddie could hear the smothered giggling.

Les Monroe was a medium-sized man who looked like he'd missed too many meals to ever catch up, and judging from the woman in bed next to him, there was a reason. For a moment Eddie was caught by the familiar dyed black hair, fleshy shoulders, and double chins, and his heart gave another clunk and shudder that this could happen twice. The terrible injustice of it came over his eyes like a thick red hood – he'd just kill her, that was all there was to do – murder her ass!

Then she turned her face defiantly toward them and it wasn't his ex, but the bartender from Douse's Inn instead. Eddie felt the anger flick its tail and slither out of him just as Ivo's breath whumped out like a thumped cushion.

Les lifted the arm hiding his eyes and grinned at them. He had a full set of teeth to match the round hard bareness of his head. His quick eyes shifted back and forth between the two of them while he adjusted the black sheet over his hips. Even his chest and legs were hairless, Eddie noticed, giving him a boyish quality that seemed odd, almost evil, against the bald head and clever old eyes.

"She's just my weekday woman, dahlin," he drawled. "You still got me on the weekend." He reached over and flicked the switch on the bucking horse lamp, illuminating the black cowboys walking around the edge of the yellowed shade. "See what she brought me?"

"You just smoked yourself right out of smarts," Ivo said. Grabbing the plastic baggie of dark green leaves off the dresser next to the door, she threw it at the bed, showering the two of them.

"Does this mean I have to do my own wash?" Les called after them, and the bartender laughed outright, followed by a piglike squeal.

Eddie was so relieved it wasn't his ex, that he opened the passenger door for Ivo without thinking. She climbed in and he shut the door. She handed the keys over without a word, crushed in the seat with her spare-parts limbs folded around her like a broken spider. He headed them back down the dirt road, then onto the pavement, feeling the mortal spills of their lives overlapping in the hum of the big engine powering its way up past 100, on through to 110, then 112, and finally 115 where they stopped hearing even the sound of the tires pulling sticky off the hot blacktop, and the pistons' pure oily rise and plunge dissolved into the roar pressing them past the limit of endurance. Suddenly he was glad he hadn't left her to run back to town on her own. If a person just had to go out and try love, Eddie thought as his foot asked for the last quarter inch of power left in the pedal, then you needed a good fast car to bind up the devil.

Dancing

KENT HARUF

Tommy Lewis was sitting in the Holt Legion on a Saturday night. He had been gone for a year but now he was back. When he had left Holt a year ago he had thought there was something more for him in Denver. That was after he and Bobbie had had their last fight.

"Go ahead," she had told him. "Don't let the door hit you on the way out."

"I won't," Tommy said. "Don't worry."

"You son of a bitch, Tommy."

"That's what you say."

"You bastard," she had said.

She had meant that; he knew that much about her. It had made him want to do something.

Earlier that morning (it was on a Sunday after a night of dancing and drinking at the Legion) she had been crying hard and weeping into a Kleenex so that her nose looked sore as it did when she had a cold, and her face had turned red and blotchy. But now, later in the morning, she was almost calm again. They were sitting in the living room. She was sitting across from him on the couch with her feet tucked up underneath her, under her blue robe. And she was talking to him. She was saying if he was going to leave, why didn't he? He said he was going to leave. Isn't that what he'd said? She wanted to know. Why didn't he go ahead then? Why didn't he go ahead if he was going to leave?

So he had stood up. He was a young man in his mid-thirties with brown eyes and black hair. "Look," he had said to her. "I'll tell you one thing. At least we didn't have any kids. That's one thing I know I'm glad of."

He had intended by saying this to make her cry again. He had wanted her to cry. Kids were a sore point between them. For a long while they had both wanted children and at least twice that he knew of, early in the marriage, Bobbie had gotten pregnant. But each time something had gone wrong and she had miscarried. Afterward Tommy had tried to be particularly nice to her; she had stayed in bed and he had brought her hot soup with tea and toast and some fruit on a tray, and he had gotten out one of the good linen napkins they had received as a wedding present. He had folded the napkin carefully, placing it beside the plate with the silverware over it. When they had gone to the doctor, though, the doctor wouldn't encourage them to think that Bobbie would ever be able to carry a child full term. There didn't seem to be anything to do about it. That's how things were.

Still, Tommy thought children might have made a difference. Children might have given them something to talk about. On the other hand, maybe this was deeper than children. Who could say?

But Bobbie didn't cry this time when he said that about kids. Instead, she simply stared at him from across the room. She picked up a cigarette from the coffee table and lit it and then, as if she had come to a decision, blew all the smoke in his direction. It seemed to Tommy a childish and mean thing to do. She was looking at him from behind the cigarette smoke. Her eyes were dark and cold, bloodshot from lack of sleep; her hair was a mess. She had thick red hair and he used to like her hair, the way it curled up in back. But now it was a mess. It looked like hell. And her eyes looked bad too. Looking at him, she didn't even seem to recognize him anymore. Here he was and she couldn't see him. That's how it seemed. And there wasn't any love left in the way she was looking. If there was, he couldn't see it.

Finally he went outside and stood on the front porch. It was late in the spring; the elm tree in the neighbors' yard was in new leaf and there was a thin patch of shade stretched across the street. The grass, where it wasn't shaded, was as brilliant as fire. Tommy stood gazing at the bright grass for a moment, waiting on the porch, listening through the screen door for what his wife would do now. He wanted to go back in; he wanted to say something more to her. But at the moment he couldn't think what it should be. Apparently she wasn't going to call him back. She wasn't going to do anything at all, only smoke on the couch with her feet hidden up under her robe while she stared across the room. But he knew in a few minutes she would get on the telephone as she always did and call someone. She would probably call Jan, or one of her other friends. She would tell them what had happened when she and Tommy had come home last night, and then they would tell her what they thought of it and how she should view this latest development in her life. Tommy could hear them already; they would make it sound like something out of a television show. And they would talk for an hour or two, for longer maybe, once they got started. He decided he no longer cared to hear what his wife would have to say. He walked off the porch and down the sidewalk and got in the car.

After that, he thought he'd try life in the city for a while. He had never lived in a city before. He thought of it as living in the fast lane. He'd work during the day and he'd play at night, and on the weekends he'd go trout fishing up in the mountains when he felt like it, and all the time he'd meet different people. That was the idea. Then he got to Denver and even after he'd been there for six months he found that it wasn't so easy for him to make people's acquaintance. They were all going someplace. Everyone had his own story. What happened was, he didn't get to know anyone to speak of, only the people he worked with at Haights Rubber, and half of them he didn't want to know any better. Then when he went up into the mountains it seemed that everybody and his brother were already there. He couldn't find a place that was quiet and undisturbed to drop his line in. The water was already stirred up and what trout there were would be as wild as cats.

At the end of a year he decided he might as well go home again. Why shouldn't he? At least he knew people at home.

Now in the Legion it was dark and smoky. It was still early yet, about nine thirty, but the place was already filling up with people. Tommy was sitting in a booth with Leo Hagemann and Milt Saunders.

When he had come in a few minutes earlier, Leo Hagemann had waved him over.

"Come over here," Leo said. "Where are you going? Sit down here."

"Hey," Milt Saunders said, "Tommy. Long time no see."

Tommy sat down. "I've been in Denver," he said.

"He's been in Denver," Leo said. "Didn't you know that?"

"I didn't think I'd seen him around here," Milt Saunders said. He slapped Tommy on the back.

Leo waved the barmaid over and ordered Tommy a drink.

Tommy looked around. All the booths were taken. Across the room men were standing up along the bar, talking to one another, leaning over people to tap their cigarettes in the ashtrays while they watched for a place to sit down. The barmaids had opened the big side room with its long tables and metal folding chairs, and the men standing at the bar could have sat in there, but they didn't want to. It didn't feel right sitting at a table with just men, as though you were at a meeting.

From the booth Tommy had a clear view of the band and dance floor. He had seen the band before. They were nothing great, although he thought the woman singing lead was good-looking and had a decent high voice. She had tight pants on and a pink blouse pulled low on her shoulders. When she sang the chorus she threw her head back so that you saw the swelling in the big vein in her neck. She never talked between songs. One of the men did the talking. He was a fat black-haired man with curly sideburns and played the guitar. The other two were a skinny drummer with long arms like a monkey and a bass player who closed his eyes when he played.

In front of the band there were fifteen or twenty couples dancing in the open space between the booths. They were moving about in circles, most of them in a shuffling two-step, although a few of the older couples knew how to fox trot and there were others who could manage the jitterbug when there was a fast song. After each song the fat guitar player made a joke or two and the people on the dance floor turned to look at him. Then all at once the band would pick up again, apparently from some private signal, and the woman would begin to sing, and once more the people would start to move about the floor. Between sets, while the band took a break, the jukebox was turned on and everybody returned to his place and drank.

It was during the break after the second set that Tommy noticed that Bobbie and her friend Jan had come in. They were standing near the bar in that crowd of people. Bobbie's hair had been cut in a new way, in a kind of bob, and she was wearing a short dress. Tommy hadn't seen her since he'd come back to town. He wondered if they'd say anything to one another before the night was over. Maybe they'd at least say hello. Later he might even ask her to dance.

Then he saw that the guitar player was standing beside her. He had a drink in his hand and he was talking to her, waving his glass while he talked; then he must have said something clever because both Bobbie and Jan opened their mouths and laughed. From across the room Tommy couldn't hear any of it, but he saw the women laugh and afterward he watched Bobbie pat the guitar player on the cheek. Then the man was saying something more, something that was funny too, apparently, and he set his glass on the bar and he took Bobbie's hand up and kissed it, bending over her hand as if he were a Frenchman. Tommy watched while Bobbie spread her dress to the man, and made him a little curtsy.

"Hey, Tommy," Leo Hagemann said, "don't look now. But isn't that your wife over there?"

"I see her," Tommy said.

"She's looking pretty good."

"We're getting a divorce."

"That's too bad," said Milt Saunders. "I hate to hear that."

Leo Hagemann said, "I didn't hardly recognize her. She looks different. Tommy, she's looking pretty good."

Tommy looked across the table. Leo was leaning forward with his arms on the table; he had both hands around his glass, turning it in his fingers. He was staring out at the dance floor.

Tommy turned back to watch Bobbie once more. The guitar player was gone now and she was talking to someone else, someone with a red shirt. He was a tall man with wavy brown hair. He was lighting her cigarette and she was holding under his hand to steady the match.

"Listen," Leo said. "Hey? What would you think if I asked Bobbie to dance?"

He didn't say anything.

"I mean, if it doesn't bother you."

"I don't know," Tommy said.

"What do you think?"

"I haven't seen her in a year," he said. "We don't even talk anymore."

"I guess that's the green light then," Leo said. He stood up. "Here goes nothing."

Tommy watched him walk across the floor. Leo looked heavier than he had a year ago. The tail of his shirt was sticking out, and he was wearing boots, shiny and black. Tommy watched while he walked over and stood beside Bobbie, patting her on the shoulder. Soon the music started up and Leo took Bobbie's hand and led her out onto the floor. Leo knew how to dance; he and Bobbie were spinning around, making dips and turns in time to the music, and people were making room for them on the dance floor. When the song ended Leo bent her over backward, as people did in the movies, and raised her again and gave her a hug. They stood laughing at one another and as the music started they began to dance again. Tommy watched for a moment longer; then he turned to look at Milt Saunders to see what Milt made of any of this.

When he noticed that he was being watched, Milt Saunders sank his head between his shoulders so that it appeared momentarily as if he had no neck. He reminded Tommy of a bird. Then Milt straightened up and raised his glass and drank from it.

Tommy watched him swallow. He had never before paid much attention to the movement of a man's Adam's apple.

By ten thirty the Legion was crowded and noisy. The band continued to play and everyone had to talk above the music if they hoped to be heard. Under the lights the thick smoke hung in the air like fog.

After a while, when Leo Hagemann went on dancing, Tommy stood up and moved to the other side of the booth. It felt uncomfortable, he and Milt Saunders sitting on the same side with nobody sitting opposite them. They sat across from one another, without talking, watching the dancers.

Later the barmaid came by and Tommy ordered another drink for himself and one for Milt. The barmaid was a young girl in blue jeans and a tight plaid shirt that had snaps instead of buttons. She was working very hard to keep up with the crowd; the hair around her face and at the back of her neck was dark with sweat and her cheeks were bright pink. When she returned with their drinks, she set them on the table on clean napkins and Tommy gave her a twenty-dollar bill. She made change and he left a dollar tip on the tray.

"Well, thank you," the girl said.

"You're welcome," Tommy said. "Any time."

She gave him a quick look; then she smiled a little and went on.

"Who's that?" he said.

"She's new," Milt Saunders said. "She's from out of town."

"Who is she?"

"She married that Simmons boy."

"Arnold Simmons? I thought Arnold Simmons was still in high school."

"He was," Milt Saunders said. "But not no more. He graduated."

Tommy watched the young girl move across the floor, moving back and forth between the booths and the bar, carrying her tray of drinks. He wondered if she were even twenty-one yet.

Then someone was pushing in beside him. He turned and it was a woman in her mid-thirties, a little too heavy but with a pretty face, and with long black hair and blue eyes and very white even false teeth. "Hey, stranger," she said.

"Hey," Tommy said. "Marla Kroeger."

"I thought that was you sitting over here," she said. "So I said I'll go over and say hello."

"How are you?" Tommy said.

Marla Kroeger was a bus driver for the Holt County School District. For a year she had come into the bus barn where Tommy had worked as a mechanic; she had been unhappy and he had listened to her while she had talked. She would talk and he would lie on his back under one of the buses and listen to her, and now and then he would look out at her feet and ankles and at her knees if she had a dress on. After they had gotten to know one another, the topic she had talked most about was her husband Darrel.

Darrel was one of the Kroeger boys, a wheat farmer out north of town. He was a huge man, with thick hands and thick wrists and heavy legs that stretched his pants legs tight when he sat down. He was older than Marla by seven years, but he had begun to date her, to take her out in his Oldsmobile, when she was only a sophomore in high school. That was thrilling to her, she had told Tommy, to have a twenty-three-year-old man ask her out and to take her places and buy her dinner and afterward to go driving in the country with him while the stars shone overhead and the radio played the top forty from Denver. It was thrilling, she had said, but by the start of the summer after her junior year she was two months pregnant. So she had to quit school.

"I didn't care about it at the time," she said, "one way or the other. I never liked school anyway. I think I was just waiting for something to happen."

"And then it did," Tommy said.

"Oh, yes," Marla said. "Doesn't it always?"

That summer she had married Darrel Kroeger and they had moved into a double-wide trailer northwest of town. Seven months later she had had a little boy. Then three years after that she had delivered another child, a little girl this time. That was enough; she had had her tubes tied after that.

So she'd had her hands full, taking care of the children, managing the house and the yard and the gardening, and doing everything else there was to do, being the wife of a farmer. But gradually the children had grown up and had become more independent, and then Marla was only twenty-six by the time they were both attending school.

"It was so quiet out in the country," she said. "At first I liked it, after the kids were gone. And Darrel, he was always gone somewhere. Darrel, he was always outside, crawling under his machinery or drilling wheat. Or driving off to some auction with his brother."

After a year and then the beginning of another year of this, it had begun to get on her nerves. She had felt raw, in some way. She needed a little excitement. She needed something for herself. "I got tired of standing in front of the picture window, looking out at the wind blow dirt across the yard."

So she had taken what was available. There was an advertisement in the *Holt Mercury* for a substitute bus driver, and she had applied for the job and was hired; and the next year there was an opening for a full-time driver and they had hired her for that position too. "It wasn't much," she said. "It wasn't legal secretary. But it did get me out of the house."

And that's where she was five years later when she had begun to come into the bus barn to talk to Tommy. She was out of the house, driving the country kids to and from school every day.

But she didn't think she loved Darrel Kroeger any more.

Oh, he worked hard and he wasn't a drunkard. It wasn't that. And he didn't hurt her, not physically, although more and more she wished he would leave her alone in bed. She wasn't interested in that with him anymore. It was getting so she felt suffocated by him. And she wished he would bathe more often. She liked things clean. What good did it do to wash the sheets and hang them out on the line so they would smell fresh of the outdoors, if Darrel wouldn't bathe when he came in at night? Well, he said he was too tired. Well, who wasn't tired, she wanted to know. Oh, she guessed she still loved him. But she wasn't certain of it. She wasn't certain how much.

"How can you tell?" she had asked Tommy. "How do you know the exact moment when love stops? That's what I want to know."

Tommy had listened to her while he had changed a tire or drained the oil or had done some other work on one of the buses. He hadn't known what to say in response to her talk. He had decided she didn't really want an answer. She had just wanted someone to talk to, someone to listen while she talked about her problems.

Now she was sitting beside him in the booth. Under the table he could feel the pressure of her leg against his own. They were turned in the booth so they could talk to one another.

"I didn't know you were back," Marla said. "I thought you were in Denver."

"I got back a couple of days ago," Tommy said. "What's today? I got back on Thursday."

"Do you think you're going to stay here now?"

"I don't know yet. Maybe."

"Well," Marla said, "is it nice to be back, Tommy? Does it feel good to be home?"

"It feels all right," he said. "Listen though: do you want a drink?"

"I already have one. Over there where I'm sitting." She pointed across the dance floor to a booth against the wall. There were two older couples sitting in the booth. "Why don't I go get my drink and come back?" she said. "Okay? Are you going to be here for awhile?"

"Yes."

"Then I'll go get my drink and come back."

"Go ahead."

"But don't leave," Marla said.

He watched her walk across the floor. She looked different in some way. What was it? Everyone in the Legion looked different. It seemed to him that everyone had changed. Bobbie looked different; her hair was shorter; and Leo looked heavier, bigger. Now Marla Kroeger appeared to be different too. Maybe she'd lost some weight. He didn't know. Then it occurred to him that he was the only one in the Legion who hadn't changed in the past year. And why was that? In a year's time something should show.

He looked across the table at Milt Saunders. Milt was turned half around, talking to the couple in the next booth. At least Milt Saunders looked the same. The couple in the other booth was telling him some story and he was alternately nodding and shaking his head, waiting for the point of the story. Milt Saunders looked as though he were prepared to laugh at any moment, as though he might sit there forever.

Then Marla returned and slid into the booth beside Tommy. She set a glass of something chocolate on the table.

"What's that?" Tommy said.

"Taste it."

"What is it?"

"It's amaretto and cream."

"I don't think so."

"It won't hurt you," she said. She was smiling at him. "You're so serious," she said. "It's Saturday night, Tommy."

Under the table he could feel her knee again. Her teeth looked very white and straight in the dim light.

Tommy said, "Who were you sitting with? Over there."

"Oh, that's my aunt and uncle," Marla said. "You know them, don't you? John and Marty Thompson?"

"Does he work at the elevator?"

"He did. He's retired now. They live over on Detroit Street."

"I didn't know he was your uncle."

"I'm staying with them," Marla said, "until everything's settled. You knew about that, didn't you?"

"About what?"

"Oh," Marla said. "Well, I left him, Tommy. Tommy, I've had it."

"You mean Darrel?"

"I couldn't take it anymore. You know how unhappy I was."

"I remember what you used to say."

"I've had it, Tommy. Do you blame me?"

"What happened finally?"

"Okay," she said. She was animated now. She sat up straight in the booth so that her knee no longer touched his. "You want to know what happened finally? I'll tell you."

She shut her eyes and took a breath. "About six months ago I told Darrel I wanted us to separate for awhile. Just try it for awhile, I said. On a trial basis, to see how we felt about it. The kids were both out of school. Marilyn had just graduated. I made sure of that. And Marshall, he was still working for his dad, but living in town on his own. Anyway, you know all that. Well, so I told him I wanted a trial separation. And that was the beginning of the end. After that things went downhill fast."

"How do you mean?"

"Okay. For instance there was this one weekend about three months ago?"

"Yes?"

"It was in the middle of this," she said. "This was in March. I decided I wanted the house to myself for one weekend. Up till then we'd been trying to live our individual lives in the same house. You know, separate bedrooms and different meals and so on. Well, you can guess how good that worked – no good . . . . Anyway, so I said, 'Darrel, I want the house to myself for once.' And Darrel, he agreed. That was okay with him, he said. He was supposed to stay with his brother and I was supposed to have the house to myself. Then on Saturday morning I was in the bathroom taking a shower and I thought I heard something. Then I thought I heard it again. So I put my robe on and came out. And of course it was him. It was Darrel standing in the kitchen. He looked awful. 'What are you doing here?' l said. 'You're not supposed to be here,' I said. 'We agreed.'"

" 'I can't help it,' he said. 'I love you.' "

" 'What are you talking about?' I said. 'Don't tell me that.' I said, 'Look, it's too late for this. You're not supposed to be here.' "

" 'It's my house too,' he said."

" 'But you agreed,' I said. 'You agreed you'd stay away.' His eyes were red. He'd been drinking, I could tell. Here it was the middle of Saturday morning in the month of March and his eyes were all red. I almost felt sorry for him. Usually Darrel, he's no drinker. He doesn't even know how to drink."

"But now he's saying, 'Don't do this to me, Marla. Honey, don't do this to me. I already told you I love you.' "

"That's what he says. Then he wants to take me in his arms, like it's okay again. Like he thinks nothing happened. He reaches out and grabs me."

"'Don't,' I tell him. 'Darrel, now don't do this. I'm telling you. I don't want this.' But he has his arms around me so I can't move. 'Damn you,' I say. 'Leave me alone.' Then he starts kissing me. I can smell it on his breath. He starts kissing my neck and face, he's kissing my mouth, and I don't know what I can do. He keeps kissing me and I can't move, I can't do anything. So finally, you know what I did?"

"No," Tommy said. "I don't have any idea."

"I bit him."

"What?"

"Yes. I bit him. I bit him on the cheek. Hard. So it drew blood. Then he slapped me. And it hurt too. It stung. But then I broke loose and ran back to the bathroom. He came after me, and I locked the door; only then I could hear him outside, breathing and turning the doorknob. I could hear him; it's like he's sobbing."

"'Marla,' he's saying. 'Honey, I'm sorry. I'm sorry, honey, open the door. Open the door, baby.'"

"'Get out of here!' I scream. 'Son of a bitch! Leave me alone! I'll call the police!'"

"And Darrel, he's still saying, 'Honey. I'm sorry, honey. Open the door. Open the door, honey. Open the door.'"

"And he could have broken it in. I know that. I don't know why he didn't. But I guess he thinks better of it. I don't know. Maybe he doesn't want to have to fix the door afterwards. I don't know what he's thinking."

"Anyway, now it's quiet. It's silent. Then I hear something out in the kitchen again. A grunt or a cry, I don't know. Then I hear something fall, something that sounds like it's heavy. And I think, Oh no, now what's this? Now what's he done?"

"And what was it?" Tommy said.

"I'll tell you," Marla said. "I didn't know what it was. Only finally I know I have to unlock the door. So I do. I unlock the door and I walk out into the kitchen. And there he is. There's Darrel. He's laying there on the floor beside the dishwasher. He's laying flat on his back and there's this knife sticking out of his chest."

"Wait. You mean he stabbed himself?"

"Yes. He's pulled a butcher knife out of the kitchen drawer and stuck it in his chest."

"And now he's dead?"

"No. He isn't dead. I might respect him if he was dead. He's bleeding a lot, but he isn't dead. He's laying there moaning and groaning and bleeding on the floor, holding this knife upright in his chest. So I bend over him and pull his hands away, to see how bad it is, and then the knife falls loose."

"And all the time he's going, 'Marla, honey. Marla . . .' Like that. And he opens his eyes at me. He has this look on his face. He's stuck the knife in the meaty part of his chest about a half-inch. It's a good cut, so it'll bleed; but it isn't deep. He isn't in any danger. But he has this look on his face and he's going, 'Honey. Baby, don't leave me.'"

"Well, then I stood up. 'You son of a bitch,' I say. I wasn't even screaming at him now. I was standing over him. I say, 'Goddamn you, Darrel. You're going to have to clean up this mess yourself. I'm not going to clean up this mess. I'm through. Do you hear?' I say. 'I'm leaving. Darrel, this is it. I don't want anything more to do with you.'"

"And that's when you moved into your uncle's?" Tommy said.

"Yes. And my aunt's."

Tommy sat looking at her. He'd forgotten how her eyes changed when she talked. Her eyes looked darker. "But what happened to Darrel?" he said.

"Oh," Marla said. "Oh, he got up in a minute and called his brother."

"How do you know that?"

"Because. I was in the bedroom packing. I could hear him. And I was just leaving when his brother drove up. His brother drove him into the hospital here in town and they cleaned him up. They gave him a tetanus shot. As for Darrel, he was all right."

"But Jesus," Tommy said. "That's some story, Marla. Jesus, that's a hell of a story."

Then Tommy couldn't think what more to say to her. There should be something more, but nothing occurred to him. He looked away.

And then it was that he discovered that sometime during the telling of this story, Milt Saunders had disappeared. Milt Saunders wasn't sitting across from them in the booth anymore. Tommy couldn't see him anywhere.

It was nearly midnight now. Marla Kroeger and Tommy Lewis sat watching the dancers.

After a time Marla said, "Anyway, Tommy, I feel better now."

"Do you?" he said.

"Yes. I'm happier now, Tommy."

"That's something," he said. "I'm glad of that much."

In the Legion the music and noise was loud around them. It seemed to Tommy that, if anything, the noise was louder than ever. It was too loud. It made it hard to think. He was having trouble concentrating.

And then, unexpectedly, out on the dance floor he could see his wife again. Bobbie was dancing again. Her short dress was swirling up above her knees and he could see that her hair was dark with sweat. She was dancing with somebody else now; it wasn't Leo. He could see Leo over by the bar talking to whoever that was with the red shirt, the man who'd lighted Bobbie's cigarette earlier. He and Leo seemed to be having a serious conversation. They were talking. Their heads were close together.

"Oh, Jesus," Tommy said. "I don't know."

"What?" Marla said. "I can't hear you."

He turned in the seat toward her. It was as if she were someone else, someone he didn't know.

"Listen," he said. "Marla?"

"Yes?"

"Listen. Do you want to dance?"

Crete

MARLY SWICK

A month after our daughter's sudden death, I came home from work one afternoon and found the house empty. There was a one-line note from my wife on the kitchen table saying that she had decided to take a trip back to Crete, Nebraska. I was dumbfounded. Not only had she not been back to her hometown since she'd left at the age of eleven, but over the years she had steadfastly and stubbornly refused my suggestions that we return for a visit. In those early days of our marriage I'd been hell-bent on playing resident shrink and believed that it would be healthy for her to see the place again – to demythologize it, as it were. But even when we were moving from Berkeley to Madison, driving cross-country on Route 80, she had violently vetoed my suggestion that we take the twenty-minute detour. Sensing my slightly petulant disappointment, she'd said to drop her off in downtown Lincoln – she'd browse through the shops while I took a drive out to Crete and satisfied my morbid curiosity once and for all. I was tempted but shrugged off her suggestion, arguing that *she* was the one who should see the place, not me. In truth, I think I was a little afraid to go alone. Even though rationally I knew that whatever there was to see was in the past and only my wife could see that. Still, years later, reading her brisk, businesslike note, I felt profoundly gypped. As if, after all my years of urging and waiting, she had sailed off to the lighthouse without me.

The note did not say how she was getting there. I had a sudden vivid image of her boarding the plane in the faded flannel nightgown she had worn day and night for the past month since changing out of the black suit she'd worn to the funeral – her long hair straggling down her back uncombed, the other passengers giving her wide berth. Ophelia flies the friendly skies. Taking a few steps down the hall, I was relieved to find the familiar pink nightgown drowning in a puddle of water on the bathroom floor. She had taken a shower. I took that at least as a good sign. Then I walked back down the hallway and opened the garage door. Clutching the damp nightgown, I sat in the driver's seat of my wife's old Honda Civic like some psychic searching for telepathic clues. That night I couldn't sleep. I went to bed early, tired from grading British Lit blue books, or perhaps I was just tired of grading blue books, because I lay there tossing and turning, restless in the bleak dawn, until finally I fell asleep for a few minutes and dreamed I was driving through wheat fields. Literally. There was no highway. The car just skimmed along, effortlessly plowing through the graceful undulating wheat – the agrarian version of the parting of the Red Sea. When I woke up, the first sunlight was just trembling through the blinds and I imagined how it would be out on the interstate with the early morning sun at my back – bright and spacious and fast – and suddenly I knew it was the thing to do. It seemed that my wife had planned it this way, testing me. Together we would go back to the moment, the accursed spot, and then we would start over again, fresh. An exorcism of sorts. I leapt out of bed. It was a ten-hour drive from Madison to Crete. My classes were over for the semester, and there was nothing to prevent me from throwing a small suitcase in the car and following my wife. I could be there by suppertime.

Before I left the house, I turned down the thermostat in the hallway and then paused for a moment outside Lyddie's closed door, my hand paralyzed on the doorknob. It seemed to me I could hear her breathing in there, but I could not bring myself to open the door. As I walked outside to my car, I had the uneasy sense that I was forgetting something, something important, and as I sat in the car waiting for the motor to warm up, I thought of all the times I had complained about the hassle of finding babysitters, of being tied down and unable to take off for New York or Katmandu on the spur of the moment (as if I ever had). And as I backed out of the quiet driveway, I remembered a painful scene with a new babysitter – Lyddie wrapping herself like a boa constrictor around my leg, sobbing histrionically and shouting "Don't go, Daddy, don't leave me!" as I resolutely headed toward the front door, dragging her along with me. It had taken all three adults to pry her loose and carry her howling to her bedroom. I apologized to the shaken babysitter, raising my voice to be heard over my daughter's muffled but persistent wailing. In the car my wife, also shaken, suggested that maybe we should stay home, see the movie or play – I don't even remember now – another evening, since Lyddie seemed so distraught. I'd pounded the steering wheel and said no, she had to learn. What kind of monstrous adult would she grow into if we always gave in to her? My wife had reluctantly agreed that I was right and we had gone off to wherever we were going that night. When we got back home, the babysitter was peacefully watching TV and assured us that Lyddie had stopped crying as soon as we'd left and the two of them had "gotten along famously." Smiling, I had turned to my wife and said, "See?" But now, of course, these are the moments that haunt me. I wish I could run the tape backward, like a home movie. There I am walking backward toward the house. There I am lifting Lyddie up off her bed, bringing her back out to the living room, holding her in my arms.

The morning had been clear and crisp in Wisconsin, cold bright sunshine reflecting off the thin hard crust of snow, but just east of Omaha the sky bleached to bone and it began to snow lightly, a few flurries every now and then. I felt myself tensing as I fiddled with the windshield wipers and negotiated the rush hour traffic after miles and miles of open country. I suppose the tension might also have had something to do with my nearness to my destination. The questions I had been ignoring for the past ten or eleven hours seemed to be waving their hands wildly in my brain like overeager students demanding to be called on. How would I find my wife? Would she be glad to see me? Was this really such a good idea? I passed a billboard for Boys Town and remembered that old movie with Spencer Tracy as the priest and Mickey Rooney as the orphaned kid, or maybe it was Jackie Cooper. *Boys Town,* The name seemed so quaint, so wholesome and Midwestern. I was surprised the place still existed. Then it occurred to me that if my wife had been a boy, maybe that's where she would have ended up. I felt a sudden coldness and moved the car heater up a notch.

My wife I will call Jane Jones. Even with a false name some readers may recognize the details of her life or at least vaguely remember having read something in the newspapers years ago. Particularly if they were in or around Nebraska in the late fifties, which I wasn't. I was busy riding my souped-up two-wheeler in the unblinking Southern

California sunshine. I had a paper route during the year that my future wife's tragedy was reported in the news, and I always get a little cosmic chill when I think of myself blissfully, ignorantly flinging those rolled-up papers, like so many diplomas, onto our neighbors' neatly tended lawns. Both my parents, high school teachers, were avid newspaper readers and sometimes I try to imagine just what I might have been doing on that early June evening while they were busy reading about the grisly fate of my future in-laws. It is the split-screen contrast that gets me: the idea that while I could have been nursing a Popsicle, watching *Dragnet*, fighting with my younger brother over some minor territorial trespass or pleading with my mother to let me stay up an hour later, my future wife – age eleven, a year younger than I – was surrounded by actual homicide detectives who offered her sticks of Black Jack gum and refused to let her go inside her own house, where everyone was dead.

My wife has never shared my "morbid," as she deems it, fascination with her past. The first and most deadly fight we ever had was over this very issue. Shortly after our first anniversary, she stormed out of a party one night, leaving me to find my own ride home, and later accused me of "putting her on public display like some freak in a freak show." She had overheard me telling one of her piano students' parents about the murders, even though she had sworn me to secrecy. "You didn't marry me," she screamed, "you married *In Cold Blood*." She'd had it, she swore. I was on probation. And I knew she meant it. I apologized abjectly and swore to keep my mouth shut, it would never happen again. And it never did. Even when the topic of conversation, as it not infrequently does in these times, turned to the latest sensational murder, I would look over at my wife and dutifully change the subject to something bland and boring.

In the meantime, I generously allowed my wife to commandeer my own "Leave It to Beaver" childhood. From time to time at some cocktail party or backyard barbecue, I have been startled to overhear her casually relating a small anecdote from my childhood as if it were her own. The anecdotes are usually rather dull and ordinary, which is, of course, precisely what charms her about them, and the listener usually looks mildly bored and impatient, having grown up safe and sound in the suburbs himself. I can never help imagining how his expression would change from polite boredom to impolite avid curiosity if my wife were suddenly to tell him the real story. To tell him how she'd been sleeping over at a neighbor friend's house when they heard all the commotion and saw all the police cars. How they ran out onto the front lawn in their baby doll pajamas, and the first thing my wife saw was Bobby Axelrod, her sister Marjorie's recently spurned boyfriend, seventeen, being dragged toward a squad car, all handcuffed and bloody. How she'd had a little sister's crush on Bobby who, unlike Marjorie, had always treated her nicely when their mother said, "And take your little sister along." How he'd gallantly bought her ice cream at the roller rink or popcorn at the movies while Margie alternated between yelling at her and pretending she didn't exist. So how her first thought on seeing Bobby like that was there'd been some accident and he'd hurt himself. How she shouted out his name, and as she ran across the street before the police could grab hold of her, he sort of smiled and winked at her and tried to wave, just as if nothing special had gone on in there. How they could all hear the dog, Taffy, barking shrilly in the backyard, hurtling itself against the chain-link fence, and hearing the dog, how she suddenly started to cry. And best of all, how as Bobby passed her, flanked by two policemen twice his size, he twisted his head back in her direction and said, "I'm real glad you weren't home."

It was dark by the time I reached Lincoln. Somewhere on the open, rolling stretch of highway between Omaha and Lincoln, I got cold feet; I decided to postpone my arrival in Crete until the following morning. The snow was starting to fall more heavily and steadily, sticking to the asphalt. The radio weatherman was predicting a foot or more before morning. I was tired now from all the driving and didn't know if there was even a motel in Crete. The car slid and fishtailed at the red light, jolting me into wide-awakeness. In the distance, through the lace curtain of snow, I could see the capitol building, beckoning like a lighthouse to a weary sailor. Cautiously, I headed downtown in search of food and shelter. I checked into the Cornhusker Hotel, took a long hot shower, and then made my way down to the dining room for dinner. As I passed the reservations desk, I noticed that a small crowd had gathered, dripping snow onto the carpet and talking among themselves about the blizzard. Seated at a quiet corner table for two next to the window, I looked out onto the deserted street and watched the sudden gusts of snow shivering against the plate glass. As I watched the parked cars vanish under a blanket of white, I wondered where my wife was and what she was doing at that moment. In my split-screen imagination, I saw her sitting at another table in another restaurant not far away, watching the snow, slowly sipping a single glass of red wine. And as I picked up my glass of house burgundy, I had the eerie sensation that our movements were synchronized.

After dinner, I headed moodily back up to my room. On the elevator with me were a husband and wife and their small blonde daughter. The sleeping girl, swaddled in a fuzzy pink blanket, was slung over the man's shoulder limp as a large rag doll. The wife reached over with a crumpled Kleenex from her coat pocket and wiped something red and sticky off a strand of her daughter's pale hair. The elevator doors opened and the family got off on the third floor. I could hear them arguing about which direction their room was in as the doors slid shut again, and I continued my ascent alone. Back in my room, changing into my pajamas, I was suddenly seized by a terrible jealous rage toward the man in the elevator – as if this man had butted in front of me in line and managed to finagle something that should, by all rights, have been mine – and I wanted to protest bitterly, to complain to whomever was in charge. I wanted to pick up the phone and dial the manager and through the sheer logic and poetry of my justifiable complaint, get the whole sorry mess straightened out. I imagined handing over Lyddie, still wrapped in that fuzzy pink cocoon, to my wife, who always cringed whenever I complained about poor service. "See?" I would say. "You have to speak up. You can't take these things lying down."

The next morning, after a quick cup of coffee and bowl of cornflakes, I checked out of the hotel. Snowplows had been working through the night. As I headed out of town toward Route 77 South, the sun was glittering off the powdery snow, the sky was baby-blanket blue, and for entire seconds I would experience a sort of false happiness, a mirage of happiness brought on by the perfect day and the exhilarating motion. For a moment, I would hum to myself, forgetting who I was and where I was going. For a moment I was a college kid, one of my students, en route to Aspen or Sun Valley for a ski trip. Then I would remember,

I would remind myself. And if I didn't remind myself, something else would. On the outskirts of Lincoln, I passed by the Nebraska State Penitentiary. A concrete wall with guard towers surrounded the stark brick building. I looked for guards armed with rifles, but the towers appeared to be empty. Even though last we heard Bobby Axelrod had been transferred to some prison in Iowa, I imagined him right here. The car seemed to slow down of its own volition as I watched the penitentiary recede in the rearview mirror and pictured Axelrod sitting at a long cafeteria table or doing calisthenics in the yard like movie prisoners. My mental picture was clear even though I'd never actually seen a picture of Bobby Axelrod. If there'd been any in the three family albums my wife had inherited, they had been removed. I suspected that her Aunt Rosemary had gone through and plucked out any disturbing photos before handing the albums over to her niece, but, unlike my own Kodak-mad family, the "Joneses" weren't much for photography and it's entirely possible there never were any snapshots of Margie and Bobby.

From Route 77, I took 33 west to Crete. I had forgotten how flat it was out here, flat as a dinner table covered with a snowy white linen tablecloth, or a vast empty stage. This road was not so well cleared. I slowed to well below the speed limit, following a safe distance behind a battered pickup. After miles of white nothing, we passed a GM dealership and a big furniture store. Out there in the middle of that lunar landscape, they seemed like relics from some defunct civilization. But shortly thereafter, things picked up. An Alpo plant, a small boarded-up motel, houses. CRETE, population 4,872. Two intersecting blocks of small shops and restaurants, a couple of banks, the library, the newspaper office, Heidi and Harold's Cafe, the Alibi Lounge – all laid out as neat and square as a Monopoly board. At the end of Main Street I could see the Crete Mills and what I took to be silos towering over the prevailing flatness. No sign of the Maidenform bra factory where my wife's father had been a superintendent. One of the few facts my wife freely offered about her childhood. Imagine, she'd say, how warping for a young girl to have to say out loud in public that her father worked at a brassiere factory.

I didn't have much of a game plan, I now realized. I suppose I'd imagined simply bumping into my wife on the street or finding her registered at some cozy little bed-and-breakfast, although it now seemed apparent that there was no such place. But, still, the town was no bigger than the town I had imagined, and I had every faith that I would find her because I knew that she was waiting for me to find her. We had been married for nearly fifteen years. I had the sense that she knew exactly what I was going to do, was orchestrating my movements just as surely as if she'd drawn me a map.

My first destination was the house. No doubt almost anyone on the street could have pointed me to my wife's family's house – even kids too young to have been alive when it happened – but I preferred to find it myself. I remembered the name of the street, Forest Avenue, because a realtor in Madison had once taken my wife and me to look at a beautiful old house on Forest Avenue, just the sort of house we'd always wanted, but my wife had refused to get out of the car when she saw the street sign. The older residential section of Crete seemed to be back out in the direction I'd come from. I drove methodically – up each street and down the next – Juniper, Ivy, Oak – solid old two-story houses with a few newer fifties-style bungalows mixed in, neatly shoveled walkways, an occasional Santa's sleigh or makeshift Nativity scene, white wood churches, brick churches, an elementary school with no kids in sight. The streets widened, the terrain sloped upward, the houses grew larger, and suddenly there it was – on the corner. I recognized it immediately from the photographs in my wife's albums. The house had been painted yellow instead of white, but it was otherwise the same. The same shutters, the same wraparound porch, the same chain-link fence erected to keep the dog, Taffy, from being run over. Only superimposed over the bare trees and snow-shrouded shrubs was a picture of green leaves and grass and vivid flowerbeds, the way I remembered it from the photo albums. In the albums, it was eternal summertime in the exterior shots; the winter snapshots, the annual Christmas gift-opening scenes, were always indoors, shot with a cheap flash camera that made everyone's eyes glow red, like demons in a horror film. I parked across the street and sat there staring, waiting for it to hit me – this was it, the cursed spot – but it looked so unremarkable, so snug and well tended. Bright curtains on all the windows, a wisp of smoke drifting from the chimney, a holly wreath hanging on the front door. I felt disappointed, let down. I suppose I had expected to see peeling paint, sagging steps, broken glass, doors banging in the wind, cobwebs and bats – a haunted house. The Bates Motel. As I sat there watching, a large orange cat leapt on top of the sofa and stared out at me, blinking in the bright sunshine. My wife was allergic to cats.

The next stop on my mental itinerary was Aunt Rosemary's place in Beatrice (pronounced Bee-at-trice), which, according to the map I'd checked at breakfast that morning, was only twenty or so miles south on 103. I looked at my watch and decided to grab a quick lunch before heading back out onto the highway. It had begun to snow again, a light confectioner's dusting. With the perfect snow and the chamber of commerce Christmas decorations suspended like tinsel tightropes across Main Street, downtown Crete looked like the set of *It's a Wonderful Life*.

It was early for the lunch crowd and the Sportsman's Grill was nearly empty except for a few old-timers sitting in the booths, hunched over cups of Sanka. I slid into a booth about midway down the dusky aisle. When the waitress appeared, I ordered a cheeseburger and a Coke. To pass the time until my food arrived, I was skimming through the song titles on the tabletop jukebox when two women and a man bustled past, their winter coats emitting clouds of cold air, and settled in the booth across from mine and up one. The two women slid into opposite sides of the booth while the man hung their coats on some pegs. Then the man slid in next to the woman with her back toward me. All three ordered black coffee. The waitress brought my food and I eavesdropped as I ate. The couple was buying a house – apparently they'd just put in a bid on some place that morning – and the other woman was their realtor. She reminded me of someone, someone whose face I couldn't place, but then the older I got everyone looked familiar; a truly original face was as rare as a truly original idea; every semester I seemed to be lecturing to the same impervious faces. The man was a nervous wreck – tapping his silverware and twitching around in his chair like some hyperactive child. The real estate agent noticed me staring and flashed me a big smile, as if to assure me that everything was perfectly all right, couldn't in fact be any better. The moment she smiled, I recognized her. Some shutter clicked and I could visualize the wavy-edged snapshots in my wife's photo albums with the neat, cramped captions: *Janie and Betsy, First Communion, 1955. Janie and Betsy, Bathing Beauties, 1956.*

And so on. The two of them seemingly inseparable. In the last snapshot – *Chang and Eng, Halloween, 1958* – they had actually bound their arms and legs together with twine and, an inspired touch, braided their long hair into a single thick plait, an exotic copper and platinum snake. The one time I'd asked my wife whatever happened to Betsy, she'd shrugged and said they'd lost touch when she – my wife – left Nebraska.

Stunned, I sat there mute and motionless as my wife's childhood friend swooped up the bill and the man retrieved their coats. She was coming toward me, still talking, not even seeing me, and then just as she passed by my booth, my hand shot out and I cleared my throat. She paused, startled, with a half-friendly smile on her face. "Excuse me," I said, "but I couldn't help overhearing you. I'm new here and might be interested in some property. I was wondering if you've got a card you could give me."

"No card," she said, smiling more broadly. "But the name's Betsy Beemis and I'm with Ace Realty, just a couple doors down. You interested in residential or commercial?"

"Residential."

The couple with her shuffled impatiently.

"I got to run, I'm afraid, but give me a call later on" – she paused as if mentally flipping through an appointment book – "say about four, four-thirty – and I'll be happy to help you. Your name's?"

"Jones," I said. "Paul Jones."

She reached out and shook my hand. "Welcome to Crete, Mr. Jones. Crete's a nice friendly little town. Safe, quiet. You got kids?"

I gripped my coffee cup and shook my head no. "Just my wife and me."

Her smile faded a little, as if she sensed she'd somehow hit the wrong note. "Well, see you later then, I hope?"

"Definitely."

I turned to watch her leave and then turned back to my lunch. My half-eaten cheeseburger was floating in a pool of rusty blood, already half congealed. I shoved the plate aside and tossed my napkin over it, repulsed, wishing I'd ordered the grilled cheese instead. I rarely ate meat. My wife was a strict vegetarian. When I met her, she shopped only at health food co-ops and her kitchen cupboards were full of strange-smelling bags of unfamiliar teas, spices, and grains. She seemed to subsist on handfuls of raw crunchy stuff. I kidded her about her Squirrel Diet and she kidded me about my Elementary School Lunch Diet – Kraft macaroni and cheese, hot dogs, canned chili. But even though I teased her about it, I was attracted by her idiosyncratic purity. When we met I saw right away that she was not like the other young women I'd known: she was stripped clean of all the baser emotions, like bone purified by fire, all the fat and gristle singed away. Before I ever managed to maneuver my way inside, I knew just what her apartment would look like: spare, modest, bare white walls, a single mattress on the floor. The mattress, as it turned out, was covered in crisp white sheets the likes of which I had not seen since leaving my parents' house. After we started sleeping together, I took to calling her "Saint Jane."

The waitress sidled over, refilled my coffee cup, and slid my plate away. "How was everything?" she asked a bit aggressively, eyeing my half-eaten sandwich.

"Fine," I assured her. "Guess I wasn't as hungry as I thought."

Mollified, she smiled and wagged a flirtatious finger at me. "You're a bad boy."

The waitress's facetious remark seemed to hang in the air after she'd gone, like some Delphic insight into my essential, unalterable nature. And she was right: I was a bad boy. I had thought at first that my wife's goodness would rub off on me and I would become a better, more generous and compassionate individual, but in fact the opposite had occurred. Balanced precariously on the edge of that single mattress covered with those chaste and snowy percales, I would try to lead her into temptation, try to make her say something petty and catty about some mutual acquaintance – a former lover, say – but she would only look uncomfortable and retreat into a noble silence. It was as if she, with her stubborn goodness, had created a deficit of spite that I was forced to balance out. It all backfired. None of it worked out the way I'd hoped. My original hazy intention was that I, a callow catastrophe-less child of the suburbs, would marry into this tragedy of my wife's and thus attain the status of tragic hero – like a foreigner marrying to achieve American citizenship – and all without actually having to shed any tears or break any skin, so to speak. I guess you could say I wanted *to have suffered* but I did not actually want *to suffer*. The actual suffering itself I would just as soon skip. I was no masochist. I just wanted – I don't know what precisely – something she seemed to have that I didn't. Some charisma possessed by the extraordinarily fortunate and unfortunate of this world.

The coffee had swelled my bladder. I got up and walked back to the men's room. On the way back out, I caught sight of a pay phone. I dug a fistful of change out of my pocket and dialed our number in Madison, just in case she'd already done whatever it was she'd come to do and gone back home, expecting to find me there waiting for her. I let it ring and ring, picturing first the wall phone in the kitchen and then the princess phone on the night table by our bed. When I hung up finally, a sudden strong gust of depression hit me. Maybe she didn't want me to find her after all. Maybe I had it all wrong. I thought about going to the police station, filing a missing persons report, but somehow it seemed like a mistake. I knew my wife wouldn't like it. I could see the reproach in her eyes, as if she were sitting across the table from me. *But what was I supposed to do?* I'd say. *I was worried about you.* Tomorrow morning, I told myself. If I haven't found her by tomorrow morning, I'll go to the police. On that decisive note, I walked back up front to the cashier. Sitting next to some miniature peppermint patties on the counter was one of those donation cans for Muscular Dystrophy with a glossy picture of Jerry Lewis and some little girl all dressed to kill in pink ruffles and leg braces. I'd always hated Jerry Lewis, thought he was a real unfunny idiot, but when the cashier handed me back my change, I stuffed it into the can, almost five dollars. For no good reason. My little girl had died of something else – spinal meningitis – a disease that didn't even have its own movie star.

At four o'clock I was standing on the street in front of Ace Realty, pacing. I had spent an unproductive afternoon driving out to Beatrice only to discover, from a neighbor lady, that Aunt Rosemary was now living in a nursing home outside of Denver near one of her sons. Then I'd driven back to Crete and spent a couple of hours hunched over a microfiche machine at the public library, reading and rereading the newspaper accounts of the murders, glancing guiltily over my shoulder to make sure my wife wasn't watching. There was a prom photo of Margie and Bobby Axelrod so close to the one I'd always imagined that it gave me the chills: Bobby in a white tux, smiling self-consciously, like a bad actor, standing at attention next to Marjorie in her stiff full-skirted dress, a crushed gardenia drooping from the thin shoulder strap. But the only new detail I gleaned was that Marjorie had not died in the house, as I had always assumed, but had in fact been rushed to the hospital where she'd died the following day, having regained consciousness just long enough to say, "Tell Bobby I forgive him." A detail that I found highly suspect, like a false note in an otherwise gripping novel.

It was cold – the digital clock on the bank said ten degrees – and finally, when she still hadn't appeared by four-fifteen, I got back in my car parked a few feet away and turned on the heater. Every five minutes or so I'd get out and peer in the plate glass window to make sure she hadn't entered by some back door, but I could see the empty desk with her nameplate facing me. At a quarter to five, as I was peering intently in the window, she tapped me on the shoulder. "I'm so sorry," she apologized breathlessly as I followed her inside. "The escrow officer was late and there was nothing I could do." Sighing, she slipped off her coat and stamped her boots. "It's really snowing out there." She sat down behind her desk and I sat down in the chair opposite her. Her cheeks glowed a rosy pink from the cold and with her bright windblown red hair she seemed altogether too vivid for such drab and businesslike surroundings. "Now, why don't you tell me what sort of thing you're looking for, Mr. Jones." Behind her easy smile, her voice sounded a little stiff, rehearsed, almost apologetic, and it occurred to me that she was new at this.

"Actually it's not Jones. It's Vilmore, Paul Vilmore." I paused, waiting to see if the name struck a chord. It did. As her smile flickered, I rushed on. "I'm looking for my wife. I thought maybe you'd seen her."

"No." She shuffled some papers around on her desk. "I'm afraid not. We lost touch years ago." I didn't believe her. She was too unsurprised. After all these years she should have been astonished, astounded at the very mention of Janie.

She glanced up nervously and must have seen that I knew she was lying. "Well, actually, she did stop in here for a couple of minutes yesterday." She looked down at the papers again. "She asked me not to tell anyone."

"And?"

"And nothing. I was on my way out the door with a client. We hardly had time to exchange two words. She said she'd give me a call." Flustered, she looked pointedly at her watch and stood up. "I'm afraid I have to pick my son up from day care. He's five and this is his first month in day care full time. He carries on like he's dying if I'm a minute late." She inhaled sharply and looked away, and I knew that Janie had told her about Lyddie.

"Look," I said, touching her arm lightly, beseechingly. "I'm worried about her. She hasn't been herself since our daughter died." I took my hand away. I could see her hesitating, mentally weighing something, sizing me up. I stood there embarrassed by what she must be thinking, resisting the urge to defend myself, to protest that I did not drink or gamble, that I had never laid a hand on my wife, that I had never even been unfaithful. As she pulled her gloves out of her coat pocket, her car keys jangled to the floor. "Please." I bent down and held them out to her. "If you know anything – "

"Look," she said briskly, taking the keys from me. "I really do have to run." Then something in my expression must have caused her to relent. She sighed. "Why don't you drop by the house around seven, after I've fed Ryan. We can talk then." I nodded as she scribbled the address on a While You Were Out memo. "Thanks. I'll be there." As I followed her out of the office, I glanced down at the address and was surprised to see that she still lived on Forest Avenue, the house she grew up in, across the street from my wife's. "I really appreciate this," I told her.

"You seem like a nice guy." She shrugged.

Watching her pick her way carefully down the icy sidewalk in her high-heeled boots, I felt a huge lump of gratitude lodge itself like a snowball in my throat. At that moment, standing there in the freezing darkness in the middle of nowhere, it seemed like the nicest thing anyone had ever said about me, the highest possible accolade.

It was snowing hard as I drove back in the direction of Forest Avenue after killing a couple of hours over a bean burrito at El Toro. I was beginning to feel like Dr. Zhivago, trudging through the Siberian steppes, weary and heartsick. The house numbers were impossible to read in the dark through the thick, wet swirl of snow, so I just parked across the street from my wife's old house and trudged up the block until I came to a modest aluminum-sided cube with a screen porch tacked on one side. It was the only house on the block that was not outlined in colored lights and the only one whose walkway was not neatly shoveled. As I ploughed my way through the ankle-deep snow, it seemed to me I suddenly knew how Betsy's life had gone: like something out of a Bruce Springsteen song.

When I rang the doorbell, she opened the door right away. Trusting. As if she'd never heard of crime. Her hair flamed in the bright overhead light of the foyer. I had always assumed the snapshots in my wife's albums must have exaggerated the shade, but if anything, they'd muted it.

"Come on in," she said, leading me into the living room. She was one of those petite perky women, high school pretty. In the snapshots Betsy is cute and sexy, smiling confidently at the camera, while my wife is gawky and thin-faced, self-consciously scowling, her future beauty a well-kept secret. The photographs always break my heart. I wish I could have been there, standing off to the side, whispering in my future wife's ear, "Relax. Smile. You're going to be gorgeous," just as the camera shutter clicked. Dressed in jeans and a baggy plaid flannel shirt, Betsy had not changed much in the twenty-five years since those photographs. She seemed to have shed twenty years along with her business suit and high heels. Suddenly it was not at all difficult to imagine her standing out on the front lawn on a warm summer's evening in baby doll pajamas.

As I was thanking her for agreeing to see me, a child's voice whined, "Mommy, Mommy, come up here. I *need* you!"

"That's Ryan." Betsy smiled. "I better go see what he 'needs.' Make yourself at home." The living room looked like a set from *Father Knows Best* – the sort of vinyl couches and waxy chartreuse lamp shades that would sell for a small fortune in the trendy shops in Chicago or L.A. A small cluster of photographs in lacy gilt frames huddled together on the mantel making a united stand against the encroaching army of bric-a-brac. I walked to the fireplace to take a closer look, thinking that perhaps I might find my wife's face smiling at me from one of the group photos. But up closer I could see at a glance that all the children were of a younger generation. As I stood there at the mantel, I suddenly had the odd certainty that my wife had stood very recently where I was now standing looking at these same pictures. I could feel her lingering presence in the room like a ghostly trace of perfume. On the mantelpiece, as in time-lapse photography of a rose blooming, a red-haired baby developed from cuddly infant in playpen to cute, grinning toddler on tricycle, to surly sneaky-faced punk on dirt bike. For a moment, I was almost relieved that Lyddie would never grow up. "That's Dale, my older boy," Betsy said, walking up behind me. "He lives with his father." She let out a sigh that seemed to sum up years of heartache. "You want coffee?"

"That would be very nice, if it's no trouble." I followed her into the kitchen, which was messy but cozy and smelled good. A pot of chili was congealing on a cold stove burner. Crayoned drawings were stuck to the refrigerator with alphabet magnets. I remembered the look on my wife's face the day after the funeral as she peeled our daughter's last masterpiece – a gaudy tempera self-portrait with two hamsters – off of our refrigerator, painstakingly easing the Scotch tape loose so as not to tear the fragile edges, and put it away in the filing cabinet. My hand shook as I took the coffee mug from Betsy.

We returned to the living room with our coffee and a plate of cookies. "Nice place," I said after the first scalding sip of instant coffee. "Homey."

"I moved back in when Mother had her stroke. She died last year."

"I'm sorry." I sighed, waiting for her to bring up the subject of my wife.

"She was old," she said, shrugging, "but your little girl" – she shook her head – "I'm so sorry." She looked truly sympathetic as she held out the plate of cookies toward me, then hurriedly set it down again, as if suddenly realizing the poverty of the offering in contrast to the richness of my loss. To be polite I took a Fig Newton.

"Do you know where my wife is?" I asked softly.

"Not really. As I said, we really didn't get much of a chance to talk." She looked down and busied herself rearranging the cookies more symmetrically on the saucer.

"After our daughter died, she didn't leave the house for a month. I couldn't get her to go to a movie or restaurant or even to the grocery store. Then suddenly I come home and find she's taken off for Nebraska." I leaned forward in my chair. "You sure she didn't say anything? No hint?" Nervously she reached across the coffee table and snatched an Oreo off the little saucer like a guilty kid expecting to get her wrist smacked. She twisted the cookie into two halves, the way Lyddie used to do, and nibbled around the edges of the frosted half. I sighed again more loudly.

"She told me not to say anything," Betsy said with apologetic stubbornness. "I promised."

"But *why?*" I exploded, then took a moment to calm myself as I saw Betsy retreat slightly in her chair. "I don't get it." My voice was soft, sad, bewildered. I held my head in my hands and pressed the heels of my palms against my eyelids, as if to force some sudden insight. "Did she say why?"

Betsy suddenly leaned over and put her hand on my shoulder, the kind of warm, spontaneous demonstrative gesture that my wife and I had always been incapable of but always affected me deeply. I fought against the urge to bury my head in her lap and bawl like a wounded, outraged baby.

"She probably just needs some time alone," Betsy said soothingly. "To get herself together. She was always that way. She never liked people fussing over her." Absentmindedly she picked up another cookie then set it back down. "I'm on a diet." She smiled a self-deprecating little smile and waved her baggy flannel shirt. "Summer's coming."

"It's only December."

"Thank you." She picked up the cookie again and took a bite. "You're a college professor, aren't you?" she said shyly, with a tinge of old-fashioned deference I hadn't heard in decades. "Janie was always smart, too. Straight A's. I was never much of a student myself." She took another bite of cookie. "You know I tried to keep in touch with her after" – she paused delicately, apparently reluctant to speak of such tragedy aloud – "after she moved away. I wrote to her but she never answered my letters. Once I even called her long-distance, when Gary and I got married. Her aunt back east gave me her number at college. Her roommate answered and took a message, but she never called me back. Or sent a card or anything. I was always sort of hurt. But I understood," she added quickly, lest I think she was blaming my wife for any petty little lapses in etiquette after the terrible thing that she'd been through.

"She doesn't like to talk about the past," I said. "She doesn't even like to think about it. You shouldn't take it personally."

"Oh, I didn't. I mean I tried not to."

"She's talked about you a lot," I lied.

"Really?" She brightened. "I figured she'd forgot all about me. With her college friends and all."

I stood up. "I better get going. Thank you for the coffee. It was a pleasure meeting you," I said with a sort of formal awkwardness that I tried to offset with a quick clumsy hug. "I'd have recognized you anywhere, from the pictures. You've hardly changed."

"Not like Janie anyway. God, I didn't even recognize her. She's beautiful."

I nodded. "She doesn't believe it though. She still thinks of herself as a beanpole with braces."

"Yeah, and I still think of myself as head cheerleader." She gave a funny little varsity leap, and we laughed for the first time.

As I was pulling on a glove, she reached a hand out and took hold of my arm – our little outburst of silliness suddenly seeming to break through her solemn resolve. "Look, I know where you can find her. But you're not going to like it." She paused as if to give me time to stop her. I pulled on my other glove and remained silent, afraid to say anything – just generally afraid – and after a moment she went on. "She's rented a house. That's why she came to see me yesterday – she'd heard I was in real estate. And she said she figured she could trust me to keep it quiet."

"A house," I repeated blankly.

"A small one-bedroom place on Ivy. Kind of run-down really, but she said she didn't care," Betsy rushed on, anxious to fill in the details now that the dam had broken.

"It was the first place I showed her. She hardly even looked at it. I told her I thought she could do better if she looked around more – there's some nice new townhouses over near the college, but she didn't even want to take a look." Betsy shrugged. "She said she wanted a house with a garage, nothing fancy."

"I can't believe it." I stood there staring at the front door, seeing my motionless hand reaching for the doorknob. Half of me wanted to drive right over to Ivy Street and force a confrontation, to have it out once and for all. The other half wanted to get in my car and just keep going, to California maybe, or New Mexico. Get a new driver's license, a new life. I took a step toward the door.

"Where are you going?" Betsy said, worried and protective, as if I were her responsibility now, as if it were all somehow her fault. I could tell she was the sort of woman who blamed herself for everything, took it all on herself, no matter what – the shiftless husbands, the delinquent son, the invalid mother, now me. "She's not there. She didn't take the place 'til Friday afternoon and there's no way she could've got the utilities hooked up. She's not going to sit around some empty house in the freezing dark."

"I just want to see the place," I said, but I wasn't so sure.

"It's a blizzard out there. You can't drive back to Lincoln in that. Why don't you at least stay and have a drink, figure out what to do." Before I could answer, she was off to the kitchen.

She had reminded me that it was Saturday night. When she came back with a bottle of Jack Daniel's and two glasses, I said, "I'm not keeping you from anything?"

She shook her head and splashed a couple of inches of bourbon into the glasses.

"Cheers." Our glasses made an ironic clink. I eased back on the sofa and looked around the room, imagining myself living there. Betsy sat down on the sofa next to me but a safe and respectable distance apart. I sighed and she reached out and squeezed my hand. We sat there holding hands like a couple in a doctor's waiting room, waiting to be summoned for some bad news. But what bad news was left? My daughter was dead. My wife was leaving me. I reached out and touched Betsy's red hair, imagining my wife's pale straight locks interwoven with Betsy's, moonlight and sunlight. "Chang and Eng," I mumbled and held out my glass for a refill.

"How're you doing? " She tapped her stockinged foot lightly against my shoe as she poured me another shot.

"Couldn't be better."

"That's the spirit." She looked relieved. I looked away. Just like my students, I marveled, no sense of irony.

She shivered. "I'm going to build a fire."

"I'll help."

She scrunched newspaper while I took a couple of logs from a crate by the fireplace and stacked them with extreme precision, absurdly anxious to impress her with my manly fire-building prowess, to show her that I was not just some effete intellectual. That wasn't why my wife was leaving me. Pleased when the fire caught easily, I sank back onto the sofa feeling a kind of simple domestic contentment I had not felt in weeks, since before Lyddie suddenly woke us up in the middle of the night, feverish and crying. It seemed more like years than weeks. I could feel myself melting. The bourbon was like a low-banked fire glowing inside me and the fire was like a warm soft blanket someone had tucked over me. Betsy leaned forward and unearthed a large photo album from a messy pile of magazines underneath the coffee table.

"I thought you might like to see these." She flipped through the plastic-coated pages. "See." She pointed. "There's Janie and me naked. A little kiddie porn for you."

I slid closer and adjusted the lampshade. There they were, huddled together in one of those inflatable backyard wading pools. Just out of frame someone was holding a garden hose. Water arced through the air, splashing them. Betsy was laughing. My wife's expression was more tentative, a mixed grill of emotions. I knew that expression all too well. "Turn the page," I said.

As I sat there looking at the snapshots, listening to Betsy's easy, open narration, I felt a growing excitement, the kind of excitement I felt when I was working with a text, making discoveries, solving the mysteries, almost as if the characters were confiding in me their hidden secrets. For fifteen years my wife had been guarding her past like a jealous dog with a bone, snarling at me whenever I ventured too close, and now it was as if Betsy had suddenly rewarded me out of the blue with a whole treasure trove of buried bones. She flipped the page and a loose snapshot fluttered into my lap. I turned it over: my wife with her normally lank corn silk hair all tortured and sprayed into a droopy confection of curls holding an older boy's hand, gazing up at him with a lovesick smile. I knew even before Betsy whispered, "That's her with Bobby Axelrod."

We both sat there staring at the photograph in silence, searching for some sign of destiny, some visible portent, but there didn't appear to be any. He was just a nice-looking boy with a sweet smile. She shut the covers of the album. "I guess that's it."

Overcome by the warmth from the fire and the bourbon and Betsy's extravagant generosity with the past, I leaned over and kissed her. "You don't know what this means to me," I whispered, "thank you."

She nestled over against me, and the album slid off her lap with a heavy clunk. As I bent down to pick it up, she wrapped her arms around me and we sat there necking in the firelight, tasting the bourbon on each other's lips, like two crazed high school kids until a charred chunk of log split off and landed with a small shower of sparks on the hearth perilously close to the gold shag carpeting. Betsy leapt up, grabbed the poker, and swept the sputtering log back toward the fireplace. Then she sat back on her heels, looking up at me with a dazed and unfocused expression. "Did you hear something?" she said, poking at the ashy wood in the grate.

I shook my head and struggled to sit upright.

"I thought maybe I heard Ryan. But I guess not." Her voice sounded small and forlorn. "Fire's about dead. What should we do?"

"Got any more logs? " I smoothed my hair down.

"In the garage," she said, pointing vaguely.

I stood up abruptly, glad to be given a task. I walked purposefully if a bit unsteadily toward the garage. In the five seconds it took to navigate myself through the kitchen to the back door, the hot liquid passion was already starting to cool off, as if I'd suddenly swallowed an ice cube of guilt that was spreading through my bloodstream. *Jesus*, I thought. This was crazy, sick. I paused and tucked my shirt firmly back into the waistband of my slacks. The instant I opened the garage door a blast of arctic air hit me.

I fumbled around for the light switch. The cold air slapped my brain awake – alert, bracing. As the overhead light blinked on, I spied the logs stacked haphazardly against the far wall, next to Betsy's beat-up Chevette. Seeing the Chevette, I flashed on Janie's old Honda parked in our garage back home and I heard Betsy's voice saying, "*She said she wanted a house with a garage. Nothing fancy*," and I froze. Scared stiff. I don't know how long I stood there like that staring at the car before Betsy appeared in the doorway and said, "What's wrong? Don't you see it?"

"Get your coat," I said. "Hurry."

When we drove up, I could see the ghostly trail of exhaust drifting out from under the garage door. The car engine reverberating in the empty garage sounded so loud I was amazed that it had not roused the neighbors, but the houses on either side were dark, oblivious, muffled in snow. I insisted on sitting in the car with my wife's body while Betsy ran next door to call the ambulance and the police. When she returned, she knelt by the passenger's side where I was sitting and tried to coax me out of the car, treating me with a tender and delicate deference, as if I were some sort of celebrity invalid. She was talking softly, her face close to mine, and I was startled all of a sudden by what I saw there. I recognized the expression in her eyes when she looked at me and the tone of her voice when she spoke to me. It was like looking at myself all those years ago. And I knew, I knew precisely what it was she wanted from me and what she would have to pay to get it. She reached for my hand. I pushed her away. "Leave us alone," I growled. She snatched her hand back as if I'd bitten it. In the distance we heard the faint wail of a siren speeding closer. Betsy walked down to the end of the driveway, glaring back at me reproachfully, as if I were some mean-tempered, old jealous dog with a bone.

As I lie in bed night after night in the dark, I see it all on the split-screen, over and over again, the midnight show: while Betsy and I are toasting by the fire, my wife is sitting in the rented Chrysler LeBaron in the cold dark garage, running the car heater to keep warm. For a while she just thinks, plays the radio, eats some candy. (There were two Milky Way wrappers lying on the seat next to her.) About the time Betsy and I are looking through the old photographs, she flicks off the car radio, having decided what she wants to say, and turns on the battery-operated cassette player she uses with her piano students. She records her message, which is short and businesslike: *I should have been home that day Bobby shot everyone else. I should have been there. I always knew that down deep. I can't live knowing that my daughter paid for my not being there.* Her voice sounds nervous and self-conscious, thinner and higher and more Midwestern than her usual voice, and when I hear the tape, it strikes me that it is the voice of an eleven-year-old. She turns off the recorder. The garage door is already shut.

About the time that Betsy pours us more bourbon, my wife turns the ignition key and rolls down the car windows. Betsy and I grope each other on the couch, my wife bunches up her coat to make a pillow and stretches out on the front seat. Her pulse slows as ours quickens.

I remained in the car with my wife. I couldn't move. The blank white garage wall was like a movie screen, and as we sat there in the front seat holding hands in some grisly parody of a couple at a drive-in, the story of our whole marriage flickered across the screen accompanied by a babbling sound track inside my head that made no sense, as incomprehensible as Chinese. I reached over and turned on the radio. Classical music, measured and civilized, filled the small car. The Chinese babble quieted. I closed my eyes and felt something pass from her to me in the darkness, some intangible inheritance, and in those few oddly peaceful moments before the ambulance wailed and screeched into the driveway, red lights flashing, rousing the neighbors from their innocent dreams and guilty nightmares, I felt that we were more in tune, in harmony, than we had ever been before – as if some slight but persistent foreignness had disappeared, some long process of naturalization had finally been completed, and, after all these years, my wife and I suddenly found ourselves citizens of the same country.

Bad Family

LEE MARTIN

Each Wednesday, Miss Chang drives downtown to the YMCA where for two hours couples practice the waltz, the swing, the Texas Two-Step. Often, she stands at the fringe of the dancers because she comes alone and must wait until she has worked up enough nerve to say to another woman, "You must excuse, yes?" Usually, the other women relinquish their partners to her graciously, but from time to time someone will hesitate, obviously annoyed, obviously wishing Miss Chang would choose some other couple to disturb. "That Chinese woman," she hears someone say one night. "Why would a Chinese woman want to learn the Cotton-Eyed Joe?"

She wants to learn because she has never been a graceful woman. When she was a girl, Mao sent people to the countryside to learn the meaning of work from the peasants. Miss Chang traveled to Inner Mongolia. She was fifteen, and for eight years, she dug ditches and water wells. She wore men's trousers, the legs rolled to her knees. She slogged through the muck, her steps heavy and thick. Even now, her feet on solid ground, she carries the hobbled motion in her legs. All day at the Mane Attraction Beauty Salon, she moves in halting steps as she shampoos, cuts, and perms. Only her hands, small and delicate, are agile and quick. She rarely drops a comb. Her fingers massage other women's scalps. Sometimes she remembers how Mao's Red Guard, because her parents were intellectuals who had gone to the University, cut her mother's hair and shaved one half of her head so when she went out on the street, everyone would know she came from a "bad" family. Now Miss Chang's customers tilt their heads back into the cupped groove of the shampooing sink. They close their eyes. "Mmmmm," they say, and Miss Chang closes her eyes, too, and tries to feel the same luxurious motion they must feel when her fingers dance across their heads.

She has tried t'ai chi, but she lacked discipline and balance; yoga, but she tired of tying and untying the knot of herself. She likes to watch *Club Dance* on the Nashville Network. She marvels over how women who have no natural claim to grace – who are too old, too heavy – can become so radiant, so lithe, in their cowboy boots and sequined shirts, bright scarves tied around their necks. The women spin and step, all of them smiling, never once looking down at their feet, as if this is a snap, this dancing, this beautiful liquid motion they have become.

"Some are water, some are stone," her mother told her when Miss Chang came back from Mongolia, her body bulky and hard with muscle, a slim, delicate girl no more. "You, Li, you shouldn't wait for a husband. You should go to the University instead."

By this time, the American president, Nixon, had come to China – Mao had opened his arms to the West – and now there were even Americans teaching English at the University. Miss Chang fell in love with one of them, a slim, gentle man named Don. No one could understand how she could love an American, but she did, and when Don promised to uphold China's socialist principles, the government gave him permission to marry her. Then they managed to leave China, a feat that thrilled both of them, particularly Don, who boasted to friends in America that he had smuggled a China doll out of the country.

And now she is Lily, a name she has chosen for herself. Lily Chang because she has taken back her father's name. Lily because she wants to think of herself as a water flower, pretty and delicate. Here in Nebraska, she sees the plains stretch out for miles to the distant horizon, looks up at the vast sky, open and blue above her, and believes all things are possible, even at her age, even now.

Since their divorce, Don has been eager to do whatever Miss Chang asks, even agreeing to allow her to attend the dance class he and his new wife, Polly, teach. Miss Chang knows he can't forgive himself for taking her from her family and her country only to divorce her. "You should come after me with a butcher knife," he said to her once. "I wouldn't blame you." She told him, "Life's too short to drag around a bitter heart. What's done is done."

She lets him take care of odd jobs around her townhouse. He changes her furnace filters, mows her lawn, tends to her landscaping. And Polly never complains. The joke among the three of them is, all it takes is a divorce to make a marriage work. "Why can't people be kind to each other?" Polly says.

Miss Chang has never been able to dislike her, because before the divorce, the three of them were friends. Saturday nights, they would go to the Plamor Ballroom to listen to music, and sometimes Don and Polly danced. Miss Chang was always too shy, and besides, she liked to watch Don dance. His steps, precise and fluent, seemed to carry him back to some ancient form of himself – the patient, humble teacher she had fallen in love with in China. He had given her, his student, words and grammar, a language with which to speak her heart, but in America, *his* land, he became boastful and pedantic. "You don't know what it's like here," he told her. "It's a different world. Everyone's out for himself. You'll have to get an edge to you if you want to get along. I'll teach you."

He lectured her on customs and conduct. If a car cut over in front of her on the street, she was to honk her horn and drive as close to the other car's bumper as she could. "Make the asshole sweat," Don told her. "He'll think twice before he cuts someone off again." When someone called on the telephone wanting money for this cause or that, she was to hang up. "We'll pick our charities," he said. "We won't have them forced upon us." And she wasn't to pay any attention to express line limits in the supermarket. "Groceries are groceries. It's all highway robbery. Who's counting?"

It was his constant watch and guard that eventually drove them apart. "You won't listen to me," he told her. "Why won't you listen?"

She wouldn't listen because she found the vulgar behavior he prescribed unsavory. She could never imagine Polly doing any of the things Don suggested since Polly was too kind, too polite. "Milk and honey," Don said once. "A real lady."

But with Miss Chang it was a different story. With Miss Chang, it was always, "You've got to toughen up. You can't let people run over you." Don harped and harped at her. But on Saturdays, when they went with Polly to the Plamor Ballroom, he was a gentleman. He held doors open for Polly and Miss Chang, pulled out their chairs, stood each time one of them left the table. He became the charming guardian he had been when he had first won her.

Even now, under Polly's spell, he is eager and quick to serve. When Miss Chang thinks of the three of them and the common affection they have been able to manage despite the divorce, she feels a spark kindle inside her, and she knows it is her heart, and she knows it fires with longing and with rage.

Wednesday nights, at the YMCA, it embarrasses Miss Chang to have to bow to the American women, to ask for their husbands. She understands what an intrusion she is, and deep down, though she knows it is meanspirited of her, she imagines that Don could see all this coming when he agreed to let her attend the class without a partner.

One night, he takes her by the hand and says, "Come on. Show me what you've learned."

Polly is strolling around the gymnasium, weaving in and out through the couples, stopping to watch this one or that. Miss Chang admires her small feet, her narrow waist, the way she steps across the waxed floor when she and Don demonstrate a dance.

But now Miss Chang is dancing with Don. Her left hand is on his shoulder; her right palm, meeting his left, is held out into the air at their side. They are doing the waltz, and she has no trouble following Don's step-close-step. But she is on the watch, waiting for the moment when he will push against her left hand, the slightest pressure, and begin to promenade her backward. "Walk your lady across the floor, gents," he said the first night of class. "Don't bore her with the easy stuff. She deserves a chance to put on a show."

Don is chewing gum, and Miss Chang can smell his sweet, candy breath. His gray hair is parted neatly on the side, and the soft knit weave of his polo shirt is pleasant to touch. She is dancing with him, and she knows people are watching. He has chosen her, Lily Chang, and she is in step with him, in time with the music, and soon he will press her backward, and she won't miss a beat. Her feet will glide back as his own come forward, and she won't stumble or hesitate. She'll escape the thick weight of herself, and even if, as her mother suggested all those years ago, she be stone, she will be, for a short time, a small stone, flat and smooth, skipping lightly across the surface of a pond.

But Don never presses against her hand. He keeps her moving in the simple 1–2-3 box, and soon she starts to feel the insult of it all. He doesn't think her capable of anything beyond tracing that box over and over, and once she knows that, she feels a great rage and shame rise up in her.

"Good," he says. "Good."

Miss Chang has already begun to despise him. So smug he is with his neatly combed hair, and his fresh breath, and his soft, soft shirt. She intentionally botches a step, and another, and another, until their dancing is chaos, all helter-skelter, and he, for the first time, looks clumsy and inept.

"All right," he says, squeezing her hand to make her stop. "That's enough."

"Yes," she tells him. "It's quite enough. Thank you."

She sees Polly across the gymnasium, watching them, her hands on her hips as if to say, "What in the world was that?"

D-I-E

Miss Chang cuts the letters from newspaper headlines and glues them to a sheet of paper. The cliché – this stunt she's picked up from some detective show on television – irritates her, but still she uses her old Underwood typewriter to address the envelope: "Mr. and Mrs. Donald Brawner, 811 South Waltz Road." The irony of the address only deepens her anger. She imagines Don and Polly falling in love with the fortunate coincidence – two dancers living on Waltz Road – and for a moment she wishes she had someone, anyone, to whom she could announce, "It's me. It's Lily Chang. I'm the one sending this note."

Miss Chang's townhouse is in a new subdivision called Sherwood Forest, but there are few trees there, only the ornamental Bradford pears planted along the driveways, and some Japanese maples in front yards. Don cares for her carpet juniper and her evergreen shrubs and the chrysanthemums that bloom yellow and red each fall. In China, Miss Chang's father had been the director of a botanical garden, but when Mao's revolution came, the Red Guard destroyed the greenhouses, torched azaleas and dwarf cedars and rhododendrons because they were bourgeois. Here, behind her townhouse, there is only a large open space of lawn that stretches, without tree or hedge, from neighbor to neighbor. The lone exception is the house directly behind Miss Chang's, the house of Miss Shabazz Shabazz, whose back yard is shaded by the only oak tree the developers must have spared and a white pine that carpets the ground with its fragrant needles. And there is a willow tree, its feathery branches sweeping down like the hair of the beautiful young girls who come to Miss Chang.

Miss Shabazz Shabazz's daughter is also named Shabazz, but to avoid confusion she is known as Buzzy. Buzzy Shabazz is thirteen, and she has skin the color of caramel, a shade closer to Miss Chang's own than to the deep ebony of Miss Shabazz Shabazz. The day Miss Chang went to their house to welcome them to the neighborhood, Miss Shabazz Shabazz explained how she had recently divorced her husband. "A white man," she said. "I'm sure I don't have to tell you anything more."

From the beginning, there was this implicit bond between them. "Women of color," Miss Shabazz Shabazz seemed to be saying. "Women warriors. We'll look out for each other." It pleased Miss Chang to think of herself and Miss Shabazz Shabazz united, but at the same time, she had no desire to poison herself with distrust. Of course, she knew there were people in the world who thought her dirty and vile. Sometimes, when new customers came to the shop and Miss Chang told them she was ready, they made up flimsy excuses – they had forgotten to put money in their parking meters, they had left their ovens on at home – and they would hurry away, never to return, and Miss Chang would know. She tried to let her anger wash over her like a wave rolling to a crest and then falling away.

But the first time she met Miss Shabazz Shabazz, she felt the woman's rage seep into her. Miss Chang saw it in the glint of the heavy gold rings Miss Shabazz Shabazz wore, rings shaped like spear points, and in her high, sharp cheekbones, and the hair, cut close to her skull and nubbed with patches of gray. "I gave my daughter my last name," Miss Shabazz Shabazz told Miss Chang. "My African name just as my father did for me. 'That way,' he told me, 'no man will ever be able to take it from you.'"

This year, Buzzy Shabazz and her friends play a game called Marco Polo. It is a game Miss Chang has heard her customers talk about, a swimming pool game carried over now from summer to autumn, from water to dry land. Each evening after school, a large number of children gather in the open lawn behind Miss Chang's, most of them, like Buzzy Shabazz, almost at an age when such games will be lost to them. There is a desperate urgency to their play, as if they know they are leaving childhood forever and must celebrate its wild, rollicking joy as often as they can.

The game, as far as Miss Chang can tell, is a frenetic, almost maniacal combination of blind man's bluff and tag. One person wears a blindfold and runs about trying to tag someone else. The rule is this: the person who is "it" calls out "Marco"; the others must answer "Polo." By repeating the call again and again and again, the person who is "it" tries to zero in on someone else. As soon as another person is tagged, that person becomes it, and the game goes on. It goes on and on until the light fades and Miss Chang can barely see the children, can only hear their feet thundering across the ground as they run and the incessant chant of "Marco" . . . "Polo" . . . until darkness finally takes the game from them, and in the sudden calm the call rattles around in Miss Chang's head.

One night, she closes her eyes and tries to imagine the children, blind to any limits of range or motion, racing across the grass. When they run, they come dangerously close to houses. Sometimes they lose their balance and fall. They frighten away the birds that come to feed at Miss Chang's patio. She misses the birds, but she loves to watch the children run, especially Buzzy Shabazz, who is sleek and fast. When Miss Chang watches her, she thinks of the marvelous bodies of athletes she sees on television. While Buzzy and the other children run, their shouts disturbing the usual neighborhood calm, Miss Shabazz Shabazz strolls about her yard, off-limits to the children because of its trees. She is regal and leonine, as if this wild abandon is somehow beneath her concern, and Miss Chang starts to resent her and her oak tree and her willow and her pine.

One night at dance class, a door slams shut, and Polly screams. "Not to worry," Miss Chang says. "It's just the wind."

B-A-N-G-! Y-O-U-'-R-E D-E-A-D

Polly comes in each Friday for a wash-and-set. She has fine hair, thinning on the top, and Miss Chang has to use a mild shampoo and conditioner and a pick to gently fluff the hair when she is done. Still, when she has finished, she can see Polly's white, white scalp shining through the airy puff of hair, and Miss Chang imagines birds plucking away the strands one by one until Polly is bald.

Goldfinches, cardinals, chickadees, doves: these are the birds that used to come to Miss Chang's patio. But now instead of their songs she hears the raucous shouts of the children – "Marco Polo" – as if they are searching for him, calling to him over the barren plains of Mongolia where Miss Chang used to watch herds of running-free horses race to drink from the rock wells she had dug, all for the good of the Party, all for Daddy Mao.

Sometimes in Nebraska, the wind's howl unhinges her. The peasants in Mongolia believed a weasel could become a spirit and come into a person and make that person do crazy things. It must be the same with the wind, Miss Chang thinks, a wind like the one that swept Genghis Khan across Asia, a wind that makes her think she can do whatever she wants, can send note after note to Polly and Don, and no one will ever know.

I-'-V-E G-O-T Y-O-U-R N-U-M-B-E-R

One night, after dance class, Miss Chang walks into the ladies' room at the YMCA and finds Polly standing at the sink, sobbing. The delicate wings of her shoulder blades flutter.

"Please excuse," Miss Chang says, and turns to leave.

Polly grabs her by the hand. "Stay with me," she says. "Stay just awhile. I don't want to go home."

"Something is wrong?" Miss Chang says. "Something at your house?"

"There are people in the world," Polly says. "Horrid people. We've been getting threatening notes in the mail."

Miss Chang feels, in the tight grip of Polly's hand, her tremendous fear, and she wants to tell her there is no need to be afraid; the notes have been a hoax. But of course she can't admit her guilt, and, too, Polly's confidence flatters her. Out of all the people she might have told, she's chosen her, Lily Chang.

"It's probably nothing," Miss Chang says. "Probably just some crank. Some cuckoo bird. Who would want to hurt you?"

"It's Don," says Polly. "He's the one they're after. He said this would happen, and now it has."

Toward the end of summer, Polly says, Don received a call from a man named Eddie Ball, the same Eddie Ball who had been a key figure a few years before in the trial of a Lincoln woman who had hired a hit man to kill her husband. Eddie Ball, the prosecutors contended, had been the one to put the woman in touch with the killer. Eddie Ball, everyone said – though the trial had never proved it – had mob connections.

"He wanted someone to write his story," Polly says, "and someone at the University had suggested Don. Well, you can imagine Don's reaction. 'I won't do that,' he told Eddie Ball. 'Not for a lowlife like you.' You know how Don is. And Eddie Ball said to him, 'You should be careful what you say to a man. You should be able to live with whatever happens now. I've got your number. I know where you live.'"

"Those notes," Miss Chang says. "Have you told the police?"

Polly nods. "They drive by our house a couple of times each night. They've told us to be careful. That's about it. Lily, I'm scared. I think it's true about Eddie Ball. I think he knows people."

Miss Chang knows practically no one besides Polly and Don. She has acquaintances, neighbors mostly like Miss Shabazz Shabazz, and there are the other hair stylists at the Mane Attraction, and her customers, but no one really she would call a friend. Other than Wednesdays, when she goes to the YMCA for her dance class, she spends her evenings alone. She watches Buzzy Shabazz and her friends race across her lawn; then, she turns on her television to catch *Club Dance*. Before she started sending Don and Polly the notes, her quiet life pleased her with its plainness and its modesty. Still, when she saw the flit and bob of a goldfinch in flight, its bright yellow could stun her, and when she watched the women dancing on television, their steps could make her heart ache for love. And now she has become a thug, a shady character like this Eddie Ball. Suddenly, it saddens her to think of all the people in the world and the ways they can find to hurt one another when all along what they want – what everyone must surely want – is to feel that they are safe and cared for, a part of some circle larger than any shape they could ever manage on their own.

In the middle of summer, not long after she had welcomed Miss Shabazz Shabazz to the neighborhood, a policeman came to Miss

Chang's door. Someone, he explained, had stolen a birdbath from Miss Shabazz Shabazz's yard. And someone had dug up a crepe myrtle and had thrown it onto Miss Shabazz Shabazz's porch. Had Miss Chang heard anything, the policeman wanted to know. Had she noticed anything suspicious? No, nothing, Miss Chang told him. "Well," the policeman said, "your neighbor is plenty hot about this. She's afraid it's because she's black. I wouldn't want to be in her way if she got started."

After that, Miss Chang stayed away from Miss Shabazz Shabazz because she wanted no part of trouble. If someone had stolen the birdbath and dug up the crepe myrtle because they didn't like the idea of blacks living in the neighborhood, how easy it would be for them to feel the same way about Miss Chang, especially if they saw her keeping company with Miss Shabazz Shabazz.

One evening, Don comes to put in Miss Chang's storm windows. "So," he says to her, "Polly told you about Eddie Ball."

"Yes," Miss Chang says, "she told me."

They are upstairs in the spare bedroom, and Don has just opened a window. She can hear the squeals and shouts of Buzzy Shabazz and her friends.

"I've always had a big mouth, haven't I, Lily?"

"You tried to tell me too much."

"I thought I had to take care of you. You seemed so frightened when we first came here."

"I'm not frightened now," she says. "You are."

"You're right," he says. "Yes. And so is Polly. And we don't know what to do."

He bows his head, and Miss Chang, from habit, does the same. So many times, in China, they sat beside each other, arms touching, as he watched her write out verb conjugations. Now, she notices that one of his shoes is untied. She remembers one day downtown, after she had come to America, a strange man asked her to tie his shoes. "I can't believe you did that," Don said when she told him the story. "His shoes were untied," she said. "He wanted someone to help him."

Don stoops to tie his own shoe; his fingers fumble with the laces. And suddenly something comes undone in Miss Chang, the knotted fist of her bitter heart, and she says to him, "You'll come here. That's what you'll do. You and Polly. You'll live with me until this is all over and it's safe for you to go home."

"Here?" Don lifts his head, and sunlight slants across his face. "Polly and I? We can't."

"You will," Miss Chang says.

"The three of us? Here?"

Miss Chang nods. "We will."

Her invitation startles her. She knows if she were telling a story, this would be the place where her listeners would frown and shake their heads and call her a liar. "You didn't," someone might say. "Well, I can't believe it." She thinks of her customers, and how they tell her things they wouldn't dare tell the people they love the most. She lets them talk until they know they've said too much and they're embarrassed by what they've shown of themselves. "You never would have guessed that about me, would you?" someone might say. "Oh, I shouldn't have told you any of that." Some stories, she knows, are too true to be told, but she can't escape this fact: she has asked Don and Polly, her ex-husband and his wife, to stay with her, and because they are frightened, they have said yes.

It is the first time since her divorce that Miss Chang has someone in the house each evening to take meals with her, to sit with her and chat, to make her feel safer in the night when she sleeps, pleased to know she isn't alone. And they are such good company. Relaxed now that they are away from their own home, they are cheerful and eager to please Miss Chang. The first night, Don plays records on his phonograph and takes turns dancing with her and Polly. Later, they watch *Club Dance* and Don shows Miss Chang the steps to the Achy-Breaky. When it is time to say goodnight, Polly kisses her on the cheek.

"I can't tell you how much this means to us," Polly says. "I'm glad we can still be friends, considering the circumstances."

"Ancient history," Miss Chang says with a wave of her hand. "Sleep well."

They sleep in the spare bedroom. They use the guest bathroom. Miss Chang lays out fresh towels and washcloths. Each morning, she rises early to prepare breakfast and sees a dove or two at the patio feeder. When she leaves the house for work, she starts to miss Don and Polly, not with the raw yearning she felt when she left her parents for Mongolia, but with a sweet, lovely anticipation that she will come home soon and there Don and Polly will be to welcome her.

"Lily," Polly says to her one evening. "My sweet, sweet Lily."

"Thank you," Don says. "Thank you for having us here."

Then one night Polly complains about Buzzy Shabazz and her friends and their game of Marco Polo. Polly and Miss Chang and Don are eating dinner, and through the patio doors they can see Buzzy Shabazz with a white handkerchief tied around her eyes. She is running wildly, her arms outstretched. She calls and her friends answer until the air is filled with their din, and it's impossible to distinguish their words. Their sound is a shriek, a siren, the wind's howl.

"That noise," Polly says. "That dreadful noise. I don't know how you live with it. I really don't. Whose children are they?"

"Neighborhood children," Miss Chang says. "The girl with the blindfold is Buzzy Shabazz. She lives with her mother in that house. There. The one with the beautiful yard."

Don leans forward to get a better look at Miss Shabazz Shabazz's yard. "Her white pine needs to be pruned," he says. "You should tell her that."

"Miss Shabazz?" says Miss Chang. "You don't know Miss Shabazz."

"I know those children are horrid," says Polly.

"They're trespassing," says Don. "This is your property. Don't they realize that? They have no right to be here."

After dinner, Miss Chang pays a visit to Miss Shabazz Shabazz. "Your trees are lovely," Miss Chang says. "But your pine. It needs pruning."

Miss Shabazz Shabazz is gathering firewood from the stack behind her utility shed, and when Miss Chang mentions the pine tree, Miss Shabazz Shabazz drops the canvas tote sling she has filled with logs and they clatter about on the ground. "Not a word for months," she says, "and now you come to stick your nose in my business? Speak up. Are you a mouse? Are you a little mouse who's crawled out of my firewood?"

Miss Chang remembers how when the schools in China finally reopened after the revolution began, she and the other students recited from Mao's Red Book. "Chairman Mao says, 'this,'" and "Chairman Mao says, 'that.'" Over and over until the slogans stuck in their heads. The one that comes to her now is, "Chairman Mao says, 'A revolution is not a dinner party.' " So she says to Miss Shabazz Shabazz, "It's your daughter. Your Buzzy. I don't want her and her friends playing their game in my yard."

Miss Shabazz Shabazz laughs. Her lips are the color of cranberries. Her teeth are white, white, white. The power of her laugh startles Miss Chang. "Don't be silly," Miss Shabazz Shabazz says. "Look at your yard." She points behind Miss Chang to the open space. "There's nothing there. Let children be children. What harm can they do?"

Each evening, after work, Miss Chang stops by Don and Polly's house to collect their mail. She brings it to them, and they sort through the envelopes. When they find nothing out of the ordinary, they give each other a hug and Miss Chang knows she is one day closer to losing them. "It looks like this is all going to blow over," Don says. "Then we can go home, Lily, and get out of your hair."

I K-N-O-W W-H-E-R-E Y-O-U L-I-V-E

When Don reads the note, he runs a hand over his head, mussing his hair. "That's it," he says to Polly. "I won't be bullied."

Polly reads the note and folds it very neatly along the creases Miss Chang's own fingers have traced in the paper. "It's your fault," Polly says, and her voice is very low and even. "You had to open your mouth. You couldn't keep quiet. I've always hated that about you."

And suddenly, Don is shouting. "You put up with too much." He is waving his arms about. "Damn it, Polly. You always have."

"I just expect the best from people," Polly says, still in that calm voice. "That's all."

"Well, I'm going to put an end to this," Don says. "I'm going to stop it tonight."

Miss Chang remembers the last night Don spent with her. He was cutting a coupon from the back of a cracker box, and he was having trouble keeping the scissors moving in a straight line through the cardboard. Finally, he slammed the scissors down on the counter, and he told her he thought he should leave. "For how long?" she asked him. "A few hours?" "For good," he said. "Not come back?" "No, Li. I won't come back."

And now, again, he is moving toward the door.

"Lily, you talk to him." Polly turns to her, and Miss Chang thinks of how Polly comes to her at the Mane Attraction and begs her to do something with her thin hair, trusts her to do what she can to hide her baldness. "You tell him, Lily. You tell him he can't go."

Miss Chang knows she should stop him. She knows she should say, "Wait. Let me tell you. You won't believe this. It's the craziest thing." But all she can think of is Mao's Red Guard and how they tore silk clothes from people on the street, how they destroyed Ming Dynasty vases, burned books, bulldozed the graveyards because burial was an old custom and took up valuable land. No more old ideas, no more old culture, no more old customs, no more old habits. She remembers the times when Don told her how to behave in America. "Toughen up," he told her. "Get mean." If she confesses to sending the notes, she imagines his smug grin and how he might say, "You see. I was right all along." When what he can never know – what he never even suspected those days at the University when she so meekly recited her verb conjugations – is the cold, cold heart she could never leave behind her in China.

So she says nothing. And then, Don is gone.

"Lily," Polly says. "You've been so good to us. And now look at what we've brought into your house."

After Don has left for Eddie Ball's, Miss Chang steps out onto her patio, and there is Buzzy Shabazz only a few feet away. She hoists her green schoolbag up on her shoulder. She is wearing hightop leather basketball shoes, the laces undone.

"Buzzy. Buzzy Shabazz," Miss Chang says. "I want to ask you something."

"My mother told me not to listen to you," says Buzzy Shabazz.

One night last summer before the episode with the birdbath and the crepe myrtle, Buzzy Shabazz came to Miss Chang's house and asked Miss Chang to please tell her about the pretty yellow birds she saw flying onto Miss Chang's patio. "Goldfinches," said Miss Chang. How, Buzzy Shabazz wanted to know, could she and her mother get such beautiful birds to come into their yard. Miss Chang remembered how long it had taken her to entice the goldfinches, how she had hung the feeding tube filled with niger seed and had waited and waited for her little goldies to find it. And now that they had, she hated to risk losing even one of them to her new neighbors. Of course, she knew it was selfish of her, but in China there had been so few birds (once Mao had even ordered all the sparrows killed) she delighted now in the brilliant yellow birds with their black caps and wings and the playful way they grasped the rungs of the feeding tube with their claws and then flipped upside down to peck at niger seed through the slots below them. "I'm sorry," she told Buzzy Shabazz. "This is something I cannot tell."

Now Miss Chang says to the girl, "Every night you and your friends run through my yard." Miss Chang points toward Buzzy Shabazz's house. "How would you like it if I came into your yard? If I was an intruder come there uninvited?"

Buzzy Shabazz's eyes open wide. "It was you," she says. "You're the one."

"I'm not saying I've ever done it," Miss Chang says. "I'd never even dream of it."

"You stole our birdbath, and you dug up our bush."

"No."

"You, you, you."

Buzzy Shabazz's voice is rising, the way it does when she plays Marco Polo. It echoes across the empty expanse of Miss Chang's yard, and all she wants is to make Buzzy Shabazz be quiet. She tries to clamp her hand over the girl's mouth, but Buzzy Shabazz grabs her arm, and somehow Miss Chang's hand ends up caught between Buzzy Shabazz's shoulder and the strap of her schoolbag. Miss Chang is trying to let go, but she can't. And Buzzy Shabazz is trying to yank herself away from Miss Chang. The two of them are dancing about the yard, and finally, the only way Miss Chang can free herself is to put her other hand against Buzzy Shabazz's sternum and push. When she does, Buzzy Shabazz falls backward, striking her head, with a loud thud, on the ground.

Miss Chang tries to apologize. "I didn't mean to hurt you," she says. "This is all a mistake."

But Buzzy Shabazz is on her feet and running to her yard where Miss Shabazz Shabazz has come out to her white pine, pruning shears in hand.

Miss Chang goes into her own house, and there is Polly sitting on the love seat, staring out the window. After the divorce, Polly came to Miss

Chang, and she asked her if she would mind if she started dating Don. "If it bothers you, Lily. I won't do it."

"Do you love him?" Miss Chang wanted to know.

She remembers how Polly ducked her head like a star-struck girl. "Yes, Lily. I think I do."

"Then why ask my permission?"

"I don't want to hurt you, Lily. You've been so good to me. Dear Lily. I love you, too."

Now Miss Chang is crying. She is thinking about Don on his way to Eddie Ball's, and how Polly, staring out the window, must be so frightened for him. Miss Chang is imagining Buzzy Shabazz telling her mother that their neighbor, that crazy Chinese woman, has attacked her.

"I didn't mean to do it," Miss Chang says.

Polly turns and rises so effortlessly from the love seat. She comes to Miss Chang and takes her in her arms. "Do what, Lily? Poor dear. Tell me."

There is a sharp knock at the patio door, the sound of metal on glass. Polly looks at Miss Chang, and Miss Chang sees the same terror she saw in her mother's eyes the day the Red Guard knocked down their door and dragged her mother out into the street.

Miss Chang feels Polly's shoulders tremble, and she remembers one day last summer when a goldfinch, convinced it saw clear passage through the glass, flew into the patio door, and fell to the step. When Miss Chang picked it up, she could feel the wings trying to open – the slightest shudder – and she wished for something she could do, some miracle, to give the bird's life back to it. She remembers the letters she cut from the newspapers, the dancing turns and dips of her scissors, her gentle, flowing rill. She sees the letters in her mind, scrambled, swirling into words she hadn't thought to form: "LOVE," "ME," "NOW." And they startle her. All along, she imagines, this plea has been rising – this sweet yearning – and now here it is, flaring up with such an overwhelming majesty and force, she can't help but confess it.

"It's me," she says, and her voice is barely a whisper. "I'm the one who's been sending you and Don those notes."

When the Red Guard took her mother, Miss Chang ran. She was just a girl, still light and fast. She ran and ran until she stopped in the botanical garden where the greenhouses were jagged with broken glass, where the azaleas and the dwarf cedars and the rhododendrons were charred and smoldering. She was so far from home. She was alone and ashamed. But she would never be able to forget the splendid motion of her swift and graceful flight. She recalls it now as Polly steps back and slips from her embrace, and all Miss Chang can do is turn, her feet clumsy and slow, to the patio door where Miss Shabazz Shabazz waits.

The Glass House

JUDY SLATER

In the fall of 1969, my father had an affair – a serious one – with an artist named Molly Chu. This story is about them, but I find I can't keep myself out of it, can't help tracing back my own role in the affair. Because, after all, it would never have happened if it weren't for me.

In the summer of 1969, I had just turned eighteen, just graduated from high school, and was waiting for my life to begin.

I was a particularly young and naive eighteen. I think my father was both relieved and horrified by my naiveté. On one hand he was the doting father of an only daughter, an only child, and part of him must have wanted to keep me safe from the evils of the world. On the other hand, he didn't suffer fools gladly, and he must have been appalled by how little I knew. I didn't know how much a pound of hamburger cost. I wasn't exactly sure who'd been president before Eisenhower. I must have sounded ridiculous when I tried to argue with him over Vietnam, about which I knew absolutely nothing.

My mother had none of the mixed feelings about me that my father must have had. If she could have figured out a way to keep me home forever, safe, she would have done it. We lived in a beautiful house overlooking the ocean – in my memory it is all windows, nothing but polished glass. The house was my father's idea, his dream – the best of both worlds, he said, commuting to the bustle and vitality of the city during the day, driving back to the solitude of the ocean at night – but it was my mother who became addicted to the life there. She gave up her CPA job in Portland and started a small tax consulting business out of our house. It didn't amount to much – not that it mattered, my father made enough money that her income wasn't needed – and there were whole days, I think, when she didn't talk to anyone but me and my father, and once a week Mrs. Shekler who came to clean the house. She seemed perfectly happy with that arrangement – she worked a little, gardened, took walks on the beach, never seemed lonely – and I think she wished I could be happy with that sort of life too. She was disappointed that it wasn't enough for me.

Fortunately for my mother, there was a very good, small, private college just two hours from home, nestled in the hills above Portland. Astor College had once been a private mansion. Liberal (what college wasn't in those days?), but not too liberal, Astor was made to order for the sons and daughters of well-heeled, overprotective parents. It had acres of immaculately tended grounds, stained-glass windows in the library, a twelve-to-one student/faculty ratio, a rose garden, a goldfish pond with a fountain. It had everything except a moat around it, and it might as well have had that. Plus, one of its trustees was an old pal and client of my father's.

It wasn't hard to talk me into Astor. My father just called up his trustee pal and asked him to send a catalog. One look at those glossy pictures of students reading Doris Lessing and James Baldwin on the lawn, the rose garden in the background, and I was hooked. I was timid as well as naive, and though I would never have admitted it, two hours away was about as far as I was ready to venture.

In midsummer the college sent preregistration forms, and I promptly signed up for yoga, an upper-level English class on the Bloomsbury group, an art class called "Form in Color," and another one called "Chinese Brush Painting." It was a squirrelly, chaotic time – requirements were being done away with right and left, and there were no rules that prevented me from taking this peculiar assortment of classes my first term instead of the standard lineup of freshman comp and intro to psychology.

It was, in fact, my father who suggested I take the Chinese brush-painting class. He was looking over my registration forms one night after dinner, and spotted the class and the name of the instructor – M. Chu. "Maureen," he said, calling my mother over. "Look at this."

My mother, still in her gardening clothes with her hair tied back in a ponytail, went to sit beside him on the sofa. They made an oddly matched couple, I suppose, though I never thought of it that way; I was used to seeing my mother in sweatshirts and jeans, my father in starched shirts and navy-blue ties. My father never seemed to feel the need to change out of his business clothes at the end of a day, and he wore his pressed gray suits with such natural elegance and grace that he looked as comfortable in them as my mother did in her grubby garden clothes.

"Do you think M. Chu could be Molly Chu?" my father asked my mother.

His passion – it was much more than a hobby – was contemporary art. He collected it. It was an investment, he was always careful to say – a kind of game, to see if he could pick up-and-coming artists and gamble on their work appreciating over the years. But I could see it was no game. I watched him sometimes in the evenings, after dinner, gazing intently at one of the paintings on the wall as though memorizing each line and brush stroke. He seemed as happy, as at peace, during those moments as I ever saw him.

"Wouldn't that be wonderful?" said my mother. "But can it be her? I thought she lived in San Francisco."

Earlier that year, while on a business trip to San Francisco, my father had gone to an art opening and been so taken with the work of an artist named Molly Chu that he'd bought one of her paintings as a present for my mother. It was a delicate watercolor of a tumbling wisteria vine, impressionistic and sensual, and it presently hung on a scroll above my parents' bed.

"She must be here on one of those one-term appointments," my father said. One of the things Astor prided itself on, and bragged about at some length in its catalog, was its commitment to the arts. Every quarter the college brought in a visiting artist, writer, or musician to teach a class, so the students would have the experience of working with someone famous, or sort of famous.

"I'm sure it's her," my father said. "How many painters named Chu can there be? What a wonderful opportunity, Jill," he said to me. "I met her in San Francisco at the opening when I bought her painting. She seems like a wonderful person, very warm, very bright."

I didn't argue. I loved the wisteria painting. I signed up for the class.

But, bad news. The college wrote back apologetically that the Chinese brush-painting class was full. It was a popular course, and upperclassmen had first choice.

"Let's not give up yet," my father said when the letter arrived. He picked up the phone, called his trustee pal who got his secretary to track down Molly Chu – for it was her, all right, and yes, it was a one-term appointment, and she was subletting an apartment in northwest Portland. The minute my father got her phone number, he dialed it, explained who he was, why he was calling. "My daughter's heartbroken. She loves your work. I wouldn't ordinarily ask for special favors, but it's her only chance to take the class. It'll be her first term at college, and it would be such a thrill for her. Yes . . . yes. That's generous of you. She'll work hard – I promise." He winked at me. "I would. I do. Yes, my business is in Portland. Maybe we could meet for lunch. I'd be interested in buying another of your paintings. My wife and I love the wisteria."

He hung up the phone. "Done," he said to me, and smiled.

When the time came, it was my father who drove me to Astor, with my new typewriter, my towels and sheets, my new bulletin board to hang over my desk, my art supplies, my brand new checkbook with a thousand dollars deposited into it, which was supposed to be more than enough to last me the whole term, and I was sure it would be. It seemed a vast amount. I had packed everything I could possibly imagine needing for the next three months. I was pretending that I was really leaving, that I was going much farther than two hours away. I planned not to return home until Christmas break.

My mother's excuse for not going along on this trip was that there wouldn't be room enough in the car for all my stuff if she went too.

At the time, I didn't know exactly what was wrong with my mother. I still don't, really, but I suspect some odd strain of agoraphobia. It wasn't that she was afraid to go out of the house; it was that she was afraid *for* the house. She was afraid it would burn down, that the neighbor would forget to feed the cat and he would starve, that someone would break in, if she left for a night. And she was getting worse; lately she hated to leave even for an afternoon. She'd get halfway out the driveway and go back, certain that she'd left the iron on, or the coffeepot, or the stove. She had Mrs. Shekler come in two days a week now instead of one, to do errands that involved leaving the house – grocery shopping, picking up dry cleaning.

She cried when she hugged me good-bye. My feelings weren't hurt that she wasn't coming. I knew she loved me. And besides, it was a treat to be with my father alone. It made the journey seem more momentous, somehow, that my handsome father in his pressed white shirt and tall military bearing was taking time out of his busy schedule to escort me to college.

As the car pulled out, I turned back to look at my mother. I carried away a mental picture of her, waving awkwardly – she was trying to wave and hold our cat Jack in her arms at the same time – the ocean in the background. She was smiling and crying, and Jack was struggling in her arms; he had his eye on some birds flocking in the ancient spruce tree in front of the house; he was dying to get down and get at them.

It was a rainy day, the roads slick, but my father took the winding road over the mountains as he always did, with confidence and grace, just slightly over the speed limit. I was never nervous when he was behind the wheel; I always felt safe with him. He made driving seem like an art, like ballet. Whereas my mother was a nervous driver – generally far too cautious but once in a while making some wild maneuver, an illegal left turn or a lane change without looking, that got her into trouble.

My father clearly enjoyed driving. He often drove to San Francisco on business when it would have been so much easier and faster to fly. And of course he drove into Portland every day to work. I think driving used up some of his nervous energy. He had his secretary, who had a rich melodious voice and some training as an actress, read poetry by Yeats, stories by Faulkner and Salinger and Fitzgerald, into a portable tape recorder, and he would listen to the tapes while he drove. When I learned that the poet Wallace Stevens was an insurance executive, I thought of my father. Not that he was an artist himself, but he appreciated creativity; he admired it, I now think, more than any other human quality.

"Write to us," he said to me when my things had been loaded out of the car and into my cell of a dorm room. Like my mother, he was going along with the fiction that I was leaving home, that I couldn't take the bus into Portland and be at his office in less than half an hour any time I wanted to. "I'll be waiting to hear how you like the Chinese painting class."

He hugged me hard and swiftly – too swiftly to give me a chance to get teary-eyed – and then he drove away in the rain. Fast, confident, lifting a hand for one final wave.

Chinese brush painting was held on Thursday nights, in what had been the greenhouse when the college was a private mansion. It still smelled like a greenhouse – musky, earthy, faintly tropical.

Molly Chu wore her thick black hair in a shoulder-length pageboy. She had a round face and dark eyes, wore black pants and a long royal-blue silk shirt. Her hands were plump and dimpled and graceful, and she was already laying out her brushes and paper, mixing ink, when we arrived.

There were thirteen of us in the class. The limit had obviously been set at twelve, and I was the extra, the interloper, though no one knew that but Molly Chu and me. We sat at long tables, two per table to give us room to spread out our rolls of rice paper. But one table – not mine, as it turned out – had to make room for three.

She sat at the front, facing us, at a table all her own.

The first thing she did was to pass around a wallet-sized picture of her family – a daughter who looked to be about my age, a son maybe a year or two older, a husband. "My husband's name is Paul," she told us. "My daughter's name is Marie. My son's name is James."

Her husband was not unattractive but certainly not striking – someone you wouldn't normally notice, and that's why I wonder now if I had some sort of premonition, because why else would I scrutinize so carefully the picture of someone I didn't know? And I did scrutinize him. I concentrated on him, not the children. I didn't give them a second glance, but even now I can see him, smiling uncomfortably into the camera.

But no, I had no premonition. It was just that what she did was so unusual, a college professor passing around pictures of her family.

I was obviously not the only one who thought so. I saw the other students giving each other sidelong amused, questioning looks. Molly went on. "I love living in San Francisco," she said. "I love the blend of cultures. My father is Chinese. My grandfather was a traditional Chinese calligrapher. He is the reason I became an artist. I worshiped my grandfather, and when he died, I cut off my hair – it was down to my waist then – to show the depth of my grief. My mother is American.

I have a French grandmother. My daughter is named after her. And so my own art is a blend – mainly traditional Chinese, but with a little Monet and Cézanne as an influence. I am telling you these things so that you will get to know me quickly, because we do not have much time together and I want to teach you as much as I can. I have been painting since I was four years old. I can do a painting in a matter of seconds" – and she demonstrated, dipping a large brush into the ink and making a few deft strokes, black birds swooping across a white sky – "but I am not doing it in a few seconds, I am doing it in forty years plus a few seconds. Do you see? I cannot give you those years of experience, but I will give you what I can. We must use the time we have together wisely, and not waste it. Now we will begin."

She showed us how to mix water with the thick black ink to get varying shades of gray. Some artists, she said, used only black ink, but we would use three shades – a pure black, a medium gray, a light gray – so that we would get subtle gradations and a three-dimensional effect. Our paintings, of bamboo and chrysanthemums, water lilies and orchids, would look as though they were alive.

She had us come up in groups of four to watch her demonstrate how to hold the brush. It was nothing like the way you held an American watercolor or oil painting brush – you held it straight up, perpendicular to the paper, your fingers arranged in a complicated way around it, and when you painted you used your whole arm, never just the hand and wrist.

Right away, I saw that I had a problem. I was left-handed, and the procedure she was demonstrating was complicated enough that I could not seem to transpose it to my left hand. What should I do? I asked her.

"It will not be a problem," she said to me firmly. "Simply use your right hand. All traditional Chinese painters paint with their right hand. You will find that you have no trouble."

I was not remotely ambidextrous. I dipped my brush into the paint with my right hand, expecting awkward movements, a shaky line. But the line of ink looked more graceful than I would have thought. Molly made a few adjustments, straightened the brush, moved my fingers a fraction of an inch this way and that. "Again," she commanded. "Good," she said. "Good."

She had brought a record player, and she played Chinese music for us to paint by. We practiced painting bamboo leaves, over and over – loading the darkest ink onto the base of the brush, the lighter ink at the tip, starting with a firm pressure at the beginning of the stroke, then lightening up as we drew the brush along. We must practice over and over again, she said, to build our confidence. The best stroke was a quick, fluid, confident one – if you hesitated at all, you lost the momentum and the line was ruined.

She passed around tiny sesame-seed cookies for us to eat during our break, and then we were back to work again. From time to time she would turn down the music and talk to us – sometimes demonstrating a particular brush stroke, sometimes just talking in general about her life.

What all did she tell us during that first class? She spoke rapturously of nights spent staying up till dawn with friends, drinking green tea, playing music, arguing about art, *doing* art together. She didn't waste her time on passive activities like watching television, she told us. She talked as though she never slept and never needed sleep. The apartment she was subletting belonged to a friend who was on an extended trip to Portugal, and she had made it her own – bringing her favorite wind chime with her from San Francisco, her special tea set, a spice jar to put flowers in. She carried these things with her always, even when she was going to spend only one night in a hotel. We should do this too, she told us, should always surround ourselves with objects we loved.

How did all these topics come up? How did they relate to each other? I have no idea. She told us that even when she was younger and hadn't had a lot of money, she always hired someone to clean her house, because housecleaning could be an art and it was better to pay someone to do something well than do it yourself in a mediocre way. No one can do everything well, she told us, and the best way to live was to concentrate on doing the things you liked and were good at.

At some point in the evening, the students who had been snickering and nudging each other stopped. We all of us fell under her spell; of course, I had been under it from the first moment.

At nine thirty she clapped her hands and told us it was time to wash our brushes. The clapping of her hands startled me as though I'd been in a trance. That was when I looked out the windows of the greenhouse and realized how dark it was.

Three weeks into the term, my roommate obliged me by having a nervous breakdown, or something, and dropping out of school. I hadn't liked her, had often wished her gone. I felt somewhat guilty after she left, as though I'd put a curse on her. But I was thrilled to have the room to myself. I remembered what Molly Chu had told us about making even a one-night hotel room your own and set about transforming my dorm room into a painting studio. I had thought the thousand dollars in my checking account would last forever, but without blinking I spent a hundred of it on a celadon vase. I spent more money on flowers to put in the vase – fresh chrysanthemums and orchids at least once a week. I moved the furniture around, putting my ex-roommate's desk against mine for a surface large enough to spread out my rolls of rice paper. I bought dozens of candles, so at night I could paint by candlelight instead of the harsh overhead light in the room.

Sometimes when I practiced, I had doubts. I had always gotten A's in art, always felt confident drawing or painting. I couldn't help thinking, now, that being forced to paint right-handed must be holding me back. If I could only use my left hand, I could paint so much more naturally. I did try it a couple of times, but I had come too far, practiced too long in class with my right hand; it seemed like starting at the beginning again, going back and relearning how to use the brush with my left hand. It didn't feel natural, as I had thought it would, but stilted and awkward. Also, I felt guilty. Molly wouldn't have approved. I decided she must know what she was talking about and went back to painting with my right hand.

Soon after my roommate left for good, I got a call from my father. It was the first time I'd had a call from him. He and my mother were both faithfully preserving the illusion that I was away – we wrote dutiful weekly letters to each other.

He told me that on Wednesday he planned to stay overnight in the city – he did this occasionally, at the Edgeware Hotel, if he had an early breakfast meeting the next day. Would I like to meet him for dinner? I could take the bus into the city. He thought he might give Molly Chu a call to see if she could join us, since he was still interested in buying another of her paintings.

I hung up the phone, elated. Dinner out with my father was always an occasion, and – I had to admit this – I was glad my mother was not coming along. My mother had very little interest in food – she just didn't see the point. And of course, going out to eat meant being away from home. When we went out for dinner, she would usually order something she thought the cat would like, and then take most of it home for him. Throughout the meal she'd be restless, always looking at her watch.

But my father delighted in the experience of dining out. Though he was a moderate, self-contained man who never drank more than a cocktail or two before dinner, never drank more than one cup of coffee in the morning, and rarely ate a second helping, at elegant restaurants he became expansive and generous, ordering appetizers and elaborate desserts.

On such evenings, his nervous energy in check, he would eat slowly, appreciatively, as though he had all the time in the world, the evening spread out before him like a beautiful fan. He enjoyed the attention of the waiters and liked to talk to them. On such nights he was not preoccupied, the way he often was at other times; he would lean toward you, rapt, interested, and charmed by everything you said.

So you can imagine what this night was like for me – my glamorous father whisking me away from the dreariness of dorm food, into the city for a candlelit feast, a table by the window overlooking the glittering lights. And the added pearl: my glamorous teacher, who had no idea of the hours I spent practicing my painting, practicing to be like her.

Their affair began that night. Molly told me that, later. It wasn't planned to happen. They were both innocent. The evening had been orchestrated, all right, but not for that purpose. My father invited Molly for my sake. He knew how the world worked; he knew the value of personal connections and knew I would be too shy to establish them. He wanted the class to be special for me, and he was afraid that, left to my own devices, I would sit in the back of the room and Molly Chu might not notice me at all – and the whole experience would be wasted, as though I were watching it from the window of a train passing by.

Molly arrived at the restaurant ten minutes late, in a flurry of apologies and laughter. "I'm sorry," she said. "It's always harder to get a taxi in the rain – why is that? And there's something going on at the Coliseum, some sports thing." She waved her hand dismissively to indicate the unimportance of sports things. My father, who had no use either for sports, smiled. "I had to wait *forever* for a taxi." But she didn't seem in the least put out. She wore a black, shiny raincoat that crackled when she took it off to reveal a silk dress in the royal blue she favored. She smelled like an exotic tropical flower.

She slid beside me in the semicircular booth, so that I was in the middle. She entered immediately into the spirit, my father's spirit, of the evening. He had ordered a dry martini, and she said, "Oh yes. I'll have one too." When it arrived, she ate the olive first, with relish, popping it whole into her mouth. "You know, I'm not a drinker. Not at all. But martinis are so festive. Who can resist the *idea* of a perfect martini?"

She was not merely following my father's lead, matching her mood to his. She was that sort of person herself; she liked a festive evening. I knew that about her already. I thought of the snacks she brought to class, the rice cakes and sesame cookies and steamed buns, and the way she presented them to us with such enthusiasm, making the eating of them a ritual. (I thought disdainfully, disloyally, of my mother, who sometimes forgot to eat entirely.) And I thought about the other evenings Molly'd told us about in class, those evenings when she'd stay up all night long with her artist friends, drinking tea and playing music. She had told us so much. I felt as if I knew her intimately, knew everything about her life. It didn't occur to me to wonder what her husband did on those party nights, whether he was with her. She hadn't mentioned him since the first night when she passed his picture around.

We ordered tiny bluepoint oysters as an appetizer. "No cocktail sauce," my father warned me when they arrived. "Just a squeeze of lemon to bring out the flavor." I nodded. I had never eaten raw oysters before. I loved them immediately. They tasted and smelled like the essence of the sea. (I have been back to the Edgeware Hotel several times since that night, and it seems in recent years to have become a ghost of itself, the restaurant no more than a glorified coffee shop, no oysters on the menu anywhere.)

"Jill is wonderful," Molly said as we ate our oysters. She sipped her martini, patted my hand. "My best student."

"I'm not surprised," my father said, and smiled at me. "She does everything well."

Basking in their approval and attention, I became suddenly brave, confessional. "I worry," I said to Molly, "about the fact that I'm left-handed. I'm afraid because of that I can never be really good. I want to be really good. I would like to be" – I had never said the words aloud – "an artist."

"Don't worry about it at all," she said firmly. "You can be every bit as good as if you were naturally right-handed." Of course, how would she know, being naturally right-handed herself? She'd never had to struggle with it. But I didn't think of that then. "What is important," she said, "is that you concentrate fully, that you have the *chi*, the life force, flowing through you as you paint. And you do have that. I can see it when I watch you."

The end of the evening stole up on me, the way it did on Thursday nights in class, like the end of a delicious dream. I saw my father push away his plate. I glanced at my watch and was amazed to find that it was after ten. We had been at the table for more than four hours. But it wasn't over yet.

There was chocolate mousse for dessert. At Molly's urging we ordered three instead of one to share, as my father and I would have done if we'd been alone. She was not as naturally moderate as my father, I noticed. She ate more than he did, and with even more pleasure. She ate bread, slathered it with butter. Only now, looking back, does it occur to me that she ate a little greedily.

At the end there was coffee (I was struggling to acquire a taste for it), and a special surprise – the waiter brought three snifters of marc, on the house. He set my snifter down before me without a blink. My father didn't blink either. Maybe he'd forgotten for a moment who I was exactly. Maybe I had fooled him, and myself, into thinking I had transformed into some older, more sophisticated version of myself.

Though my parents often had a cocktail hour before dinner, I was as innocent about alcohol as I was about everything else. I'd had a beer or two urged on me by high school boyfriends, but on those occasions I'd only pretended to drink. I'd never been drunk, never even tipsy, in my life. So it didn't take much. I sipped the warm golden liquid in that snifter and the world turned rosy and slightly out of focus. I even giggled, embarrassingly, but softly enough that nobody seemed to notice.

It had to have been obvious that night that something was happening between Molly Chu and my father. Any fool could have seen it – I can see it when I replay the evening in my mind. I didn't see it then.

It was still raining when we went outside. My father hailed a taxi for me. My memory is that, though it was a busy night – that sports thing just letting out at the Coliseum, and lots of disgruntled umbrella'd people on the sidewalk, peering in vain for a cab – my father lifted a hand and a taxi materialized out of thin air. He gave me twenty dollars for the fare, hugged me goodbye in that swift hard way he had.

And then, of course, he and Molly must have turned to each other . . . and that was the moment. They went up to his hotel room or to her apartment – I don't know which. Molly told me a lot, later, but she didn't deal in such specific details, and though I was hungry for them I was too shy to ask. One place or another, though, they spent the night together.

The dinner, which my father had planned so carefully for my benefit, did have its intended effect – Molly did single me out for extra attention from that night on. I became the one she asked to help her pack up her brushes and paper, the one she walked out with after class. The other students began eyeing me jealously, but I didn't care. I could feel it – she was beginning to treat me as her friend instead of her student.

I've never felt again the way I felt that term. Evenings, days, weeks seemed to float by without my being conscious of time passing. I stayed up all night, often, painting by candlelight. I don't know if what I was experiencing was what Molly had in mind when she talked about the *chi*, the life force, flowing through us while we painted. I do know that it sometimes seemed as if I painted in a waking dream.

Between painting, yoga, and reading *To the Lighthouse*, I was as whacked out as if I'd been experimenting with seven different kinds of drugs – which I never did. I knew my classmates were doing drugs – all I had to do was walk past other dorm rooms and smell the pot and patchouli wafting out at all hours of the day and night. Not me. I was oblivious to all of that.

In the distant background, the war went on. At Astor, we were all against Vietnam, but we protested the war not by bombing buildings or demonstrating, but by holding candlelight vigils around the goldfish pond. We petitioned the dining hall to serve nothing but plain rice and tea one night at dinner – to what practical end I have no idea. It wasn't as if the college planned to send the money it had saved on our one dinner to the troops in Vietnam. It was the concept of sacrifice that appealed to us, I guess. Most people went out for hamburgers afterward.

My other art class, "Form in Color," fell by the wayside fairly early on. The bright acrylics the teacher used seemed jarring and garish after Molly's class. In Chinese painting class, Molly told us we weren't nearly ready for color yet. It would take months, maybe years, to master the art of those subtle variations of grays and blacks.

I still went faithfully to yoga, but the Bloomsburies faltered sometime in mid-November. Even Virginia Woolf's considerable charms could not compete with Molly Chu's. So I would be getting an Incomplete in that class. But I wasn't too worried about my less-than-stellar first-term performance. My father, I was sure, would understand, and that was all that mattered.

I was getting to be good at Chinese painting. I would have been supremely untalented not to have developed at least some measure of skill, considering all the hours of practice I put in. I'd developed enough confidence that I'd dared to do a painting – in black and those subtle gradations of gray that Molly prized – of the ancient spruce tree in front of our house, which I planned to have mounted on a scroll as a Christmas present for my parents. I had asked Molly's advice about this; my parents had never been the sort of parents to hang their daughter's finger paintings on the refrigerator door, and it seemed presumptuous to give them a painting of my own when they had a collection of work by real artists worth thousands of dollars. If I gave my parents a painting, it had to be a good one, a real painting.

"It is a fine painting," she said firmly. "The best you've done. He will love it." She amended her statement. "They will love it."

As the term came to an end, I felt something magical, irretrievable, slipping away. I could not take Molly Chu's class again – she would be going back to San Francisco. I might never see her again.

When I went home for Christmas break, I left my brushes, my rice paper, my ink block, in the dorm room, also my tea set and the celadon vase. I remember feeling very ambivalent about this decision – but in the end I was afraid, somehow, that if I didn't leave these traces, these artifacts, of myself behind, the dorm room would no longer belong to me, and I would come back to find it as stripped and bare as it had been the day I moved in.

On a more practical level, there'd been mention of my being assigned a new roommate the following term, and I had some vague notion that if the dorm director came in and saw how completely I had overtaken the room and made it mine, she would realize how much it meant to me and would let me keep it all to myself. (This was, of course, another of my naive notions. I was indeed assigned a new roommate at the beginning of the next quarter, and no one – including my new roommate – was shy about telling me to move my stuff, pronto, back over to my side of the room. But that was later.)

At first when I went home it seemed that nothing much had changed, except that my mother seemed to have grown more obsessively attached to Jack, the cat. Also, the scrolled wisteria painting had moved from its place above my parents' bed and was rolled up and standing in a corner of my father's study, but this didn't seem especially unusual. Artwork in our house was often in transition, older pieces making room for new.

The storm arrived on the Saturday before Christmas.

There was nothing, at first, to indicate that it would be anything other than a normal winter storm. The ocean was dark and roiling, the wind blowing fiercely, the rain blasting down, but I was used to that. It probably ought to have occurred to me that, even with the wind and rain, it was unnaturally dark for midafternoon, but somehow it didn't. It must not have occurred to my parents either, because nobody moved to turn on any extra lights.

My mother and I were sitting at the dining table, putting together a jigsaw puzzle. Or rather, trying to put it together. The problem wasn't only the dim light. The other problem was, we had no idea how many pieces might be missing. My mother had quirky habits concerning money. She would often decide to buy something – an Oriental rug, a sofa, a coffee table – without even asking the price, but then she would turn miserly when it came to small things. The jigsaw puzzles were in this category – she had found a flea market that regularly sold used ones for fifty cents, and one of Mrs. Shekler's duties on errand day was to go there and see what bargains she could pick up.

This particular puzzle was a cloying, sentimental picture of puppies and kittens in a basket, roses in the background.

My father was pacing the house like a caged animal. I know the reason for his mood, now. I didn't then, but I think it must have scared me a little, subconsciously, the way the unnatural darkness in the afternoon must have scared me without my quite realizing something was wrong. For all his nervous energy, my father was never bored, almost never irritable. He always brought work home, even on holidays, and he was happy being at home, working in his study, or gazing at his paintings or out at the ocean. But now he didn't seem to have any work to do; he didn't seem to have anything to do. He wore a thin gray sweater and khaki pants, and he looked uncomfortable in them. He poured himself a drink, which I'd never, ever, seen him do this early in the day. I glanced at my mother, but she was absorbed in the jigsaw puzzle.

The jigsaw puzzle clearly irritated him. The ugliness, the overblown sentimentality of the picture, must have offended his sense of taste. Not to mention what a complete waste of time it was.

But from my point of view the puzzle was not a total waste of time. While we worked together on the puzzles, my mother and I were able to converse after a fashion. She had cried and hugged me when I arrived home, but after she stopped crying she didn't seem able to think of anything to say to me. We had always had our troubles communicating, but it seemed to me she was even more distant and distracted than usual. I would come upon her idly flipping through magazines or staring off into space. Her cooking, which had never been especially good, became disastrous. She served us steaks cooked to leather, baked potatoes cold and hard in the middle. I had begun to miss dorm food. It was only when she was working on our puzzles that she seemed focused, that she seemed really in the room.

"I'm looking for a completely black piece," she said now. "Sort of like a flower shape. See here? For the dog's nose."

I searched, but didn't find one. "Maybe it's missing."

"Oh, I hope not. It will spoil the whole picture if it is."

My father gave a snort of disgust.

I remember that clearly, his snort of disgust, a split second before the storm hit in earnest. Rain smashed against the windows. The two dim

lights we'd had on flickered and went out, and suddenly it was dark –
as dark as seven or eight o'clock at night. The wind blew harder.

I remember my mother's face across the table, shadowy. My father,
standing by the window looking out at the sea, was just a dark shape; I
couldn't see his features at all.

The cat was the first to realize what was happening. He'd been dozing
on the sofa, and he suddenly leaped onto the coffee table, sending an
expensive crystal figurine spinning across the table and onto the floor,
smashing into a million pieces.

"Goddamnit!" my father, who never swore, shouted.

Jack's eyes were wild, his fur electric, his tail puffed out fat. My
mother, so attuned to the cat's moods, realized then too, and cried out
harshly, "Graham! Get away from the window."

Even then, I wasn't afraid. I'd seen plenty of rough weather over the
years. Living on this isolated stretch of coastline, the winter storms
offered just about the only excitement there was to be had here. I would
watch them from our picture windows, feeling the same thrill, the same
sense of pleasurable fear, that I got from watching a horror movie.

And, of course, I wasn't afraid because my father wasn't afraid.

"For God's sake, Maureen," he said. "It's nothing. Just a storm."

"Please," she said, and he sighed and stepped away from the window –
more, I'm sure, to forestall any hysterics than because he thought there
was any danger.

"Calm down," he said. "We'll listen and see if there's a weather report
on the radio." But he'd forgotten; the power was out.

I went to my bedroom and searched for the old transistor I'd gotten
for my thirteenth birthday. I couldn't remember having turned it on in
years. Its batteries, though weak, amazingly still worked. We leaned close
to the radio – it was hardly bigger than a pack of cards – and listened
for a weather report. The battery was just about dead when a wheezy
announcer's voice came on and said, "A special report. Residents of
the northern coast from Twin Rocks to Arch Cape are advised to take
extreme precautions. Gale winds expected over the next twenty-four
hours up to eighty miles an hour. Mud slides have been reported."

"You see?" said my mother.

"Extreme precautions," said my father. He took a calm, deliberate
sip of his drink. "We're taking extreme precautions. We've got some

candles, right? We'll just stay inside where it's safe and wait out the storm."

There was the crackle of static, and then, just before the battery went dead for good, the announcer's voice came on again, barely more than a whisper. "Residents of homes west of Highway 101 are advised to evacuate. We repeat –"

My mother looked up at my father. We were both waiting for him to tell us what to do, but he didn't say anything.

I thought of his driving skills, his perfect confidence behind the wheel. "Daddy," I said – I hadn't called him that since I was ten – "why don't we drive into Portland? Stay the night at the Edgeware till the storm blows over." I thought, we could eat oysters, drink marc. We could be safe.

My father didn't answer at once, and I thought he was considering my idea. But then he said, firmly, "There's nothing to worry about. We're not going to panic over nothing."

Another blast of wind and rain shook the windows. *People who live in glass houses*, I remember thinking, but the saying didn't fit.

"Graham," my mother said. "Please."

And then I thought, *the eye of the hurricane*, because that's what it felt like – the house a dark square of silence, the wind and rain swirling and shrieking outside. "All right," my father said finally. "Get your coats and get in the car. I'll be right behind you."

"What do you mean?" my mother asked. "Why aren't you coming now?"

He spoke calmly. "I just want to check on a few things, make sure all the windows are shut tight so there won't be any water damage. And I might bring out some of the art work."

"Graham – "

"Just in case. The paintings are irreplaceable, Maureen." He repeated the word. "Irreplaceable. Besides, there's nothing to worry about. This is just a precaution. Get in the car. Jill," he said when I didn't move. "Do it. I'll be right along. I promise."

I got our coats, and a blanket to wrap Jack in. I remember that I felt sorrier for Jack than anyone. He was so terrified of riding in the car.

We waited there in the cold car, my mother and I, Jack in his blanket. The wind rocked the car, and the rain crashed down so hard it felt like someone hurling heavy rocks down from the sky and onto the roof. My father, getting soaked to the skin – he hadn't bothered to put on a coat – brought out in total three armloads of paintings, till the trunk was full, and he had to put some in the backseat with me. When he tried to go back again a fourth time, my mother grabbed his arm and cried, "No!" He leaned in then, patted her hand, and said, "I'll be right back. Stay here. I just want to check to make sure the deck posts are holding firm."

The rest is a jumble I try not to think about. There are the sounds of splintering wood, breaking glass, but I have to strain to hear these sounds because the sounds of wind and rain are so much louder. All of it happening so quickly there's no time to think, to make a decision. My mother stayed in the car, holding Jack, and I stayed there too. We stayed because he had told us to. It was only at the very last second that I pushed open the car door – the wind fighting to slam it shut again – and got out. By then it was too late.

When it was all over, I saw that the ancient spruce tree by the front door had been ripped out of the ground and was lying flat, its tangle of roots exposed like (this is the way my father would have thought) a giant piece of abstract sculpture. It may have been the spruce tree that killed him. It may have been the house itself – a falling beam, a brick, a pane of heavy glass. That was Molly's theory – it was the house itself that killed him – but how can anyone know for sure? It was hours before they could get in and extricate his body from the rubble of wood and glass – what was left of the house. The rest of it had slid down the cliff into the sea.

You could say Molly shouldn't have told me anything at all – and maybe she shouldn't have. But who else was she going to talk to about him? I didn't blame her. And besides, isn't it better for me to know the truth instead of being left, always, to wonder?

She knocked on the door of my dorm room one day during the winter term, sometime in February. Fortunately my new roommate was away for the weekend. I didn't like this roommate any more than I'd liked the first one. If my father had been alive, he would have made a phone call, would have found some way to get me back my single room, my art studio.

I almost didn't recognize her. She had cut her hair.

And then I knew – the last, the missing, piece of the jigsaw puzzle, the picture finally making sense. Molly said, "You understand, don't you, why I couldn't go to your father's funeral," and I nodded.

I invited her in. She was wearing her crackly black raincoat, a black dress underneath. I even brewed some green tea on my little hot plate, to be hospitable. We sat side by side on my narrow dorm bed.

My father had broken off his affair with her the week before the storm hit, Molly told me. "He had tried to leave your mother. He had told her he was in love with me, that he wanted a divorce. She said he could have his divorce, but that she would fight to keep the house."

Apparently – amazingly – my father had not anticipated this, had not expected that my mother would defy him in this particular way. What had he been thinking of? Had he really thought that she would give in, go away so quietly, that he could have Molly and his perfect dream house too? But maybe he did think that. My father, always, was a man used to getting what he wanted.

My mother's insistence on keeping the house changed everything, Molly said.

"I told him, let her have it. Let her keep it. Let her keep everything. My God, Graham, I said. We can work. We're both hard workers. We can start over, and in a few years we'll have a house you'll love more than this one."

She would have left her own husband in a minute. She wouldn't have cared where they lived. She could live anywhere, so long as she had a flat surface to paint on, so long as she could have her wind chimes and a jar of chrysanthemums on the table.

They had talked all night long. She'd cried – not weak, pleading tears, she told me, but angry tears. She knew she could make him happy; there was no doubt in her mind of the course they should take, and she was furious with him that he couldn't or wouldn't see it.

In the end, they left things unresolved. He asked her to give him some time, a week or two. He would talk to my mother again. Molly was leaving anyway, for shows in Los Angeles and San Diego. She said she would talk to him when she got back.

But then in L.A. she heard a brief news flash about the storm in the

Pacific Northwest. No details were given, but "I knew then and there what had happened," she said. "I knew at that moment he was dead."

I wasn't sure whether to believe that last part or not – it sounded false and overdramatic. But what did it matter whether she'd had some psychic connection with my father at the moment of his death? He was dead, all the same.

"But I know what his decision was," Molly said. "He chose the house over me. He chose the house over his own happiness. It's clear what he was doing. He was trying to save the house. And in the end, the house killed him."

That too sounded melodramatic. But I think she was probably right that his final decision had been to leave her. For one thing, her wisteria painting was not among the ones my father had tried to save. I can't help wondering if he would have tried to save my painting if he had known it existed, but he didn't know. It was rolled up – Molly had helped me mount it onto the scroll – under my bed, tied with a Christmas ribbon.

I stayed friends with Molly over the years – first in a furtive, secretive way out of deference to my mother, then later, when it didn't seem to matter, openly. Who else could I talk to about him, besides Molly? We are friends to this day, all these years later, at least she would say that, does say that, though we do nothing anymore beyond exchanging Christmas cards. "To my dearest friend Jill," she writes on them, and signs them, "Always, Molly." She has stayed married to Paul. He's a genuinely nice man – I went to visit him and Molly once, years ago, in San Francisco, and he greeted me graciously, as though he didn't know whose daughter I was. For all I know, Molly still passes his picture around to her students on the first night of class. She still teaches now and then, though she is past seventy.

I kept painting off and on during the rest of my freshman year, practicing at my cramped dorm room desk. Without the class and Molly's strong-willed presence, without her looking over my shoulder, I gave myself permission to begin painting with my left hand. It didn't work, though. I kept feeling ambivalent, guilty. And besides, how could I be sure that her praise of my work hadn't always been, at its heart, a way to get to him? I lost confidence; my brush began to falter in midstroke. Finally I gave it up altogether, though I still have the brushes and the ink, the leftover roll of rice paper. I keep them in that boring, ordinary way of people who take up hobbies and then abandon them, always vowing to get back to them "someday."

I still have nightmares about that winter storm, but in daylight I try never to think about it. I do think, sometimes, of that night at the Edgeware Hotel when I ate oysters for the first time and drank marc, when I imagined myself sophisticated, older than my years, poised on the threshold of a glamorous adult world. I think of my father, conjuring a taxi out of thin air on a busy rainy night, and I wonder how I could ever have been that innocent.

Sounds from the Courtyard

TIMOTHY SCHAFFERT

The women sat in a circle in the hotel lobby examining the hosiery Seymour brought. The woman to Seymour's left, a teacher of math, held a blue stocking before herself. She held it at the very tips of her fingers as though handling the skin of a freshly skinned snake. "Hose shouldn't be this color," she said, and she uncrooked her fingers a bit to let the stocking slip back into Seymour's open suitcase.

But Seymour paid little attention to the schoolteacher; his mind was on the woman sitting directly across from him. This woman wore a short black robe with a dog-faced dragon stitched up the sleeve. A line of bruises, like a knobbed serpent tattoo, twisted up from her shoulder and along her neck and jaw and up to her cheek. When she crossed her legs and her robe parted some, Seymour saw that even her thigh was purple and red and black. She flipped the flap of her robe back to cover her upper legs. Because she wore dark glasses, Seymour didn't know if she watched him watching her.

Mrs. Lope, the manager of the Hotel Juliet for Women, brought Seymour a thin Italian cigar and a cup of Earl Grey. Seymour, as a traveling salesman of ladies' hosiery, had visited the hotel often in the last few years, and he believed Mrs. Lope had a crush on him. But he hadn't any interest in her – he considered her too old. Because of the way he looked, he had trouble convincing Mrs. Lope of the age difference. Within the last fifteen years, his wife had died, he'd suffered the Depression, and all color had been shocked from him. His hair and skin were chalk white, his lips and fingernails just barely pink.

Mrs. Lope leaned over to stir the sugar in his tea. The heavy powder she wore only emphasized the cracking of the dry skin of her face. Seymour took one short sip of the tea and put it aside. He didn't like Earl Grey, because it tasted, strangely, of Mrs. Lope's perfume.

The bruised woman still looked in Seymour's direction, her eyes still hidden, and Seymour became conscious of his every inch of appearance. He could feel the air on his exposed calves above his socks, and he pushed at the knees of his trousers in his attempt to cover the skin.

A woman who sang jazz at a club called the Blue Kitchen sat squirming, her rustled taffeta noisy as she pulled a pair of peppermint-striped stockings from Seymour's suitcase. Seymour had seen this woman perform once. He'd gotten a headache trying to understand the words of her song – she'd slurred and muttered like a pained drunk. Seymour had leaned forward and squinted at the dark stage, to interpret. It had been like trying to read the label of a spinning record.

Everyone in the lobby politely took no notice of the rattling of the cup and spoon against the saucer of a nervous woman in the corner. This woman wore a bleach-stained smock and a plaid skirt, and she worked days in a wood shop, painting still lifes and pastoral scenes on headboards and the drawers of dressers and china cabinets. Whenever Seymour visited the hotel, this woman would sit there at the edge of the seat, shaking like that, her eyes wide as though she needed to reveal something hideous and astonishing about herself or someone she knew.

Even after this nervous woman went up to her room, the lobby was still noisy. The wind and rain shook the glass of the window, pushed open and slammed closed the front door. It was early spring, the season for storms, and every night this week the weather had been bad.

Earlier, as Seymour had driven into town, there had been hints of tornado weather – the wind, then the stillness, wind, stillness. As he'd walked up the front walk of the Juliet, someone had tossed remnants of an old life – clothes and books and photographs – from an upstairs window. A magazine, its pages flapping violently, swooped down like a hawk and knocked off Seymour's hat. The howl and shrill whistle of the wind produced a cacophony to which a blue dress did an angry dance before catching and tearing in the branches of a lilac bush. From the flower garden, Seymour picked an old photo of a young woman. She posed beside a vase of lilies, looking off remorsefully, and Seymour could imagine strains of the Paragon Rag, could imagine the smell of pickled eggs and spilt beer. Seymour had grown up cleaning up messes in his father's tavern – a dark, back alley place where the kind of women who weren't bothered by being alone in a dark, back alley place collected. These women would descend like fresh ghosts confused and battered by a sudden loss of life, and Seymour's father would work what magic he could with his colored bottles and bawdy songs. After the tavern closed, the women would stand out front, unsure of where to move on to. They'd stand in the light of the gas lamps, their many pale shadows gathering at their feet and clinging to their ankles.

Though the bruised woman in the dark glasses was too young to be this woman in the photograph, she had the same haunted expression. Seymour might have asked if it was her mother in the photo, might have asked if that was her dress caught in the lilac bush, but she disappeared as Seymour was distracted by the jazz singer wordlessly paying for her striped stockings.

Because it was so late, and because of the bad weather, Mrs. Lope invited Seymour to stay on for the night in the room behind the front desk. From the window beside the bed, Seymour could see the walled-in courtyard – its gazebo and grape arbor and stone fountain. Mrs. Lope brought him yet more of that Earl Grey tea, and she sat with him for a moment in the room. She noticed him looking out into the courtyard, and she explained the tree. It was a diseased pear tree that had one autumn deeply disturbed the women of the hotel by dropping its stunted fruit in the middle of the night – as a pear would fall it would rustle leaves, snap branches, would thud against the ground. But to remove the tree would leave a stump always in their courtyard – something more ominous than a season of last fruit.

"I don't much care for this tea, thank you," Seymour said, smiling, replacing the cup on the tray.

"But it's Earl Grey," Mrs. Lope said.

"I know," he said. "I don't much care for Earl Grey."

"I think I've always brought you Earl Grey. Well, you should have said something a long time ago. I could have brought you something else." She put her own cup on the tray and said, somewhat defensively, "I just think it's very strange that you didn't say something a long time ago."

Seymour became a little defensive then too. "Well," he said, "I never drank any of what you brought me. I've always left the cup full."

Mrs. Lope's face sank with the weight of a new understanding. The fact that she had remembered always bringing him Earl Grey, but had never once noticed he hadn't drunk it, seemed to disturb her. She sighed with resignation, then stood to pick up the tea service. "I'll leave you to sleep," she said.

As Seymour lay in bed, he felt bad, feeling he should have just drunk the tea. But then he drifted off to sleep, thinking of the bruised woman, and he wondered what it could be about her that hinted so of life, though so much about her physical nature suggested only death – her bruises and her feverish-pink skin, and her limp, and the way she'd reclined in that lobby chair as though she was weak from just lifting her bones all day. And what about those dark glasses she wore. He didn't even know if she had eyes in her head.

Seymour woke the next morning to the sound of splashing water in the courtyard. He sat at the edge of his bed and watched as three of the women of the hotel – the schoolteacher, the singer, and the bruised one – all washed their hair in the rainwater that had collected in the fountain. Their voices were strained, their laughs husky, as they tried to speak with their heads bent, their chins near their necks. Soap bubbles skimmed the top of the water and spilled over the edge to drip against the brick base. Their hair washed, the women went to sit in the best sunlight. They pushed their hair about, combed it out with their fingers, as it dried. Seymour became dizzy at the sight of this, at the sudden intimate knowledge he believed he'd just gained of these women, and he lay back staring at the ceiling and thinking of his wife again.

For months, after his wife's murder, he'd slept on the floor of her closet. Before he had drifted off to sleep those nights, he had studied the imprint of her foot on the insole of her shoes. Her dresses had still retained a bit of her shape. And so much of her character and personality had caught in her hats. "Oh, that hat is *you*," people had said to her when she'd worn one. One night, he'd wakened to the sound of a moth thumping against the wall. Upon sensing something alive in the closet, he'd grabbed at an empty dress, desperately needing his fingers to wrap about a leg. He'd cried and cried then.

Now Seymour got up, got dressed. He decided he'd be bold and ask the bruised woman to spend the day with him. He worked some cream through his hair, then combed his hair into place. He sprinkled on some cologne that smelled faintly of wood chips. The man that killed his wife must have been allowed a comb, cologne, hair tonic, Seymour thought. This man, while confined to a hospital for the criminally insane, got married to one of his nurses, and there was an article about him in the paper, next to a photo of him looking groomed and handsome on his wedding day. The article quoted the nurse as saying she recognized in him "a sweet regret." It seemed unjust that someone was allowed to fall in love with this man, that special pains weren't taken to prevent such a thing from happening.

This man had been a butcher and had been standing out front of his shop when Seymour's wife, mistaking him for the grocer, asked him How fresh is the fruit, or How much for a head of lettuce, or some such thing, when the butcher just lifted a cleaver above his head and brought it down against her shoulder, then against the side of her neck. Afterwards, the man couldn't even explain why he had felt inclined then to kill this stranger. It had just been something he had had to do, he'd said. It had been like an itch in his hand.

Shortly after the murder, Seymour, who'd been working in a tailor's shop, lost his job. Things just got worse and worse, and for a few weeks he'd even been without a home or belongings, spending his nights in the halls of ramshackle hotels. One day, he saw a businessman leap from the top floor of an office building. Halfway down, the man's shoes had popped from his feet and had hit against a closed window as though in one last effort to save at least themselves. Seymour had stood across the street from the building, just watching as the police and ambulance arrived, then as night fell, and the police and ambulance left. But the shoes were still there, near the alley, and they were a rich man's shoes, so Seymour wore them as he looked diligently for a job in an effort to save his own life.

Seymour stood in the lobby at the bottom of the stairs, next to a plaque – "no men upstairs, please" – the word "men" italicized. The bruised woman approached the top of the stairs and slowly started her descent, wearing her dark glasses, a long baggy coat, and a scarf wrapped around her head. Seymour was reminded of a fortuneteller he'd visited at Capital Beach a few years ago. The way the purple incense smoke had licked at the open flaps of the tent, he had expected to look in and see something festering, something seething and feral. But inside had been only an unlearned sibyl in dark glasses and scarf and long robe, and she'd stood leaning, her back straight, her arms and wrists crooked, like a praying mantis on a twig. Seymour no longer remembered what that woman had spoken of then, but he did remember that her words hadn't been spoken with a special poetry, or in a practiced accent, and he'd wondered what power she might have possessed had she had more talent for her work. He'd wondered what sort of amazing things a woman like that could make him understand.

"My name is Seymour," he said, greeting the bruised woman breathlessly, holding out his hand. She touched his hand lightly, the dry and harsh skin of her fingers brushing his like a cat's lick.

"Nadine," she said.

"I was wondering . . . ," he said, "I was thinking about going to Capital Beach . . . have you been there before?"

"Capital Beach?" she asked.

"Yes."

"Yeah," she said, "I've been to Capital Beach."

"Well, I was wondering if you'd be at all interested . . . if you would like to go there with me today. Would you be interested at all in something like that?"

Nadine smiled and sort of shrugged as she looked to her left and looked to her right. "Yeah, sure," she said. "I guess I could go to Capital Beach with you."

It thrilled Seymour that Nadine was a woman of such leisure, that she could walk downstairs and quickly accept an invitation without hardly considering why she'd come downstairs in the first place, why she'd put on her coat and scarf.

In Seymour's car, they rode in virtual silence, occasionally looking over to each other and laughing quietly, both amused and tolerant of the awkwardness. "So you sell hosiery," Nadine said, and they both nodded and were silent for the rest of the drive.

At Capital Beach, Seymour watched the dark clouds, and he watched the people. A dance platform extended out over the lake, like a wide dock, and some of the men would jokingly dance their partners to the edge and hold them there, threatening to push them off. It was a common joke, but each man would act as though he was the first to do it. Some of the women would look at the men with mock horror, others would laugh and beg for them to quit fooling around. One big-armed man with a spindly girlfriend held her by the shoulders just off the platform, and the toes of the girl's shoes were splashed by the gently breaking waves beneath her.

Seymour and Nadine sat on a bench near where the fortuneteller's tent had once been. There, now, was a man with a collection of cages – mostly birds and lizards and mice for sale. Seymour had looked at one of these lizards and he'd wondered what burdens such a small creature might bear to look so morose in the face. Now a man walked in front of Seymour, a lizard perched smartly and ornamentally at the front of the brim of his derby hat.

Nadine's hair was a mess. They'd ridden the Jack Rabbit three times. Seymour had splinters in his hands from gripping the front of the wooden car. On the second ride of the rollercoaster, Nadine's scarf had whipped away from her head, and the wind had knocked her curls this way and that. Her wild hair had fit her expression of amused fright as the cars were lifted and dropped.

Exhausted from the rides, Seymour sat forward on the bench, resting his head in his hands. Then he told Nadine, almost unthinkingly, about his life, about his wife and the man that murdered her, then he watched the beach again. People stumbled and staggered from the Fun House, in disarray. They were dizzied by the bent mirrors and the spinning floors, their hair and clothes mussed by the fans and air vents. It took them all a moment to get used to the absence of fun, then they'd walk in straighter lines.

Nadine told Seymour of her husband: "He was a man on fire. He had orange hair and wore a red suit coat you couldn't stare at for too long." Nadine told how he'd offer a guy a stick of gum, then would fold a tiny paper swan from the wrapper. "Pour me some likka," her husband would say, "likka," with a snap of the tongue. He had a loud collection of Saturday night ties – some with dots or stripes or paisley, some with skinny dogs, skinny women, blue fish. When he'd drunk enough, he'd dance, his arms and legs flailing like someone had given him a hot foot.

"When he was beating me up once, it was then I realized I've lived other lives." She had memories of things she couldn't have experienced in this life. She could remember, quite vividly, standing at the window of a pink convent, the juice of the orange she was slicing spotting the front of her habit. Outside, two nuns stood speaking beside a cactus that resembled a dancing Mexican girl – a purple flower in her hair, one arm up, the other at her hip. The back of the habit of one of the nuns was caught on a needle of the cactus, and lifted slightly, and neither woman noticed. The cactus, though mouthless, seemed to be smiling in a way, delighting in a devilish prank.

"I also remember," Nadine said, "something in a cellar, some cellar, I was cutting wax away from a wheel of cheese, and there was a man there turning the wine bottles on the rack, checking the labels, blowing away cobwebs. He said something very sweetly to me in a language I don't know now. But the strangest memory I've had – everything was dark, and there was howling, and I think I was crawling around on the ground. Well, at the base of a tree, I found a bug and I ate it. But, for some reason, I was very happy having found the bug." Nadine took a handkerchief from her coat pocket and held it over her nose and mouth. "When I started having these memories I began to feel foreign to this place and time. The air was different to me, it pained my lungs to breathe. The sky's a different shade of blue too. It gives me a headache. And I can feel the heat of the ground right up through the bottoms of my shoes, if you can believe it," and she lifted her feet slightly from the ground. The sun, which had shone for a moment, went back behind the black clouds and Nadine took off her sunglasses. Even before Seymour saw her eyes, he knew everything she said was true. He believed that she'd lived and died before.

It broke Seymour's heart that this woman had been hit so hard that she now had difficulty breathing the air of the world she lived in.

They decided to see a movie in town before Seymour took Nadine home. As the movie played, the wind outside picked up, and Seymour could just imagine what sort of havoc they were being sheltered from in this theater. When he listened closely beyond the ticking of the projector he'd catch sounds – a scream, he thought, or the crackling of a fire, or the screeching of metal as an automobile was twisted. But no one stopped the movie and told them to take cover. The electricity didn't go out. But then a wind worked through the theater.

The doors at the back frantically swung, and the heavy, weighted curtains in front lifted and shook. The light fixtures on the wall beside the exit glowed brighter, then dimmer, then brighter, giving the shadowed cherub at the edge of the screen the illusion of taking wing. But the movie still ran, Carole Lombard still whined, and Seymour took out a cigarette and hoped to relax. He lit a match, and the flame seemed to be lifted for just a moment from the tip, then replaced. He looked over to Nadine then, and saw she was as afraid as he was, and they instinctively grabbed at each other, wrapped their arms around each other and clutched and clawed. They kissed, their teeth knocking together, their lips pulled away from their gums.

The movie stopped, the lights came up and there was absolute silence, as though the rumbling at the walls had just been a product of the projector. Seymour and Nadine stepped dizzily to the aisle, and as they walked to the doors, Seymour saw a stocking draped over the back of one of the seats. He picked it up and he could imagine his car outside mangled, and all his trunks broken, hose and socks spread along the street. His whole livelihood destroyed again.

Seymour wound up the stocking and stuck it in his pocket, and he noticed Nadine blushing at his familiarity with the garment. She glanced down to check her ankles as though she believed the hose might have been peeled from her leg and carried back here by the strange wind without her knowing. Both her legs were still stockinged and she laughed a little with a sense of foolishness, the first laughter Seymour had heard from her. Seymour didn't care then if they ever left the theater. He didn't care if he ever learned the condition of his car and trunks and everything outside.

Alternative Lifestyle Alert

Excerpt from *The Quality of Life Report*

MEGHAN DAUM

My first impression of Prairie City was that it seemed not to be there at all. The "city," which, as Sue Lugenbeel had assured me, truly was a city with crime and drugs and "plenty of night life," wasn't visible from the air. We descended into wide patches of brown and green fields. Only two airlines served the place and despite the smallness of the airport and the relatively small number of people getting off the plane, I had never seen so many friends and family members waiting at the gate. At least half of the women had babies on their hips. They gave us curious looks as we pulled the video equipment off the carousel, or maybe it was just that I was wearing a leather jacket even though it was close to one hundred degrees. Everyone else had on shorts and tank tops. The cameraman, Ray (Faye frequently called him Roy, and sometimes even Raoul, which incensed him), was close to retirement and considerably put out, at having to make the road trip. "I'd like to see some of these chicks in thongs," he mumbled.

We rented a car and drove into town. Nearly every radio station played classic rock exclusively. Peter Frampton's "Do You Feel Like We Do" came on twice. We passed the welcome sign that said OPEN ARMS, OPEN MINDS and pictured a group of racially diverse individuals holding hands. Along the highway, stretches of land gave way to factories and big concrete silos with train tracks running alongside them. Billboards seemed to stand in for trees and the vehicles on the street, most of them mammoth pickup trucks or SUVs, rolled to careful stops at intersections, even when the lights were yellow. Ray, who was driving, barreled through all the yellow lights until we reached the Ramada Inn, a slablike building in downtown Prairie City. At fifteen stories, it looked to be the tallest structure in town. We checked into our rooms and I called Sue Lugenbeel. Outside my ninth-floor window, the town looked so lifeless and depressing I wanted nothing more than to do the interviews in under two days and go home.

"Lucinda!" Sue Lugenbeel chirped. "Welcome to P.C.! I have seventeen fabulous women who are dying to be interviewed."

Prairie City, it seemed, was one of those towns that went by its initials, like D.C. or L.A.

After surveying the women, I selected the five thinnest ones and conducted on-camera interviews with them for the next two days. During this time, an odd sensation crept upon me. Though "fabulous" may have been an overstatement, the women proved themselves far worthier interview subjects than any of the boutique owners, dietitians, Pilates trainers, bagel makers, and relationship experts on whom I had cut my teeth as a journalist. Despite my plan to talk to them for no more than ten minutes each (and despite *Up Early's* unofficial interview edict: "make 'em cry, say good-bye") I let the women talk for hours and hours. I loved them. I couldn't get enough of them. When Ray went back to New York I called Faye from my room at the Ramada Inn and told her I needed to stay and do additional research. Then I got out my microcassette recorder and passed another three days interviewing the remaining twelve women by myself. Something almost mystical had happened to me. Even though Prairie City was hot and dreary and the food, at least at the restaurants near the Ramada, tasted like lunch at a school cafeteria, something about the blandness of the town and the flat land that surrounded it were making me feel alive and exotic. Almost like another person.

This was, after all, serious country. The real heartland, the plains. Not necessarily Prairie City, itself, which, at most intersections, could have passed for Long Island, but the land surrounding it, *that* was serious country. It was Willa Cather–novel serious. It was Sissy Spacek–movie serious and documentary-film-about-poor-conditions-in-meat-packing-plants serious. It was a place where, according to my early observations, not only did substance trump style but a very nuanced and therefore quietly sophisticated style was born out of the substance itself. What I meant by this I wasn't sure. All I knew was that observing the people of Prairie City, particularly the beleaguered women at the recovery center and the careworn case workers who pressed empowering novels by women writers into their hands and encouraged them to eat soy products, made me feel for the first time like it might be possible to become a good person. Not that there weren't plenty of opportunities to be a good person in New York. I'd just never bothered to take them. I had never worked with homeless kids, never adopted a stray animal, never volunteered to rake leaves in the park, never even, come to think of it, attended a church service. No one I knew had ever done any of these things, either. Was it laziness, busyness, distress over not having the right outfit for such activities? What did it matter? It was shameful. Not that adopting animals or going to church automatically makes you a good person, of course. And not that I was necessarily a bad person. It was just that I had come to view my moral status as a quantifiable entity that was measured solely against one person. That person was Faye. And the fact that I did not start fires and throw things at people had always firmly positioned me, if not in the "good" zone, at least in the "not remotely as bad as Faye" zone. But now, as I drove past the cornfields along the outer stretches of Highway 36, fresh from an interview with a woman who worked on an assembly line at the Firestone tire plant, an interview during which we'd *really bonded*, during which she'd told me her troubles, and I, treating her as an equal, had told her some of mine, like the rent increase ("you poor thing," she'd said), I felt I was more than just not remotely as bad as Faye but actually *good*, at least potentially. And goodness, I realized, not only felt good, it felt *cool*. It *was* cool. The substance became style, the kind you can't fake. Any truly stylish person will tell you that's the only way it works.

It's possible, however (and looking back, it's not only possible but true, and it makes me wince), that I just felt superior. As I interviewed the methamphetamine-addicted women, listening to stories of bad boyfriends and accidental pregnancies and cars repossessed by the bank, smugness coursed through my veins like a narcotic. Of course, I didn't see it as smugness. I was merely *interested*. I was engrossed by the stories of other people's screwups, mostly because, though I didn't realize it at the time, they made my own screwups seem minor in comparison. After years covering the toe ring craze and announcing to New Yorkers that "scones are the new muffin," I felt that I'd finally found my niche. I was a socially conscious reporter passionately committed to the true-life health crises that affect thousands of women nationwide.

With every press of my record button, feelings of righteousness released themselves in me like an Alka-Seltzer tab in water. And when it came to feeling not only righteous but heroic, there was nothing like ordering a room-service breakfast at the Ramada and then navigating the rental car to a trailer park with a name like Shadowland Estates for hours of heart to heart with some woman whose misfortune – husband got her hooked on methamphetamine and left her destitute with three kids and two minimum-wage retail jobs – was about to be rectified by what this woman believed would be a heart warming, nonexploitive segment on *New York Up Early*.

Besides, methamphetamine was an easy story. Given the constraints of your average *Up Early* segment, there wasn't much more to say about the drug other than that it was a very bad thing and that even though it might help you lose weight (a fundamental concern of the show) it might also rot your teeth and/or land you in jail. Later, the promos for the segment would scream, "The party may never end, but your life just might. Find out about the dangerous drug that's sweeping the not-so-innocent heartland and heading straight for New York!"

Of course, there was already as much meth in New York as there were opportunities to do good in New York. It's just that no one I knew had anything to do with either. That was another reason the story appealed to me so much: it was guaranteed to lead me in the opposite direction of my actual life. There was little chance of encountering a publicist, plus I noticed that people in recovery had a way of telling you everything, including things they really shouldn't tell you (like that they're high this very moment), which produced, in addition to the previously established feelings of superiority and righteousness, a tertiary sensation of omniscience. Thanks to the interviewees' own stupidity (and my disarming interview technique – what a pro!) dozens of disadvantaged waifs with no concept of the term "on the record" were putting themselves at the mercy of my compassion. And I would not let them down. They were safe. I would not quote the things they said about smuggling. I was Mother Teresa, a credit to my despicable profession and the snide, backstabbing metropolis I called home. Suddenly, I loved my job.

I also loved Sue Lugenbeel. She was the executive director of the Prairie City Recovery Center for Women and she wore batik harem pants and dangling silver earrings and had spiky bleached blond hair that she claimed to have cut herself. She said she lived on a farm outside of town. I suspected she was around fifty. I also suspected she was a lesbian, which, given the farm, I found fascinating in terms of, as Faye would have said, her "cultural context." In addition to setting me up with seventeen recovering addicts, Sue also assumed the role of ambassador for Prairie City. The first night after Ray returned to New York, Sue met me at the Ramada and drove me in her Saab to a Japanese restaurant in a strip mall, where we met two of her colleagues and discussed women's issues. Generally I wasn't up for discussions of women's issues, having filled my quota in college, but there was something thrilling about the juxtaposition of the vaguely 1970s-sounding rhetoric – the word "empowerment" kept coming up – and the decor of the restaurant, which had a huge freestanding fish tank and was carpeted a deep red to connote "an Asian flair." I liked the warm, self-deprecating nature of the other two women. I liked the way the piped-in Kenny G music weaved in and out of their conversation. They segued flawlessly from sanctimony to cattiness, from the subject of rampant meth use among women in their community to gossip about who had slept with whom in the county health department. After dinner, we retreated to a modular sofa in the bar area, where Sue smoked a cigarette, a gesture I found admirably rebellious in light of her work as a health advocate.

After my third day of further research – there had been a redheaded truck-stop waitress whose teeth had rotted from drugs, a nineteen-year-old mother who'd lost both her children to the state, a dental hygienist who, having tired of prescription drugs stolen from her office, had resorted to smoking meth in the basement every night while her husband watched *Jeopardy!* – Sue invited me for cocktails out at her farm.

I got lost on the way to Sue's place. Off the highway, there was one gravel road after another, roads with names like Little Mud Creek Road and Northwest 317th Street. Finally I found a farmhouse with a Saab in the driveway. It was old and rambling like something out of a Hallmark Hall of Fame movie except it had an aboveground swimming pool with rainbow windsocks on the deck and a rainbow beach umbrella on the patio table. Acres of tilled cornfields spread out in every direction.

Tractors hummed in the distance. k.d. lang played on the stereo inside the house. Sue ran out to greet me, followed by three large dogs with rainbow collars.

"Welcome, Lucinda!" she cried, hugging me even though she'd seen me two hours earlier. "This is the old homestead."

There was an END HATRED sticker on the front door. The dogs were jumping all over me, covering my J. Crew Capri pants with drool.

"Stop that, Willa! Stop that, Chloe!" Sue yelled at the dogs. The third one, an ancient-looking black Lab, cowered behind her legs. "This one's Isaiah. He's a little shy. He was abused by his old owner."

Another woman emerged from the house. She was wearing Birken-stocks with the same harem pants I'd seen on Sue. She had long, slightly frizzy, dirty blond hair that she'd tied up on her head and pierced with chopsticks.

"This is my partner, Teri," Sue said. "She has to take off, unfortunately. She's taking a Chinese medicine class at the college."

Teri gave a quick wave and climbed in the Saab and drove off, kicking up a trail of dust on the road.

"Wine?" Sue asked. "I just went to Shop 'N Save. I have some Triscuits, too."

Sue and I drank approximately two and a half bottles of wine that night. Because I was in interview mode, I asked her a lot of questions. And because what little inhibitions she had were erased by the wine and at least half a pack of Merit filters, she told me what seemed like everything about herself. Her life story read like an entry in *Our Bodies, Ourselves*. She had turned fifty-two that year. She was in the process of planning a menopause shower for herself and a number of other women – "it's like a baby shower except you get calcium supplements instead of teething rings!" Sue had grown up in Prairie City, taught health at Prairie City High School for several years, and, upon realizing she was a lesbian, attempted to open a gay cocktail lounge, which had ultimately failed because of competition from the more established queer hangout, the Thirteenth Street TGI Friday's. Given her interest in women's issues, she began working at the Prairie City Recovery Center for Women and was eventually promoted to executive director. She'd met Teri at TGI Friday's and, a few years later, they'd bought the farm, where they'd recently installed track lighting and a subzero refrigerator. Sue had twice received the League of Women Voters' Antonia H. Kubicek Award for excellence in community service in the interests of women. She was on intimate terms with all of the city's left-leaning elite. The liberal county commissioner and his wife, a former all-state women's softball champion, were her best friends. She was also very close with her brother, Leonard, who drove a garbage truck for the Prairie City Department of Sanitation. He was Native American by blood but had been adopted into Sue's family as a toddler.

"He took back his Indian name," Sue said. "So now he's Leonard Running Feather. You can imagine how my mom felt about that. It made my being a lesbian seem about as big a deal as getting a D in math! But they got over it."

"Do you ever get, like, harassed?" I asked, now a probing journalist in the Katie Couric vein, unafraid of raising the tough questions. "I mean, being openly gay and living out in the country and everything."

Sue looked bewildered. "No."

She said this as if I had asked whether coyotes ever came near the house, opened the door, and sprawled out on the couch to watch *Friends*.

In the adjacent field, a farmer drove by on a John Deere tractor, a bright headlight guiding him through the dark. He extended his arm in a giant wave.

"Hi, Joe!" Sue called out.

So why was it that every time Sue went inside the house for more wine or Triscuits I could do nothing but look out at all that farmland and, with the mixture of fear and exhilaration that accompanies a dare, wonder if the solution to my problems, the problems that began with my apartment lease and ended somewhere around my growing feelings of shallowness and moral worthlessness, was to move to Prairie City? Why was I so stirred by the selection of magazines in Sue's bathroom: *Country Living, Travel & Leisure, Mother Jones*? Was it merely amazement that someone living on a farm in the Midwest would subscribe to *Mother Jones*? Or was there truth to my mounting suspicion that I had discovered a secret pocket of American society, a place farmers waved at semi-butch lesbians, a place where women threw menopause showers and the sky – I'd noticed this even from my hotel room – seemed to eclipse the earth itself. It could have been another planet. It was certainly a cheaper planet. As I scanned the classified section of the local newspaper I picked up at the airport on my way home, I noticed that houses rented for as little as four hundred dollars per month. Prairie City was, if not an obvious paradise, a bizarre and intriguing idea.

My one-room, one-window apartment in New York had mice and hardly any kitchen. Though I'd never even attempted to entertain more than two guests at a time, I was considered an obstreperous tenant, mostly by my downstairs neighbor, Bob, the longtime lover of my upstairs neighbor, Yuri. They'd lived there at least twenty years and both of their apartments were rent controlled. Neither paid more than three hundred dollars a month; so instead of getting a place together they moved between the first and third floors as if they had one apartment, padding up and down the stairwell in their robes and slippers like college lovers in a dormitory. It was as if my existence on the second floor was that of a guest who would not leave a dinner party. My apartment itself seemed an infringement on their rights as private citizens. Bob was forever shoving notes under my door. "You walk so heavily on the floor. Could you please remove your shoes upon entering your apartment?" "Would it be possible to lower the ringer on your phone?" "Your overnight company is shall we say, a bit vocal. Have you any idea what I can hear?"

This last was so mortifying I vowed never to run into Bob or Yuri again. I scampered down to the lobby to fetch the *New York Times* and the mail, terrified of the sound of Bob's unlocking door at the foot of the stairs. I lingered on the sidewalk if either of them happened to be walking ahead of me into the building, Yuri holding the door for Bob like a patient grandfather, his jet black toupee sweeping across his deeply creased forehead, his imitation silk ascot tucked in his shirt like a Russian lounge singer, which he may well have been at one time. I would watch them from the entrance of the Korean grocery a few doors down, counting the seconds until I could walk toward my building without their seeing me, clutching my plastic container of deli salad and wondering exactly how a person gets to be twenty-nine and still finds herself hiding from her neighbors before going to her apartment and eating tricolored pasta salad in front of a TV with barely any reception. I experienced this sequence of thoughts almost weekly.

On the evening I flew back from Prairie City, I dropped my luggage off in my apartment (a glance in the darkened kitchen area revealed two dead mice in overturned traps) and took the subway downtown to meet my friend Daphne at our favorite cocktail lounge, Bar Barella. Daphne was usually my favorite friend, though not necessarily my best friend (my best friend was Elena Fein, with whom I was usually angry or vice versa). Part of Daphne's appeal, part of the reason I was willing to come home from a long trip and meet her in a bar that was forty-five minutes from my apartment and one block away from hers was that she was notoriously unavailable. She would disappear for months at a time. She would retreat to Maine, staying in some cottage owned by her relatives, and not call anyone. She would go to Africa for six months as a relief worker, then slink back to New York, sublet an apartment, and wait weeks before letting anyone know she was around. Her dominant characteristic was her lightness, her lack of rules, her ability to perceive individual stupidity as a natural response to global stupidity. During a time several years earlier, when I was briefly dating a guy who netted hundreds of thousands of dollars a year running a high-end escort service that catered to Wall Street brokers, Daphne was the only person I told. Years later, when Daphne dated a guy who netted hundreds of thousands of dollars a year selling high-grade marijuana to rock stars, I was one of many people she told. That was the difference between us. She could do stupid things and actually come off looking cooler for it. For this I worshiped her.

When I arrived at Bar Barella, Daphne was sitting on a Victorian sofa in a dark corner. A flickering candle on the table reflected in her Armani glasses, for which she'd paid four hundred dollars despite difficulty making her rent. I wanted to tell her about Prairie City, about Sue and the farm, and my thought of moving there, which, by the time I picked my bags off the carousel at LaGuardia, had evolved from a thought to a full-fledged, terrifying plan. But she needed to talk first.

"Oh my God," she said.

"What?"

"My fucking life."

It seemed that in the week I'd been gone, Daphne had managed to sleep with two different men. This was after a year and a half without sex.

"Rock on," I said, which isn't the kind of thing I usually say. But it seemed a less offensive cliché than "You go, girl." Given the census data, the seven hundred thousand surplus of single women, two men in one week was less an act of sluttishness than of stockpiling. We hardly ever got laid. My "vocal" overnight guest had been an anomaly. As for Daphne, two men in one week, especially two men taller than she, merited a glass of Champagne.

But no. One of them was an ex-boyfriend, a struggling actor who'd dumped her long ago for an actress with a trust fund and a SoHo loft. The other was her ostensibly platonic friend Ira, who had been in love with her for years and to whom she wasn't attracted. Somehow she'd gotten drunk and spent the night in his apartment because she didn't feel like taking the scary D train all the way home from Brooklyn. Neither had called her since.

"Fuckheads," she said. "I have to move."

"Move to the Midwest," I said.

"Really?"

"Oh, sorry," I said. "We're not done with you. Keep going."

"No, I'm finished," Daphne said, sucking down her last bit of Pinot. Her eyes darted around for the waitress. "And even more disgustingly," she continued, "Ira has a single bed. He's too cheap to get a grownup bed. And I can't believe I'm even admitting this but he has *Smurf sheets*, like a child's sheets. Like it's ironic or something. Like we're still in college. I mean, he's fucking thirty-three."

"I met these lesbians in the Midwest," I said.

"There are lesbians in the Midwest?"

"They live on a farm and drink wine and read *Mother Jones*," I told Daphne. "You can rent a house for four hundred dollars. I don't know. Something's happened inside my mind."

"I thought *Mother Jones* went out of business."

"And," I said, "the town is called Prairie City. How cute is that?"

"No fucking way!"

"Way," I said. "I think I might have to move there. I think the train has left the station. I have the idea. I can't not do it."

"Uh oh," she said. "Alternative Lifestyle Alert."

When my friends and I were not discussing the lack of available men, we were usually discussing moving out of New York. Again, the subjects were related, though not entirely. Someone was always coming up with an escape plan, a way to lower the cost of living, a way to increase the odds of meeting a guy who actually knew how to hammer a nail into a piece of plywood. The plans varied according to the books we'd recently read, the movies we'd recently seen, the city most recently featured on *The Real World*. We'd say Austin, Seattle, Paris, New Delhi. When somebody came home from an unusual location – a wedding in Nova Scotia or a snorkeling trip in Australia – and spent two weeks obsessing about moving into a yurt on the Bay of Fundy we called it an Alternative Lifestyle Alert. The guiding principle of the Alternative Lifestyle Alert was that it was never acted upon.

Until now. No, I thought as I rode the subway back to my verminous apartment, this time it would be different. I, Lucinda Trout, would break the pattern of Alternative Lifestyle Alert inertia and actually alter my lifestyle. That night, as I unpacked my clothes, which still smelled like the country air and cigarette smoke of Sue's farm, I entered a kind of trance. It was an intensified version of the kind of trance I'd occasionally enter on nights when I'd catch some kind of heartland movie on TV, *Country* for example, which starred Jessica Lange and an especially scrumptious Sam Shepard, and, despite the fact that it was produced by Disney, had always been a secret favorite of mine. Out of this trance would always arise the same question, a question that asked what would be left of me if I uprooted myself completely. What would happen if I removed myself from the crowds and the money and the constant talk of who had been featured in articles in *New York Magazine* with titles like "Under 35 and Over the Moon: Gen-X Internet Moguls Cash In and Take the Real Estate Market by Storm"?

I bring this up because in the stack of mail by my door was that very magazine with that very article. And one of the underthirtyfives was a woman I'd known in college who had taken what basically amounted to a personal Web page chronicling her sexual exploits and sold it to Time Warner. Then she'd purchased a seven-hundred-thousand-dollar loft in TriBeCa. A full-page color photo showed her reclining on a leopard-print Victorian sofa. The caption read "Haley Bopp (née Alice

Sterngold), creator of the cyberdiary *This Broad's Sheets*, might have given up creative control of her Web site, but she now seeks artistic expression in her 1500-square-foot loft, which she's decorated with the help of the red hot design firm Home Planet, known for its innovative approach to feng shui."

My trance was briefly interrupted by an outburst of envy and disgust. I considered calling Elena, who was an early riser and might have taken a 3:00 AM phone call as an opportunity to get a head start on her workout. But then, like a light breeze, the trance returned, bringing with it the realization that no amount of leopard-print Victorian sofas or feng shui consultation from Home Planet could justify fifteen hundred square feet going for more than ten times the amount of Haley's and my tuition at Smith College, a place where we had been required to take courses with names like "Gender, Power, and Commerce," courses from which I, who was still paying off my student loans, had obviously garnered fewer benefits than she. It occurred to me that Sue and Teri's farmhouse, purchased in 1991 for sixty thousand dollars, would probably sell for close to a million were it located within a seventy-five-mile radius of New York City. It then occurred to me that the *2 BR, 1.5 BA, c/a, fenced yard, w/d hookups, gar, gorg. woodwork, $475/mo* listing I'd spotted in the *Prairie City Daily Dispatch* would not only reveal what would be left of me if I uprooted myself but would leave me with enough extra funds to fly home and have drinks with Daphne at Bar Barella every month if I felt like it.

But there was more to it than the cost of living, more to it than the male-to-female ratio and lack of chivalry from men who had Smurf sheets. Though I couldn't put my finger on it (and, indeed, would never be able to articulate whatever "it" was, even years later) my reasons for wanting to go to Prairie City, for *needing*, as I was now convinced, to go to Prairie City, had something to do with my relationship to what I could only describe as "real life." Even in childhood, which I'd spent in a middle-class suburb of Philadelphia, I'd had the distinct feeling that nothing that surrounded me, not the boxy Cape Cod houses of my street, not the multiplex at the mall where my friends and I had skulked around on weekends, certainly not the chemically maintained grass of my parents' small backyard, was ever quite the stuff of "real life." There was a neither-here-nor-there quality to my existence. We were neither rich nor poor, neither city dwellers nor country dwellers, neither athletes nor intellectuals (we played a bit of tennis, but not enough to ever join a racket club). My parents had been old when they'd had me, my sister already at Penn State by the time I was three. Though they'd never have admitted it, I was an accident and, as if rising to the occasion, they delayed their retirements until I got through Smith, after which they promptly moved to Florida. After that, I'd scarcely seen my family again. In keeping with the overall impermeability of my life, this was neither a loss nor a relief, just the way things were. My sister got married and then eventually divorced somewhere near Pittsburgh. My parents retreated into a world of halfhearted tennis and early cocktails. And I had moved to New York, a world that, despite its endless opportunities to experience "real life," I had managed to make as trivial and petty as the social politics of my own high school. As hard as I'd tried to enter the "real world," I was still eating from plastic containers and reporting on thong underwear. Though I considered myself semi-intellectual, I was also semi-attractive, semi-successful, and semi-happy. Not a bad state of affairs, when you thought about it. But in Prairie City (though I still hadn't fully admitted this to myself) there seemed the possibility of being (or at least appearing) very intellectual, very attractive, very successful, and, if not very happy, at least in possession of a bigger apartment. And if it didn't work out that way – and no doubt it wouldn't – I could always come back. Except for the small matter of my job.

I looked out my window at the building across the alleyway. Though it was just past 4:00 AM, the sounds of shouting and the occasional ring of a telephone still punctuated the night. In one apartment, where the lights were on, a couple was unfolding a futon in their one-room apartment. I watched them throw books on the floor, pull out the frame to where it rammed up against their dining table. The air was muggy and they took their clothes off with the curtains open; it was too hot to bother with privacy this time of year. I watched them shut down the computer and climb into bed. There was a tiny television set on their night table and on top of it a towering stack of papers. The man reached up to turn off the light, and the papers fell to the floor. I heard the echo of his "shit" across the courtyard as the window went dark.

Then it all came to me. The key to what I wanted, the way to get out without really leaving. Like a math formula passed under the desk by a much smarter student, I now had everything I needed, and it was so much simpler than I'd ever imagined. I turned on the computer and began to type.

To: Faye Figaro
From: Lucinda Trout
Re: Idea for Segment Series

My trip to the Midwestern town of Prairie City, where I conducted a number of probing interviews with methamphetamine addicts, proved useful in more ways than just producing the meth story (which, btw, I have no doubt will be emotionally resonant and really groundbreaking). While in Prairie City, which is a town of just under 100,000, smack in the middle of the country, where the flat prairie stretches out to meet an endless sky, I had a startling and potentially ratings-boosting revelation: this place represents the American Dream. Far from the cramped quarters and moral compromises of New York, a town like Prairie City, with its surprisingly diverse population and plethora of old farmhouses that sit on acres of natural grassland, is precisely the kind of setting New Yorkers imagine when they think about "escaping New York."

So, in keeping with Up Early's *new initiative to expand coverage into national issues, I propose a yearlong series that allows New Yorkers to live out this fantasy without actually having to do it themselves. I propose that I, as Lifestyle correspondent, move to Prairie City for one year and produce weekly dispatches that show New Yorkers exactly what it's like to trade apartment life for a farmhouse, Chinese takeout for steak flanks, and rude drivers for friendly farmers on tractors who wave as they drive past. I could also feature interviews with quirky locals, such as, for example, a farmer who is a champion ballroom dancer, a ranch hand who writes poetry, or a garbage man whose larger goal in life is to conserve energy by installing (for free) solar panels in people's houses. Slice of life stories aside, however, the real essence of this series is that it taps directly into New Yorkers' concerns over the idea of "quality of life." New Yorkers think they don't have it (or must pay a lot for it). In Prairie City, quality of life flows like water. What does "quality of life" really mean? What does it say about our identity as New Yorkers? Our identity as Americans? After all, more and more people are leaving the big city for places like Prairie City. Is it a trend?*

I will be the one to bring Prairie City into the homes of New Yorkers. I will be the guinea pig for their escape fantasies. And they'll be able to see it only on Up Early. *If this doesn't appeal to you, I'd be happy to pursue the cell phone rage story we discussed at last week's meeting.*

So jazzed now by my trance that I could feel actual sparks in my body, I skimmed my memo; found it to be frighteningly brilliant, and e-mailed it to Faye, even though she wouldn't get it until she arrived at the office, which was never before 11:00 AM. I didn't bother unpacking the rest of my clothes.

At noon the next day, Faye called me into her office. Two grande cappuccinos were sitting on her desk and her temporary assistant was trying to pour packets of Equal in them without knocking anything off.

"Is this your resignation?" Faye asked.

"Faye," I said, "you may think I'm kidding but this is potentially huge. There is a wide, wide market for this kind of thing. Because what I'm tapping into is not only a fantasy; it's an anxiety, a crisis. It's a conflict. And because so many people feel it, it's a trend."

"It's a trend to move to some backwater shit hole?" Faye said. "Where everyone's a drug addict? Plus they're fat. I saw the footage from the meth story."

"Those were average-sized women!" I said. "Besides, that was just one marginalized group. But get this, there are just as many men as women there. Not like here. And I met some cool lesbians."

"There are lesbians in the Midwest?" Faye asked. Her eyebrow, tweezed to the width of an extrafine pen, arched slightly. She picked up one of her cappuccinos and the lid fell off. Foam rolled onto her hand and dribbled on her desk. "Fuck!" she yelled.

"Look, just try it," I said. "Send the memo upstairs to see what they say."

"They'll never go for it," she said. "We're supposed to pay you to do a couple stories a month about fat people? There's no way it's a weekly thing, Lucinda. There's a reason Roseanne's show got canceled, although in talking to her I see she had a real vision. It was quite scatological really. She's coming out to the Hamptons this weekend."

"Hell," I said – was it time to resort to begging? – "you could keep me on, like, as a freelancer. You wouldn't have to pay me quite as much. The cost of living there being, you know, lower."

Faye looked startled. "Well, obviously we'd pay you less," she said. "Obviously."

"I mean, not that much less," I said. "I mean, I'd be constantly researching stories."

"I'll send this upstairs," Faye said. "But you really do appear to be having some sort of crisis. And I would encourage you to get into therapy rather than working it out on company time. In the meantime I want you to do a story on jungle gym safety. John McEnroe's kid fell off some climbing thing in Central Park. He's pissed. I think he might talk. And can you bring me a paper towel?"

Four hours later, fate stepped in. Because fate is what steps in when you take charge of your fate. Or something like that.

"*Lucinda!*"

When I walked into Faye's office, Bonnie Crawley and Samantha Frank were sitting on the love seat drinking bottled water and looking vaguely disgusted. They shushed each other when I came in.

"Well, you got your wish," Faye said. "They accepted your resignation. I mean your proposal."

"Are you serious?" I yelped.

"What? Now you changed your mind?" Faye said.

"No!" I said. "No, I think this is great. This is going to be a great series. And of course I'll still come back for meetings whenever possible."

"Don't bet on it," said Faye. "They want to do it, but the budget is tight. Now, Samantha had an idea for the name of the series and Upstairs likes it so we're going to go with it."

"I thought it should be called 'The Quality of Life Report,'" said Samantha. "It's sort of the lifestyle equivalent to barometric pressure. It goes up and down. You've got good days and bad days. Except here, 'quality of life' refers to the larger concept of the good life, the life New Yorkers feel deprived of. As Faye pointed out in her memo."

"That was my memo," I said.

"You're brave, Lucinda," Bonnie said. "But that's the whole point, right? Courage. Risk taking. Kudos, I say! At any rate it'll be great to have you stationed in a remote."

"'Cause it will add some freshness," Samantha said. "Not that we won't totally miss you and be sad."

"I have to meet my trainer," said Bonnie.

The hosts departed. Faye sat back in her chair. "Okay, here's the thing, Lucinda," she said. "If you want to do this, you're going to have to, like, give a little.

"Yes."

"I mean, like cooperate."

"With?"

"The budget," she said. "We're going to have to pay for editing facilities and a cameraman from a local station out there. Your salary is going to be, like, cut back a little."

"To what?"

"To adjust to your lowered living expenses."

"Well, sure, of course. But I still have student loans and everything."

"Is that my problem?" Faye hissed.

"What am I going to be paid?" I asked.

"You're going to be paid by the segment," Faye said. "Per segment. But look at it this way, if you do forty-five segments you get paid for all forty-five. It's ipso facto."

"Do you mean quid pro quo?"

"Don't be uppity."

"And what do I get paid per segment?" I asked.

"A thousand dollars," Faye said. "But we're going to cover an HMO. So that's really a pretty good deal when you think about it."

"A thousand dollars?" I said. I felt sick. "Well, then, I'm going to do a story a week, right?"

"Whatever we work out," she said. "Come on, what does it cost to rent an apartment there, a couple hundred a month?"

"Well . . ."

"I have a doctor's appointment," Faye said, looking at her watch. "Or a lunch. I have something. You should be happy. You got your way. They want you on site by the end of the month."

"Wow, okay."

"Just don't get fat!"

So the American Dream began. At least my version of it, which didn't stir up a lot of envy.

"I'll come visit you," said Samantha Frank, who had never even come to my apartment when I lived ten blocks away from her on the Upper West Side.

"I'll come visit you," said Daphne. "Maybe, anyway."

"I'll come visit you," said Elena, who, since turning thirty a few years earlier, had gotten LASIK eye surgery and braces put on the backs of her teeth, which caused her to lisp. "But not until you get indoor plumbing."

Elena and I were having coffee at The One; a café near Elena's yoga studio whose main attraction was that it had binders filled with profiles of single people looking for dates. Elena was sweaty from a yoga class and her curly black hair was springing out from under a floppy hat she'd purchased in an effort to copy Jennifer Aniston on *Friends*. She'd bought one for me, too, but it just gave me a kind of Peppermint Patty appearance, which Elena had pointed out and suggested I use to land a well-heeled lesbian who might give me room and board for a while. Elena was usually looking for a boyfriend, but since she felt she was above actually filling out a form she went to The One only to scrutinize the bios of the other women. "Just sizing up the competition," she always said.

"Look, this twit thinks it's worth mentioning that she prefers Hatha yoga over Ashtanga," Elena said, slurping her soy latte through the rubber bands behind her molars. "Translation: lard ass!"

"I find it interesting that you only ever read the women's profiles when you come here," I said.

"The men have atrocious handwriting," she said. "And if I hear of one more software consultant who aspires to write for *The Simpsons* I'll buy him a one-way ticket to L.A. Why won't they grow up?"

"That's exactly why I'm moving to Prairie City!" I said. "I mean, not exactly. But it'll be a perk. Not having to deal with the backward baseball cap set."

"Yeah, you'll just have to deal with the chewing tobacco set. You'll have to deal with wannabe truck drivers," Elena lisped. "Can you imagine? Single male, age thirty, works as bricklayer but dreams of long-haul trucking career and possible membership in North American Man Boy Love Association!"

"Maybe I can date one of my movers," I said.

"Lucinda," Elena said, "you better tell your movers to wait in front of your house for the first night. Because that's how long it's going to take you to realize you're coming right back to New York! I mean, it's one thing to go to Nepal, like Daphne. But this is beyond the third world. I mean, they don't even do Backroads Adventure trips there!"

My parents, for their part, thought I was going to graduate school. Since their associations with the Midwest were almost completely limited to Big Ten universities, they could not imagine anyone moving there for any other purpose.

"I'm doing an extended assignment for the show," I said to my mother on the phone. "It has nothing to do with getting a master's degree."

"But maybe you could at least take some classes," she said. "It will give you something to do. It's also a good way to meet people."

My mother had a long-held belief that the reason I was relegated to the thong underwear beat was that I lacked a postcollegiate education. She was under the impression that senior-level news anchors – even those on *Entertainment Tonight* – held Ph.D.'s. She also felt that the reason I was never able to upgrade beyond a studio apartment was that I couldn't type sixty words per minute.

"If I have to take a class it'll be a driving class," I said. "I haven't driven a car in eight years."

"Well, honey, I wish we hadn't sold the station wagon."

On the eve of my departure, I lay in a sleeping bag on the floor of my studio and cried for exactly seventeen minutes. Small apartments have a way of looking so much better when they're completely empty and something about the echoing space that now surrounded me, the white walls with marks where the pictures had been, the naked oak floors, the curtainless window that now offered a direct view to the apartment across the courtyard, where a woman was stirring something on the stove while talking on the telephone, knocked the wind out of me like I'd fallen hard off a bicycle. During the month that I'd spent preparing to move to Prairie City, I'd maintained an alarming composure, not allowing myself to second-guess a decision that the whole world was waiting for me to second-guess and then, with my tail between my legs and a few self-deprecating comments to save face, totally renege on.

Now, the tears came like a train that was creeping into the station weeks behind schedule. As sincere as they were, they were also perfunctory and I gasped through the sobs until I began to feel like I was wasting time. The movers had come only that day, the last possible day they could come. There had been a delay because my furniture, being a partial load, needed to go on a truck with several other loads and they couldn't find a truck that was going anywhere near Prairie City. When they finally found a truck they claimed it was too big to turn the corner from Broadway to West Ninety-fourth Street and they had to bring in a smaller truck and then transfer my stuff to the bigger truck. Though I barely had twelve hours left, I still had to take everything out of the medicine cabinet and either throw it away or pack it into one of the three duffel bags I was carrying with me. I still had to take a bunch of canned foods out of the cupboards and put them on the steps of the church down the street. It was already getting dark. So I stopped crying. The nighttime summer air sat motionless outside the window; there was no breeze to bring it in. Car alarms and sirens hummed outside as they had every night of the last nine years. Yuri's phone rang upstairs. The elevator clanked through the building. Doors slammed shut. Someone outside yelled an obscenity. Someone else laughed. A garbage truck went by. The apartment looked so big without the furniture. It occurred to me that maybe I just should have lived in it unfurnished.

The next morning, as planned, I got up before 5:00 AM, stuffed my sleeping bag into one of the duffel bags, brushed my teeth, got dressed, walked out of the apartment, and took the bus to LaGuardia. *Up Early* had not even sprung for car service. Dawn broke as the bus ambled through Harlem and over the Triborough Bridge. Looking back toward Manhattan, the sun glinted off the redbrick housing projects that bordered the East Side. Behind the projects, the skyscrapers where earlier in my career I'd worked more temp jobs than I could remember jutted out into the sky just like they do in the opening credits of movies about people who come to the city and suffer a million knocks before something happens to them that is so spectacular, so redeeming, and so much a testament to their unrelenting passion and hard work that it's like the knocks never happened, it's like they sailed in and the city greeted them as though it were heaven and they had died trying to rescue someone who'd fallen onto the subway tracks.

Though it wasn't yet 7:00 AM, planes were climbing and landing from every direction. The terminal was packed. I waited in line for half an hour and checked my bags. I got coffee at the Starbucks stand. To calm my nerves, I pretended I was going on a business trip. I pretended that *Up Early* had sent me off on a story, a story concerning, perhaps, women who had been fondled by their gynecologists. I got on the plane, we took off, and the island of Manhattan shrank away behind the clouds. Four hours and one airport connection later, we descended into a patchy prairie. From the plane I could see tiny boxlike farmhouses, sectioned-off fields of crops, the occasional factory flanked by a huge parking lot, which was flanked by acres of cornfields, then acres of prairie grass, then a highway with barely any cars on it.

What was I doing in this place? Then I slapped my wrist with the plastic coffee stirrer. I wasn't allowed to ask. That had been the pact, no getting upset for six months, no breaking down, no admission of error. Besides, it was beautiful down there. Land and sky and nothing in between. This place seemed less a place than a huge amount of space, enough space to see what you'd do with yourself when given so much room, enough space, I later realized, after it was much, much too late, to get yourself in a whole lot of trouble.

Our Passion

ANNA MONARDO

The night my daughter, Veronica, was born, her father, Kenn, was on a date at the Café Bientôt, or one of those places he was taken to in the late '70s whenever he was being courted. Those days it was Edo, whose real name was Eduardo.

Earlier that evening, when Edo arrived with orchids for Kenn and more orchids for me, I was still feeling fine. Kenn had my head on his lap and was stroking my bangs. There was no pain yet. I was just sort of weepy.

"But, Delilah, what if it's time to go to the hospital?"

"Kenn, go." I just wanted them out of my apartment so I could cry alone for five or ten minutes. "Go, you have a reservation."

Edo, with that accent full of vowels, told Kenn, "We leave the number to the cafe. Maxi, the man there, he know me. Delilah could have us by phone in two minutes."

"Call me for whatever, even if you're just feeling blue." I started singing, "I'd rather be blue, thinking of you . . ."

"Delilah, come on, if you're scared or lonely or if the pain starts."

"Leave the number. If you're not there I'll talk to Maxi."

Edo had been standing in the archway to the living room, waiting. Relieved when it was clear I was going to let them go, he told me, "You are a handsome woman, Delilah." He was handsome himself, but short. Short and dark and perky and rich. Edo was Brazilian. His business was jewels. He had provided the rubies for an ad Kenn was shooting, and that's how they had met. Kenn told me he thought Edo could be the love of his life.

Kenn put a pillow under my head, stood up, and Edo watched the back of Kenn's jacket fall open as he bent to kiss me. I sang louder, "Blue o-ver you." Edo grimaced. I didn't care. When I sing big, I really sound like Barbra Streisand to myself. As always when he left for the night, Kenn patted my stomach. "Later, Buster," he said.

"I'm almost sure it's a girl, Kenn. Don't call her Buster." He covered my feet with an afghan. "Bye, love." They left without writing down Maxi's phone number.

As soon as the elevator was taking them away, as soon as we were alone, before I could reach for Kleenex, Veronica let me know it was time; she wanted to be born.

I woke up the next afternoon in the hospital and there before me sat Kenn with pink roses on his lap. "How could you?"

"Kenn, I'd never call anyone from a date to come to the labor room. I wanted you to have fun." Really, I'd been afraid that if Kenn came for the birth he'd have brought Edo with him.

"So, tell me," Kenn demanded. "It was awful, right? Who helped you breathe?"

"Luis helped me."

"Luis? The doorman?"

"He was getting off his shift when I went down for my cab. He's still all excited about that son of his who was born last month. He insisted on coming."

"In the delivery room? He was there?"

"He was wonderful. You should have heard him. '*Mira, Mira*,' he shouted as soon as her head popped out. '*Qué bonita*, Mrs. Delilah!' Luis says she's even more beautiful than his son was. But his son was more powerful, he says. He wants them to get married. He promises that his son will become a doctor."

"The doorman saw you give birth to our daughter but I didn't?"

I started to cry.

"Oh, baby, what?" Kenn came and sat beside me on the bed.

"We were supposed to shave my legs yesterday and we forgot. Everyone, even Luis, saw my legs."

Just then the nurse rolled in a Plexiglass bassinet; in it was our baby. "You know," the nurse said, "I been watching this here baby. Her eyes all open all the time. She don't miss a thing, this one."

So much the worse for her, I thought.

Kenn stared down at the baby. "The redness goes away, right?"

"Just be glad she ain't all yellow with that jaundice," the nurse said and lifted her from the bassinet.

"She's so small," Kenn complained, but when he got Veronica in his arms, his face went slack with wonder. "Delily, Delily, look what we did."

I wiped my eyes. "I know, Kenn, I know. But it'll be all right."

From the start I began composing in my head the story I would eventually tell Veronica of how Kenn and I became friends. It was in high school, 1962, in the career-placement office, when I asked Kenn if I could see the University of Chicago Catalogue when he was done with it, and he told me, "No, I'm taking it overnight," which wasn't allowed. Kenn had a reputation for being a jerk, partly because he was, and partly because he was a genius in a Vermont town where intelligence was valued but brilliance was considered show-offy. I was the first student in five years to get near-perfect college-board scores, but that was because I studied all the time. The next week I told Kenn about St. John's, the great-books school, which interested him, so then he trusted me. It was one of those intense friendships between kids who really don't fit in. Besides, we both had secrets.

Kenn was having an affair with our physics teacher, a woman. I had a boyfriend no one knew about, a married gas-station attendant, a high-school dropout. Meanwhile, I was practically engaged to a guy I'd known all my life. I was letting him fill out applications for married students' housing at the state university, but every other weekend when he came home to visit me, no matter how he tried, I wouldn't let him unzip his pants in my presence. A little miserable, mostly pleased, he'd say, "Oh Delilah, it means that much to you, doesn't it, to wait until we're married?" I'd nod a bit, yes, but the real truth was this: I just could not give into sex that would lead to anything as boring as marriage.

All my older brothers and sister were married and living so close to home that their chimneys or garages or garden sheds could be seen from the window of my parents' kitchen. My sister had too many kids and no money, and she was always coming over to borrow my clothes. One night she wore my raincoat to PTA, put her hand in the pocket and found my panties, which I'd inadvertently left there after a date at the gas station. On her way home, she tossed my coat into a Goodwill bin. The next morning, early, she called. "What kind of a person are you?" she asked me.

I was a passionate person – both Kenn and I were. Neither of us was particularly happy – each date at the gas station, each visit to the physics teacher's house was too brief, never enough – but talking about our lovers brought us close, led us into high-blown discussions about Love and Art. We agreed on this: Passion comes only to those who are willing to break the rules. You saw it in abstract art, for example. For hours we compared our lovers' moods and blemishes and lovemaking to our favorite paintings by Picasso and Miró. That guy I was supposed to marry – Kenn called him the Dutch Still-Life.

One Sunday night in February, senior year, we were sitting in a booth in the twenty-four-hour coffee shop. We were both in black turtlenecks – Kenn in jeans, me in a kilt – and we drank our coffee black. Kenn was reading the *Village Voice*. I was sitting across from him sketching his profile, trying to figure out his good looks – was it nose, chin, jaw? – but the handsomeness was all over Kenn's face. Only his dark brown hair was a mess, getting long around his neck. Recently it had started to fall into his eyes so he'd got scissors and hacked away a chunk of hair without even looking in the mirror. People said it was one more way Kenn was trying to be surly and cool. But I thought the angry haircut was fantastic, the way it off-centered the classic alignment of his fine features and made for more compelling sketches.

That night in the coffeeshop was a night of heavy snow, so we heard her snow chains, jiggling like too much jewelry, before the physics teacher's baby blue Volkswagen appeared. This was Kenn's signal.

"Gotta go," he whispered as soon as she passed, but instead of reaching for his coat, he took my hand, rubbed at the charcoal smeared on my fingers. Kenn leaned toward me in the booth, whispered again, "Why'm I doing this? Except for class she hasn't shown her face in weeks." Wiping out the toughness of his haircut was his voice, which was watery and full of fear. "Why'm I going to see her, Delilah?"

"You said she was kinetic, like Martha Graham choreography."

"Oh, yeah," he said, "I forgot."

We sat still another minute, both of us leaving charcoal fingerprints on the white place mats. Finally Kenn stood, pulled money out of the pocket of his jeans, dropped a dollar and some change onto the table.

"So, you're going?" I asked.

"It's not to be believed, is it, what a guy's got to do to pass physics these days."

Sunday morning a few weeks later, I was standing at the sink scrubbing the pot my sister had cooked the oatmeal in. I had just got off the phone with Kenn. He was on his way to the physics teacher. She'd asked him to come over before lunch, so that afterward she could settle in to correct quizzes and lab reports. I was watching a residue of oatmeal skin slip out of the pot, get caught in the drain – whitish, gelatinous – just like what my boyfriend had left in my hand the night before, when we were in the back seat of his wife's car. And I knew that if Kenn and I stayed in Vermont we'd be sneaking around for the rest of our lives.

It had been three years since anyone from our high school had gone to college out of state, but that year Kenn took off for Stanford, and I left to take classes at the Art Students' League in New York City.

Twelve years after high school I was a book designer, working out of my apartment on the Upper West Side. I was pretty much just making ends meet, but I had won a few publishing awards. Kenn was in Hollywood doing marketing for a major film company – an odd detour for someone who had been a philosophy major in college, but he'd found he had a knack for business.

Kenn and I had had a flurry of late-night phone calls when he had his first affair with a man. Then we had more long phone calls a year or so later, when the guy walked out on Kenn during their Baja vacation. But years had passed since Kenn and I had seen each other. During that time I'd been ashamed to tell him I'd managed to get myself engaged again. This time it was Oliver Twinning, a manic-depressive percussionist who lived in my apartment building. We'd met in the elevator one morning when he was in a manic phase and my hair was chopped down to a half-inch crew cut. "I have to touch this tiny haircut," Oliver had said that first time we ever laid eyes on each other.

The elevator was small. We stood close, face to face. I asked how come I'd never seen him before. He said he traveled a lot. He was brown-skinned, with the highest, brightest cheekbones. "Can I touch?"

I asked, but my fingers were already climbing the Himalayas on his face. To give us more time, he kept pushing the elevator buttons, sending us up and down. I should have known.

Oliver was half-Nepali, half-British. He loved to cook, and his apartment always smelled exotic. Curry one day, hashish the next. No one before him had ever taken me so far from Vermont. I knew no one with such voluptuous moods. When he had migraines we had to pull down blackout window blinds; some weeks at his apartment were like living through a war. Then, maybe, the very next week, undressing him, I'd find he had a new tattoo.

A terrific musician, he played with lots of bands, which is why he traveled so much. Or so I thought, until I ran into him downtown with his other fiancée. She flipped, I flipped, and he checked himself into the hospital, promising us both that he was very close to a decision. Oliver and I had been breaking up for three years when Kenn came to New York and called me. He said he'd got a new job – with an advertising firm – but I hoped he had arrived to take me back to Vermont. I was sick of passion. Oliver was on new medication and had just left town.

The night Kenn came to dinner my haircut wasn't grown out yet. A hennaed nubby ponytail on the top of my head was the best I could do. Since he was coming from Hollywood, I had wanted him to find me in something slinky, with cleavage, but I ended up in my usual leopard-print Lycra bellbottoms and a huge black sweater I'd been dragging around in for years.

"*That* is my sweater!" Kenn said when I opened the door, and I thought, He's still sort of a jerk. But then he smiled and we hugged and he pulled back to look me over.

Kenn looked so clean I couldn't believe he'd just walked up Broadway. His face was closely shaved; moisture, fresh as dew, lay on his cheeks. Mahogany-dark hair clipped short, much neater than in his senior yearbook picture. Kenn was dressed like a Vermont boy – leather hiking boots, a plaid flannel shirt, tight jeans – but his clothes were impeccable and ironed, boots polished. He was wearing the smallest gold earring.

We sat in my kitchen and talked that first night. After a while, Kenn admitted that it was bad love, not a new job, that had sent him from L.A., so I told Kenn about Oliver's apartment above mine. "Oliver and

I aren't sure how definite this split is. He says he needs time." Oliver wasn't sure yet what that meant. Days, weeks, a different incarnation.

The Upstairs apartment – fireplace, archways, wooden cabinets in the kitchen – reminded Kenn of Vermont. What he didn't know about yet were the bulging pipes and the roaches, the street noise after midnight, the cold showers on most weekday mornings. "What if I wanted to stay a long time?"

"Probably you'd be able to. Either Oliver will crack up and stay away, or he and I will get back together and live in my place – it's bigger. Either way, you could get the lease."

Oliver did crack up. Kenn moved in upstairs. And that is how far, more or less, I've prepared the story of Kenn and me. I'm always wondering how I'll explain to Veronica what happened next. "It was like this," I'll say. "A few years after Daddy came from L.A., these apartments went co-op. It was the night of the closing, and he and I went out to dinner to celebrate." Actually, the two of us ran from our apartments as soon as he got home from work – we were afraid, suddenly, to stay put in those homes that were now all ours. Since we felt poor, we went for Cuban Chinese. Since we felt hopeful we talked about the maid's rooms.

Each of our apartments had a maid's room off the kitchen. Kenn said they were our dowries, for when we found our perfect boyfriends, so we hadn't fixed them up yet. As we shared a plate of fried plantains Kenn asked me, "So, what will you do now with your maid's room, my sweet maiden?"

"A nursery," I said. I hadn't had a real boyfriend since Oliver, but I was thirty-four and determined. "I'm going to make a nursery, with the walls all soft green, like grass, and the ceiling pale blue, like sky."

"Poor Delily, how much you want to be a mother." He took my hand.

"What will you do with your room, Kenn?" I asked, taking my hand away.

"Have a son who'll take care of me in my old age." He was still in his business clothes, tie loosened, top button undone, cuffs rolled up showing his good gold watch. It had been a while since I'd noticed how good Kenn looked. There was gray in his hair, which was long and slicked back. Lines between his eyebrows had roughed up the young man's prettiness of his huge round eyes, and they were maybe a chillier shade of blue now, quicker to turn away, impatient. But in the New York advertising world, Kenn's occasional surliness was seen as a sign of high competence. He commanded respect. Looking at Kenn, I realized that we had, to some degree, become as good as we were ever going to get. I reached across the table, pulled Kenn's gold pen out of his shirt pocket. On my napkin I began sketching Kenn with a cigar in his mouth. I drew a cartoon bubble over his head and in it, I wrote, "*It's a boy!*"

I could feel Kenn looking at me. When I glanced up, his diamond earring winked and he said, "Do you know who I'd want as my son's mama?"

I shook my head.

"You, Delily. You."

"You're just kidding, Kenn," I said, testing.

"Not really, Delilah." He took my hand again, pushed up my bracelets and leotard sleeve, held my wrist, rubbed. "Let me kiss your wrist," he said. "I've always wanted to do that to someone in public." I let him kiss my wrist. Then he kissed it again. "From time to time, I imagine us having a child." He was still busy at my wrist.

"Yeah," I said, "you think of it, but only when you're between men."

His eyes opened wide just above my palm. "Honey, when I'm between men, I don't think about anything."

Without lying, I'll be able to tell Veronica that she was conceived during a night of passion. A cold winter night about a month after the co-op closing, Kenn called me. "Come on up. And bring your wallet." Artie, an ex-lover of Kenn's, had stopped by with some pot. We all made dinner and drank wine. Artie rolled joints. We had coffee-and-Heath-bar ice cream, then smoked some more. Artie fell asleep on the couch. Kenn and I were sprawled out on Kenn's dhurrie rug, giddily rolling into and away from each other, all over the wine-colored surface.

"We're caught in a bottle of Chianti," I told Kenn.

"Hold on," he said. "We're drowning." His arms fell around my waist, his face in my hair. "We're going to have to breathe like fish. Here, I'll teach you how." Kenn's legs behind my legs; we moved together, as if we were treading water slowly. "Artie's not as cute as he used to be, is he?" Kenn whispered.

"Not as cute as us fishes," I whispered back.

Still treading invisible wine-colored liquid, we sang, softly, all the songs on Side One of Carole King's *Tapestry* album. Kenn behind me the whole time, his newly grown mustache on the back of my neck. Then hands under clothes. "Hey," he said, "this isn't fish skin." Talking through dazed sleepiness, he moved his legs against mine. Slowly, jeans lowered, skirt lifted, skin stretching into the darkness; that short-breathed adolescent wonder of giving into something, finally, for the first time. It was all hands on skin, it was all rocking together, apart. "S'okay," the voice behind me kept saying. "S'okay, we'll just stay here like this in the wine, oh, keep swimming."

We floated easily, just touching and rocking. Then, quickening a bit, like a swimmer determined to take the lead, I moved faster. I reached down and eased Kenn forward.

"Aaaaa," he said.

When I turned to look at him, Kenn was asleep, his black eyelashes dropped onto the white skin under his eyes, a velvet curtain closed. His face was flushed red and tensed, his lips on the verge of a smile. Kenn looked both alert and amused, as if the dream he was watching was some kind of *Roadrunner* cartoon. "See," I said under my breath, "it's not so bad."

Veronica was born with Kenn's eyes, sharp blue and evasive. Even as an infant, she'd drop her lashes when she'd had enough of my kisses, but she was beautiful to me that way too.

"This child," Edo said, "will grow to be a princess."

"No, she won't, Edo. She'll be a little girl. Nothing more, nothing less." I was trying so hard to like Edo, but I didn't trust him. Kenn said I was projecting. "He's not Oliver, Delilah. Give Edo a chance."

By now the two of them were living together, in Kenn's apartment, right above mine. Still, Kenn did come through for the baby and me, just as he had promised a year earlier when, timidly, expecting the worst, I told him it no longer had to be a fantasy – he would have a child, I was having a baby. Back then, Kenn had promised to share the responsibility, thirty-seventy. Now, he was doing at least thirty-five percent of the work. Even Edo helped out. It was his idea to drill a small hole between our bedrooms so Kenn could hear if Veronica was crying a lot at night. Every third night or so, Kenn came down in his robe, fixed a bottle, took Veronica from me – "Sleep, Mama," he said to me, "sleep" – and in the chair by the window, he rocked her.

When Edo and Kenn had been together one year, Edo offered to build a staircase between our two apartments, from living room to living room.

"Why's he doing this for us?" I asked, more thrilled than suspicious.

"He knows how much you and Veronica mean to me. He wants us to be happy. Delily, I'm beginning to think this man is it."

Construction went on all through July. When Veronica and I got back from visiting my family in Vermont, Veronica's home was connected to her father's by a carpeted winding staircase and separated by a door at the top that latched twice.

For Veronica's second birthday Edo had emerald earrings sent from Rio. I wore them the next week when I went out on a date, my first in three years. At the end of the evening I walked up to my apartment alone but happy from a chaste yet promising kiss in the lobby. I didn't know then that the man was only separated, not divorced, so I felt hopeful when he said, "We'll do this again."

"What," I asked, "the dinner or the kiss?"

"I'll call you," he said.

When I got upstairs and opened my door, Kenn was on the phone, pacing, making soothing sounds in Portuguese, which I didn't know he could speak so well, and Veronica was watching David Letterman. A few minutes later Kenn hung up and threw the phone across the room.

"Kenn! What happened?"

"That," he said, "was Edo's wife."

"He's married?"

"There's a family crisis in Rio and they need to reach him. His oldest daughter is in premature labor. It's the first grandchild. His New York office gave Mrs. Edo our phone numbers."

"Edo has children?"

"He's supposed to be in Madrid on business but he hasn't been in his penthouse all night. The wife's a mess about the daughter and the baby. I'm thinking to myself, Stay cool. All this poor woman needs right now is to find out her husband's got a boyfriend in New York, and she says to me, 'In confidence, please, does my Edo have a girl friend in Madrid?' "

"*Her* Edo? She asked you that?"

"He's lying to everybody, that shit. I thought I had a life with him."

"You did. You *do*. He built the staircase, didn't he?" But then I understood, so I didn't say anything else.

Kenn pulled Veronica up onto the couch, hugged her, apologized to her for tossing the phone. I sat down and put my arms around the two of them. "Come on, Delilah, don't cry. Listen, you were right. He's like Oliver. Even worse."

"Oh, but Kenn, will everyone always leave us?"

Mimicking one of Letterman's guests, Veronica said, "No way."

With Edo gone, Kenn and Veronica and I began to live somewhat like a family. Actually, we were more like the Riccardos and the Mertzes, running back and forth between apartments. We ate dinners and weekend brunches together in my kitchen, because that's where the highchair was, but usually Veronica ate only if Kenn was holding her. Before coming down, Kenn always hollered from the top of the stairs to ask if we needed anything. His door stayed unlatched later and later in the evening. Veronica learned to pull herself up those carpeted stairs before she even attempted waddling down the hallway, grabbing at the wall. As Kenn says, she is perfect. We can dress her up and we can take her out. She's invited to come along wherever we go: art openings, movie screenings, book parties in lofts. Kenn and I watch her pattering around, dressed in her little black stretch pants, schmoozing here and there, not leaving anyone out, working the room better than a publicity assistant looking for a new job. Her godfather, Luis, calls her *Milagrita*. Little miracle.

A few years ago, when Veronica was almost three, just as she was starting to be able to converse on the phone – asking our friends about their lovers, their pets and vacations – a few of the men started to get thinner and pale. Some weakened so quickly they couldn't lift her anymore, and she'd cry. We never took her to the hospitals to visit. She never went to the memorial services.

Kenn and I got tested. We were okay, but the doctor told us we had to retest in six months. Then she told us Veronica should be tested. "ASAP," the doctor said. I started to cry right there in her office. Kenn cried that night, lying across my bed while I sat, sleepless, at my drafting table drawing nothing, with black ink. "Did you hear her?" I asked him. "She said ASAP."

"Delilah, Delilah, what were we thinking?"

We hadn't been thinking. We'd been too happy. It was during that last month or so, right before Veronica was born. I couldn't sleep at night, neither could Kenn. Who could sleep? Suddenly there was so much to discuss. Mostly we couldn't get over it. Having a baby was the cleverest thing we'd ever come up with together.

A few nights, just a few, three or four, after Edo was asleep, Kenn came down to my place and we lay on my living-room floor below the fan. We talked. I was getting so big. "My God," Kenn whispered as he reached his arms around me, "you're a globe. It's like holding a globe." And as I was filling up his arms I was thinking, Kenn and I keep being together and being together, and I wanted to say it out loud – honey, look, this is our life – but Kenn was whispering into my neck, into my hair, and he moved in as close as he could. "Delily, I feel the baby. I feel her moving." She was right there, between us, kicking, doing things neither of us had ever felt before. Kenn wanted to get closer. He slipped off my dress.

Like I said, it was just three or four nights, maybe one or two more than that, always on the floor, never in bed. On the floor it didn't seem to count, and it was so early in Kenn and Edo's relationship. Edo never found out, but we did have to tell the doctor. She was silent a long moment. Then she asked, "The man, Edo, what happened to him?"

"He died," I told her. "We heard that he died."

On the bus going to the doctor's for Veronica's first test, I thought of all the things that terrified me before I had a child – loss of limbs, suffocation, death by fire – and I realized those things were nothing now.

Veronica behaved beautifully while the doctor took her blood. But later, leaving the office, she accidentally rammed her elbow into the doorframe, felt for the first time that spinning pain, that weird assault. She started to cry.

"Oh, honey," Kenn said apologetically, "that's your funny bone."

She kicked his boot. "You're being a liar."

"Sweetie, no, he's not." I kneeled down and tried to look in her eyes.

"It's just a name for your elbow. Your funny bone. Everybody hates to hit it. It always hurts, I know."

"But you . . . you . . . you," she was stuttering over her tears, backing away from us, edging herself into the sucking center of a full-blown tantrum. Kenn's eyes met mine for the sos: Beware! Big, messy scene in public. Finally, she wailed, "You didn't tell me it hurts!"

"Sweetie, we didn't know you were going to hit it."

"Yes," she howled. "You do know!"

Kenn looked at me and we smiled. Then we had to turn away because we were laughing. We can still laugh, I thought. What a relief to know our love for her was still bigger than our fear. It's been eighteen months since the first blood tests. Next week we go for the third time. "Have faith," Kenn says. "Remember, Delilah, you and I have always tested well."

The worst is the time between when we get tested and when we go in for the results. During those days I keep hearing a voice (sounding disconcertingly like my sister's), the voice is interviewing me, asking terrible questions, like "Now if there were only one last thought you could leave with your daughter, what would it be?" I know I shouldn't think this way, and it only happens during that week of waiting. Most of the time I think about when Veronica will be older.

And I do see her older. I imagine it. I have to imagine it, fiercely, like a prayer, to make sure it comes true: Veronica at eleven, twelve, fifteen, twenty. Please, let us all get there together. Please, I'll do anything. But no matter what happens, there is this one thing. I want Veronica to know that since her father and I were young, two kids who knew nothing but what our bodies knew, we had been traveling toward her. She is it. She is the passion. For years, we'd been looking and looking.

My Communist

RON HANSEN

I am conscious of the lacks at my English, which is my least language, so you will please correct my errors. My story is happening in California during 1982. But it is beginning far, far away in my country of Poland where I was born and growing up in Kraków and where I matriculated in philosophy at famous, six-hundred-year-old Jagiellonian University. In fall, 1975, I have begun four years of theology studies at Rome's Pontifical Athenaeum of Saint Thomas Aquinas, which is called "the Angelicum," and in 1979 I was ordained a priest for the diocese of Kraków by its former archbishop, Karol Wojtyla, who is then just a few months Pope John Paul II. We have much in common, such as homeland and schoolings, and as friends it is day of great happiness for us, my ordination.

My first parish is in difficult times. We are oppressed country and hard-working people who cannot afford government price increases of sometimes one hundred percent on meats, and waves of strikes for social justice and freedom from Soviet Union have begun at shipyards, railways, bakeries, milking farms. Many priests such as me join the strikers and preside at outdoor Masses for many thousands of workers. A revolution, which is called *Solidarno*, is underway, and there is nearly a military invasion by Warsaw Pact countries to "save socialist Poland," but it is halted by interventions from the Pope and warnings from the United States. Even so, priests are kidnapped and murdered to scare and make sad the strikers. In fall, 1981, General Wojciech Jaruzelski becamed first secretary of Polish Communist Party and it is December when he declares state of war in my country. Martial law there is put on us, and many thousands of Solidarity activists without warnings they are being arrested like with Nazis in Occupation.

I can hear the question, "Why this histories?" I will answer the asking in a small while, and you will find out why is necessary. Also in December it was a bad news that my cardinal archbishop finds out the name of Stefan Nowak is on a list of party enemies, and I am invited to his excellency's residence. There I hear a communication from His Holiness himself that his young friend, Stefan, not even yet three years from his ordination, is to go to California as a missionary. A big surprise, belief me!

I disliked to leave home so soon after joining my first parish, and if I open my heart to you I will confess I was thinking my friends would consider me coward. To die like Christ for my faith is a dear wish since childhood when I am reading about old-time martyrs, so I am prepared to stay. But also ever since seminary I have dreamed to work in countries where Catholics suffer without the sacraments. Initially my thinking is Africa, Latin America, or Russia, but California is also still missionary country. And obedience to the Pope is no question.

With one week spending in Chicago city, giving lectures about my country in parishes and visiting beautiful churches and museums, I board an aeroplane for its fly to San Francisco, first time to visit in my life, though I have seen it, naturally, in the cinema. I am met at San Francisco International by the wonderful old pastor of All Souls parish, whose family name when I first heard in Kraków was sounding very homely for a man from Poland. Smolarski is very typical name there. Monsignor Smolarski asks I address him Joseph and admits he does not know Polish language. A disappointment. I promise to teach him some sentences, and songs too, and Joseph promises to correct my broken English. My much in pieces English.

All Souls is not old, old parish like in Kraków or Warsaw, but from beginning of twenty century. Forty kilometers south of San Francisco, and in the number of two thousand people, maybe less, the church has only fourteen parishioners from Eastern Europe, and none who speak my dear-to-my-heart Polish. Immediately upon learning, my soul cries out, *Why have I come to this far place?* The first nights there are long for me. Hours and hours I pray. I write hundreds letters home. But I feel silenced and not as much useful. I have looked up the word: I am forlorn.

California, so big a state and rich in different beauties, I like very much with its weather always in a good mood and its people friendly because not cold or persecuted. The Mass is familiar even in English, though I am embarrassed by my "charming" accent and I am frustrated to be sounding unintelligent with homilies too like a child. At first many humiliations, as in Italy and first year theology.

And such wealth here is horrifying, really. I have a day off and all afternoon I walk through a gigantic proportion supermarket. I have arrived in America with one luggage. With how many shall I leave? The both sides of the building seem a distance of a kilometer as up and down the aisles I am wandering, seeing fruits and vegetables even in winter, so much different foods to be sold, such plenty, but not wanting to buy even a chocolate piece for thinking of how much people in my homeland must do without. And that is when I first see him. In a gray trench coat, no kidding, and gray homburg hat, holding a shopping basket in the vegetable aisle but watching me, for sure, the face maybe from cousin to Leonid Brezhnev, the pig eyes, the slicked black hair. Weighty. You would not think: *A Californian!* This is herring man, a favorite to vodka. He is like to have hammer and sickle tattooed on his chest. Well, I am making it sound funny, but it is not so then. Here for what is this spy? A friend of mine was found in a northern forest with a bullet in his brains. Has this fellow gun in pocket? Little hidden camera? Wanting confrontation, I walk forward but he is too fast away. On a bin for green cabbage that is being rained on he has left behind his plastic basket and inside it are kielbasa, piroshki, and from delicatessen a carton of *kutia*, which is Polish Christmas pudding. My father would buy such at the market.

Is fat man waiting for me outside? I do not wish to be surprised in lonesome place, so I rush opposite to his going and push through a steel door. I find myself in storing house where a garage door is lifting high overhead as outside a fruits truck backs up, a horn beeping. I hurry out and jump from the dock, and I do not stop hurrying until he for sure cannot be behind me. I say nothing to Monsignor, for he is old man with conditions of heart.

On Sunday again I notice my spy, looking hard at Stefan in my long white alb and green stole and chasuble after the ten o'clock Mass, and the not-yet-thirty priest is smiling because a sweet girl of sixteen has taught herself enough Polish to say, "Good morning, Father Nowak," and it is not so bad, her accent. I glance across the street and the Communist is standing in a wide circle of shade, for the sun is miraculous even in March, and he is in many clothings and homburg hat, his hands behind his back, just watching me. I am certainly not an amusement to him. I am some hunter's offal, some striker's wreckage that must to be removed. I lift my right hand high. Half a hello is it, and half a salute. My spy holds onto his expression, like his face is inflexible, and then he strolls away.

I find less and less I am afraid as weeks go by, and he is around now and then only. I have no idea his thoughts, if he wants me dead, if he is KGB and I am only his idle hours, his hobby, and his main jobs is military secrets. But I have decided for sure he is Polish, and it pleases that whenever he is watching me he is thinking of me in the same language that I am thinking of him. I do not care the words he uses.

We are now last week of March, and he sends in mailing four photographs of me and back of each he is labeled in Polish handwriting: "S. N. at local bookstore," "S. N. in front of All Soul's rectory," "S. N., funeral on 20 March," "S. N., home of Mrs. Kaniecki." Was this to harass me? Was he just getting rid of? The photos are nice of me. One I send to parents. Others I hang them in my office.

But I am thinking: I like my pastoral job very much. I have a fine rectory to live in, my first car ever, friendly priests who join us for drinks or nights at the cinema, invitations to dinners with families, the joy and honor of my vocation. And how much could my Communist have? A flat maybe with small television, food he cooks for himself and eats lonely, a hundred worries and secrets, and no god to pray to? Was I a priest to have luxuries while another has so little?

With April, quite suddenly he is not spying on me anymore. I find myself looking and looking, but he is like I invented him. Poland is still in a "state of war" and my mailings from homeland tell of jailings and intimidations, but I seem to be no longer of interest. I am surprised by the loss I experience. To "stew and fret" is good slang for my feelings. I miss him, this Pole. Has he been recalled to Europe, or is he ill with no one to help him, or dead with no one to find him until the smell is bad? I pray it is not so.

On first day off, I decide to investigate. I have habit of visiting a fine bookstore in Palo Alto where I read for free – please to excuse me, lovely store owners – their French, German, and Italian newspapers so to find out more about Poland, which is not so well covered in America. Many Europeans must do the same, for sure. I go to very nice woman at bookstore counter and describe, "My old friend whom I have lost touches with." Smiling, she remembers a man also with my charming accent who fits exactly my describing. Oskar, his name. She thinks he lives not far, since he drinks espresso in next doors café as he reads journals each mornings. She has not seen this Oskar lately.

Let me tell you, are fourteen apartment buildings within few blocks of bookstore. It is quite a job for me until I figure to go to cheapest apartments first, for this is Soviet system, not CIA. The Spirit is leading me, for in third place I look I read his handwriting on the mailbox: "O. Sienkiewicz." In Poland a very typical name. Weird that I am so happy, as if I have forgotten evil and murderous regime.

Up an outside flight of stairs to Apartment C, with no signs of life inside. I ring the doorbell many time and shade my eyes to peek through kitchen window, seeing nothing but a heap of dishes. Oskar's bathroom window is frosted glass and like venetian blinds, each cranked open an inch for California air. I look in through slit and find his foot in pajamas as he sits on the bathroom floor, and when I stand taller there are his hands in his lap, and then just a slice of his square head can I make out, tilted toward his right shoulder, some trickles of sickness around his mouth.

"Oskar Sienkiewicz!" I shout, and there is a flutter like he wants to waken. "Are you ill?" I ask in Polish.

He a little nods and answers in Polish, "I'm resting," and just the one sentence in mother's tongue puts me in happiest mood. I walk to the flat's front door, try the handle, and find it is unlocked, no problem. His flat inside is torn furnitures that Monsignor would call "shoddy." Loud on small television is noontime sex opera. On food tray beside a stuffed chair is feast for a hundred flies and a half-full bottle of Polish vodka.

Oskar is on hands and knees on the bathroom floor when I get there. His stink is hard to take, for sure, but I help him stand and he lets me, then my hands he hits away. We speak in Polish from now on. With sarcasm, he asks, "Why aren't you praying?"

"Are you so certain I'm not?"

He falls into the bathroom wall and just there he stays for a while, like he is drunk. But he is ill instead. He recites: "'But I say unto you which hear, Love your enemies, do good to them which hate you. Bless them that curse you, and pray for them which despitefully use you.'" With satisfaction he smiles. "I have the quote right, no?"

"If you meant the Sermon on the Mount."

His forehead he taps. "I'm smart." And then he slides a foot or so until I catch his hot-with-fever weight and heave him to the hallway and onto his bed, its sheets in riot and still wet with night sweats. He sits there, his head down, his hands useless beside him. "We are not friends," he says, "but I am glad to see you."

"I have missed speaking Polish."

"A hard language for outsiders," he says. Oskar squints at me. "I am from Wambierzyce. Have you heard of it?"

"Naturally. It's in Lower Silesia. A shrine to Mary is there."

Oscar falls to his left. "I have to lie down," he says.

Lifting up his white feet, I ask, "Is there anything I can do for you?"

His left forearm covers his eyes as he sighs and gives it some thought. And then he says, "Die."

"I could find a doctor for you. And medicines. Wash your clothes and dishes."

"Were you to die," he says, "that would make me happiest; that would be quite enough."

And that is when I tell him how even in such a terrible times it was to me pleasing to have him around. We shared thousand-year history. Wawel Castle meant to him. Rynek Główny, he knew, is a marketplace. Mariacki Church. The scent of the Vistula river. Hiking in the Carpathians. We are feeling nostalgia for identical things, and for these reasons he could never be my enemy.

With irritation he stares at me. "I was a Catholic once," Oskar says. "But I grew up."

Why this is hilarious to me is not clear, but he is infected by my laughter. I find a spot on the foot of his bed for sitting and he glances at me from under his forearm before shifting his legs to give me more room. "I found the kielbasa you left behind. And the delicatessen carton of *kutia*," I say. "And I was sure you were a real Polander."

"Oh, say nothing of Christmas pudding! My belly aches for it even now."

"And roasted walnuts?"

Oskar groans.

"And the pastries from that shop by the Jagiellonian?"

"Stop it, Stefan, or I shall weep!"

And so I go on naming foods until we both are crying.

Bad Jews

GERALD SHAPIRO

There were only a few perfect spots in the world, and Leo Spivak had finally found one of them, right here in Mendocino. He was stretched out just inside the screen door of the brown-shingled beachfront cottage he and his wife, Rachel, had rented for a week – just the two of them, alone in all this peace and quiet. It was as beautiful and peaceful as a postcard. An adorably disheveled burst of nasturtiums framed the screen door and tumbled down across the tiny lawn of shaved English grass to their own private redwood hot tub. Ocean breezes, tangy with salt, washed over Spivak's face, and through the mist he could hear very clearly the wet, hypnotic slap of water as it lapped at pilings across the cove. He'd been looking for this very spot – these flowers, this breeze, these gently lapping waves – all his life. And now here he was. He found himself seriously mulling over the possibility that he'd never move again – that he would lie quite happily in this precise position, right here by the screen door, until he died.

And then the phone rang. Spivak closed his eyes. "Honey?" he moaned. Rachel was snoozing on the couch; the phone was exactly halfway between them, but Spivak wouldn't have wanted to answer the damn thing even if it had been nestled next to his cheek. Their daughter Elena, sixteen, was at a tennis camp in Wisconsin that they couldn't afford, and she'd called them twice already in the past three days pleading for more spending money. "C'mon," he said, "you get it, okay? If it's Elena asking for another two hundred bucks, I'm liable to say something I'll regret. I'm not kidding. And anyway, I can't move. I'm in the perfect spot."

Rachel caught the phone just after its third ring. She listened a moment, then her face went slack, and she handed the phone to her husband silently, despite his raised eyebrows.

"Hello?" he said, and sat down heavily next to her.

"Leo? This is Inez. Your father's friend in Tucson?" Though she'd lived in Tucson all her life, the intonations in her voice were Hispanic. Spivak had always been proud of the fact that it didn't matter one bit to him that Inez was Hispanic. His father, on the other hand, the bigoted bastard, had always given Inez a hard time about her heritage, joking with her about Mexican farting contests and calling her a wetback to her face.

"Inez, hey, how are you? How's my father?"

"Oh," she said, and then her voice caught. "That's what I'm calling you about. I'm so sorry to have to tell you this news. Your father's dead, Leo. I'm so sorry."

"He's dead?" Spivak's heart leapt, and then, immediately ashamed of itself, it plunged back into the dark cavern of his chest. "He died? Oh, my gosh, no. When?"

"Last night. I don't know when. They didn't call until this morning."

"Who? The nursing home? Tell me – what happened? What did they say?"

"He fell," Inez said. "He slipped and hit his head. I don't know, they didn't tell me too much. They asked me to call you. I told them I didn't want to do it, but they asked again."

"He just hit his head and died?"

"That's what they told me. He's gone, Leo. He's gone." She was crying now, this old woman – her voice sounded thin and silly to him, suddenly soaked with tears, as though she'd stepped off a ledge into deep water.

"How did you find me at this number?" Spivak asked. As soon as he'd said it he realized how inappropriate it was at a time like this – but he couldn't help himself: he was curious.

"Oh, I called your house," Inez told him. "I spoke to your house sitter?"

"Okay, well, I'm glad you called," he said, though that was, of course, a lie. "Sit tight, Inez. I'll handle everything."

"Do you want me to arrange for a funeral announcement? In the newspaper?"

"Oh, gee. Yeah. Good idea – go ahead and do that. Sure. That'd be great."

"What should I say? About your dad, I mean? For the announcement?"

"What should you say?" Spivak asked. "I don't know." His mind was completely blank. "You knew him. Just say whatever you want. You can make something up."

Over Spivak's objections, Rachel came along with him on the drive from Mendocino to San Francisco, then flew with him to Tucson; why, after all, in the name of God, she asked him, would she have wanted to stay in Mendocino by herself? But once they'd arrived in Tucson and had checked into their motel, Spivak announced his firm intention to take care of all the details of his father's personal effects and funeral arrangements by himself. "You didn't even like him," he reminded her. "I didn't like him, either, but he's my father, so I'm obligated."

"I'm your wife – I'm obligated, too."

"Absolutely not. It's out of the question. Stay right here," he told her. "Go swimming – they've got a great pool here. Work on your tan, read a book. I don't want to hear about you doing anything but relaxing. And whatever you do, don't try to get involved in this funeral thing. We're on vacation. We didn't go on vacation because my father was alive, and now that he's dead, that doesn't mean our vacation is over."

"You're not making any sense. Come on. This is your father we're talking about."

"We've waited for this vacation for two years. I'm not going to have it ruined, and that's that. It's not Mendocino, but at least there's a pool and the sun is shining. Okay, so it's a hundred and eight degrees and there's no ocean. But shut your eyes, use your imagination, you're right back in California. Smell that surf. Just work on your tan and practice your backstroke, and let me handle this my way, okay?"

So while Rachel lounged nervously by the pool at the Marriott, daubing sun block on her shoulders every five minutes, Spivak, his face set in a grim mask, drove to Desert Angels, his father's nursing home. He stood impatiently in the reception lounge, waiting as the woman behind the counter rummaged through a pile of papers. A moment later she thrust a clipboard full of documents at him. "We're all going to miss your father," she said, her voice full of cheery compassion. "He was such a lively, lively guy. You can fill these out over there." She pointed to a nearby couch.

There was no denying it: the place smelled frankly of urine. Near the door, an old woman sat in a wheelchair, her head sunk so low that her whiskered chin nearly rested on her chest. Her eyes were open, but she seemed to be staring at nothing. She was nodding her head slightly and grunting, making a sound that resembled "uh-huh" – like some sort of relentless, monotonal benediction. *Lively,* Spivak said to himself, rolling his eyes as he filled out forms. *Lively compared to what?*

From where he sat, he could see into the dining room: a morbidly obese woman stood at a lectern reading bingo numbers into a microphone, while a few residents of the nursing home sat like zombies in wheelchairs, some of them hooked to oxygen tanks. Attendants stood by, helping the residents keep track of their progress. "Bingo!" a male attendant said in a loud voice. Somewhere down the hall, someone was screaming.

He handed the clipboard back to the receptionist, who said, "Just sign this release form and you can take your father's personal papers." Spivak scribbled his signature, and she handed him a manila envelope, which he immediately ripped open. Inside were his father's honorable discharge from the army, a copy of his Social Security card, fourteen dollars, and a typed and notarized last will and testament. The will was worthless; his father had scrawled his own name on both of the lines reserved for witnesses' signatures. Spivak stuffed it back into the envelope and shoved the whole thing into the hip pocket of his shorts.

"Before I go," he said, "would there be anyone available who could talk to me for just a moment about my father? You know – just for some sort of closure? I'm kind of curious about his death. To be perfectly honest with you, I'd sort of convinced myself he'd live forever."

"Of course," she said, and bit her lip. "Just have a seat and I'll get your father's nurse."

In a moment a large woman with masculine features appeared and sat next to him.

"You're Mr. Spivak's son?" she said. "I'm Mrs. Mitchell. I stopped in to see your father almost every day. He talked about you all the time. Leo this and Leo that. He was very proud."

"Well, thank you. That's very nice to hear."

"You wanted to know about your father's death," Mrs. Mitchell said. Her eyes narrowed.

"Your father slipped and hit his head." Mrs. Mitchell coughed into her hand. "He'd had an accident, and the floor was slippery."

"An accident," Spivak echoed, and nodded thoughtfully.

"Yes. This may be painful, Mr. Spivak. He'd – lost control of his bowels." She saw the look on Spivak's face, and quickly added, "That's not at all unusual among our patients. It happens every day. Apparently he was trying to get to the bathroom." She coughed again.

"You mean my father slipped in his own – ?"

"Yes. That's right." She looked away for a moment, and knotted a handkerchief in her lap. "A fall like that . . . internal bleeding, cerebral hemorrhage." She shrugged. "Your father hadn't been well, you know. He was frail. He'd fallen a number of times in recent months. You have to understand, Mr. Spivak, we have a hundred and sixty residents here at Desert Angels. Orderlies were on their way to his room when the accident occurred. We try to respond to all incidents like this one as rapidly as possible – your father rang the call button and it couldn't have been even five minutes later when we got there. We're all very sorry."

"He slipped in his own shit," Spivak said, his voice soft and full of awe. "Gee, that's really something." He stood up and shook her hand limply, then walked away.

Outside, the heat was like a brick wall. He walked through it bent over, trying to avoid the glare of the sun. As he crossed the parking lot he felt the pavement sucking at the soles of his shoes. He tried to remember what his rental car looked like, but all he could think of was the phrase *he slipped in his own shit*, which echoed in his head like a dull gong. There it was, the rental car, a deep maroon something-or-other. All he knew about it was that the air-conditioning worked. What did people do out here, he wondered, before there was air-conditioning? Probably nobody lived here back then. Probably Tucson was just a couple of adobe huts stuck among the cacti and the scorpions. Probably people slipped in their own shit all and time, and nobody was there to clean it up except a few coyotes.

At his next stop, the Marshak Jewish Funeral Chapel on Orange Grove Road, he waited for nearly half an hour on a Roman bench in the cool, marble-floored lobby until Stan Marshak, the funeral director, was free. A receptionist brought Spivak a cup of weak coffee, which he sipped while he listened to the dim sounds of weeping that came from behind the handsome mahogany door of Marshak's office. He stared at a large stainless steel sculpture that hung on the wall across the lobby, and realized after a few minutes that it was supposed to be a menorah. Finally the door to Marshak's office opened, and a huddled family group walked out, gripping each other and sniffling.

Marshak came out behind them, wringing his hands. He was a tall, spare man dressed in an expensive-looking black suit. "Mr. Spivak," he said slowly, his head cocked to the side.

"Stan Marshak. So sorry for your loss." He clasped his hands at his throat and stood frozen there for a moment, remorse dripping down over his long, ravaged face. Then the moment passed, and he waved Spivak wearily into his office, which was festooned along its paneled walls with framed certificates of merit from various Jewish organizations.

"Well, I've gone through our records, and the good news, Mr. Spivak, is that your father provided for everything," Marshak began. He let the word "everything" slip through his lips in separate, breathy syllables, as if Spivak's father had shown shocking, unprecedented foresight – the first person in recorded history to ever pre-pay a funeral.

"Is that right," Spivak said.

"Absolutely." He flipped through a pile of paperwork. "Yes, here it is. Just look at this, will you?" He shoved the papers across the desk. "You see there? Sol Spivak – right there, that's his signature." He tapped a finger on the top sheet. "Everything's paid for in advance. Your father did that several years ago. Burial plot – he even picked out a casket. Will you look at that. Very considerate, indeed." He shook his head and tssked.

"Well, that's good news. I'm relieved – and frankly surprised, I have to tell you. My father wasn't usually one to think ahead."

"Well, you can relax, because everything's been taken care of. Except of course for my fees, and for a few other odds and ends. Your father was orthodox, was he not?"

"My dad? Oh, no. I don't even think he belonged to a synagogue, as a matter of fact."

"Are you yourself a practicing Jew?"

"No, not really. I mean . . . no. But I know he'd like to have a Jewish burial."

"Yes, of course," Marshak said. "I understand perfectly. We'll make sure everything is done strictly according to Jewish law. So for starters, then, there will be the additional fee to have the body watched until the funeral. That's traditional. Then there'll be the ritual washing and wrapping in a shroud – again, it's traditional. And then there will be the rabbi's honorarium. Traditionally, five hundred is suggested. The cost of the casket has gone up, of course, since your father made his arrangements. Everything's gone up-up-up. The cost of fine woods like mahogany – "

"Wait a second. I thought in orthodox funerals the casket was just a pine box."

Marshak looked up at him under lavish snow-white eyebrows and held the pose for several beats. "Yes. Well. If you'd like to go that route."

"Isn't that traditional?"

"Your father pre-paid the cost of a fine polished mahogany casket. But of course you as the surviving son – you are the surviving son, are you not?"

"Yes, I am."

"Well, of course you're free to do what you'd like. These were your father's wishes, but – "

"What are we talking about, in terms of price difference? Roughly, I mean."

"Between the pine and the mahogany? About five hundred dollars."

Spivak sat back in his seat. "Are you absolutely sure my father wanted the mahogany?"

"Oh, yes. It's right here in black and white."

"Well, that's a mistake. I bet he just circled the wrong box or something. All my life I've heard that Jews get buried in plain pine caskets. I've always admired that, you know? It seems so much more sensible than something fancy. *Goyim* go crazy with their polished caskets and open viewing of the dead and all of that. It's disgusting. Who'd want anything like that?" "So you're saying you want the plain pine? Is that it?"

"Yes. That's definite. Let's go with the pine."

Marshak cocked his head and pursed his lips as he scribbled a note of his pad. Then, not bothering to look up, he said, "Fine and dandy. Let's just do a little figuring here, shall we?" At that, he fell into a five-minute frenzy of calculations, scribbling furiously on a pad, muttering to himself, transposing figures onto other sheets of paper, pounding out nervous, staccato rhythms on an adding machine. Finally he rested, and leaned back into the plush leather cushion of his chair. "Well, are you lucky," he said, shaking his head in admiration. "Isn't this something."

"Oh, yeah?"

"Just look at how this has worked out," Marshak announced, and pushed a ruled pad of paper under Spivak's nose. "Now first you'll see I've given you the 15 percent discount on my own fee – we call it our Out of Towner Special. It's a little something we like to do here at Marshak – so many of our bereaved are from out of the area. Then you'll notice that I've waived the traditional fee for having the body watched until burial. That one's 'on the house!' But wait, this is the nicest part – you'll notice the fifteen percent deduction off the standard rabbi's honorarium. A perfectly fine, highly qualified rabbi I happen to know here in Tucson, unaffiliated with any congregation at the present time, looking for a few extra functions to perform. And will you just look at those savings!" He beamed and stroked his wrists, which were long and bony and matted with dark hair, like a chimpanzee's wrists.

The total came to nearly two thousand dollars over the amount his father had already paid. Spivak stared at it. "Did you figure in the savings on the casket?" he asked sharply.

"Of course. Didn't I mention that?"

"No, you didn't. Jesus, that's a lot of money. I thought you said it was all paid for. I thought you said my father had thought of everything."

"And he did, he certainly did, Mr. Spivak. Except for the items we've just discussed."

When he got back to the motel he found Rachel out by the pool and stood sweating over her, blocking the sun, describing to her the manner of his father's death. "I mean, tell me, is that death with dignity?" he asked her. "Is that any way to exit this sphere – this plane of existence? Slipping in your own excrement? Is that a way to die?"

"No, it's not, Leo. It's awful," Rachel replied. She adjusted her sunglasses. "I'm really sorry. I wish you would've let me come along with you. I really wanted to. No kidding. I'm serious – I really did."

"Why? What good would that have done? What would it have changed? If you'd been there, you think they would have said he died peacefully in his sleep, listening to Mozart?"

"That's not what I meant." Rachel shaded her eyes and gazed up at him. "It's awful, honey. They shouldn't have told you. What's the point in knowing that?"

"I don't know. Listen: the funeral's tomorrow, and I don't want you to come. That's absolute. This is my job – he was my father, and it's my responsibility. You're on vacation, I want you to go buy some jewelry or something – maybe something turquoise. Go have a massage or a facial. Pretend you're still in Mendocino." He thought of telling her about the issue of the pine casket, but then decided not to bring it up. What if she told him she would have voted for mahogany?

"Are you okay, Leo?" Rachel asked. "You look awful."

"Well, I'm hot. We're in Tucson, it's summertime. This weather really takes it out of a person. I wish we were back in Mendocino."

"No, I mean – you know."

"Listen: this is my version of grieving. I know it's not the way I'm supposed to be acting, but I can't help it. My dad lived for eighty-five years and now he's dead. Period, end of sentence. And get this: the funeral's going to cost me two thousand dollars. Can you believe that? I don't want to be a bastard about this, but my God, that's a lot of money just to put somebody in the ground." He wiped his cheek. "That's sweat, by the way," he said. "I'm not crying. I'm sweating to death." He paused. "I'm serious about tomorrow. I don't want you anywhere near that funeral."

This was the same motel he and Rachel had stayed in fifteen years before, on their first trip to Arizona. In the wake of Spivak's mother's death, his father at the age of seventy had suddenly gone haywire, quitting his job selling children's clothing and moving to Tucson from Kansas City. "I'm tired," he told them. "I'm sick of the ice and snow, I'm getting the hell out of there." He had next to nothing in the bank, no pension at all, just his pathetic Social Security and the pittance he'd gained from the quick sale of the house. Alone and friendless in the desert, baking in the

sun, over the next couple of months he called Spivak every day or two
– mournful, remorse-laden conversations, which seemed designed to
elicit sympathy and money from his son. Then the phone calls petered
out, and when Spivak called to check up on his father in Tucson after a
silence of several weeks, the old man seemed transformed. He drawled
like a cowboy, spoke of needing to "go get some grub," answered Spivak's
questions with "yup" or "nope."

Spivak stewed over this new development for another month, his
anxiety mounting, then finally he couldn't take it any more. "We've got
to go down there and make sure he's okay," he told Rachel. "He's my
father – I can't stand him, it's true – I've never been able to stand him,
even when I was a kid – but now he's the only parent I've got left, and
he's turning into Gabby Hayes." So just after St. Patrick's Day, when old
drifts of brown-crusted snow were still heaped in the alley behind their
house in Winnetka, Spivak and Rachel parked their infant daughter
Elena with Rachel's parents, the Sperlings (who had flown to Chicago
just to babysit), and went down to visit the old man in Arizona for three
days.

When he and Rachel got off the plane in Tucson that first time, the
air was rich and fragrant with desert flowers, the sunshine so bright it
hurt their eyes. The elder Spivak, his face as pink as scar tissue, clomped
up to greet them in cowboy boots. He wore a shirt decorated with gold
piping and brass studs; low-slung jeans hung beneath his belly, held up
by a belt with an enormous silver-and-turquoise buckle, and a well-
aged straw cowboy hat rode askew atop his freckled bald skull. "Howdy
there," he announced in the same twang that Spivak had heard over the
phone.

"Dad?" Spivak asked. He peered at his father carefully.

"Y'all hungry?" his father asked. "Let's mosey on over to the Steak
Stampede – I could eat me a hoss." At the restaurant, while they were
waiting for their food to come, Spivak and Rachel trotted out their
pictures of Elena, but his father fanned through them disinterestedly,
then shuffled them as if they were a deck of playing cards, and handed
them back across the table. After they'd finished their lunch and the
plates had been cleared away, the elder Spivak leaned back into his
seat, sucking on a toothpick, and regaled them with stories of old time
Tucson, his twang growing more noticeable with every sentence. Finally

he suggested they all might attend a rodeo that afternoon. "More fun than a barrel of monkeys," he told them.

"We're not going to any rodeos, Dad. That's out of the question. Look, what's going on?" Spivak demanded. "What's with that hat!"

"Keeps the sun off my head," his father said, shifting his gaze to the floor. "Lotta sun out these parts. Man's got to take precautions."

"Listen to the way you're talking. 'These parts.' What's got into you? You think you're a cowboy? Well, hello – reality check. You're a retired salesman from Kansas City, you're seventy years old, remember? Whatever happened to aging with dignity?"

"Your mother aged with dignity, and now she's dead. Dignity doesn't count for much in the end. I loved her, but she's gone, Leo. She was a good woman. The best I ever knew."

"You don't have to tell me that. I know she was a good woman. She was my mother."

Spivak's father turned his gaze to Rachel. "We lived our whole lives for *him* – for his happiness," he said, pointing at Spivak. "Leo wanted something, he got it. We made sure he never lacked a thing. We may not have had the fanciest house on the block, but – "

"What's that got to do with anything," Spivak said disgustedly, and shook his head. He'd heard this spiel before, and so what if it was true, or nearly true? It was ancient history! What was he supposed to do, hang himself out of guilt, just because he'd had a decent childhood? Okay, he admitted it freely now: at one time, *many sacrifices* had been made on his behalf. This had all occurred during his childhood, when he was a *child*, for Christ's sake, and he hadn't noticed any of it; he'd been too busy watching stupid television shows, playing capture the flag and King of the Hill, building model airplanes, blowing holes in the yard with illegally obtained firecrackers, camping out at the neighbors' house, getting sick on candy – he'd been masturbating and learning to ride a bicycle by falling off it repeatedly, hoarding *Mad* magazines and pretending he was James Bond, masturbating some more – and so he hadn't had time to keep a running tally of all the things his parents had done without on his account. So okay, already! He felt bad about it now; he cringed to recall his childhood – the shopping trips during which he'd pleaded for new toys, the tantrums he'd thrown on the way to the synagogue on Saturday mornings, the tears, the *kvetching*, the whining for a trip to Wimpy's for hamburgers even though he'd known well enough that the money for such frivolity simply wasn't there. But what was he supposed to do? Travel back in time, get a job at a glue factory at the age of six, so he could pull his own weight in the family?

"I joined the Elks Club last week," Spivak's father said.

"The Elks? Why?" Spivak shook his head. "What's wrong with the Jewish Community Center? Join the temple, or something. Join B'nai Brith, why don't you."

"Listen to you. What are you, Mr. Jewish Culture all of a sudden?"

"I just thought you might like to join a temple, that's all. It's a place to meet people. They've got temples out here. Don't you want to have a place to go on Rosh Hashanah?"

"Why would I want that? Your mother was the religious one, not me. All that *davening* and breast-beating. *Oy, oy, oy!* A bunch of pathetic crap – six million Jews *davened* all the way into the ovens at Auschwitz, look what it got them. Anyway – you can go dancing three times a week at the Elks. And I'm a pretty good dancer." He stared at Spivak sharply now. "You probably didn't even know that about me, did you? My own son, and you don't even know I'm a good dancer. Take my word for it, ladies out here line up to get the chance to foxtrot with Sol Spivak. Widows are crazy about me. Look at me: I'm clean, I take a shower every day, I walk a mile every day at the mall, I do my own laundry, I iron my own shirts. I get hungry, I heat up a Swanson TV dinner. You want to stay back there with all that snow every winter? So stay. I want to live out the rest of my life in the sun. Is that a crime?"

And so the ensuing fifteen years had passed, first one widow and then another, sometimes several of them at once accompanying Sol Spivak to the Elks' dances. Spivak had met a few of them over the years during his brief trips to the desert to visit his father; though he fought the impulse, he couldn't help comparing them to his mother, and inevitably found each of them wanting – some were stupid, others bitter and cynical. All of them struck him as desperate: corseted, pinched into outfits too small for them, their faces daubed with makeup, their hair dyed a spectrum of unlikely colors. Still it was a mystery to him that they put up with his father, who seemed to have decided to use his advancing years as an excuse to seek the worst inside himself – to let go of the rope that holds us tied, no matter how loosely, to the pier of decency and respectability. He lied incessantly. He shoplifted until he was caught and given a suspended sentence. He grew a Fu Manchu moustache and wore fake gold chains around his neck. He ran up thousands of dollars on his credit cards and then called Spivak in tears, begging him to pay off his debts. He bought a hairpiece that looked like it was made of yak fur, and insisted on wearing it backwards. He cheated relentlessly on every woman he met, then cried and fumed and cursed them when they left him because of it.

But gradually as the years had gone by, his father's health had failed; the sun slowly turned his skin to burnt parchment, the heat sapped his strength so that nine months out of the year he hardly saw the outdoors at all; his dancing turned to feeble shuffling and then stopped altogether, and in its place the elder Spivak turned to the daytime TV talk shows for entertainment. The yak fur hairpiece and the fake gold chains sat on the coffee table in front of the couch, gathering dust. His personal habits grew shabby. For days at a time he would eat nothing but crackers and peanut butter, washed down with prune juice. He occasionally lost control of his bowels in the shower, and each time called his son to tearfully confess what had happened.

Along the way, of course, the parade of widows thinned out, until finally over the last couple of years there'd been only Inez, who put up with Sol Spivak through seasons of discontent, as he moved bitterly from one cramped, fetid apartment to another. They saw each other at least once a week, when she drove them to a restaurant for an early bird dinner (he'd finally given up his driver's license at the age of eighty-one, after creaming a public bus broadside in the middle of the afternoon). Inez called Spivak to complain to him about his father every six months or so. "All my friends tell me, they say 'Inez, what are you doing with that man? He's no good, he's mean to you,'" she would moan to Spivak. "And so I tell them – 'Yes, I know, you're right, he's no good for me, he's too mean.' He's so mean, Leo. What made your dad so mean? Why does he have to be so bad to me? But then I think he's just so scared, he's lonely, he doesn't have nobody else, you're too far away to help him. So I stick with him. I can't help it. I like him. I don't know why, but I do."

Finally, incapable of bathing himself without falling in the tub, unable to keep himself clean or make any of his own meals anymore, his ever-growing array of medicines a bewildering maze to him now, the elder

Spivak put up at Desert Angels, a nursing home in the foothills of the mountains on Tucson's northern edge, where for the last year and a half of his life he'd proceeded to go kicking and screaming down the final hallway of his life, shouting curses at the staff of nurses and orderlies as he went.

Tall clouds gathered over the mountains the next morning. Spivak went down for a dip in the motel pool with Rachel before breakfast – the only time during the day when it was truly comfortable outside – and it was only when he was back in their room toweling off after his swim that he realized he'd brought nothing even remotely appropriate for a funeral with him. Look at him: he didn't even have a *belt* with him, for God's sake. To hell with it – he wasn't going to go out and buy anything at this point. Why should he? Already they were two thousand dollars in the hole – not to mention airfare for the two of them to Arizona, plus the cost of this motel, plus the rental car, and don't forget the cost of the car and the vacation cottage in Mendocino, all of it non-refundable, money down the drain.

The best he could come up with was a clean pair of hiking shorts and a yellow knit shirt with a little polo pony over his left nipple. He put these on, then looked at himself in the mirror. "What do you think?" he asked Rachel.

"Oh," she said with a sympathetic frown, and put her hands on his shoulders. "Well, what could you do, Leo?" asked Rachel. "We were in Mendocino when you got the call. What were you supposed to do, go buy a suit on your way to the airport?"

"I don't know," Spivak muttered, and gathered his wallet and keys.

On the way to Marshak's Funeral Chapel he tried halfheartedly to recall the prayers he'd learned as a boy, but all he could dredge up were tattered fragments, a shred or two of melody, a few unintelligible sylla-bles. Well, who was he kidding? He'd just have to admit it to the rabbi right up front – there'd be nobody saying Kaddish, nobody lighting any *yartzheit* candles, nobody laying any *tefillin*, nobody attending services to honor Sol Spivak's name. The plain fact, Spivak told himself, was that he was a bad Jew. He'd *always* been a bad Jew, even as a child, when at his mother's behest he'd suffered through several years of Hebrew school in preparation for his Bar Mitzvah. Nothing the rabbis told him meant a damned thing; it all seemed about as profound as a game of tiddlywinks, in fact, and though he recognized that he should be ashamed to feel this way, he wasn't. This was Spivak's sense of his destiny, his lineage: though he had nothing solid to back it up, no hard genealogical evidence per se, he felt sure in his heart that he was descended from a long line of bad Jews, an age-old dynasty of skeptics and know-nothings, eaters of *treyf*, nose-thumbers and back-row snickerers, dregs and dropouts, stretching back through centuries of squalid tenement flats and mud-and-straw-hut *shtetls*, tattered tents in the middle of goddamned nowhere, all the way back to the golden calf itself.

Marshak was waiting for him in his office, dressed in a suit even more funereal than the one he'd been wearing the day before. He gave Spivak a quick deadpan head-to-toe glance, then raised his eyebrows and inhaled through his nose.

"I'm sorry. I didn't bring any funeral clothes with me. I know it's inappropriate. I was on vacation with my wife in California when I heard about my father's death, and this is the best I could do," Spivak said. He crossed his arms on his chest to hide the polo pony. "I was in Mendocino," he said, and then before he could stop himself he added, "It's gorgeous there."

"Yes, I'm sure it is," Marshak said. "Was your wife unable to accompany you? I thought I understood you to say yesterday – "

"She's back at the motel. I told her to relax," Spivak said. "It's so damn hot out, you know? Anyway, she hardly knew my father. We're not exactly a close-knit family."

Marshak gazed at him silently, his head cocked, and he seemed to be on the verge of a comment of some kind when a knock sounded at the door. He opened it, admitting a florid, pudgy man with receding red hair. "Ah, yes. Perfect. Mr. Spivak," Marshak announced, twirling his long, bony hands around, "may I present Rabbi Adrian Fink."

Spivak shook the rabbi's hand. "Not a word about my name, okay?" the rabbi said quickly. He flashed a brief, mirthless smile. "Sorry, I always say that – it's a preemptive strike." Marshak excused himself and left the room, rubbing his hands together as if it had suddenly turned cold in his office. Spivak and Rabbi Fink sat down in slippery leather chairs. "Forgive me, Mr. Spivak. I know you're in mourning and all. I'm just very sensitive about my name," Rabbi Fink said. "I've had a rough life. I'm awfully sorry for your loss. And I'm glad you agreed to let me perform the service for your father. I didn't know him at all, so I'll need to ask you some questions in order to prepare a few remarks in the way of a eulogy." He took out a pen and a scrap of paper.

"Ask away."

"What was he like?"

"He was a jerk."

Rabbi Fink laughed nervously. "Well, well," he said, and clicked the pen a few times.

"You asked."

"Yes, indeed. How old was your father at the time of his death?"

"Eighty-five. He was born in Lithuania. He always claimed that he couldn't remember the name of the town. But my guess is, he just didn't want to think about it."

"And how long had he lived in this country?"

"Seventy-three years. He lived in New York originally, got his start in the garment industry, then moved to the Midwest after the war. I was born in Kansas City, Missouri. Now I live in Chicago – Winnetka, actually. It's on the north shore. My wife and I have a daughter, Elena. That's some name, isn't it? She's sixteen. At tennis camp up in Wisconsin – Camp KeeTonKee." He leaned forward and before he could stop himself he added, "She's spending money up there like you wouldn't believe. How much can a can of tennis balls cost? You know what I mean? I think she's putting most of it up her nose, to tell you the truth. My wife's in deep denial about all of this. 'Cocaine? Not our daughter!' Oh, yeah."

"Okay. Right," Rabbi Fink said, though his eyes were wide. "Isn't that something. Now, about your father, for just a minute . . . what was his line of work?"

"He sold children's clothing, wholesale. His territory covered most of the upper Midwest. He didn't enjoy it very much, and so he didn't do very well at it, to be honest. When you don't enjoy what you're doing . . . well, you know. But anyway, it was a living."

"And his hobbies?"

"My father didn't have hobbies. Well, wait a second. When I was a kid he liked to watch the Friday night fights, the Gillette fights, on television. He'd sit in the den and have a beer and let me take sips from it. He liked to dance, too, although I didn't know that about him until after my mother died. She died of cancer fifteen years ago. They were married forty-two years. It wasn't a great marriage, but it was very long."

"I understand," Rabbi Fink said, drawing big, nervous circles on the scrap of paper.

"No, I don't think you do," Spivak said. "See, the fact is, he really wasn't all that great a father. He was gone a lot, and that was bad, but what was worse was that when he'd come home from a trip he was usually in a rotten mood, because he wasn't earning a lot of commissions, since he really didn't have much of a gift for sales – and he'd say stuff that really hurt my feelings. He called me a little creep once, when I was about ten. I can't remember why he did it. Nobody'd ever called me a creep before, and to hear that from your own father – well, listen, it was very depressing. Another time, I broke a window with a tennis ball and I couldn't get it fixed before he got home – I was maybe eight or nine – and when he saw it, he told me I wasn't his son anymore. I cried for days."

Rabbi Fink ran his tongue around over his top front teeth, as if rooting around for the remains of his lunch. "That sounds awful," he said. "I'm really very sorry."

"Oh, that's okay. I survived." Spivak fell silent, and sank back into his chair.

"Is there anything you'd like to add – anything about your father you'd like me to know?"

"No. I don't think so. I mean, I don't want to sound abrupt, but he lived for eighty-five years, and then he died. You know? He wasn't exactly cut off in his prime."

"All right, then." Rabbi Fink pulled an embroidered yarmulke out of his pocket and clapped it on his head. "I have a confession to make," he said, wringing his hands. "You opened up to me a bit just a minute ago, so I feel like I can tell you this. This is my first funeral. I'm a little nervous. I've been a rabbi for twelve years, and it's been tough, tough, tough," he said, pounding his fist into his palm. "You think your father hated his work? Well, talk to *me* about on-the-job frustration. I've never caught on. I don't know why. I'll get a three-week tryout at a congregation, and at the end of three weeks they pat me on the shoulder and show me the door. I've been everywhere. You want to know what it's like being a rabbi in Sitka, Alaska? I did three weeks there. I think it's my name, you know? They hear the name, Adrian Fink – *boom*, they're against me. 'Adrian, what is that, a *girl's* name?' 'Fink, hey Rat Fink, Rabbi Rat Fink!' Ha, ha. Everybody's such a comedian."

"I'm sorry to hear that. Don't worry about the funeral. It should be a snap," Spivak said. "Nobody's going to show up, anyway. The notice was just in the paper today, and besides, except for his friend Inez, I don't think anybody in Tucson was still speaking to my dad. He was a hard guy to like. And as for a eulogy, you don't have to say too much. Just say he lived a long time and now he's dead, and that ought to do the trick."

"Well, thanks. You're holding up very well under the strain of your loss, I must say. I haven't spent a lot of time around bereaved families, so what do I know about it? But you seem like you're doing great so far, in the grief department, I mean. I suppose it's because you didn't have a very deep or meaningful relationship with your father anyway."

Spivak bristled, sensing that his capacity for feeling had been called into question. Meaningful? Who'd said anything about deep or mean-ingful? "We all grieve in our own way, Rabbi," he said, then he shut up, because he didn't know what the hell he was talking about. What did he know about grieving, anyway? Oh, sure, he'd felt a terrible loss when his mother died – for months afterward he thought of calling her every Sunday, as had been his habit, but then each time he realized she was gone, and he'd have to talk to his father instead, he hung up the phone and sat by it, lost and utterly bereft, tears welling up in his eyes. He'd liked his mother, had even admired her, to the very end. She was a woman of true faith, and while Spivak didn't understand faith, and didn't respect it very much, either, he admired it in his mother, because he saw quite clearly that it gave her a cushion, something firm and comfortable to lean against in her final days when the pain grew intense, and it let her die with something that looked like dignity.

This, on the other hand, was something altogether different. As hard as he tried to summon up grief of a similar kind in response to his father's death, all Spivak could think of was the fact that from now on he wouldn't have to send the old guy any more money. For years he'd been sending his father dribbling amounts, a hundred one month, two hundred the next. It wasn't the money itself that bothered him, he told himself. But then he asked himself: what kind of bullshit was that? Of *course* it was the money. After all these years toiling away at Bowles and Humphries, his salary was still stuck in the high five figures – unlike other guys his age, like Adelman in Media, Kinsella in Accounting, and the Bobbsey Twins, Bob Luther and Bob Delgado from Creative, all of whom were vice presidents already, stockholders in the firm. Christmas rolled around, these guys got smacked with bonus checks that had *Mercedes* written all over them. But not Spivak – no, never Spivak, no bonus checks for him. God, it would feel good to stop writing those damn checks to his father. Maybe now he could start saving for something. He didn't know what, just yet – but he could figure that out later. There must be something out there that was worth having.

Marshak tapped on the office door and then a moment later opened it a crack. "May I intrude?" he asked in an unctuous voice.

"I think we're done in here," Rabbi Fink said. He stood up and put a serious, businesslike expression on his face. "Thank you for your candor, Mr. Spivak. I'm sure you loved and honored your father, and I know you revere his memory. I'll do my very best to convey all of that in my remarks."

"Mr. Spivak?" Marshak said softly, in a voice full of steely tenderness. "I'm sorry to seem abrupt, but we have another service scheduled for this afternoon. Please – this way. I'll show you the family viewing room."

The viewing room turned out to be a low-lit curtained alcove off to the side of the chapel. Through a gap in the curtains, Spivak could see his father's casket up on a platform at the front of the chapel, near a lectern. The casket looked pretty nice, considering that it was a plain pine coffin and obviously cost five hundred dollars less than the one his father had ordered. The wood was as pale as cream, and the casket's contours were smooth and rounded; clearly it had been built with genuine skill and care. But still, there was no denying it: this thing didn't pack the wallop of a polished mahogany casket glinting under the lights. There might as well have been a large price tag on it, *$500 LESS THAN THE MAHOGANY!* scrawled in big red letters. Spivak peeked out a little farther to see if there were any mourners. Surprisingly, a group of them sat there, a sorrow-beaten band of arthritic old *cockers* his father had called his friends. In addition to Inez, there were elderly women in attendance, as well – a small sampling of the widows his father had courted in past years. The duffers were a fragile, shabby bunch, just as decrepit as his father had been of late. They were tieless, dressed in soiled double-knits outfits, their shirt collars out over their jacket lapels in the style of Israeli *Knesset* members. One of them had fallen noisily asleep, his mouth open, his dentures slipping out. The widows were sitting in furious, hennaed, clench-jawed isolation, each one occupying her own separate row. How had these people managed to learn of his father's death in time to come here? They must grab the early papers every morning and search the obituaries for familiar names. Maybe they hoped a buffet would be included.

Inez sat by herself in the front row, her bowed head covered in a doily. She was a plain woman with a rough, battered face. She was weeping now; he could tell by the jerky way her shoulders moved.

"Listen, do I have to stay in here by myself?" he asked Marshak. "I feel a little ridiculous peeking through a curtain at all of these people. My father's friend Inez is out there."

"It's traditional," Marshak replied, and handed Spivak a black yarmulke.

"No, I mean, do I have to? Is it required? Is it in the Bible or something? Thou shalt peek through a curtain at thy father's funeral?"

Marshak sniffed. "Of course not. As with everything else, it's your decision."

"Well, fine, then," Spivak said. He slipped out through the curtain and sat down by Inez.

Rabbi Fink opened the service nervously with a hymn that Spivak didn't recognize. It might have been a soothing melody, but Fink's voice cracked several times as he sang, and at one point it seemed he might be on the verge of tears. Spivak sensed that his father's cronies were staring at him from the pews further back in the chapel – he could feel their rheumy eyes boring into his shoulder blades – but he didn't care. He couldn't stop gazing at his father's casket. The casket seemed very big for such a little guy; his father hadn't stood much over five-six, and in the last few years he'd lost weight, shriveling like a piece of rotten fruit. Inside that box lay the already moldering remains of the man whose lap he'd slept in occasionally as a small boy – the man who had taught him the ins and outs of manhood, starting with how to pee standing up. Once upon a time they'd played catch together in the front yard night after night, pegging the ball back and forth under the oak tree for hours, until they were called in for dinner or it grew too dark to see. In the years before baseball games were regularly televised, Spivak and his father would sit together on the couch listening to the old Kansas City A's on the radio, eating peanuts and mocking the anemic voice of Monte Moore, the team's dipshit announcer. Sunday mornings in summertime, they washed the car together in the driveway, squirting each other with the hose. When Spivak was fifteen and developed a moustache, his father showed him how to shave, standing behind him at the bathroom sink while Spivak's mother wept in the doorway. He realized now as he stared as his father's casket that he might be embellishing some of this stuff, blowing an isolated incident into something grander, more enduring – but still, he couldn't be making it all up from thin air.

When Rabbi Fink was done singing the opening hymn, he gripped the podium and stared in wide-eyed wonder at the audience of mourners, as if he'd just realized they were there. "What can I tell you about Sol Spivak, that you don't already know?" he asked. "What, finally, is there to say about such a man?" He slipped a hand into his coat pocket and withdrew a scrap of paper, which he now consulted. "That he was from Lithuania, came to this country as a young man, moved to Kansas City and lived there many years? That he was retired, a single man, a widower? You knew all of that. That for many years he made his living, such as it was, selling children's clothes? You knew that, too, I'm sure. And anyway, what does it matter? He wasn't that good as a salesman, and his career's been over a long time." Inez, who'd already been weeping gently, now burst into tears that seemed ready to tear her to pieces. "He was a simple man, Sol Spivak," Rabbi Fink continued. "Not a good man – no, let's not kid ourselves, not a hero. He wasn't a saint – far from it, in fact. He said things he shouldn't have said, did things he shouldn't have done. And now he's gone." He crumpled the scrap of paper and shoved it back into his pocket. "There will be no plaques in this man's honor. No one will ever pray in the Sol Spivak Memorial Chapel. No one will send their child to college on a Sol Spivak Scholarship."

"Christ almighty," one of the duffers in the rows behind Spivak muttered, "what the hell kind of a eulogy is this? Who is this rabbi, anyway? What's his name again?"

"It's a common story, isn't it? Ashes to ashes, dust to dust," Rabbi Fink continued, pounding the podium to emphasize his points. "Whoever heard of Sol Spivak? Nobody. What did he have to recommend himself? Not very much. In a week we'll all have forgotten him."

Spivak could stand it no longer. "*And yet!*" he cried, rising to his feet as if bouncing off a trampoline. He stood stock-still for a moment in shock, his index finger pointed toward the ceiling as if to emphasize an upcoming rhetorical point. Rabbi Fink stared at him blankly. "And yet – he was an Elk!" Spivak said, his voice calmer now. "That's right – an Elk! Isn't that remarkable? Can you get a load of that? He loved it – being an Elk, I mean – the dancing and all. I thought he was crazy, I really did – but he adored it."

"Thank you, Leo, loving son of the deceased – thank you for sharing that with us," Rabbi Fink said. He flashed a beaming, insincere smile at Spivak, and then opened his prayer book as if looking for the proper place to reenter the service.

"Wait a second. One more thing, and I'll be finished," Spivak said to the rabbi. "I'm sorry, I should have mentioned this to you before, in the office." He turned back to the audience of mourners in the chapel. "Give me just a second here. I think he wanted to be a lawyer when he was a kid. It didn't work out, but that was what he dreamed of when he was young. He told me that once. Oh, and he loved sauerkraut. It was his favorite food, but it had to be ice cold or he wouldn't eat it. He loved borscht with sour cream, too. And he had a weakness for pretzels."

"Thank you very much, Leo. I'm moved by what you've said, and I'm sure everyone here is moved, as well," said Rabbi Fink. "And I'm glad you felt able to speak up this way." When he saw that Spivak had no immediate intention of stopping, the rabbi shut his prayer book, glanced briefly at his watch, and rolled his eyes.

"When I was a little boy we'd go to the swimming pool at the Jewish Community Center and play a game called King of the Corner," Spivak said. He inched toward the podium now, and rested a hand on it as he spoke. "It was my favorite game. My Dad would get in the water at the shallow end and wedge himself into a corner of the pool; he'd wrap his arms around this lip of tile so he had a good grip, and I'd try to pull on his legs to yank him out of that corner. He'd kick and splash, and I'd hang onto his legs and pull. He never seemed to get tired. We'd go for hours, and then whenever I wanted to play King of the Corner again, he'd always say okay."

Rabbi Fink cleared his throat. "Mr. Spivak? Are you finished now? We should move along," he said, and reached out a hand to caress Spivak's shoulder.

"I wish I'd remembered all of this earlier," Spivak said. "I just thought they'd want to know some of this stuff. Every year at Passover," he began – then, when he felt Rabbi Fink's fingers tighten slightly on his shoulder, he karate-chopped at them fiercely until they loosened their grip. "Every year at Passover," Spivak began again, "my Dad would go into a big harangue about leaving an extra wine glass on the table for the prophet Elijah. He'd tell me to keep my eye on the wine glass so I could watch Elijah come in and take a sip, and I'd try to keep my eye on it – I mean I'd watch it like a hawk – and somehow every year, every year without fail, at some point late in the seder after my attention had wandered, he'd cry, 'Look, Leo!' and there it would be, Elijah's wine glass, sitting there half empty. It used to knock my socks off, every year. He did that for me," he added. "He didn't believe in any of it. He didn't believe in a goddamn thing, but he did that for *me*. I don't know why he did. I think he wanted me to believe in something. It didn't work, but at least he tried." Spivak filled his lungs with air, and sighed out a deep breath.

At that moment Stan Marshak burst into the chapel through the back door, clapping his hands. "All right, everybody," he announced, "let all who mourn this man rise now to recite the Mourner's Kaddish. Up, up, up! We've got another service coming in at half past three, and we need to move forward, please. Let's keep it going, please, and thank you very much!" He glared at Spivak, then at Rabbi Fink.

Biting his lip, his head hung low and his cheeks stinging, Spivak resumed his place in the audience and stood with everyone else. He felt as if he were in kindergarten and had been caught poking Rabbi Fink in the ear with a crayon. It had been years since he'd heard the Kaddish – years, for that matter, since he'd stepped foot inside a synagogue –

but now as the meager, forlorn group of mourners began hesitantly to recite the words, the melody came back to him quite easily, and the words, as well: *Yiskadahl, v'yiskadosh, sh'may rabo*, all of it dredged up from some bittersweet well of memory inside him – the same place he kept all the Top Forty love songs from his youth. Not so bad for a bad Jew, he told himself. He could hum along, at least, and that had to count for something.

Inez stood by his side, tears streaming down her rough cheeks, leaving black mascara tracks through her rouge. She wasn't reciting the prayer; even with the transliteration spelled out in English on the facing page, how could she hope to wrap her lips around these unfamiliar guttural phrases? It must have sounded to her ears like a fitful effort to bring up phlegm. Spivak put a comforting arm around her shoulder and pulled her closer as he recited the Kaddish. She pressed against him, and in a moment it seemed to him that she'd melted into his side.

Although it was late afternoon, the drapes in their room were drawn when Spivak got back to the motel, and Rachel was deep asleep on the king-size bed in the cool darkness. He had to shake her roughly to wake her up.

"I'm back," he said. "I'm an orphan." He sat down heavily at the edge of the bed.

"How was it?" Rachel murmured. She rolled over and looked at him a moment, then switched on one of the bedside lamps.

"I don't know. It was okay," Spivak told her. He swung his legs up and lay back against the pillows, then he arranged his arms and legs just so, and stared up at the ceiling.

"You were gone a long time," she said in a tired voice. "I was worried."

The telephone rang on the nightstand.

"Don't answer it," Spivak said sharply, and Rachel pulled her hand back from the phone. He watched her intently; if she made a move for the phone, he was prepared to intercept her – to break her arm, if he had to.

"It might be Elena calling," Rachel said. "I called today and left a message for her to call. She'll be worried. Let me just – "

"No," Spivak said, and moved between Rachel and the phone. "No more phone calls. Let it ring."

And so it rang. The intensity of his gaze softened; he really wanted to tell Rachel about Rabbi Fink and that lame excuse for a eulogy, and about Marshak and his Out of Towner Special, and about Inez and the other widows and the miserable pack of *joskies* who'd showed up in their polyester *shmattes* to mourn his father. Most of all he wanted to tell her about the pine casket and the five hundred dollars.

The phone kept ringing. "Leo?" Rachel said, and put a hand on his arm. "Honey?"

If he could just get the part about the casket off his chest, he thought there was a chance he might be able to breathe again. He could just blurt it out, make a joke of it, even, and Rachel would tell him he'd done the right thing, he was sure, and he would know she was lying, but he could deal with that part, he really could. The part he couldn't deal with was that she'd know that he'd fucked up once again, and sometime soon he'd catch her looking at him with that expression he'd seen in her eyes before: *Leo, Leo, why are you such a shmuck?* And anyway, what was he supposed to do about it now? Was he supposed to exhume his father's body and confess his sins? Face it: the thing was over and done with. Finished. So why mention it to Rachel? Why even bring it up? What good could it possibly do?

"Leo? Speak to me, honey. C'mon," Rachel said. The phone abruptly stopped ringing, leaving a metallic, echoing silence in the room.

No, Spivak told himself, there wasn't anything to be done about it now. It was too late. And there was no going back, no second chance, no rewinding the tape and getting to do it all again: it was going to *stay* too late forever. Now he could finally get on with the business of living the rest of his life. The only hard part would be learning to breathe with this goddamn weight on his ribcage. The rest of it was going to be a piece of cake.

'Orita on the Road to Chimayó

LISA SANDLIN

When Good Friday fell in March, it often snowed, and next day the *New Mexican* ran photos of pilgrims trudging into the white flurry, heads bent, cold hands shoved up their sleeves. But this Friday landed three weeks into April. The sky glowed like a turquoise bowl, from the Sangres to the Jemez Mountains, over the piñon hills, over the tiny, toiling people. They streamed from the south, from Pojoaque and Santa Fe, even Albuquerque, walking the sides of the highway to keep out of the way of cars.

Back here, on this particular jog of a shortcut off U.S. 285, they had to keep out of the way of three young firemen who were running to Chimayó. The firemen wore gym shorts and football jerseys cut off at the ribs. One wore a turned-round *Lobos* cap. They had dark, slim-muscled legs without much hair, and their stomachs were flat now, but not for much longer. Their barrel chests would plump out. They called to people *Gangway*! or they ran around them so close that people jumped over, stumbling and sliding on the gritty shoulder.

The firemen hadn't yet caught up to Catherine Sachett, a woman with the long, sad face of an El Greco count. Catherine was dedicating the first mile of her pilgrimage to the exorcism of her ex-husband. She was well now, except for those traces of Pete. Her sickness and the loss of her breasts had just . . . erased him. First to go was his great jackass laugh, then eye contact, then his voice faded so that she kept after him, repeating, "What, babe?" He had managed to make love to her after the operation, give him that. And it wasn't that he turned her around; she liked it that way. It was how he touched her – his hands fast, lifeless, quickly withdrawn. Pulling up the sheet, she'd leaned against the headboard and asked him, "Where's my husband?" A few days later

Pete disappeared for real, giving Catherine, in a backhanded way, her lone advantage: her rage at him outweighed the fear of cancer.

She used to dress up in dreams – sequined minis, always Caribbean Blue – slip in the C-cup breast forms, and go kill Pete. Shooting him was good for her, she found: fury and pain swarmed from her belly, her forehead, from far down beneath her scars. She woke up with a wetness on her body, broken through the skin like dew.

Catherine sighed and shooed her ringless hands around. *Out of here, out.*

She'd promised her second mile to the sick people she visited now. To Loretta, Erlinda, and Roy, curled like children in wide white beds. And the third mile was for . . . In Mexican Spanish everything little – *chico* – can be made even littler. *Chiquito, chiquitito,* that just means something's really there. Catherine Sachett hardly knew it but she was walking a part – *lo más chiquitito* part – of the third mile for herself, because she was still alive.

Sweat from those running firemen flicked on Benny Ortiz, and he hurled them a few words. Benny was good-looking but jittery, a twenty-nine-year-old weightlifter with no Life Plan. Sometimes, really pumped, with four or five guys psyching him, he freaked himself – glided from under the iron and spread into the mirror's thin brightness. His mother thought he was walking the pilgrimage because her folded hands guilted him into it: let his father come back to them. Right. What Benny really wanted – what he'd ask for in Chimayó's little santuario – was the guts to tell his mother to give it up. Tune in. Get some strength. The old man wasn't ever coming back. Once, when Benny was still dumb, he'd gone to a house where his father was staying with a girl and her baby. He'd brought a bear for the kid; hey, it was his brother. And the girl – Benny could still picture her dead spider eyelashes – told him not to come around again. His father shrugged, winked, like he'd fix it later. Who's asking? Benny knew the rule: don't ask your father for nothing. He shot a swift finger to fireman number 19's back.

About that time, as Benny's finger still goosed #19, the wind jacked up. Light started sliding from the blue bowl sky.

Because the sky had darkened, it was easy to see the man fly up as the car veered to the shoulder and caught him. He was wearing a white shirt and a white straw cowboy hat like a real Mexican, and he sailed up in a gainer except his arms weren't tucked but flung out. He landed on his back well off the road, on a piece of ground tended by a tall piñon. The driver wavered, but then nosed the car – low-slung Buick, metallic green – back on the road and hit the gas.

Two of the firemen pirouetted in their tracks and took out after the Buick. The third, once he wasn't mesmerized by the flying man, spotted a roadside cross held up by some decent-sized rocks. Should he EMT the poor guy now or bust that fucker's back window? Smoke one *pow!* right down the pipe. "Hold on, don't move him!" he called, scooped up a rock and ran off.

Catherine Sachett found the victim first, on a hard swell of ground behind the piñon. She knelt beside the hurt young man, a boy really, of eighteen or nineteen. The next person to run up, a man about Pete's age but with an easy brow, took one look, repeated after Catherine, "Ambulance," and sprinted out toward U.S. 285 for help.

The hip was mangled, but worse, the boy seemed not to feel it. He didn't respond when she pressed her palm to his groin, through his raveled jeans, which were growing wet and red. He gazed up at Catherine as to a face in an alarming dream.

Aquí está, oh no, Brother Teo the historian, whom he'd always displeased. Though Brother begged him to memorize the blessed lives, the boy could never remember which saint had burned, which had been ripped by lions, which had her breasts sliced off, which sat old and feeble in the temple door repeating to the heedless, "Love one another." Brother Teo reported him to his mother. Then they exchanged expressions: Brother, eased, departing to coach the soccer team, and his mother's face drawn long and sad. When he saw how sad she looked, the boy thrashed.

With one hand, Catherine stroked his chest until he calmed and even smiled at her. With the other, she pressed a clean handkerchief to the bleeding. She didn't know much first aid, but growing up in south Texas had taught her some Spanish. The wind was rising; she bent close. "*Dime, chulo, cómo te llamas?*"

The boy told her, his tone straining a beat, urgent, and he gestured. Verdiano, his name was Verdiano. When he flashed a nervous smile, his kid mustache looked even wispier, like a teenage Zorro's, and he stared up at her with eyes that were big, dark, and clear. But he didn't know where he was – she could see that. Other pilgrims discarded their staffs in the ditch, tracked over from the road, and gathered by the piñon, asking questions. One old man, his cheek stapled in on itself in a deep scar, crossed himself and hunkered down at the boy's head. "Hey, let's get the wind off him," he said. Those who'd happened to be on this shortcut shuffled together, elbow to elbow.

Turning his head slowly to take them in, Verdiano murmured, "*Frío, hermanos.*" He spoke so familiarly that people hurried to pull off sweat-shirts and windbreakers. When Benny Ortiz stripped off his MANPOWER T-shirt, a couple of women raised their eyebrows. The staple-faced man, already squatting, took it on himself to receive the clothes, duckwalked a step and spread them on the boy. He tucked some gray sleeves beneath the boy's worn-down Chihuahua heels.

Swiveling his head again, Verdiano addressed them "Gracias . . . gra-cias." He fixed on Catherine. Her hollow cheeks, how lines were worn all around her eyes but not her mouth, made him comfortable. Catherine told the bystanders, "He says he could have lived in the trailer with the others, but to save rent he slept in the restaurant's storeroom, so then the only thing anyone tells him is what table to clean. He says he hasn't talked in six months."

"Yo, Ms. U.N.," Benny growled, "save the translation." Benny didn't usually put himself forward, didn't pay. But he was ruffled. He was upset. Who died and left her boss? Pectorals bulged as he knelt down, squinting at the Anglo woman. Bony, they never stopped dieting. Raw eyelids. "You a nurse?" he asked her. To keep focused, he really bored in on her. Because there was one little more thing – the way the boy said *Cold, brothers* barbed his chest. Benny'd been hit by an urge he didn't know what to do with: to make sure the kid got warm now, got an ambulance, got a doctor with some brains.

"I'm not a nurse," the woman said. Benny craned around at the bystanders. "Anybody here a doctor or a EMT?" Everybody shook their heads. "Bunch of plumbers," he muttered; the woman heard. She cocked her head at him, asking, "Look, you know first aid? You want to do this?" Benny jerked back – hey, not him. And for making fun of how he didn't know anything, he'd give her the needle back. He jutted his chin at her. "You got a pretty good hold of his privates there."

She spread her fingers so the blood seeped through, then closed them up again. People winced and murmured over the injured boy, whose olive face was a shocky white, like they were seeing it by moonlight. The handkerchief was soaked. A woman in a sunhat offered another.

Benny passed the handkerchief, then spoke in the kid's ear. He couldn't keep the Anglo woman from hearing, but he could let her know she wasn't included in any way. "Bro. Ambulance'll be here soon. Don't talk." The kid nodded at the English, smiled, turned his head until he located Catherine's sad face, and began to talk.

They were startled by the boy's thanking them for listening. "*Es que . . .*" he felt like talking, he said. He looked from Catherine to Benny and his eyes softened and he choked. The onlookers flinched, but no blood came up. He just cleared his throat and started to talk again. He told them about his family back in Mexico, his four little sisters and his mother who was tranquil now that an aunt had died and left them two rooms in her house. He told about his *novia*, his sweetheart, who was sick. She coughed too much and when the wind blew, she had to lie down. Her name was Ana Luz, and she sewed Ford seat covers, Verdiano said, and though he had family, she had no one but him. "Thank you, señores, but I'd better stand up now." *'Orita*, he said, meaning he'd stand right this second, in this tiny bit of now. His head lifted as though the rest of him would follow but it didn't and his mauve lips formed an O. For a moment, they thought he might cry out.

Verdiano knew he had something urgent to do, but not what it was. Then Brother Teo's exasperated voice lanced his confusion. Staving him off respectfully with *Sí, Hermano*, oblivious of his own fingers rising in a jerky ripple, Verdiano cast about in his jumbled mind for a saint to report on. Who came to his aid, inching forward with eager, earthy hands, but the least likely of luminaries – Simplicio.

Simplicio was a kitchen worker, just like him. Simplicio was a kitchen worker to the priests, but he took no vow himself because he loved a girl and wanted her, and besides, he was mostly Indian and couldn't read.

Benny, who'd ordered Verdiano to "C'mon lay back, man," recoiled at the sight of the kid's hands. They reminded him of caught fish quivering. "Hold here," the bony woman urged him to take over. Why'd she do that if she thought he was so stupid? Benny held his breath when he

received the rag, feeling the trickle, the suggestion of a beat *thum* . . .
thum . . . under his pressure. The woman captured Verdiano's hands
and smoothed them down. She asked the whole crowd to go through
what pockets they had left for another handkerchief and then resumed
pressing the wound. She passed the soaked rag to Benny, who couldn't
help squeezing it and shuddering before he threw it away.

"*Una vez*," Verdiano said, when the cook's knife slipped and cut the
back of his hand and the little strings there, Simplicio put down some
carrots and clamped the cook's hand between his. When he let go, the
strings were whole and the bloody cut sealed pale pink like baby veal.
"*Hijo*, like veal!" exclaimed the staple-cheeked man, and the boy turned
up his eyes toward the voice and smiled. "Sí, señor," he said. "*Y otra
vez*," the cook's helper spilled boiling fat on his shins and feet. Simplicio
knelt down and blew on the burns. He rubbed some spit on the blisters.
They went away. That time the cook told the head priest, who told the
bishop, who called Simplicio before him and ordered him not to do
those things anymore.

Wind tossed a piece of Verdiano's hair on and off his forehead until
Benny licked his fingers and combed it back. Every so often, another
curious pilgrim would cross to see what was happening behind the
piñon, see the boy on the ground and stay. At first the people had
shifted foot to foot, anxious. They scanned the sea of hills, the piñons,
the arroyos, stared hard toward the highway they knew was on the other
side. But then they'd just crept in closer to hear the story. What else
could they do? All run off in a crowd to get an ambulance? If somebody
didn't hear a phrase, Catherine repeated it in English. Verdiano would
wait for her to finish before he went on. Talking calmed him, though
the corners of his mouth crusted white.

One day when Simplicio was coming back from the garden with
onions and garlic, he heard a scream from the church wall where some
masons were plastering on a scaffold. A man was falling, so Simplicio
stopped him. He didn't save him because he'd been forbidden. He just
stopped him upside down in the air.

"How did he do that, Verdiano?" asked the woman in the sunhat.

"*Lo mismo*," the boy said, licking his lips. The same as before. It was
good to hear his name called. He breathed in deeply, breathed out
deeply, like a fat man after a fine dinner, and said it again, "It's so good

to hear my name." The little wind-tears flying out of his eyes roused a world in the sunhat woman's head. She should have had children this boy's age. Those children, her own blood, now found themselves alone, hurt in some strange land, like this boy. Tenderly she promised, "Listen, Verdiano, we're here." The staple-faced man asked, "So what happened? Did Simplicio save the mason?" The woman jabbed him with her elbow. "Let the boy save his strength."

Verdiano meant to gesture as he spoke, but his hands moved apart from his words; that frustrated him. He shrugged and laid them on his chest, as though they were gloves he'd taken off.

Simplicio had to go ask permission to save the man, Verdiano told them. He was only a kitchen worker. So the mason stayed in the air upside down while Simplicio found the bishop. When he doffed his hat, he saw how his hands were dirty from the garden; abashed, he hid them behind his back. He would obey his superior. Yet . . . he wanted to save the mason. The man surely had a wife and children to feed. And then. Then he craved . . . Say the truth, Simplicio: you crave the time during these occasions when all runs out and all flows in.

Simplicio lowered his head and advanced. "Do I save this man, your grace, or let him fall?" he asked the bishop.

"I told you to stop doing these things," the bishop said.

Simplicio begged, "I can't help it, holiness, they go where I do."

"Nevertheless, you don't have qualifications."

Verdiano took a long time saying that word *cal-i-fi-ca-ci-o-nes*; once he'd gotten it out, he seemed spent. His lids fluttered, showing the whites of his eyes. People groaned.

Benny cursed, thumped Verdiano's chest, hollered at the woman across from him. "Fix it, fix it, lady, get a new rag or somethin'!" She looked at him – *híjole*, what eyes, like bruises – unzipped her yellow sweatshirt, reached under a T-shirt, and handed him one of two round pink jobs with pooches like sofa buttons on them. She applied the other to the bleeding – it fit perfect.

Connection, Catherine knew too much about why people stick around not to sense a connection. She'd seen them, patients who'd become friends, holding on at seventy-nine pounds, waiting for the grandbaby, the son on the midnight plane. Catherine cupped her free hand to call him back. "Verdiano!" She had to yell. "Verdiano! This long story! Do you mean you left your *novia* in Mexico waiting for you?"

Verdiano returned. "But that's it," he said. "*Mi novia*, I left her in Mexico, hanging in the air." The chalk corners of his mouth frowned in dismay, stretching the wispy mustache. The clear brown eyes spilled.

Catherine understood the beauty of resignation – a way to go forward – but now she found herself coughing up its other half, the beauty of not being resigned. As a plain matter of fact, she would not allow this situation to exist. "Do something," she commanded to no one in particular. The wind whistled; a fat, wet snowflake landed on the piñon. She looked at the muscled man across from her.

Benny's features had gone a little slack after he verified to himself what exactly the woman had given him: the pink job was supposed to be her breast. The woman's gaze seared each bystander and returned to the staple-faced man at Verdiano's head. "Do something for this boy!" she shouted.

The crowd began emptying their pockets, but because they were pilgrims that day on a route with nothing to buy, they didn't have much money. Benny nodded gruffly toward Catherine, so they stuffed the money for Verdiano in her yellow sweatshirt pocket.

He said, "Look, bro. That's for your girl," but Verdiano didn't understand so he put it in Spanish "*Pa tu novia*," and then Verdiano tried to touch his white cowboy hat in thanks but it had blown away long since, and besides, his hands were gone. He only closed his eyes, showing how long and thick his black lashes grew, and opened them again.

The old man with the scar still wanted to know about Simplicio, did he save the mason or not?

Benny crowded the narrow old face. "Cost you to find out, *jodido*. How much you got?"

The sunhat woman raised a dyed eyebrow and said about the old man, her husband, "*¿Ése?* He owns seventy-nine apartments in Santa Fe."

"*Cállete, mujer*, what does that have to do with anything?"

"And five houses all on the same street. *Y* one *por acá* way up on the hill. That one has a historical plaque."

The old man blinked and shifted a little in the wind, like a stunted piñon.

Benny pulled out his pockets so the wind would flap them. "Anybody else here got money?" Everybody said No, Uh uh, that was it. They'd given it all. For a minute, like he was straining at the limit – two hundred seventy-five pounds of iron chin high and wobbling – Benny couldn't figure what to do. But then *Eeee, this is it I'm a genius*, he loomed over the old man. All the shivering still didn't make his muscles look any smaller. "Give him a house, Mr. Monopoly."

"A house?" The old man looked at the people, and they looked back at him. "Give my house? That I worked all my life for?" He thrust out his hands so they could see the pad of callus from gripping the trowel, but that was years ago and the people saw only smooth skin.

"Well, let him live there, then. Give him some rent."

"Yeah, rent." "Rent's okay." People's heads were bobbing.

The old man's eyes got slick and his face as chamisa green as the spring roadside. He held his stomach down with both hands. All the time his face was working, rubbery, like the staple was being pried open.

"Evaristo, *qué pasa?*" cried his wife. "What's happening with you?"

Coughing, Evaristo managed to sputter, "A year's free rent."

Benny gave him some breathing room, smiled. "No, you don't get it. As long as he wants."

Evaristo grunted. "It hurts like I swallowed a cleaver, five years," he said.

The bystanders rumbled approval. Catherine informed Verdiano, whose face, by now as white as a Japanese dancing girl's, didn't change. Two more spring snowflakes lumbered down. Everybody hugged their own arms. "Look, take this." Catherine gave her sweatshirt to Benny who tugged it on, the cuffs hitting him mid-arm. He zipped it up tight, and by main force did not look to see how level the pocket on her T-shirt lay.

Once he'd made the hard decision, old Evaristo's next one was surer. "He can live in the little casita on Scissors Street, the first one I bought. Let him bring his *novia* there. *Cómo se llama?*"

All the rest had gone past Verdiano like so much chatter, like restaurant conversation; he couldn't quite attend to it. But *novia*, Verdiano heard. "Ana Luz," he said.

"No, not that house!" Evaristo's wife had his number. "That one is falling down."

"Hey, a little mud." Her husband threw out his arms. "I will provide." Saying it, he was an actor, but with the little sentiment echoing, bouncing off people's impressed faces, he began to believe, *un poco, un poquito*, you know? He liked how it sounded. He cleared a single snowflake above Verdiano's head. "I will provide."

"They'll have children, Evaristo." His wife enlarged the world – now Verdiano and Ana Luz had dear little babies the ages her grandchildren should be. "Get them a new roof, a washer-dryer. Some carpet, *entiendes*? Some of that champagne color, it goes with everything."

Evaristo's half-face bloomed out. "No problem."

Benny grumbled, "Okay, you paid, you can ask now."

The old man was blank. Ask what? Ay, the curse of old age, he couldn't remember anything he needed to know. "Ask what?" he said.

"The story. Did Simplicio get the mason down or not?"

So they turned to Verdiano and asked him, and he was about to answer when the car drove up.

A green Buick with the back window smashed coasted to a stop by the ditch. Those runner firemen, they'd caught up to her. One scared her foot off the gas with a rock hurled through her rear window; the other two ran alongside until the car stopped rolling. They had to make her raise her head off the wheel and hear what they were telling her. They had to get her to unlock a door. They had to talk her into unclenching her fist and giving them the car keys. It took some time but finally they'd made her do all those things. Then they slid in and turned the car around.

Three men in wet gym shorts lunged out the doors and dragged over a girl by the tender part of her arm. The crowd melted back, all except Evaristo's wife who pointed a red finger, "*Mira*! Look at the blood on her headlight. Look at the dent! It was her, all right." A hissing noise came from the people and just then a cop car approached and they cheered. "Hey! Hey! Here they come," people yelled, and "It's about time," and "Where's the ambulance?" but even though a fireman loped out from behind the piñon, semaphoring and whistling, the cop car drove right by. "Eeee, those guys are more stupid than dirt," the fireman said. He left the girl and took off chasing the cruiser.

Another fireman hauled her through the crowd of people right up to the hurt boy. She took a lot of little steps because her white lace mini cut any natural stride and her white high heels made her sink and trip over the uneven ground. A second after the girl stumbled by, they could smell her. She smelled like piña coladas and peach daiquiris and crème de menthe with shaved chocolate and amaretto sours with extra cherry juice. She stared down at Verdiano, her huge brown eyes smudged all around with flicks of mascara.

Nobody said anything. Some of them stood on their toes to see what she was going to do. They thought the girl would fall on her knees in her white Easter mini, clench her hands, and cry. Say she didn't see him. Say it was an accident, she didn't mean to hit him. Never in a million years did she . . . that's what they were expecting. But the girl just curled her lip, breathed through her mouth, and tried to back up. Her wide eyes kept jerking away from the boy on the ground to the people around her. She twisted her head like someone was poking her with a stick.

Finally a fireman narrowed one eye and nodded his heavy head two or three times to show how serious he was. "If he dies, you're a murderer," he pronounced to the girl. The bystanders agreed with him. They had some names for her, and they weren't just mumbling. They were making sure she heard. Somebody reached past the fireman and shoved her. "Hey, don't do that," another person said and shoved her back. Evaristo's wife dug two red fingernails into the girl's lace shoulder blades, giving her a pinch. This one here, this very girl broke her children, never even looked back as they bled on the road. "Little puta hit and run," she accused. The girl whimpered.

The girl and the whimper made Benny Ortiz kind of sick. Couple a years ago it might have been fun to shove her, but not now. The kid was still going to be lying here with most of his blood leaked out, wasn't he? Benny made the first speech of his life. "Hey, back off," he told the bystanders. "She's lost it. Like if your dad was poundin' your mom and you climbed up in a chair and clocked him with the steam iron, then when he woke up you swore you didn't. I mean, you stared at that iron, and you truly believed you didn't. It's too big to handle. Look at her, man, she ain't got her lights on."

But nobody paid much attention. "*Mira*, kid," a fireman hooked his thumb at the girl and spoke past Benny to Verdiano. "This is the one did it to you." People stopped muttering and watched to see what would happen.

Verdiano opened his velvet eyes on the girl. Pink, the most delicate pink, a drop of red in an ocean of white, tinged his cheeks.

"Ana Luz," he said.

The fireman yelled in frustration. "No, no, man, wake up! This is the one hit you!"

"Ana Luz, I can smell your cough syrup."

The girl surged back, but the fireman had her clamped.

"It's good you drank it because the wind is blowing."

She shook her head, her pretty face contorted.

The sunhat woman cried, "Little bitch hit and run! You ought to get down on your knees and beg him you're sorry." With that, the woman stepped up and pushed her to her knees, so that when she fell forward the girl's black-streaked cheek touched the boy's white one.

Verdiano's eyes glittered. His chin was trembling. Here she was, his *novia*, all dressed up. After a grinding day shift, she must have sneaked in at night to make this dress. He could see how it must have been. Ana Luz with her bowed neck, hiding far in the back where the seat cover foreman never inspected, her foot speeding the machine's pedal. For her health, for the bounty of her love, he had walked the pilgrimage – and now this. How had she managed to find him? Softly, through a froth of rosy bubbles, Verdiano praised her name.

"Ana Luz. Who could have done this but you?"

It was like the girl had been electrocuted. She leapt to her feet and broke the fireman's grasp. Flailing her arms, she beat her way through the bystanders, who reeled back from her blows, her scent of curdled sugar. She made it to her car, where a fireman leaned leering against the Buick's door. The girl threw back her head and howled.

Evaristo hoisted himself up and limped over to her. First he got her by the shoulders and gave her a few shakes, then he talked to her. After a while he took the girl's arm like they were crossing a busy street or he was escorting her down the aisle in her soiled Barbie bride dress, and he walked her back to Verdiano.

The girl's face kept changing. Her eyebrows would draw together and apart; from wide and blank her eyes would focus. Finally her shoulders sagged. She wiped her face with her hands, looked down at Verdiano, and her red lips parted like a little slit heart.

Verdiano's brow furrowed the slightest degree, as if he were listening hard. He breathed in, eating the rose bubbles. Then, like someone taking his picture told him to stop goofing around and get serious, c'mon freeze for the camera, he was still. People drew forward, waiting for him to let the breath out, but Verdiano kept it.

The girl's eyes rolled back then, and they had to grab her and hold her for maybe ten more minutes until the cop car, with ambulance trailing, screeched up in a fishtail stop. The doors burst open, and two state cops sprang out. Taking his time, a fireman slid from the back seat and bent over to massage his hamstrings.

Flashing and whooping ("Aw, man, what *for*," said a fireman), the ambulance sprayed them with grit and pebbles. People kneeled down where Verdiano had lain, picking through the pile of sweatshirts and windbreakers to find their own. Shrinking the world to regular size, oh much better, Evaristo's wife sent a prayer for the *pobrecito*, the little *mojado* dead so young, and set about provoking her husband. "*Bueno*, that dump on Scissors Street, you got your rent back, are you happy?"

Evaristo blew on his hands and rubbed them, rubbed his face, yeah, he was still there. "Hey don't call it that, okay?" His first house. A million adobes he'd laid, a million cinderblocks fit and grouted, miles of scaffolding climbed, saving up for it, his little cornerstone. Yeah, he decided, it was a terrible thing what happened here but not so terrible to have his casita back.

Benny peeled off Catherine's yellow sweatshirt; it was way stretched out. He found his bloody T-shirt in the pile. People who'd carried staffs retrieved them from the ditch and stood by the road, trying to clear their heads before they continued their walk.

Who felt like going seven more miles to Chimayó? Nobody, but were they supposed to turn around and walk back to Santa Fe? With all the world heading the other way? Besides, the day was warming up again. The wind had dropped. The sky was lightening into blue ribbons, and see – there on the wavy piñon hills a little gold was shining. "Poor kid," a fireman crossed himself before jamming on his *Lobos* cap. Another one slapped his flat belly and did a few calf stretches. They all ran off, slim muscles prancing. "*Híjole*," a voice carried back to the last two left, "this damn weather is so crazy."

Catherine lowered herself to the roadside and propped her head on her knees. She needed to sit a while, allow her breath to calm. As she wiped her streaming face with the hem of her T-shirt, she saw the muscleman shoot her a glance. He stood in the dusty road shifting his weight, rubbing his forehead. Then he squatted down, and barely meeting her eyes, held out her pink breast. Because his face was so serious, she didn't laugh – though it was funny how he handled the foam rubber. With unease but with respect. Reluctant but wanting something – like Simplicio advancing on the bishop.

When the woman smiled to herself, Benny found her face less weary, her eyelids less scraped, less blue, her wide mouth harmless. In order to stick the breast in her sweatshirt pocket, she had to remove a wad of money. "Oh no," she said, fanning the bills of Verdiano's collection.

An idea struck Benny – it was just that *'orita*, he couldn't shape words – could they find Ana Luz? Because the money belonged to Ana Luz, and of all the people there, Verdiano belonged to him and to this woman. She had no breasts. She really had no breasts. Benny was having this crazy sensation of his hand reaching out, simultaneously seeing in his mind how it would be – smooth, sealed, her pink chest. Like it would hurt him to touch it. And what was weird was he didn't flinch, didn't grimace. She was clasping his wrist, whether to slap him back or to keep him with her, Benny couldn't say. He couldn't get out even one word.

It was like he'd been falling, hurtling down headfirst, only to be stopped mid-air and set down . . . shocked, dizzy, dumbfounded by the rescue.

St. Anthony and the Fish

RON BLOCK

The road where Ned had discovered the nun connected Dunning, Nebraska, to Arnold, Nebraska. Rand McNally took it off their maps a few years back, but the road's still there, and it's still got a pretty good surface. It runs by Ned's farm and ranch and two others. There's not a reason in the world for anyone who's not from around there even to be on this road unless they're lost. The way Ned had it figured, the nun must have been driving through late at night because she was there in his driveway at eight in the morning, sleeping in the front seat. She was already sweating. Her license plate said Pennsylvania, which made no sense at all, no matter which way you were going.

"You got problems, ma'am?"

She rolled down the window a crack and said, "I've run out of gas."

"Well, that don't sound too serious," Ned said. "But I do think your problems will be a lot worse if you stay in that car with the windows rolled up." Ned considered the fact that what he had just said perhaps sounded like a threat, so he added, "What I mean is that you might get heatstroke."

He caught a glance of himself in her window: he hadn't shaved in days – saw no need to, really, since his wife left him, and he hadn't felt much need even before.

"I'm fine," the woman said. She kept the window up, the doors locked.

He tested the weight of the gasoline can in the back of his pickup and said, "I can get you back on the road, but I'm going to have to go into town for gas. I'd siphon you off some of my own, but the last time I did that I nearly went blind, so if you don't mind I'd rather not take the chance. You can ride with me if you want. Be a damn sight cooler than sitting in that car with the windows rolled up."

"I can wait," she said. She was dressed in a heavy black dress buttoned

273

up to her neck, with a white collar and white cuffs, all soaked through with her sweat.

"Well, I'm serious, ma'am. If you feel like you're getting too hot, you'd better walk up to my house. Door's open. Don't take any chances, okay? At least get out into the open air, maybe sit in the shade of that tree over there." He pointed at the tree, the only tree.

"I'll be fine," she said, and rolled up the window.

In town, Ned pulled into the gas station where a large-headed chocolate Labrador named Walrus was sleeping in the shade of the pumps. Ned knew the name of every man, woman, and dog in this town. The owner of the station was on his back with his head under a car, so after Ned filled up the red gas can, he walked over and grabbed the man's ankle, causing him to thrash and bump his head. "Damn it, Ned!"

"Sam? If I were a criminal, you'd be dead. Is your cash register open?"

Sam rolled out from under the car and said, "I hope to hell you have exact change. I haven't had time to get to the bank."

"You mean to tell me you don't even have change for just a ten?"

"Just write yourself a tab, will ya? I'll bill you when it's enough to be worth my time." Sam slid back under the car.

"I've got a woman out in front of my farm who's out of gas," Ned said. "I'm helpin' her get back on the road. It's too wet to mow hay anyway. Fact is, from the look of her, I think she's a nun. I'll put a six-pack of soda pop on my tab, too, if that's okay."

Ned wrote up his tab and put that in the empty cash register. Sam hadn't been kidding. He put the six-pack in his beer cooler. The ice had turned to water overnight, but it was still cold, the beer cans resting at the bottom like bright stones in a clear pond. Before going back to his farm, he stopped by the Cattlemen's Cafe to pick up something for the nun to eat, experiencing a great deal of indecision about what kind of thing he should feed a nun. The waitress suggested tuna melts. By the time he got back to her car, she wasn't in it. Squinting his eyes, he scanned the horizon. She wasn't under that shade tree, either, and he didn't see any black shape hunkered over in the grass. He drove up to his house, but she wasn't anywhere about. He might have considered this whole episode a dream or such except for the car. The car was still there. So where in the hell was that nun? Finally he walked into his barn, and there she was, seeming to be asleep and lying in the hay. "Ma'am? Are you all right? You okay?"

When he tried to help her up she called out, "Oh! Lord! Oh!"

"Land sakes, I'm not goin' to hurt ya. You're gonna hurt yourself if we don't get you in the house, so don't argue."

She blinked and looked around. "I thought this *was* your house," she said.

"This is my damn barn, lady," he said, growing impatient. "I don't know where you come from or where you got the idea that we put hay in our houses, but I've got half an idea to pack you in ice as soon as we get you inside."

With his shoulder under her arm, he walked her across his farm lot. Occasionally, she started and tried to pull and twist away from him. "I'm gonna run a cold bath, " he said, deciding to be tough about it. "And you're gonna get in."

"Please," she said, "no, please."

"I'll put you in, dress and all if I have to. And I've got soda pop here, too," he said. "But drink it slow or you'll get a headache."

He got the nun a soda out of the cooler and, after pausing for a second, decided he wanted a beer. The woman stared at him while he drank it. "It's maybe a bit early," he said. "I'll own up to that. But you've given me quite the scare." She had a look about her like she hadn't been outside in a year, like she could tan in the moonlight. Her skin had a faint blue, almost transparent look to it.

Ned took some steel wool into the bathroom with some dish detergent. The tub was almost gray and black, and he had to work quite a while before it was acceptable to anyone but himself. He could hear his floors creak as the woman finally got up and started moving around. When he'd finished scrubbing, he found that the woman was staring at a photograph of his ex-wife.

"I'm divorced," Ned explained. "I'm not proud of it, but that's how it is."

While she was bathing, he took the opportunity to feed his pigs and make sure they had enough water. The pigs were all waiting on one side of the pen. Their breakfast was long overdue and they knew it. They were mad at him. They nudged and pushed, nipping at his pant legs.

Ned's wife had left him for many good reasons, but none of them serious. Simply enough, Ned wasn't a very clean man. He wasn't a very smart man. His farm never made much money, but he didn't have any debts. He drank too much, but not much too much, and he wasn't mean about it. He worked hard, from sunup to sundown. Winters he didn't have much work to do, so he made work, but none of it was geared to making life any more comfortable. He mended fences and he checked on his cattle. He was a dull man, maybe. His wife really had only one friend in town, and when that friend moved away, their life together fell apart. It wasn't really that nasty a divorce. His wife moved away more to be closer to her friend than to get away from him. She still liked him and told him so whenever she wrote him, which wasn't very much. And so the main reason why his wife left him was that their hometown had little to offer, and Ned did little to add to the nothing. A few more inches of rain each year and maybe they would have had something. A little trip now and again – even to the Black Hills – might have helped, too.

At night, sometimes, Ned could feel that nothing creep right up to the house and almost stare in the windows. In the morning Ned could still feel the nothing hanging around, like the old men in the Cattlemen's Cafe. It didn't bother him, though. Nothing-to-do was like room temperature to him. But in a way he felt sorry that his wife had moved out before this nun had showed up. This was the kind of thing his wife always looked forward to happening, when it never did. Not that she wanted to get a visit from a nun specifically, she just wanted a change of some kind, any change, really. Ned couldn't understand this, even though he wanted to. He couldn't understand wanting a change for its own sake. It made no difference to him. It was like some strange food that he never acquired a taste for, and so he never craved it, never missed it.

For a long time after getting out of the tub and dressed again, the nun surveyed the living room, occasionally sniffing at the air. Watching her, Ned became aware of whatever she was looking at. There were Christmas cards from many years back, magazines his wife subscribed to that he hadn't cleared away, junk mail opened by his ex-wife's hand with the unopened junk mail piled on top of it. Ned saw that anyone with a detective's mind could pinpoint the month and year when his wife got fed up and left. All the clues were here.

"I don't keep a very clean house," he finally said. She smiled and continued to look around. There were mourning doves moaning in the yard, cows moaning farther away. Ned became aware of what sounds she'd hear, what smells she might smell. She walked to the window and opened the curtain, and sunlight fell into the room.

"Rained here all last week," Ned said. "Kept me out of the fields or else I'd be mowing hay right now. It's gonna make a good second cutting, though."

She grew very still as she stood in the sunlight, which was streaming with dust.

"Yes?" she said. At first Ned thought that she was talking to him, but then she again said, "Yes?" and he hadn't asked her anything. She closed her eyes and put her arms out. With her standing there in the stream of sunlight, he felt like he was watching an old home movie of someone he was supposed to know but didn't recognize anymore. With his parents dead, his wife gone, there was no one he could even ask about it. She turned and looked at him. At that moment, he realized that she hadn't looked at him directly before. Suddenly she reached out to touch his forehead, and he stepped back from her, too shocked to do anything but smile.

Ned took a load of hay out to his pasture and spread it on the ground for the cattle there. It was hot, an unusually muggy day, and the air buzzed with cicadas. Grasshoppers splashed around his legs as if they'd been riled up by the recent rains. He drove across his field and discovered a ruptured fence line, which he mended. In this field there was a huge puddle that wasn't there a week ago. There were sandpipers strutting on the shore, and there were cattle in the water up to their knees. At the end of the day, he drove back to his house, seeing her car still in the driveway. She was cleaning his kitchen. He didn't know what else to do except offer her a room for the night, although it bothered him when he heard her praying out loud, at the top of her voice. At one point, he woke up with a jolt, because he thought she was praying right over his bed.

The next morning, by the time he got up, she was already making breakfast. When he came into his house later that afternoon, the living room was full of light. She showed him an old cathedral-like radio she discovered in the basement, which turned out to work just fine, pulling in stations from far away, and she stayed another night. The next day, she showed him an old farm tool she discovered in a shed nearly lost in the cedars and underbrush of the shelterbelt. He told her it was an old-time corn planter. "It's what my grandfather used when they still planted corn by hand," he said. "I'd never bothered to plant corn about here myself because it'd just shrivel up anyway. It's too dry."

"But this tool, can it still be used?"

"Well, sure, but it's way too late to plant corn," he said.

The next day he discovered that she'd found a bag of old seed corn in the barn, and she was planting this corn right next to his house. It bothered him. He didn't like to see her work as hard as this and all for nothing. Of course as the weeks passed there was talk around town about this guest he had. Sam gave him strange looks, and whenever he walked into the Cattlemen's Cafe the crowd went silent, but soon enough it seemed natural that she was there. Most nights when he came home from the fields, she would be out walking about in his pasture. Her hands would be clasped behind her back as if she were thinking about something. Or she'd be out near that pond that had risen with the recent rains, staring at the water. When she'd see him, she'd wave, and start on back. After a while, she started talking to him. She started slowly at first, as if she weren't that used to it, but then she started talking a lot. She told him about her order, its mission, their silences and songs. Ever since she was a child she had planned to be a nun, she said. She was frequently disappointed. Work was prayer, she said. Her greatest temptation was that she longed to be extraordinary.

Sometimes after supper, she'd show him something she'd discovered in his attic or basement or one of the extra rooms that had filled up with junk over the years. Almost every day, she found whatnots and keepsakes that she packed into the china cabinet where the china had long ago been harvested for everyday use. As the summer wore on, the hay was thick, the cattle were fat. More rain than he remembered in years, and the pond in his pasture had become the habitat for pelicans, beautiful white pelicans.

What's more, the old seed corn she had planted was starting to grow. No way would it mature, but that hardly seemed to matter. For the first time, as long as he could remember, Ned wondered what would happen next. He felt ill at ease but in a pleasurable way, as if he were letting a horse he was riding run as fast as it wanted. One night she asked him if he believed in miracles, if he knew what they were. He had to admit he'd never given it much thought. In his life, it had been more a matter of taking day by day and accepting what came. She laughed when he told her that, and then she told him the story of a man who couldn't stop preaching. Whenever people gathered around him, he preached to them. He couldn't help it. One day he traveled to a deserted shore to rest his voice, but when he saw the fish he started preaching to them, too. He couldn't help preaching, and the fish couldn't help listening, their heads poking out of the water to listen, their pink lips puckering as they concentrated on his words.

He smiled and nodded, more at the joy she took in telling the story than the story itself. In fact, he didn't really know if he understood her meaning. But that didn't mean the story had no effect on him. In fact, ever since first hearing that story, he started to wonder if there were fish in his cattle pond. The pelicans seemed to think so. They stepped lightly on the shoreline and studied the water, and every time he saw this, he thought about her story.

As the summer passed, he ordered chicks through the mail for the first time in years, and they all survived shipment. Cats wandered onto the farm and stuck around. When the fall came, the pelicans left. The pond froze over, and he was glad for that. It would keep its secrets locked up through the winter. Usually he didn't have much to do in the winter unless he had cattle and pigs. That winter he sold them off, the chickens too, so he could spend more time working on his house. When he tore out the old lead pipes, he found the wedding ring of his great-grandmother, caught in a water trap. When he moved the ancient refrigerator, he found an old closet door behind it. There was a wedding dress inside, his great-grandmother's wedding dress, and layette gowns and bonnets and booties. Without her he would not have known these words.

One day in February she began packing her car. He followed her around the house, letting her pile her few possessions into his arms, and when they were finished, she said to him, "Ned, you're a good man, but I don't think you even know what that is." She reached out and touched his cheek, and he blushed, his face continuing to feel warm in the cold as he watched her drive off. She left fresh tracks in the snow. Darkness fell. He tried to make himself a supper. He burned his eggs. He noticed that the bread had molded and the milk was rancid. He noticed that the melting snow from his boots had soiled the carpet. He was afraid that his house was returning, almost before his eyes, to the state it had been in before she arrived. Later he walked out to the frozen cattle pond where they had walked almost every night. He looked for fish frozen in the ice, their heads sticking out, their mouths open in astonishment.

He knew she was gone for good when she hadn't returned by midnight. The farm was empty. Even the cats that made their summer appearance had drifted away, and the nothing that had always been just outside his window had finally made itself at home. He stayed up late, listening to the wind, waiting for it to speak to him. He wrote a letter to his friend Sam. "All the cattle are gone, the pigs and chickens, too," he wrote. All at once he knew that he had been preparing for this moment, selling his farm off piece by piece. "I'm gonna be gone awhile, too, so look in on the house every once in a while if you can. Make sure it doesn't leak. I'd hate to see all my good work spoiled."

At the first sunlight, the snow a pale red, the sky a deep blue, he carried a bag out to his pickup and drove away, making more fresh tracks. Hers had already been covered over, since it had been snowing all night. He did not know where he was going or how he would find her. As he drove through town, he saw that there was nobody on the street. He stopped at Sam's Service Station and left his note on the door, and he noticed that the old Labrador, Walrus, was standing on the wide street looking at something that he couldn't see, the snow coming down, seeming to circle its giant head. Ned took this as a sign: the dog was staring down the town's only road, so he followed it. He drove forever. Small creatures came out of the fields, came right up to the road to watch him drive past. There were wild geese flying ahead of him, guiding him. There were sundogs in the sky above him. There was a warm wind rushing out before him, brushing the new snow out of his path.

This Is the Last of the Nice

BRENT SPENCER

I am a man of mild manner. But lately I've been a little unwell, a little punk, a little – you know – crazy. Not Patsy Cline crazy. Not thrill-kill crazy. Just crazy crazy. Hell, I don't hang from a flagpole forty stories up, or anything close. What I am is tired. Very, very tired. It's the economy. It's the greenhouse effect. It's the millennium. But it sure the hell isn't me.

The big plate-glass window in the hospital lobby, with its black miniblinds slicing up the scenery, that would make anyone nervous, right? And the dangerous revolving door. And the hallway at one end of the room leading to the real hospital, the hallway at this end leading to my destination, the mental health center, Club Cuckoo. Who wouldn't feel a little off his feed?

My miseries are so ordinary. I'm a cold-caller for an insurance company, reminding the elderly that they're more prone to robbery, disease, and accidents than the rest of us. But I don't want to talk about that. And my wife ran off three weeks ago, but I don't even want to think about that. Up to then we were always together. Ned and Naomi, like a team of draft horses.

It was supposed to be nothing more than another white-water vacation with her women's group. She'd go off with them once in a while, down the Colorado, the American. But this last time she decided never to come back. Just like that. She let me know by postcard. *I can't come back.* That's all she wrote. I laughed when I read it. It was like some wild river had finally gotten the better of her, and now she and her raft were too lost to find the way home. But it wasn't a joke. Well, let that go. Let it go.

Across from me sits a large woman, asleep, an oxygen tank pumping and hissing at her feet. Her face inflates and deflates with each wet breath. Her limp blonde hair has a greenish tint. The clear tube hooked over her ears and under her nose looks like a necklace that won't fit.

Another woman, younger and almost as heavy, sits next to me. Her hair came out of the same bottle. A two-year-old totters back and forth between them. She's wearing purple tights and a red-and-yellow striped shirt. It's so short it shows her soccer-ball belly. And those legs. She collapses against her mother and breaks into hoarse laughter.

The mother tickles her under the chin. "Annie-fanny-funny-face!" The baby giggles. Her hands are bright red, as if they've been dipped in gore. When the mother sees me looking, she says, "Finger paint." She catches a hand and picks off a few flakes while the baby tries to wriggle away. "Didn't have time to wash up after Lotta Tots, did we, Annie-fanny?" The baby flashes her greasy grin and rubs her face on her mother's knee, which is as large as a throw pillow, then breaks free and hobbles over to Grandma.

The mother glances outside at the pale blue sky shredded with dark clouds, like smoke from some catastrophe, and says, "Weather coming." She peels her hair away from her face and drapes it behind her ears. "Looks like the last of the nice." The horizon is shaggy with dark clouds. They're coming closer. Grandma's sleeping with her back to the weather. How can she do that? It's the most frightening thing I've ever seen. The woman asleep and the weather coming, coming.

"Yes sir," the younger woman says, "it's supposed to get cold as old Sam Scratch. They already got six inches in the panhandle."

I hate it when Nebraskans describe the western reach of the state like that. Panhandle. More like a stump. I screw up my mouth to let her know this.

"Almanac's promising the hardest winter in twenty years." She shakes her head. "Only September and already a killing frost. Now, I ask you – is that fair?"

Overnight, the flowers have blackened in their beds. The leaves of the young dogwood are black at the tips. They don't know they're already dead. I say it out loud: "The dying has begun."

The woman's eyes tick to my face. She gives me a wide broken smile. "Well, that's one way to put it."

It's the only way. The birds know it, weighing down the branches of the dogwood. They're distraught, they're over the edge, they're pissed. The wind is gusting twenty miles an hour, and everything's bugging them. The sound of their outrage seeps through the thick hospital glass. They're flapping and shrieking. They can't sit still. They want to pull the spindly tree clear out of the ground. Never speak your heart. Never.

But the only thing that really worries me, the only thing that kind of ties my knickers in a knot, is the feeling I get once in a while that if I turn my head too fast I'll flip ass-over-tea-kettle straight across the cosmos. But that's pretty common, wouldn't you say? Everybody feels like that, right? Lucky for me, I'm prepared for every eventuality. I figure the angles. I know the degrees of freedom. I look sharp. I stand clear. I am, after all, an insurance man. And don't get me wrong – sleeping in the closet, that isn't a regular thing with me. It's silly, but I like the dark. And besides, it's bigger than you think. My only regret is telling the therapist. I admitted that sometimes the day is stacked against me so, I don't even come out. But I'm not worried. I'll be fine. I think maybe there's something wrong with my diet.

It's my job to point out how many ways the world can kill and maim. We have coverage for all of it. We're especially generous for dismemberment, which is so much worse in the imagination than death. "You live on a farm, Mrs. Hinkle? With machinery?" Mostly they hang up. Sometimes a word or two is enough to sell them – *combine*, *thresher*. Sometimes a lie. I'm a messenger bringing the bad news that hasn't happened yet.

She catches me staring. "You're looking at those little bowlegs on Annie?" It's true. The baby is the bowleggedest thing I've ever seen. "We're here to have those legs all broke so she can walk straight. Go on, Annie, go get on Grandma. Snatch her oxygen tube!" The baby runs to her grandmother. It's like watching a pair of pliers run. She pulls herself up the side of Grandma. Her crooked legs seem built for climbing. When she's high enough, she snatches at the tube.

Grandma snorts awake and bats playfully at Annie. Her nervous laugh crumbles into a volcanic cough. Tectonic plates are bucking. The crust is cracking. Magma is surging. I hook my foot around the leg of my chair.

"Now punch her," the mother says. "Punch Grandma!" The baby delivers several body blows before the grandmother, gasping, can pry her off and lower her to the floor.

A week after Naomi left, I got another card: *You deserve the truth – I have fallen in love with Buddy, our raftmaster. Please be happy for me.* And a few days later, another: *I'm so crazy in love I won't even come home for my clothes.* Just let it go, I tell you. Think about something else. The sign at my end of the lobby:

St. Regis
Mental Health Center
and
Addiction Recovery Center

Up and down the words read: "Mental Addiction" (yes), "Health and Recovery" (you wish), "Center Center" (what the hell is that?). Try the words in different combinations: "Mental Recovery," "Health Addiction." I want a message. I want a witness. I want a drink. I want, very badly, to beat the living shit out of something. I do not want to go through this embarrassing group-therapy nonsense.

As if she's heard my thought, my therapist appears in the corner of my eye, gliding across my retina and out the door in the far wall. I let my gaze go slack so I won't have to exchange looks with her, but still I can feel the heavy drag of her eyes over my face.

I've been seeing her for a couple months. Janet, call me Janet. A tall woman in her late forties who has a habit of screwing up her mouth when she wants to show she's unhappy with something you've said. It's where I picked up the habit. I'm trying it out. It hurts my mouth muscles. Like French. And besides, I have very few honest opportunities to make the gesture. Nothing much bothers me. Not really. Sometimes at night the line of light under the closet door. But I can stuff a towel into it and make the darkness complete. What I like is to make it so dark there's no difference between my eyes open and my eyes shut. What I like is to take in the faint scent of Naomi still clinging to her clothes – sharp as ozone, tender as sin.

It bothers me sometimes the way Janet talks as if there are several people inside me all fighting to get out, monkeys in a cage. "Not *that* one," she'll say. "I don't want to talk to the *nice* one. I want to do battle with the *mean* one."

The first time she said it, I said, "The mean one wants to know if we can get a group rate for these sessions."

She made her mouth, a demented kiss. I remember thinking, we are not getting out of this alive.

It's true I have a bit of a crush on her. Not much. I'm being very professional about this. Hell, you can like your therapist, can't you? Without it being all Freudian and everything? I like the way she reacts sometimes to my stories about my father – the time he locked me naked outside the house, the time he tied me to the toilet. Ordinary extremities. "Son-of-a-bitch!" she says, nearly jumping out of her chair. I don't tell the stories to learn anything about myself. What's the point? Such a long time ago. I only want to entertain her. But what happens when I run out of stories? I'll lie, of course.

"Where is it?" she said yesterday. "Your rage?" She handed me a piece of construction paper and a box of crayons. "Draw me a picture of your rage." I stared at the blank sheet for a long time and then, before I knew what I was doing, I tore it into careful squares, smaller squares, smaller yet. "I don't have any rage," I said, letting the paper dust fall from my hands.

"I'd like you to consider joining a group I'm putting together." She scratched a comment on her clipboard. "It's a Men's Post-Traumatic Stress Disorders Group."

"But I wasn't *in* Vietnam."

She stopped writing and looked up. "There's all kinds of wars out there."

The group room is strange. I expected the molded plastic chairs set in a circle, but not the totem pole made from papier-mâché and tinsel, or the brightly colored drawings pinned to the wall. Despite these efforts to brighten the room, I can feel it, the leftover sadness, like a smell.

My therapist is making coffee. She's wearing a calf-length blue dress with a design of small white flowers no bigger than gnats. Very matronly. She knows my mind. On each drawing is a name painted in sparkles, a few words crayoned under it. RON – *that I have nice hands,* SUSAN – *that I have a nice car,* CHAZ – *that I'm good in sorry.*

"Do you run a group for kids?" I'm trying to be nice, right?

Janet shakes her head. "That's our wall of pride. They were done by children, yes, but not the kind you're thinking of." She points at the long wall, from which three blank sheets of butcher paper hang ceiling-to-floor. "After a few weeks, you and the others will fill this wall with your own words and pictures."

It's all I can do to turn my back on the blank wall and sit in the circle. Next to the pride pictures is a window looking across the garden to the other wing. The blinds of the window opposite are partly drawn, but I can see the silhouette of a man pacing, his head shifting mournfully from side to side.

I've been afflicted with tests, the most cruelly named of which is the SCIDS test. It's a measure of how dissociated I am, that is, *we* are. Do you talk to your appliances? (Only when they get out of line.) "Do you talk to yourself? (Exactly which one of us are you addressing?) "Have you made a real commitment to therapy?" (I'm here, right?) "Does it ever seem to you as if you do things against your better judgment?" (I'm here, right?) When the test-giver stopped looking me in the eye, I knew I was flunking with flying colors.

Next, in the dismal way my luck runs, I flunked Prozac. They started me on twenty milligrams a day, then upped it to forty. After three weeks, there seemed to be no effect. Secretly I raised my dose to sixty, but without results. They promised me an oceanic high. They promised me days filled with sunlight and grace. But after six weeks, everything still tasted like cardboard.

A tall thin man comes into the room and perches on the chair across the circle. Neatly trimmed black hair and a moustache so delicate he probably has to feed it with an eyedropper. His name, he says quietly, is Alston. He makes his living developing computer games. "I was the principal designer of Lunatics at Large." His eyes go out of focus. "There was a time when I thought that was funny."

Bill, who comes in next, has a rugged face and closely cropped hair. He supports himself as a freelance referee for high school basketball and football games. He has big blocky hands, hands that like to signal penalties. I wedge my own hands under my thighs.

"Ned," I say. "I own a bar on the west side."

Janet shoots me a look.

"More of a night club, really."

Things are off to a bad start. It's junior high. We're backed up against the emotional gym wall, knowing we'll never get invited to dance. We sit there for a few minutes smiling dumbly. When the coffeepot wheezes itself full, we make a big show of helping ourselves to it, grateful for something to do.

When we're seated again and sipping, Janet says, "Bill, how about you? You've been through the routine before. Maybe you can get us started. What brings you here this time?"

Bill's face struggles for words. He squares off his idea with those hands, planes it flat, turns it back and forth.

"All right," he says, "Okay." He acts like Janet's beaten a confession out of him, which is what a lot of my sessions with her are like. "You want to know about pain? About hurt?" He looks at us with frightened eyes.

I say, "What do you think we're going to say – 'Thank you, Bill, but we're not interested in your pain?' Go for it. Let's get this over with." Janet's eyes have turned to stone.

I am immune. I have no feelings. It's the one thing I thank my father for. Someday, from her cellular phone, just as her dinghy goes twisting over the falls, Naomi will ask for forgiveness. But even then, there will be nothing on my heart's oscilloscope but a dead-even line. Farewell, my love. *Bon voyage.*

Bill says, "OK." He says, "All right. I play in an adult softball league. I don't know how much you know about the game, but I'm batting and the count is three-and-oh. I'm supposed to take, right? I mean, *I* know this. But can I help it when a fat pitch comes right down the line? I go for it, right? I miss, of course. And miss. And miss again. Back in the dugout, the guys are on me: 'What're you doing going on a three-and-oh? You're supposed to take!' Man, that hurt."

"That's it?" I say. "Are you kidding?"

Janet ignores me and looks at Alston, nodding slowly. "Sound familiar?" Alston smiles and nods back at her. I feel a surprising stab of jealousy. I've let myself think I'm Janet's only patient. Client. Client. I don't like the thought that she spends time with others, listening to their stories, stories that might be better than mine. From now on I'll lie. Dream up some tale of woe to make this guy's pain seem like so much pocket fluff.

Janet has to say it twice before I hear her. "What about you?" It's her great talent – timing.

"I'm not interested in sports," I say.

"That's not what I mean."

Pity. On all their faces. Pity. "Am I the only one who doesn't want to be here?"

"Talk about that," Janet says.

"I feel fine," I say. "I just get a little edgy now and then." A nerve in my eyelid is twanging. Can she see it? Stop it. Stop it.

Janet can be very mean when she wants to be, and it looks like she wants to be. She folds her hands in her lap and sets her head. "Why don't you tell us about that death-trap you drive?" She smiles like a movie villain.

My turn to make a mouth. I drive a Pinto – orange with black interior – I bought for five dollars. Worth every penny. I hung a pair of fuzzy dice from the mirror and set about driving it into the ground. Things keep going wrong. Headlights burn out two months after I put them in. The exhaust pumps thick white smoke. Every time I use the heater, water drips onto the floor. And of course at every stoplight I wait for the rear-end collision that will turn me into Detroit flambé. But the damned thing just won't die.

"My wife left me," I say. "That's why I'm out of sorts. It's as simple as that. You want to dig through my past. You want me to get in touch with my feelings, my hidden motives. But all I want to know is how to deal with this." I fish out Naomi's last postcard, the one from Mexico. Uncrumple it. Show the front, a picture of an Aztec temple. Read it. Just read it. *"You haven't lived until you've DONE IT on an altar where hundreds of virgins were sacrificed!* What are you supposed to do when your wife sends you a card like this? That's what I want to know. That's all I want to know."

A silence blank as butcher paper. Then Janet says, "That isn't what she wrote, is it, Ned."

"What do you know about it?" I stuff the card into my pocket. *I'm tired of the way you let me take responsibility for your happiness. I'm tired of feeling alone in my own house. How can I come back to that?*

Alston says, "I've never even *been* to Mexico. I've never been *any-*where."

"Let's stay on task, gentlemen," Janet says.

Bill's hands fly out and he says, "Ned, what is it you want from us?"

I give him my dead-level voice. "I want you to shut up, Bill. And I want you to sit on those hands."

Janet looks at me as if I've derailed the entire recovery movement.

I say, "You think I'm out of my head. Is that it?"

"No," she says very carefully, "but I think that's where you'd like to be."

"I don't have to sit still for this." Get up. Stop shaking. "I'm hardly like *that* basket-case." Point at the window, at the inconsolable silhouette passing in the far hall. "I mean, I'm hardly some kind of drooling catatonic sub-specimen, would you say?"

Janet claps. "There he is – the mean one!" She holds her hands palms up and claws the air. "Come on out," she says. "We're ready for you."

Go home. You kept your promise. You came. The silhouette moves sorrowfully past the window. "This farce is over." I turn to go. Synchronous as trained seals, the grouplings bark, "Talk before you walk!" I'm halfway out the door when Janet touches my sleeve. There it is, the mouth. I've flunked group. That's all right. I'm prepared for her, for any kind of pleading. I want to be gone, far away from here, far away from phones and mailboxes, far away from everything. I want to be somewhere in the dark, in a room so small I can't fall down.

She looks into my eyes. "Are you safe?" It's the most intimate thing anyone's ever said to me. "Are you?" she says, pulling lightly on the sleeve of my jacket.

For a second . . . for a second . . . but then I regain myself. I whisper so as not to disturb the swift recovery of the group. "The world is full of danger," I say. "*Nobody's* safe. Don't you know that by now?"

Outside the room, I feel as if the back of my head has floated open. Ten minutes. That's all I could take of group. I'm already embarrassed by the sorry spectacle of my rage, the untamed thing of me. But then I get an idea. I head down the hall toward the other wing. I'm going to save a soul the old-fashioned way. I'm going to shake the life back into that silhouette. No sorrow is so deep that a good, hard slap won't put you right. Right? But when I round the corner, there is no silhouette, only a maintenance man pushing a floor-buffer, guiding it carefully back and forth, side to side.

"Yeah?" he says, shutting off his machine and dialing down the opera on his cassette player. "Can I help you?"

Turn slowly. Walk back down the hall, toward the angry birds, toward the dangerous world.

Right before Naomi left, I went to Kansas City for a two-day insurance seminar. When I got back I said, "Did you miss me?" "No," she said, "actually, I didn't." And it wasn't her words so much that scared me as the touch of surprise in her voice. She was already gone.

I never got mad. I never had a wild hair. I never developed unforgivable appetites or quirky habits or ungovernable interests. But I never woke her up at two in the morning with my mouth on her mouth, my hand on her breast. What I did was keep to the wall, stay out of the way. I thought that's how it was done. In the end, living with me, she said, was like living with no one at all. Can't win. Either there are too many people inside or too few.

Death and dismemberment. All the world's dangers. I sold Naomi without a word. Made her feel how little there is to trust. A chemical in the brain dries up, and you're no longer in love, can't imagine being in love. Toward the end she followed me from room to room, waiting for the words that would make sense of everything. I couldn't get away from her. I only wanted to be left alone. One day I got my wish. I couldn't bear the possibility that love like ours might end, so I ruined it.

Grandma has fallen asleep again, the respirator pumping softly at her feet, her loyal pet. The daughter is throwing dark looks her way and yanking through a magazine.

Annie, the bowlegged toddler, pliers over to me. She looks up into my eyes. I stare back at her. In a voice too deep for a baby, she yells, "Hey!" She holds out one bent leg, then the other. "Hey!" Her voice is raw, like she's been standing naked in the cold, screaming at a locked door for hours. It's the voice of someone who's about to say, Everybody suffers, everything hurts, get over it. Then she squats down and crows, "See? See? Shoes!" I look. They're brand new, her shoes, red as ripe apples, shiny as silver.

The bad weather is closing in. Big dark rollers tumbling like bodies through deep water. As I watch, a stiff wind crosses the parking lot. The dogwood throws up its arms, leaves flying, wings flapping. What makes someone buy new shoes for a baby whose legs are about to be broken? I swear the birds are pulling the tree straight out of the ground. I want it. More than anything. But the birds settle, the branches relax, the tender leaves go limp, and everything falls strangely still. This is the last of the nice. The count.

Believing Marina

MARY HELEN STEFANIAK

I met Marina Zoltar on a Greyhound bus out of Chicago, a Saturday
night bus so crowded that young men in baseball caps and nylon jackets
colorful as flags were sharing seats with children in fuzzy sleepers who
looked like stuffed toys in their mothers' laps. I was on my way home to
Davenport from Milwaukee, where I traveled once a month to get my
scalp shot up with cortisone because my hair was falling out. Marina
Zoltar was sitting in the aisle seat, third from the front, when I changed
buses in Chicago: a woman about my mother's age, well-padded, with
a round face and the kind of milky skin that made you want to ask
her what she used. I don't know what it was about me – my snazzy
fedora? – that made her pluck at my sleeve as I sidled down the aisle.
She had a bad leg, she said, with the barest trace of some place far from
Chicago in her speech, and offered me the window seat beside her.
"Miss," she called me. I hesitated. The last thing I needed on my way
home from Dr. Borkowski's was a three-hour stint as designated listener
while someone like Marina Zoltar talked herself into existence the way
people do, especially on Greyhound buses. My first choice would have
been the empty seat behind hers, next to a little girl wrapped in a plaid
cocoon of blankets. She had long braids and big glasses, and the minute
I looked at her, she fell over sideways to take up both seats, her eyes
squeezed shut. Marina Zoltar shifted her knees obligingly to one side.

As soon as I sat down, she began to talk. She tapped the side of
her face and told me this was the cheekbone that was broken when
a mugger, having knocked her to the ground and stolen her purse,
had stomped on her face for good measure. It was the fourth time
she'd been mugged, she said. She'd lost three good leather bags with
important documents inside (she did translations, she said, for lawyers,
journalists, government agencies) before she wised up and began to

carry a cheap vinyl purse like the one in her lap. "My money and ID? They're here." She patted her breast, then lowered her voice. "The police say to carry some kind of bag, too, or else they know you got it somewhere on you."

She didn't want me to get the wrong idea about her. She wore the big flowered scarf around her shoulders, three flannel shirts, and not one but two dresses, she confessed, lifting up the hem of a black and white check to reveal the paisley underneath, "in case it gets freezing cold on the bus, you see. Last month it was so freezing everybody complained. Listen," she said. "Feel." She leaned across me to pass her hand over the vents along the bottom of the window. She smelled like cooking, oregano maybe, a little garlic. "Does that feel like heat to you?" She told me she owned three houses – one in Chicago, one in Kalamazoo, Michigan, and one in Des Moines, Iowa. She, Marina Zoltar, occupied the second floor of her Chicago property, and she visited the other two every month to clean or garden or see to repairs, and to collect the rent in person. She leaned toward me a little, holding on to the purse in her lap. "If they know you're absentee," she said, "they wreck the place on principle."

Finally, she paused for breath. My scalp was itching and aching under my hat, the way it always did after a pounding from Dr. Borkowski's Dermashot. To resist the urge to scratch, I reached down carefully – not wanting to break Marina Zoltar's sudden silence – and pulled *Anna Karenina* from the backpack at my feet. I was near the end of the book and eager to get to the part where she throws herself under the train. The Dermashot treatment tended to put me in that kind of mood.

"Tolstoy!" Marina Zoltar said, and a gold incisor gleamed. "What a coincidence!" Did she mention that she had a Ph.D. in Slavic Languages and Literature from the University of Chicago? For years, she had taught Russian Literature in Translation. Pushkin! Turgenev! Gogol! Tolstoy! Dostoevski! And of course, Chekhov. "I show them 'The Lady with the Little Dog,'" she said. "I know the translation says, 'with the Pet Dog,' but it is a diminutive ending – thus, a little dog. Chekhov doesn't tell you everything. He is subtle. He gives clues. The students, they can't figure it out. You know how this goes."

"Yes," I said. By now my scalp was itching so fiercely that I'd broken out in a sweat. Unable to bear it any longer, I left my book in my lap and lifted my black felt fedora straight up off my head so as not to disturb my concealing hairdo. Cool air bathed my scalp, and I sighed.

"Do you want me to put your beautiful hat up top?" Marina Zoltar asked. She had it out of my hands already and was hauling herself to her feet with the help of the seat in front of her. (The old man in it groaned. He wore an overcoat with huge epaulettes, and wild white hair circled the dome of his head like an untrimmed hedge. He, too, had a seat to himself.) When she dropped back down, Marina Zoltar said to me, "You got some thinning there, I see. A few patches."

My hand flew to my French twist. She was right, of course. I was suffering from what my dermatologist called alopecia *areata*, which means *areas* of hair loss. I had discovered the first area back in October – a bald spot the size of a quarter behind my right ear – and in spite of consulting a half-dozen dermatologists on both sides of the Mississippi, I was now on the brink of alopecia *totalis*, which means exactly what you think it means. The only bright spot (aside from gleaming patches of my scalp) was that my baldness was mostly in the back, so if I wrapped my formerly luxuriant hair around my head and then tucked it into a modified French twist secured with a big barrette, nobody was supposed to be able to tell I had a problem – yet. "I used to have the same trouble," Marina Zoltar said.

Still fingering my barrette, I looked at her. She had a head full of brown curls generously threaded with gray, flattened in the back but otherwise normal looking. She turned toward me also, and I saw for the first time that the cheekbone she said the mugger broke was higher than the other. The asymmetry made her look as if she were winking at me.

"I can help you," she announced. "I am a practitioner of the old medicine."

"Home remedies?" I said, keeping my voice down.

Leaning toward me, Marina Zoltar said, "I'll tell you. I never was a child. My mother – who was also a medical doctor in Ukraine – she started to take me out when I was only three. She showed me plants for our practice – herbs, roots, sap. Also minerals, animal parts, and venoms. By the time I came to this country, I could cure malaria, cholera, tuberculosis, ulcers, hardening of arteries, heart attack, night blindness, and brain stroke. Also prevent."

From the corner of my eye, I saw two circles of light flashing. The little girl's glasses were turned our way.

"And – hair loss?" I said.

"Easiest thing in the world to fix. Five or six different treatments I've got, depending on the person. They all work like a charm. There is no reason on earth for any person to be bald." Marina Zoltar smiled, her teeth twinkling at this happy news, and seemed again to be winking at me. I was unable to keep myself from hoping that her cure for baldness did not require venom or the body parts of endangered species. She sensed this and leaned a little closer, adding, "It runs in our family, this problem, but you would never know to look at us. Except for two that don't believe in the old medicine."

"These treatments," I said.

"*They're* both bald like an egg."

"Do you think one would work – for me?"

"I'll tell you," Marina Zoltar said. "I came to this country in 1949. All alone. I was twenty years old. My sister and her husband had already fled before the war. They were in Brazil. My mother and my brother, they stayed in Salzburg, where we were after the war. She spoke no English, my mother, but I spoke the Slavic languages, including Russian, and also English, so I worked for the Americans. The Americans were taller than we were, but my mother said, 'Look at their bellies, how fat they are. Why does nobody take care of them?'"

Here the man in the seat in front of us coughed, a long phlegmy business. I wished Marina Zoltar would hurry up and get to the roots and the venom. To move things along, I asked her, "So did you and your mother take care of the Americans?"

She gave me a sharp look. "I came to Tacoma, Washington," she said. "All alone. I worked in the biggest paper mill in the world. I was typist, secretary. One hundred people worked in that office. So many trees there were then in Oregon and Washington. Now, much of it is bare." She glanced at my head, then continued. "One day, I was standing outside on my lunch hour, and a lady, a supervisor at the plant, asked me my name. She said she thought I looked as if maybe I was a religious person. She said this because I didn't wear so much makeup – the style then was like Marilyn Monroe, so much lipstick and paint – and my hair was up in braids that are wrapped around the head. I told the lady that it just so happened that I *was* religious and that, even though I liked to paint – I studied art one year in Vienna – I didn't like paint on the face."

"You wore your hair in braids?" I said hopefully. "Wrapped around your head?"

"The lady asked me if I would like to come and live with her," said Marina Zoltar. "Her daughter, who was about my age, had just got married and moved to Portland, Oregon. Even though you could see from Tacoma to Portland across the bay, there were no bridges and it was a long way around. This woman, in her fifties, had health problems – high blood pressure and phlebitis – and her daughter was ringing up big bills on the telephone, calling her mother every night to check on her. So she was very glad when I went to live with her. I was glad, too, because now I could start making the documents ready to bring my family to the U.S. I couldn't sign the documents to sponsor them because I was not a citizen, but churches were sponsoring people, DP's they called them, and this woman, my landlady, she belonged to a big church. Do you know what it is – a DP?"

"It means Displaced Person," I said, and Marina Zoltar scowled – whether at me or the concept, I couldn't tell.

"As soon as I found someone at my landlady's church to sponsor my family," she continued, "I applied for the visas. I tell you, I went to bed very happy on December 30, 1949, thinking that 1950 was a special year, my mother and brother would be coming to America. We would be together again. But in the dark hours of the morning" – here her voice dropped to a minor key – "on the last day of 1949, I had a vision that came in a dream. I saw that there would be another war. I saw that my mother and brother would not come to me, and that I myself would go someplace far away and be unhappy there. I woke up trembling, with tears on my face." As if the tears were still there, Marina Zoltar picked up a corner of her flowered scarf and held it to her cheek.

"A vision," I said.

Marina Zoltar gave me a sidelong look. She dropped the scarf. "I can see," she said briskly, "that in some ways you are like the lady I was living with. Her name was Frances. She had been a beauty when she was young. She still dressed very nice, very attractive, but she would get angry at me for many things. I tried to tell her, with her high blood pressure, don't eat so much meat, so much salt. Oh, she got mad. 'I go to the best doctors and my doctor says eat meat, it makes you strong,' she said. 'Who are you to tell me he is mistaken?' When I told her about my dream, she said, 'Visions! Visions come from the devil!' The priest had told her that. 'And on the radio they said there will be one hundred years of peace.' I should kneel down with her right now, she said, here, in the front room, and pray that God would free me from such things."

Marina Zoltar sighed. I pictured her and the landlady kneeling on faded carpet, Marina's braids hanging down her back.

"I was very sad for a long time after that," Marina Zoltar said. "Then, in March, I got a letter from the State Department. It said, here are the visa numbers for your mother and brother. Expect them within two months. I was reading that letter and my landlady Frances was looking at my face and she could see that it was something good. She said, 'What is it? What is it? Oh, let me read it myself.' And she read it and danced me around the kitchen. Sometimes she was very nice to me. 'Let's go out and celebrate!' she said. So we did. We went out to eat.

"While we were eating, my landlady said, 'You see? You and your silly visions. It was only a dream. Everything has come out all right.'

"I said, 'My mother and brother are not here yet.' I ruined the whole evening by saying that.

"But you know what, I'll tell you. In the U.S. Consulate, there are crooks. They will sell a visa to criminals and murderers, anyone who has the money. The visas they come with just a number, not the name, so they can put someone else's name on it for the right price. And those crooks at the Consulate, they sold my family's visas to someone else. Every day in Salzburg my mother would go and ask if the visas had come and they would tell her, 'Not yet, not yet – soon, very soon.' And then one day they tell her that the quota for immigrants from her country to the U.S. is filled, and they will have to go somewhere else. 'Why don't you go to Brazil?' they say. 'You have family there. Brazil is giving visas. You'd better go.'" Marina Zoltar's hands closed into fists. "Don't you see? My vision had come true!" she cried, in a voice so sharp the bus driver turned his head, and behind us, the little girl's glasses flared.

Marina Zoltar folded her hands in her lap. "It was *not* a dream," she added more quietly. "Soon I get a letter from Paris. My brother says they are waiting for the train to Marseilles and from there they will go to Brazil. Oh, how I cried! And one day I came home and there my landlady Frances was sitting at a table with a telegram, weeping. I say, 'What's the matter?' She says, 'You are a prophet!' and hands me the telegram. The war in Korea had broken out and her sister's son was killed. Only then did she believe me at last." As if overcome by the irony of it all, Marina Zoltar gazed past me, toward the window. The reflection of her round white face floated in the darkness outside.

I waited a moment before I said, "The war broke out and her sister's son was killed the first day?"

"War," Marina Zoltar said hoarsely. "It's a terrible thing. In Salzburg, after the war, the soldiers would come and grab the people and say, 'Oh, he is a criminal!' 'She is a spy!' 'They collaborated with the Germans!' But it wasn't true. They just wanted to kill people. Ten thousand Slavs they killed after the war. Excuse me please." And she heaved herself out of the seat. It was a bumpy time to go to the restroom. I turned to watch Marina Zoltar stagger down the aisle, holding on to the backs of seats. (The little girl in the seat behind us was watching her, too, twirling one of her long, brown braids like a jump rope.) By now I knew that if I'd said I had AIDS or Alzheimer's, Marina Zoltar would have come back just as brightly, "Easiest thing in the world to fix." There were no treatments that worked like a charm. I had fallen for the old bait-and-switch. As if that weren't bad enough, when I turned around to face the front, the old man with the hedge of white hair had popped up to glare at me over the top of his seat. He had rheumy blue eyes, red-rimmed and so malevolent that I glanced over my shoulder to see if he might be looking at someone else, but the little girl with the glasses had ducked out of range and the occupants of the seat behind hers were slumped and veiled in grainy darkness. For reasons I couldn't imagine, I seemed to be the old guy's target. This is why people don't take the bus, I thought. He snorted in disgust and dropped back down out of sight.

When Marina Zoltar returned, landing solidly in the seat beside me, she said, "Where was I?"

I expected the old guy to pop up again any second. I said, "Your hair was falling out."

Marina Zoltar didn't buy it. "I went to Brazil," she said, "to see my family. I had a six-month tourist visa so I could return to the U.S., but while I was there, in Brazil, something happened. In my sister's beautiful house, I had another vision. I saw my mother dead on the bed in my sister's beautiful house!"

She paused, looking for a response. I thought I heard snores rising gently in front of us, a sound like a motor wrapped in cotton.

"How would it happen?" Marina Zoltar asked the darkness. "Sickness? An accident? The streets were very narrow in Brazil and the drivers were crazy. If they couldn't get by on the street, they would drive on the sidewalk. Would my mother get hit by a car? I worried all the time. Would she catch some sickness from the poor people we used to treat, my mother and I, with our herbs and medicines? The old medicine was illegal there, too, but nobody cared what you did for the poor.

"Then, one day, my mother said to me, 'We should keep the first-aid kit downstairs in the kitchen. Accidents usually happen downstairs.' She showed me a cut she had on her finger. 'See?' she said. 'I cut myself the other day when I was killing the chicken, and I was too lazy to go upstairs and put iodine on it. Now it's inflamed.'"

Marina Zoltar stopped. She bowed her head and put one hand over her heart, as if she were about to pledge allegiance.

I waited as long as I could before I asked, "What happened?" She lifted her head. "She died, my mother."

"From a cut finger?" I wanted to sound skeptical, but suddenly I was picturing gangrenous limbs, festering sores, terrible things. I don't know why.

"From cancer, she died," Marina Zoltar said. "Cancer was not one of the things we knew how to treat then because it was so rare. In all her years of practicing medicine, my mother saw only three cases, and one of them was a poor woman with cancer in her female parts that we saw at this time, when my mother had her cut finger. I know how to beat it now. I have cured myself of cancer, as well as several others."

"The *hell* you have," said a gravelly voice.

The old man wasn't asleep, after all. His head rose slowly above the back of the seat like an ugly sun, but Marina Zoltar only sat up straighter. As if he hadn't spoken, she said, "I have a thousand pages I have written on the old medicine and other unusual things."

"The hell you *have*," the old man repeated. His voice was like rocks in a tumbler.

Marina Zoltar continued to pretend that he did not exist. She looked at me instead, her eyes hard.

"A thousand pages," I said. "That's a lot."

The old man hooted. Marina Zoltar narrowed her eyes. "I'm going to divide it into five books," she said defiantly.

By now, the old man had hooked his fingers over the back of the seat and pulled himself up until his head hung over the top, facing us. On one side his hair stood straight up above his ear, like a finger raised to make a point. "Always, always the same," he said to me. "She can see the future. She can cure cancer. She can grow hair on an egg." The old man snorted again, and I pressed myself into the seat, backing away from his breath. His voice, too, had a trace of some place far from Chicago in it. "Oh, and she has a *bad leg*," he said. He wagged gnarly fingers at her sturdy support stocking, which ended in a man's dress sock and athletic shoe. "Does that look like a bad leg to you? Does it?" He raised a shaky fist and cried, "I'm telling you, people on this bus are trying to sleep!" He treated us to another long, rattling cough. Then, as if exhausted by his efforts, he sank back into his seat.

I waited for Marina Zoltar to say something after the dome of his head disappeared, but she stared straight ahead, stony, silent. Minutes passed without a word.

"She won't talk to you no more now," a small voice whispered right into my ear. It was the little girl with big glasses standing up behind me, her head squeezed in next to the window. "Every time *he* says something" – I felt her chin lift and point toward the old man – "*she* freezes. Look." A small hand appeared between my head and Marina Zoltar's and did a poor imitation of fingers snapping. Marina Zoltar didn't blink or budge. The small hand disappeared, and I felt the little girl's breath behind my right ear again. Her braid swung forward and touched my shoulder. "See?" she said.

"I never was a child," Marina Zoltar said suddenly.

I looked at her – the white cheek, the sculpted cheekbone.

"She's not talking to us," the little girl said. "She says that every once in a while." The little girl hung back for a moment, then curled closer to me and confided, "We seen a man in Texas once. He could cure cancer. He could make the lame to walk and the blind to see."

Behind us, a sleepy woman's voice said, "Jennifer?"

"Right here, Mom," the little girl said. She leaned still closer (I felt her fingers flutter against my neck) and whispered more urgently, "I seen them get on the bus in Michigan."

I twisted around as far as I could toward the window.

"She was limping," the little girl said.

"You saw them?" I don't know why I whispered. "They're together?"

As if I'd missed the point, the little girl repeated, "She was *limping*. I *saw* her. With my own *eyes*."

"Stop bothering people, honey," said the little girl's mother.

I was going to turn around and say, brightly, that she wasn't bothering anybody, but the old man snarled again, louder this time, "People are trying to *sleep!*" and the little girl tumbled back into her seat.

After that, they all quit talking, and the sounds of the bus ride rose around me as if someone had turned the volume back to normal. I listened to the engine clearing its throat and changing its tune, to the faint buzz of nearby headphones, and after a while, to the old man's cottony snores. Amid the percolation of coughs and murmurs behind me, one little voice was doggedly singing the theme from Sesame Street, the words going blurry and then snapping back, all the way to Davenport. Most of the passengers got off there, although the old man stayed on, sleeping, and so did Marina Zoltar, sitting up straight as a pillar, an oracle turned to stone by her unworthy listeners. Hemmed in by her, I watched the little girl with glasses and her parents go by – first the girl, then the mother, then the father, each with a hand on the shoulder of the one in front, making a little train. I was already in the aisle myself, retrieving my hat, when Marina Zoltar looked up, with her wink that wasn't a wink, and spoke to me once more, a single word in a weary voice.

"Garlic," she said.

"I beg your pardon?"

"Pull one toe of garlic from the bulb, cut it to bring the juice out, and rub it on the bare spots three times a day. In a week, maybe two, you'll feel something." She ran her fingers up from the nape of her neck, through her curls, to show me where. The old man snorted in his sleep.

Inside the station, I headed straight for the restroom to tighten up my French twist. That was it? Garlic? No venom? No toads? A thousand pages about the old medicine and other *unusual* things, and the best Marina Zoltar had was *garlic*? I took off my hat and saw that my barrette had slipped. Garlic was not an unusual thing. Four out of any five grandmothers – including, as a matter of fact, one of my dermatologists – recommended it. I knew I'd try it sooner or later, after I gave up on the Dermashot. I undid the barrette and watched my hair fall to my shoulders, wispy and translucent like angel hair. I gathered a paltry ponytail's worth and twisted it up, but the barrette clasp got caught somehow, and when I pulled it out to try again, a rope of hair came out with it, so I hid in a stall and cried. This was not an unusual thing either. I'd been crying daily since the middle of October. Since October, I'd been trying to talk myself into believing that I could exist without hair, that I wouldn't turn into somebody else, wigged and invisible. I didn't need Marina Zoltar showing me how hard it was, how much fast-talking was required just to keep from disappearing.

I came out of the restroom, still sniffling, in time to see the little girl with glasses walking through the bus station with her parents. She was wearing shiny black tap shoes – I hadn't noticed on the bus. Here they clicked on the terrazzo floor. The little girl had both her parents by the hand. "No, Mom, this way," I heard her say. There was something unusual about the way they were moving, the three of them, something tentative but brave, and suddenly, as I watched, the clues added up: the little girl's parents were blind. She was leading them through the bus station, holding their hands, because they were blind.

I stopped right there by the lockers and watched the little girl walk her mother into the restroom while the father waited a few paces from the door. Then the little girl came out and led her father past the video games, slowly, to the vending machines, where she handed him over to a bus station employee – a black man with a brilliant hairdo like ramen noodles lacquered to a shine. By this time the mother was standing at the restroom door, so the little girl hurried back, clicking and tapping. I saw the mother lean toward the sound, but when the little girl reached up to take her hand, the mother snatched up the little girl's braids instead, holding one in each hand for a moment, like reins, before she let them slip through her fingers. The little girl stood very still for this, gazing in my direction, one eye huge through the thick lens of her glasses and the other squinted shut, as if she were drawing a bead on something.

I went to call a taxi then, thinking that Marina Zoltar was not the only one who never was a child.

When I came back from the phones, the parents were sitting down and the little girl was standing by the video games, tap shoes in hand. She was watching two big boys with shaved heads and wrinkled flannel shirts play *Urban Warrior*. I saw her dodge one boy's elbow to put a quarter down, staking her claim. That's when she spotted me and asked, "You waiting?"

"Yes," I said. I guess I was thinking of the taxi.

"I'm next," she warned me, loud enough for the boys to hear over the sounds of battle.

I missed my taxi waiting for them to relinquish the game, but it was worth it to see the little girl play, to watch her pounding the buttons and leaning into the joystick, tugging and pushing it, her elbows all over the place, and her braids – they were something – whipping and writhing like snakes around her shoulders. Her braids made me think of stories Dr. Borkowski liked to tell me while the Dermashot pinged and thwanged against my scalp, stories about brave and resourceful bald people, unusual things, like the woman who answered the door with her cat draped over her head.

You know, I had never believed those stories.

Anything You Want, Please

PAUL EGGERS

Six months after moving in together, Reuben Gill revealed to his fiancée Joanne that his application for Peace Corps had finally cleared. "Don't feel guilty," she said. Then she blew her nose and smiled at him beautifully. "You want this," she said. "Go. You've been waiting a year." He had, that was true. But there was no Joanne a year ago. He was head over heels, and when he handed her a tissue he started crying, and they held each other and rocked back and forth.

They lived in a boxy adobe house in Buckle, Arizona, where the smell of asphalt rose from the interstate at night and settled over the silverware and china. They had no money and no prospects, and the highway for miles each way was empty, but they loved the emptiness: every touch, every look had weight, and even from a distance their voices were clear and sharp. When Reuben showed Joanne his packet from Peace Corps, she stood motionless by the front door so long he excused himself and went to the bathroom sink to wash up. She came to him then. Her hands were moist on his back. She said love was baroque. She said if she could, she'd step out of her skin for him and let the whole smelly mess plop onto the floor. That's how baroque love should be. That's why he should go.

So he did. At Subang International, in Malaysia, he phoned her and covered the receiver with kisses when she answered. Later he referred to Madeline, then Kate, both in his Peace Corps training group, as Joanne. On the bus south, down to Seremban for training, he talked to Hank and Reggie, and when he said Joanne's name he saw his hands move, as if caressing. The reflex startled him, but no one was paying much attention. Hank told Reggie the air was heavy as a paw. Rounding a corner, the bus narrowly missed a naked child urinating in an open sewer. Then a lorry almost hit them, or seemed to – the Malay driver just braked hard and stopped inches from a ditch, kicking up dust. For miles, the fruit trees along the road were spiky and red, and when Reuben smelled them he was suddenly hungry.

In the second week, everyone bought hats with wide, floppy brims and spoke with Australian accents during breakfast. Reuben, laughing hard, wondered what he was really doing. He bicycled up to the Peace Corps training site, still wondering, and sat in the language classroom, saying *woo-woo* each time the Oxford-tie Malay up front whacked the vowel chart. Hank and Reggie chanted along, whispering jokes out the sides of their mouths to Kate and Madeline. Reuben couldn't follow their banter. He was wondering what section of his brain would be lit up if he had one of those synapse-activity dyes the instructor had talked about. His mouth was making noises – *woo-woo, woo-woo* – but in some corner of his mind, some insistent, demanding corner, he was asking how, last night, he could have staggered past a woman sweeping rat pellets into a pile and then fallen down drunk in a wicker chair, yelling "Whiskey, boy!" snapping his fingers, mouthing a stubby Thai cigar into pulp. He wondered how he could have sat like that all night, queasy with chloroquine, slapping at smoke-stunned geckos, singing dirty lyrics to "Oh Suzanna" with Chinese alcoholics, the whole bleary bunch of them an arm's length from a hacked-up sow dying in the doorway. Or how, earlier, at a roadside breakfast stall, he could have rubbed the chest hair of a fat Sikh ("is lion hair," the Sikh said; "is good luck"), then let the man pretend to shave him with a tiny, pearled dagger, kitschy as a Monopoly marker, dangling from a keychain. How, he wondered, could he feel his body tremble with recklessness when his head was still buzzing with Joanne?

After class he walked to the trainee bunkhouse with Hank and Reggie. They were all frowning from the heat. Reuben's hair was stiff with sweat, and when he came in out of the sun and saw Geronimo Donaldson in the far corner, soaking his feet in a laundry tub of beer bottles and cold water, his scalp started to tingle. Geronimo was naked, except for a dirty plaid sarong bunched loosely around his waist. He was the cultural orientation leader, an up-country volunteer who earned extra cash by showing newcomers the ropes. Even now, sloshing his feet in the tub, he was unnerving. He had no body hair, his skin glistened like plastic, and he was always staring, bug-eyed behind thick horn-rims with an elastic strap, what he called his oil baron look. His real name was George, but he said Oak Park, Illinois, had been so dull that simply leaping up from the dinner table made him yell *Geronimo*.

"Gentlemen," Geronimo said, grinning. "Everyone make their beds this morning?"

What Reuben saw folded on his pillow looked at first like a gift of cloth. It was yellowed and creased; it had a design. Then he understood: it was a newspaper. An article had been circled in red. The headline was "Amok Injures Estate Workers."

"Amok," said Reuben, tapping the paper.

"That's right," said Geronimo. "Same as English. To run amuck. They use the noun form here."

Reuben swayed a moment, alarmed, recalling his night at the bar, then his roadside shave from the Sikh. No one had seen him, not even Hank or Reggie. Hank, from New Jersey, always smelled like garlic, even after bathing, and his blubbery presence was announced the minute he began wheezing or wiping his face with his shirt. Reggie was still jet-lagged and spent most of his spare time sleeping. He was bald and sweaty, with a dimple on the top of his head; he would have stuck out in a crowd like a balloon. As for Geronimo, he had been holed up in the conference room all week, arguing loudly with the program director about training procedures. Yet there was the article – *amok*, it said, *amok* – on his bunk.

"Rube, it's for you," said Geronimo, pointing to the paper.

Reuben felt the heat from his roommates' bodies. They were behind him, probably craning their necks forward to read the circled article. He imagined them breathing silently through their mouths, so as not to announce their snooping. They would feel bad for him: his behavior was being questioned. Perhaps he would be sent packing, put on a bus to Kuala Lumpur with a ticket back to Buckle in his pocket.

"Hey, not to worry," said Geronimo. He wagged his finger at Reuben, as if to say *I know what you're thinking*, then splashed water in his direction. "It's just titillation," he said. Then he leaned forward and spoke in a low voice. "Rube," he said, "paste it in your scrapbook."

No one made a sound. Geronimo just sat there, glistening, his lips drawn tight, eyes steely behind his horn-rims. Hank and Reggie stood motionless by the door. The sun was so bright the jacaranda blooms outside had turned the color of chalk.

"Yeah, I can paste it in," Reuben said, lifting his head. He heard his voice quaver. "Sure. Just a sec."

From his travel bag he withdrew a pair of baby scissors – for his toenails, for pulling out splinters – and set to clipping. Splashing came from the tub. Geronimo lifted his feet from the water and ambled over, leaving wet tracks on the cement. His sarong was wrapped around his waist like a towel.

"Hombre," Geronimo said, pinching the scissors closed with his thumb and forefinger. Hank and Reggie still hung back, standing by the window slats, feigning interest in the insects smeared on the glass. Geronimo spoke softly so only Reuben could hear. "White boys in Buckle cut," he said, bending at the waist. He shook the scissors. "White boys in the bush *tear*."

"I know where I am," said Reuben.

"Yeah?" said Geronimo. "So tear, Rube. Titillate yourself. Get her out of your head for a change."

"What is this?" Reuben whispered. "What do you know about me?"

"Hey," Geronimo said. "I've been there. Personal experience, you know?" He tapped his head. "I can read your mind."

The words were astonishing, especially coming from Geronimo's mouth. This refugee from Oak Park, Illinois, this virtual stranger, a man perhaps with little loyalty to another life: this man had somehow grasped the problem in clear, if reductive, terms. Titillation as antidote. It was like snorting cocaine to stop smoking.

"Listen," Geronimo said. He put his mouth to Reuben's ear. "A little titillation, it's like giving her a vacation. From your head. You know what I mean? You don't have to evict her. Just let her out sometimes. Give her some air and clean your noggin up."

Reuben pictured his letters to Buckle. He had licked the stamps and re-checked the address. He had personally dropped them down the Out of Country slot at the post office, safe from prying eyes. "Who told you this?" he said. "No one," Geronimo whispered. "Come on now. You know you want to. Come on. Just tear. Just a little."

So Reuben tossed the scissors on the bed and placed his fingers at the bottom of the paper. He tore, straight up, ripping the paper cleanly, all the way to the article, then around. Geronimo cocked his head like a dog. Reuben leaned forward, listening. The newsprint was cheap; it made a sound like brush parting. The paper felt dusty in his hands, and the fibers dangled when he tore them, pulpy as tiny buds. Before he knew it, he had ripped a ragged hole out of the middle, and the hole framed the room like a window. He held the paper out stiffly and looked through the opening. He saw Geronimo rocking slightly, eyes closed, lips curled in, rubbing his fingers together hard, like mandibles, and by the door he saw Hank and Reggie, their faces pinched and alert, looking out across the trainee compound into the trees, as if they heard something rustling about.

Mail didn't catch up to the trainees until the third week. When Joanne's first letter came, Reuben set his face with an expression of brooding. He had never seen so much of her handwriting before. He traced his fingers over the words, then stuck the letter in his pocket and walked along the road, alone, sweltering, smelling the diesel drifting in from the logging trucks, and he became nostalgic and quiet. When he ate that night he thought of ice cream and chicken potpie, and in the warm night air he swore he smelled spaghetti. The moment turned him weepy: Joanne's dinners were clouds of steam and pasta; the food made them drowsy and they slept without blankets on their big red couch.

That was her first letter. The second was covered with butterfly stamps. *To remind you of home*, the letter said, but Malaysia had more butterflies than he had ever seen in his life. There were so many, they made the field by his bunkhouse move, and when they flew, their wings left a fine dust in the air that settled on the plants. The letter made him teary – *I miss you so much*, it said, *I say your name into my hand and hold you all day* – and so he stood in the field, mice scuttling underfoot, bicycle tires blistering against the gravel in the compound, and just looked at the butterflies. "Now that's titillatin'," he said to himself. "Titillates me to the bone." Later he napped on a palm frond big and cushy as a blanket. By an Indian temple the next day he put his nose to a crumbling wall. It smelled like chutney. He scraped it with his finger and a brick fell apart. Wedged in the mortar was a yellowed slip of paper, filled with hearts and inky Chinese script; dark stains dyed the wall in patterns that looked like faces. He felt eyes on him. He stepped back and saw a naked Malay boy crouched like a cat by the entrance, resting on his forearms, just watching. He wondered if he were hallucinating.

Titillation: The restaurant bins were dumped in the sewers, and before the sun burned off the morning mist, the air in town was sweet and buttery as cornbread. In the afternoon, the heat soaked into his pores and pressed for hours like a hand, a woman's soft, insistent hand, against his skin. Some days he swore a tongue was licking his ear. The women wore tight polyester dresses; they thought he was exotic; they flirted outrageously. The old men doubled over with laughter when he sneezed, the stars were in the wrong place, and the spiders grew big as saucers and in his shoes they laid quivering egg sacks the texture of sponges. At night, the frogs' mating calls were so loud they seemed to be coming from his bunk. When everyone slept, he looked out the window and saw the silhouette of the palms lank against the night sky, and in his dreams the trees whispered to each other and made kissing noises, and sometimes they leaned through the bunkhouse window to touch him.

Some days he imagined himself as a bead of water on a griddle. He was jittery and feverish all the time, and he walked faster than he ever knew he could walk. After the rains, when steam rose from the fruit rinds heaped in the streets, he felt so light he had to cinch his belt for fear he would walk out of his pants. He looked into the outhouse mirror one day and couldn't believe the white face reflected back at him was really his. He put his fingers to his face. His skin felt hard and wet. His whiskers had stopped growing. It was a trade-off, he said. You feel a little strange when you learn things.

He learned, for example, that Geronimo followed him around. Once, walking past one of the outbuildings, Reuben yelled when something grabbed his arm; it was Geronimo, sneaking up from behind. "Don't bumble in the jungle, hombre," Geronimo whispered, shaking his head. Sometimes at night Reuben heard what he swore was Geronimo's motorcycle whining in the distance, but then he'd look up and see Geronimo peeling fruit, gobbling rambutans or lychees, staring at him. Or Reuben would be at the well, taking a bucket bath, splashing cool water over his head, when he'd sense someone nearby. There would be

Geronimo, naked except for his sarong, covered in leaves and tiny bits of wood.

"Don't you bathe?" said Reuben.

"Sure I do," said Geronimo, picking off a leaf. "The trails are bad here. Real dusty. This stuff sticks to you."

Geronimo told him a cross-cultural story that apparently no one else had heard. Reuben was flattered. He kept the story to himself until one night Madeline came into the bunkhouse, steaming. She called Geronimo a pig. He had leaned back against a tree, she said, and scratched himself immodestly, right in front of her, and when she brought it to his attention, he said, "That's the lesson. Just say what you want." Then he stopped scratching.

"I don't like being tested," Madeline said. "He's got no right."

"He gave me the Roseliana story," said Reuben.

Madeline had never heard it. "It's not so good," he said. "It's just a list, really." Madeline insisted. She wanted evidence that Geronimo had some sort of problem.

The story was Geronimo had taught in a tiny school up in Trengganu State, where he was in love with this Malay woman, Roseliana. She was the school secretary. She always looked at him coyly, face down, eyes up. Geronimo said all the Malay girls acted that way when they wanted to drive the white boys crazy; even his students did it to him when they handed in their papers. He walked into the office one day between classes and asked her if she could order some fluorescent lights for the boys' bathroom. There was no one around. She stood up and leaned against the wall. "Anything you want, please," she said. She looked at him. He stared a moment, then took her clipboard. "How about this?" he said. She said OK. He took the stapler off her desk, then a calendar off the wall. OK.

He could see students milling around between the classrooms, but he took her watch off, then a barrette from her hair. She was doing pouty things with her lips, laughing. He took a pencil sticking out of her pocket. His heart was pounding. He opened a file drawer and took out personnel files, stacking them on her desk. He lifted a globe of the world and set it on the floor. It was all OK. He took out a slat from the window; he took a drink from her water glass, then threw the sponge for the mimeograph machine onto the floor. She moved around some, little motions with her fingers on the sides of her dress. She was smiling.

"Please don't tell me they went at it like rabbits," Madeline said.

"No," said Reuben. "The punch line's not very titillating. The ending was he couldn't figure out what to do next. He started thinking, If I go any further, there's no turning back. And he started wondering what exactly she meant by 'anything you want.' Maybe she just meant she would go order any equipment he wanted. Or maybe she wanted to do it, right there on the desk. Or maybe she was being passive, just going along with everything until he crossed a line. Maybe something else."

"So we learn that Malays are hard to read," said Madeline, folding her arms. "Gee. Impressive."

"Maybe," said Reuben. "He said the class bell went off and all these students came running in with lame excuses. Roseliana just stood there for a minute, kind of flustered, and then went back to business. Like it's no big deal, right? But he says he started thinking about what he could have done. All those possibilities. He couldn't get them out of his head. He could have just . . . I don't know. Done *anything*. You know what I mean?"

"I'll tell you what," said Madeline. "Around my neck of the woods, you don't get any damn thing you want. I got rules."

"Well, sure," said Reuben. "It's just, I guess I feel sorry for the guy." He pictured Geronimo telling the story. Geronimo had been leaning against the flagpole in the courtyard, drinking an orange crush, rolling the bottle across his belly. Geronimo said things got sour between him and Roseliana after that. He kept thinking about what he could have done, and it scared him. His voice sounded raspy. He stopped once and placed the mouth of the bottle over his left eye, then over his right, rotating the rim slowly, not pressing hard. His chin quivered a little. He was probably crying. He looked so lonely propped up against the flagpole in his filthy sarong, the sun behind him, gnats crawling on his face, that Reuben invited him in for a game of Othello.

≥⁶

Reuben wrote to Joanne about life in the bush. *Three months already!* his airgrams said. *The culture is much different. The men hold hands, and the women don't smoke.* The words seemed so empty he held his head in his hands and pressed it hard, the way he would press a melon in the supermarket, squeezing here, knocking there, and when he felt his fingers tap against bone he laid his head down gently on the table, imagining himself back in Buckle, moving on to another bin of fruit. He wrote her lots of letters. *When I get back, yeah baby*, he wrote. *Keep a candle burning. I got one burning for you.* He had a picture of her in his wallet. When he wrote, he laid the picture out on the bunk before he picked up a pen. The words came easier when he could see her, and when he rubbed his finger over her face he made sure not to press hard.

One night the program director played blindfold chess in the common room: no board or pieces, just calling out the moves. It was an amazing feat, beyond belief. Memory so clear and pure you could bring it alive, have it come pouring from your lips. The tips of your fingers felt it; you could touch a tiny chess piece and move the plastic to a square, and everything would be right where your mind said it was. It seemed heroic as love.

He asked her for more pictures, then a lock of hair. *Hair?* he wondered. He looked at the word his hand had just written. It seemed a reasonable request, not desperate, though when he thought later about what he had asked for, he felt a little foolish. On the way to language class, he bought a rambutan fruit. It was covered with wispy strands. He stroked them, then plucked a few off and tucked them into his shirt pocket. In class he heard Tuscany pirates had once held Malay princes for ransom. Suddenly his request made sense. He asked so many history questions Reggie jabbed him in the ribs. Ransom. His letter to Buckle was ransom: give me things, and you'll live. A trade.

Nights, they all drank beer and prepared for practice teaching. The compound, a vacant boys' school, had a kitchen with a row of giant steel rice cauldrons, big enough to sleep in, and they did their lesson plans sitting in them, their bare feet sticking out, drinking Anchor. Reggie and Kate shared a cauldron one night, snuggling like teenagers on a carnival ride, rubbing their legs together. Everyone grew quiet, and after a while Reuben heard only breathing and his own lips sucking on the bottle.

"Madeline," said Reuben. He patted the sides of his cauldron in invitation. "Come simmer with me."

"Women aren't interchangeable," said Madeline, craning her neck forward. Her cauldron was at the end of the line, near the counter. All

Reuben could see of her was her head and feet. She had painted her toenails red, and she jangled with bracelets when she walked.

"Here, here, Mr. Letter-A-Day," said Kate. "Someone cool him off."

Reuben wriggled in his cauldron. He put his hands on the rim and let his lesson plan book fall to the bottom. He got out of his cauldron so quickly it tipped over, clanging, then he walked down the line to where Madeline was. His face was red; he was breathing hard.

"I never said you were interchangeable," he said. "I got a fiancée."

"Just not here, huh?" said Madeline.

"Gotcha," said Hank. Only his head was visible; he was smoking clove cigarettes, and the sweet smoke rose like steam over something edible.

"All I said was 'simmer'," Reuben said, eyeing Madeline's bare feet. "Just simmer, that's all." Her toes wriggled, as if in acknowledgement. He was suddenly afraid he might cry if he said more.

"Oh, come here, Rube," said Madeline, lightly. She patted the side of her cauldron and moved over, propping the lesson plan book over her shirt like a bed sheet. Reuben climbed in, careful not to touch her when he grabbed the rim to steady himself. Her pants leg was warm against his, and when they went back to filling in the blank pages of their lesson plan books, they wrote funny notes on each other's pages and let their bare arms touch.

❧

In his letters, Reuben grew demanding. Send me your business card, give me your bracelet. Send me a tape of your voice. Give me the scent you wear.

She sent him everything he wanted, and more. The first time it was the button he had nibbled off her silk blouse. Then there was a mug, wrapped in tissue: the first cup they had both drunk from, the time she put cinnamon in the coffee. He could not recall when that was, and his failure to remember caused him such confusion he wrote her back immediately, talking about nothing, just happy to finish and write WITH LOVE in big block letters above his name. She wrote him back about her sex dreams and her crying fits. She filled a whole page with *I love you*, over and over, in big letters pasted onto the paper. The letters had been cut out of money. Each one, she said, was from a different ten-dollar bill. He didn't know what to think. "Guys, I shouldn't show this to you," he said. He showed it to Reggie and Hank anyway. They called him a five-hundred-dollar stud. They gave him high-fives. "I'm just a cad," he said, but when he spoke his lips lingered over the word, and he said *cad* to himself in private just to feel his mouth say it.

"If you're a cad," said Reggie, "then let's get some poontang."

"Use it or lose it," said Hank. "Big Brother Peace Corps don't slap your wrist on Saturday night. I know a place in town."

"How do you know a place?" said Reuben.

"Geronimo," said Hank. "The man knows a certain house of ill repute."

"Some place," said Reuben.

"Coming or not?" said Hank.

Reuben shook his head. "Hey, I'll be there in spirit," he said. He watched them bicycle from the compound, down the dirt road. He could see their headlights move faster and faster the closer they got to town. "Don't let the bedbugs bite," he yelled, but when he saw Kate and Madeline staring, squatting by a tub of soaking clothes, he was ashamed, and he walked away.

Joanne sent him her diaphragm next. "Jesus," he said quietly, then turned around in his bunk so no one could see. He threw it in the trash. He told Reggie and Hank he had gotten moldy brownies. Then he got a tube of her red lipstick. At first he was alarmed, thinking it was blood: the tropical sun had melted the contents like a crayon. He laughed about it. He showed it to everyone, and when they laughed too, he laughed even harder. "*Ain't* that something?" he said. "*Ain't* it?" He threw the tube in the trash bin, and when he saw the next morning that dogs had knocked the bin over and carried the tube away, he wondered if he would see her diaphragm on the street some day. He couldn't imagine anything funnier. He laughed all through breakfast. He felt dangerous, and when Madeline and Kate bet him a beer, he drank hot onion curry straight from the bowl on the table.

Joanne's letters were so full of sex he was aroused when they arrived. But as he read them again later, his head swimming with beer, he was stirred not with arousal but with something else, something quiet and strange. He had the sense he was reading her words through two pairs of eyes: the pair that read and the pair that watched him read. The onionskin paper seemed filled with hieroglyphics, with passion meant for someone else, for someone not even present, like a heart carved into a tree, containing names he didn't know. How? he asked. How can anyone live with such desire? Where can it go?

He sat at night in his bunk composing letters back, acknowledging to himself his own confusion. He sat stripped to the waist, the mosquitoes feeding at will; he nodded constantly, as if in agreement, and drank beer so quickly he got headaches. He told her nothing: his letters were full of anecdotes and turns of phrase he knew she would interpret as clumsy declarations of love. *Joanne, I saw the sun come up. Was it the same sun for you?* Or, *The women here are beautiful, OK, but so is chocolate cake. So are whiffle balls. It's not the same.* He wanted his other pair of eyes to see what he wrote. He would hold his letters up to the light. What his other eyes saw was deceit, and when he told himself he was writing deceit, when he said the words out loud, he felt light as a bubble, as if he would float to the ground if someone pushed him from an airplane.

When he received a pair of her panties, Reggie and Hank were standing over his shoulder watching him tear the package open. "Hey, hey," he said, holding the frilly silk aloft. "The letter's mine. Hands off." Reggie and Hank grabbed the panties, then threw them on his bunk, whooping. Were they new? he wondered. He left them there and went off for language class; when he came back the cleaning boy had straightened their bunks. His was empty, and when he checked under his bunk and in the small suitcase in the corner and found nothing there, he whistled in relief.

So the next Saturday night he bicycled into town with Reggie and Hank. They smoked dope in an alley, leaning against a wall that left their shirts brown and wet. They told vicious stories about everyone, then walked to the whorehouse. Its walls were covered with burlap sugar sacks; the cloth had been hammered through the cement. Inside the main room was a bead door, and when they pushed through, a Chinese man with a cyst on his neck leered at them questioningly and made an obscene gesture with his forefinger and hand. When he met his girl, Reuben spoke his desires harshly. He saw the look on her face; she thought he was joking. "So what you do?" he said then, imitating her speech. He felt himself scowling, as if he were sucking a lemon rind. "How much?" he said. He slapped his wallet against his palm. "How much you want? What you do?"

Reggie and Hank met him later in the hall. A table had been shoved against the wall, and the man with the cyst brought over beers. Reggie and Hank couldn't stop talking about their girls. They lined their empties like a picket fence on the table. They were sweating hard, so they took off their shirts. The hallway smelled like a crawlspace. "Ooh-*ee*, am I wasted," they said. Reuben looked at their nakedness. He was high and drunk, but he stood and called them liars. He knew what they were doing. He was sure of it. They were picturing themselves in Iowa and New Jersey, perhaps lined up for a wedding photo, perhaps eating at a picnic, or crossing their legs in a crowded theater. They could feel the hands of their girlfriends warm in theirs; they could smell the stale skin of white-haired relatives, hear the affectionate words of their neighbors, touch the hair of small, trembly nieces. They sensed everyone nearby, somewhere just out of sight, and they were saying *I don't know you anymore*. They might as well have been plucking their eyes from the sockets.

Later, walking alone, staggering past the Cantonese drunks, Reuben saw a man sitting on a piece of cardboard, peeling a large spiky fruit. The man leaned against a giant, bulging sack, driving a spoon into the fruit to extract the pulp. When the fibers broke against the husk, Reuben heard the little tearing sounds, like stems being yanked from the ground. He held his arms out, as if to take the fibers in his hand, to roll them between his fingers, but he felt only the air, thick and warm with the exhaust from the diesels barreling past. The night was sticky and damp. When he woke in his bunk the next day his lips tasted of cloves and mud.

One day Madeline had a package for him. She walked into the men's bunkroom and smelled what they were smoking. "You can get kicked out for that shit, you know," she said, waving her hand like a fan.

"Smokes from Geronimo," Reuben said. "From the man's own hand. You going to say no to that?"

She looked at him with one eye shut and crinkled her nose. "Did you want the Peace Corps or the Marine Corps?" she said.

The men laughed. They aimed invisible guns at each other. Ker-*pow*, they said. Ker-*pow* and ker-*pow*. Reuben groaned as if wounded; he pushed back his chair and laid himself out on the cement floor. Hank staggered over to the beer tub and dumped the water out, then sprawled in the puddle. Reggie grabbed hold of the table and shook it. He brought his forehead down hard on the Formica top. "I am slain," he said.

"It's from Joanne," said Madeline, holding the package out. "Reuben," said Reggie. "I'm serious. I think my head's bleeding."

"So bleed, already," said Reuben. Then: "The Marine Corp's it exactly, Madeline." He held out his arms and she threw him the package. He put it under his head as if it were a pillow.

"Reuben," Madeline said, looking him in the eye. Her lips were parted as if she wanted to say more, but she just folded her arms and walked out. Reuben watched her go. She was righter than she knew. He wanted to be a killer.

"Reuben," he whispered, in a high, far-away voice.

"Hey," said Hank. "I can do Madeline better than that." He said Reuben's name in falsetto. Reggie said he could imitate her even better, and the two men rocked their heads back and forth and started saying Reuben's name over and over.

But it wasn't Madeline's voice Reuben had imitated. It was Joanne's. He whispered his name again, accenting the first syllable, the way Joanne spoke when she wanted his attention, and he put his finger to his head. He pulled an invisible trigger. He imagined Joanne sitting up in bed, yanking the sheets up over her knees. She would be wrapping a package with twine, stuffing – what? her breakfast? her bra? – into a box, nibbling at her long hair. She would whisper his name, and he would go ker-pow, ker-pow, ker-pow and she would see his clunky body laid out stiff on the floor.

❧

Reuben kept packages and letters from Joanne in a cardboard box, grown soggy with water from the beer tub and the occasional rain. The box was stuffed with clothes on top, and when he received letters he first read them, then plunged the paper through the shirts and pants like a white-hot poker. The letters said *Reuben*, but now he could feel the pleading in the word. *Reuben, where are you?* the letters said. *Where are you, Ruby?* He had a whole boxful of pleading. He put a canvas backpack over the box, but still he heard it rustle at night with small, mewling sounds that disappeared only when he stared at it hard.

Later he gave packages from her to the cleaning boy. Most of the boy's teeth were missing, so when the boy smiled, Reuben saw his gums. He imagined the boy gnawing the packages open, wetting them first with his tongue, his hands shaking with excitement, his nose flat against the paper, sniffing.

Geronimo put his hands on Reuben's shoulders early one morning and began massaging. Reuben was seated on a bench, eating steamed noodles with his fingers. "Bro," Geronimo said, "how'd you like to see a real Peace Corps house?"

"Bro?" said Reuben. "Since when am I your bro?"

"Hey," said Geronimo, "you don't want, I won't say it."

Reuben shrugged. They left in the evening on Geronimo's motorcycle, veering past a convoy of logging trucks on the main road, then bounced down a dirt path near a fence post. The trail was patchy and full of snakeskins and scrubbrush, and the leaves and dust blowing up from the tires stuck in their sweat, matting their arms with dirt and tiny sticks. They passed piles of rotting foliage in a clearing and, farther back, a circle of shacks on stilts, lit by lanterns. The road began again by a row of shophouses with tin roofs, then ended suddenly by a heap of sewer grates in a ravine. In a clearing, Reuben saw a lean-to. A lantern had been looped around a pole, and in the light he could see the ground was covered with lumber, as though walls had been torn down and laid flat in the dirt, like a sidewalk. A tiny Malay man in a Muslim skullcap rose from the darkness and waved. He was stirring a wok. Reuben heard a cleaver click against the metal. Against the tarp he saw the shadow of something long and thin, like a tail, and then the lean-to was gone, replaced by jungle, and the footpath grew so small Reuben thought of veins: tiny ropes burrowing into dense, fatty palms, the knuckly banyan roots underneath, a wall of bark and vines on either side.

Geronimo's house was nothing much: it had shuttered windows, and the planks were so old and wormy they looked like straw. The stilts were missing in places. Piles of muddy bricks supported the floor.

"I thought this was going to take hours," said Reuben. "That's what I heard. 'Geronimo's place is *hours* away.'"

"You know how it is," said Geronimo. "All the scenery looks the same off the main road. People lose track of time. It's different for everyone."

Inside were tiny red stuffed chairs and a wooden desk, the type used by Malaysian schoolchildren. A few watercolors of water buffalo had been taped onto the wall planks, along with a stained calendar advertising a tractor. "Kitchen, so-called, down there, bedroom over there, well and wash-up floor out back," said Geronimo, pointing. "Johnnie Walker cabinet here." He nodded at a chest of drawers in the main room, with a cassette player on top, a wadded tissue stuck to its side. Geronimo pulled a lantern out of one of the drawers, then lit the paraffin wick.

"This is wonderful," said Reuben. "This is Peace Corps."

They sat down in the red chairs and drank Johnnie Walker from stained plastic cups rimmed with chew marks. Reuben thought he had never heard a man talk so much: Geronimo told him how the movie theaters were too cold, how The Beach of Passionate Love, up north, was full of chiggers and sand crabs, how in Bangkok you could ride elephants on the street and buy a girl for the price of American shampoo.

Reuben reached for his cup, but his aim was woozy, and he knocked the liquid onto the planks; he could see it collect in the cracks.

"No prob, bro," said Geronimo. "I got the best vacuum cleaner in town."

Reuben was drinking from the bottle cap when he heard Geronimo call him. "Out back, Rube. Come see the vacuum." Down the back steps was a cement floor surrounded by a wall of corrugated tin. Geronimo was standing by a stone well, turning a rope crank with both hands. It creaked; the rope was frayed, patched with something shiny and black, like tar. "Shh!" Geronimo said, and kept turning. Reuben peeked into the well. It was pitch black. The air smelled fetid, as if something were rotting in the water. Reuben stepped aside, crinkling his nose in disgust, suddenly aware of screeching in the air, a tight howl, and when he realized the sound was coming up through the well, he turned to warn Geronimo, who just shook his head. Reuben saw fingers clawing up the sides of the bucket. Geronimo held the crank with one hand and reached down into the well with the other, and his extended arm began to shake, as if something had grabbed hold.

"Hey!" Reuben said. He stepped back.

"Relax," said Geronimo. "It's the vacuum cleaner." He pulled his arm up, and holding onto his wrists was something tiny and thin, with a tail. It had a pruney, shrunken face. Its skull was round as a ball.

"It's a monkey, hombre," said Geronimo, smiling. "It's my little bro',

Hoover." It opened its mouth wide and screeched at Reuben, baring its teeth, then used the top stone as leverage and held Geronimo loosely around the neck, like a baby. "I put Hoov in the well when I'm away," said Geronimo. "He likes to tear things up. He sleeps in the bucket when I'm gone."

"God, he stinks," said Reuben. The air was putrid and sweet.

"He takes some getting used to. But I'll tell you, Hoov's the one to call when there's a mess. He'll suck up anything your little heart desires."

Back in the living room, Geronimo threw Hoover to the floor. "This way, Hoov," he said. "There's some yum-yum for you." The monkey put its face to the floor planks and stuck out a long tongue, lapping.

"*That*," said Geronimo, "is titillatin'. Huh, Rube?"

Reuben nodded. He couldn't keep his eyes off Hoover.

"Tunes?" said Geronimo. He handed the cassette player to Reuben, then bent over and stroked Hoover's head. Hoover looked up and chattered a little, then stuck its head into Geronimo's cup, lapping up more Johnnie Walker. "That's a good Hoov," said Geronimo. "Give big bro' a kissum." He kissed the top of its head. "Oh, he's a hungry little guy. Did you hear that stomach? We gotta get Hoov some munchies."

A tape was already in the cassette player. Reuben pressed the Play button, but was disappointed at what came out. It was a woman's voice, whispering. The tape was so scratchy he could hardly hear her over the roar in the background.

"So who is it?" Reuben said. "I could swear. . . . Who is it?"

"I don't know," said Geronimo. He was sitting cross-legged on the floor, holding Hoover in his lap, tipping the cup up to its tongue.

"Come on. Who?"

"It was a gift." He shrugged. "The cleaning boy. You know how he is."

"I know this voice," Reuben said. What he heard didn't seem to be music at all, just roaring and this woman's whispering, and when he looked up questioningly, eyes roaming the house, he saw the shutters were closed, even though the evening was hot. Winged insects were struggling in through the cracks.

Geronimo stood, folding his arms. "You know it really?" he said. Hoover squatted by his side, eyes shining.

"Yeah," said Reuben. "Really." He frowned in concentration.

"Listen. Listen real close."

"I don't know," Reuben said. "It's like Joanne, almost." He felt light, as if his feet weren't touching the floor. He was dizzy, his breath shallow. He thought he heard her whispering his name, but the roaring in the background crackled so loud he couldn't be sure.

"You think? Maybe it's just a voice out of nowhere," said Geronimo. "Spooky stuff, you know? Like how I know what you're thinking. I mean, I can just get *in* there." He grunted. "You just got to make up your mind, that's all. What do you want? Really?"

"Is it her or not?"

"Which you want it to be?" Geronimo said. He opened his hand, then closed it.

Reuben held the cassette player out and watched the tape move from reel to reel. That whispering. What was she saying under the roaring? Her voice was breaking, as if she had the hiccups.

"Your wish is my command," said Geronimo. He squinted into the lamplight. A leaf was stuck to his cheek. Small twigs dangled from his shirt.

"Please," said Reuben.

"Hey, sorry," said Geronimo. "I'm just a jungle junkie, not a love broker." He bent down and let Hoover crawl up his shoulder. In the lamplight, Geronimo's face was half in shadow, and when he spoke his lips hardly moved. He stroked Hoover's tail, and the monkey closed its eyes and laced its fingers around the earpiece of Geronimo's glasses. It gnashed its tiny teeth. It grabbed hold of Geronimo's hair and put its mouth to his ear, chattering.

"I just . . . I'm hearing something," said Reuben, pressing the cassette player to his ear. "I got to know what."

"All right then," said Geronimo. "All right. Now we're getting somewhere. Just put the tape player down. Right on the desk. Don't give it to me. Just put it down. Right there, put it down. Nice and slow."

Reuben felt his body tingle, and he saw his hand holding the cassette player, caressing the plastic window lightly with his thumb. Hoover began to screech and bare his teeth, and when Reuben tried to raise his arms to shield his face, Hoover lunged forward, for him or for the tape he couldn't tell, and Reuben's limbs just flopped at his sides. He felt Geronimo's hand on his. He looked down and saw the man's fingers around his wrist, guiding his hand to the desk. Together, they put the cassette player down. Geronimo ejected the tape. Reuben felt Geronimo's arm around his waist, moving him toward the door, helping him down the steps. He saw a flashlight beam illuminate the ground. He saw his body move, his feet step over roots, his hands pull aside brush. He felt himself walk awhile, staying inside the beam, and sometimes he caught glimpses of Geronimo at his side, holding Hoover's hand. He had no idea how far they walked. He knew only when they stopped, they stood in a clearing. There were thousands of flecks in the air, fuzzy as static, suspended in the flashlight beam. Reuben saw Hoover run into the beam, opening and closing his hand and stuffing his fingers into his mouth. Flying ants, Geronimo said. They swarm this time of year. Hoover loved to gobble them. Reuben felt the tickly wings on his hands, his mouth, his eyes; he felt a blizzard of wings. They sounded like whispering. He ran forward into the swarm, straining to hear, but Hoover leaped up and straddled his neck and started to screech and screech and wouldn't stop.

Why Won't You Talk to Me?

RICHARD DUGGIN

The couple across the hall in Number 4 were fighting again. The young woman's voice was shrill with recrimination. Even with the hallway as a buffer between the two apartments, and with the doors closed, the sound carried to Dowd like an alarm. The first time he heard it he thought it was their television up too loud, that he was hearing a rerun of *I Love Lucy*. The woman's voice had that same nasal timbre as Lucy's keening. The couple had been married not quite a year. They'd moved into the building a month after Dowd.

Almost from the beginning Dowd had heard them. Mostly it was the young woman he could hear. The young man was very soft-spoken, unexcitable. That was one of his wife's indictments as time went on. Her husband seemed not to care enough for her; he was not demonstrative enough in his caring for her liking. "You never *say* anything," she reproached him in her strident voice. "You won't *talk* to me about anything. I'm trying to make our marriage work, Ben. I'm trying the best I know how to be a good wife. But if you'll never talk to me about anything . . ."

It wasn't that Dowd was nosey. For the most part he had lived a quiet and respectable existence, and he had never been one to pry into the affairs of others. But the young woman's voice was so lucid with affliction that he could not help himself. He was not yet accustomed to living with people above, behind, and beside him. He couldn't ignore the presence of strangers in the sounds that trespassed through the walls, in the pipes, in the ceiling. He had spent all forty-seven years of his own marriage in houses buffered for privacy with plenty of space and foliage between neighbors.

Before the young couple moved in, a frail old woman lived in Number 4, a widow, Dowd guessed, in her mid-eighties. She kept parakeets. He could hear their metallic chittering whenever he stepped out in the hall. He encountered the woman just twice, both times during the first week he'd moved in. The first time, they each exited their doors at the same time to check the mailboxes in the front entryway. She had reacted as if she had caught him spying on her: she clutched her letters to her bony chest and fled past him, locking her door behind her. Two days later, he startled her again when he happened upon her in the laundry room in the basement. That time, she had let him know in no uncertain terms, her hand flattened over her heart. "You gave me a terrible fright," she said. Her eyes did not betray alarm; they were fiercely accusatory.

Dowd was distressed by the woman's reaction. Even after a year, he still mourned his wife Elizabeth, feeling dislocated and unmoored without her, and like the old woman, he was alone by force of circumstance. He knew she would not have reacted that way had she known he was a married man. But she acted as if she had seen something else, something loathsome, and Dowd felt ashamed and resentful.

The third week Dowd was there, she died.

From his own apartment, he had listened to the clump-clumping of the firemen's boots in the hall, the rattle of the paramedics' metal-framed stretcher being wheeled in. For the longest time, he could hear the steady thump-thump-thump and intermittent asthmatic sigh of the resuscitation machine, and the hushed voices of relatives called to the scene. After an hour, the firemen left and then the relatives. The birds, who had been quiet during all the commotion, commenced their trilling again.

That was the worst night Dowd had spent since he moved in. He was sure he had made a terrible mistake letting Father Liotta, their priest and friend for over fifteen years, convince him to put his home on the market and seek reprieve from his grief in new surroundings. "Simplicity," the priest had said. "Let others take care of maintaining for you, George. Reduce your space to what is comfortable for one, and live with other people around you – be aware of life all around you. Get out and travel while you still have your health. Go visit your boys, and let someone else cut the lawn and replace the worn-out washers in the faucets." His sons lived on opposite coasts, Ronnie and Mark in California, Richard in North Carolina. Each was married, with his own family and concerns, and Dowd didn't wish to complicate their lives with his just now. It was enough to take Father Liotta's advice about moving into a smaller place with other people in the same building with him. But so far, he'd only been reminded of solitude and death, and he could not escape the dreadful feeling he'd abandoned Elizabeth, some essence of her left behind yet in their house, doubly empty now for his absence as well. Residents in apartments were transient, and mostly what he was aware of in the sounds of life around him were the closings of doors, the slipping of deadbolts.

Apartment 4 was empty for three more weeks before the young couple moved in and shattered the early evenings and weekends with their arguments.

One time the woman complained, "Every place we go, we hardly ever go where I want. Whenever we have any time to go anywhere at all, we see all your friends, but I haven't hardly seen any of my friends, not once since our wedding."

The young man must have said something in return, but Dowd did not hear it.

"Oh yeah, I'm sure, and what do you do when we go over to my parents? Huh? Tell me that, Ben, what do you do?"

Again, there was no response Dowd could hear but what he might have taken to be a clearing of the throat.

"You're right, Ben. Exactly *nothing*. All the way in the car you won't say a word to me. I could be carrying on a conversation with a corpse. How do you think that makes me feel? How long do you think a person can stand someone who won't even talk to his wife?"

Within five months of their moving in, the young woman was gone. Dowd hadn't seen her leave, but by some intuition he was aware of her absence. The silence pressed behind her door, and he sensed it like a seismic depression from across the hallway each time he unlocked his own door. For a period after that, Dowd occasionally observed the young man come or go from work, and in the evenings some of his friends – from his single days, Dowd surmised – dropped by with six-packs of beer. At those times there would be laughter and sounds of celebration, perhaps over a football game they were watching, or a prize fight; or perhaps it was over nothing more than getting together to drink beer, boisterous in their freedom the way young men are who haven't quite abandoned their adolescence. Dowd could recall such occasions before he got married, when he still preferred the company of males his own age. Fifty-two years ago, before the war, when he had graduated from high school and was on his own for the first time, working for the Union Pacific as a clerk in Freight Accounting. He had not yet met Elizabeth, who would have been in junior high school then.

Still, he did not actually hear his neighbor, Ben, join in his friends' chorus. With them Ben remained quiet, his voice no louder than usual – indistinguishable through the walls beyond anything more than low reedy phrasings, like an oboe among brass. Dowd could not gauge how seriously Ben was taking the absence of his wife.

She stayed away for several weeks. Then one day she returned. Dowd happened to be sitting on his patio in front of the apartment, reading a mystery novel – his favorite form of relaxation – and he watched her make several trips from her car to the front door of the building, carrying armloads of clothing on hangers. By her third trip it was obvious to both of them that he was observing her, and so he felt compelled to say something. "Moving in, or moving out?" He tried to keep a friendly, understanding tone.

"In," she said in a voice that revealed nothing. "Again."

Dowd felt relieved. He did not like to see young people troubled as they were over marriage. There was so much of that today. It seemed half of them were pining to find love, the other half wanted to let go of it. It all seemed selfish and pointless. In his last years working for the railroad, a supervisor in the Traffic Division, he had seen the marriages of several of his younger employees end for reasons that were shockingly trivial. They needed more "personal space." They had discovered "different priorities" for their lives. "We made a mistake," one of his female clerks told him in the lunchroom one day when she asked him for time off to go to court. "It wasn't what we expected it was going to be like together." She had been married two years. Dowd could not imagine what might have gone wrong so soon. How could you know it was a mistake before you'd even begun to share a whole life with someone? Just what did they expect marriage was going to be?

Shortly after the woman's admission, Dowd had occasion to introduce Elizabeth at the annual Traffic Division banquet. It was during that moment just before the invited speaker gives the keynote address, when all the employees are called upon to acknowledge their spouses or guests. "This is my first wife, Elizabeth," Dowd proclaimed to all assembled. Even though he was being humorous, it was his way of expressing disapproval over the younger generation's ready failure to honor their commitments.

He had married Elizabeth when she was seventeen and he was twenty-one. She was a child then, he not much more. It was right after the war. She had just graduated from Central High School, he was newly out of the Army with his old job back as a clerk in the Freight Accounts Office of Union Pacific Railroad in Omaha. What was there to know about personal space or expectations? They had a life to get going. Three sons to bear and raise up to their own marriages and families; two houses to transfigure into homes; forty-six years to live together, and longer still, if death had not split them apart. A *mistake*? What was it people expected?

For a time after the young woman moved back into Number 4, she and her husband seemed to settle in with one another. They behaved the way Dowd remembered marriage could be: the uneventful comings and goings of two people who shared the same domicile. They both worked, the husband in the day and his wife in the evenings, and their common hours at home were seldom the same each week, except late at night.

Ben continued to have a few of his friends over, and at different times, friends of the woman, whose name, Dowd learned, was Jill, came by to visit her, too. They dressed smartly, like department store clerks or young account managers, in crisp skirts and gray or navy blazers with padded shoulders. They came to shower the single among them who were about to become married also, or to buy housewares or lingerie at home parties which Jill hosted. Dowd heard their laughter, the shrieks of surprise. It reminded him how his own wife had loved to socialize. Sometimes he craved the sound of women in his home, their voices red with gossip.

When he was quite young, the only boy in a family with four sisters, the very existence of women had sometimes vexed him: his mother's friends were quick to dismiss him with an inclined nod of their heads, a tolerant smile; his sisters and their girlfriends – especially his youngest sister's friends, who were his contemporaries also – embarrassed him with their shrill laughter and simpering taunts, the way they made fun of their boyfriends in sarcastic tones as metallic as iron. They were voracious in their derision of how boys behaved and spoke, and, riddled by their talk as he often was when they were in his house, Dowd believed that girls were harder than boys by virtue of their scorn. Still, they seemed vulnerable, too: they wanted boys to like them even as they mistrusted them. They could not help themselves, and it was all they talked about. His own sisters had grown up in a house with a father who did not talk to them. He left that to their mother. "You watch out for yourselves," was as much as he had to say to them. "You go out with a boy, you make him keep his hands to hisself if you want to keep your respect." Dowd could see how their attitudes had to do with a mistrust of *all* men, and he learned, in time, to be tolerant of them out of sympathy for their lot.

Lately, across the hall they were fighting again. Apparently, Jill was not coming home at night when Ben thought she was supposed to.

"I stayed for a while after work. It was Lisa's birthday, and we had a drink to celebrate, is all. What's wrong with that?"

Dowd could never make out what Ben said in his soft oboe voice. Even when he opened his door and stood in the hallway outside their door, Dowd could hear only Jill's side of things.

"Before that? When before that? Last weekend to talk with Michelle and Betty Ann and Michael. These are my friends, Ben. I can have a drink with them if I want to."

Even with his ear to their door, he could only hear Ben mumble.

"Oh, poor Ben. Poor put-upon Ben. Why don't you just admit it – why don't you have the honesty to just out and ask me directly: Jill, are you having an affair?"

Dowd couldn't make out if Ben asked his question.

"The answer, Ben, if you really cared to know, the answer would be no. I'm not having an affair with any one of the guys I *work* with. None of *them* is my type of guy."

Dowd wondered at her ambiguity. Was she clever enough for intentional equivocation?

"The fact is, Ben, the plain fact of the matter is you don't care whether I love you or not. All you care about is your pride. You're just worried what it might look like to your precious friends if I found someone else to sleep with – someone else who cared enough about me and wanted me – how your pride would be hurt. Otherwise *you* don't care."

The oboe protested, a little four-note riff.

"No you don't. And you know you don't. Because if you did, then I wouldn't feel this way."

It went on like this for several days in a row. Each time Ben came in the door in the early evening, it was something. Once it was about her waiting meals for him to get home from his job.

"All you have to do is call me or something, just tell me when you're coming home, or leave a note before you go off in the morning. Maybe then I could have something ready for you, or make you something when you get here, if there's ever any time before *I* have to go to work. Your hours are always different. I've thrown meals away, Ben, because I get home from work and find them all dried up in the oven waiting for you. All you have to do is maybe tell me an hour I can expect you to be here. Is that asking too much? But instead you just get mad at me and take it out on me with your silence. You never tell me what you want. You only sulk if I don't do everything just perfect for you. There are times, if you care to know, when I cry about it when you aren't here. I *cry*, Ben, because it hurts me that you don't care any more than that about your own wife. I've had a lot of hurt, Ben. But you don't care, do you? Well, I'm sorry, but I've got news for you. Just maybe I don't care anymore either."

And always it returned to the familiar lament:

"I'm sure, if you'd just talk to me once in a while . . . I'm sure you can do that, if you wanted to, Ben."

Occasionally when he saw her during the day passing by on the sidewalk in front of his living room window, he thought she looked in some way defeated, littler even than her stature. He wanted to let her know that he sympathized. He supposed that loving someone who was indifferent was undoubtedly worse, even, than enduring someone's anger. Several times when he ran into her on the way out his door he almost said, "If you'd like to talk to someone about it . . . I understand the problem." But the plain truth was, Dowd wasn't at all sure he did understand. Nothing like that had ever happened to him. Elizabeth, who had died at sixty-two of a disease of the heart, had never worked outside the home, and except for her garden club and bridge group, she had never spent an evening in the company of others without him. Neither had she required he talk to her at any length, nor indicated she was displeased if he were silent. In every respect, they had a good marriage. In spite of that, however, there was a coal of guilt, which smoldered yet beneath the rubble of his grief, and he could neither smother it nor quite bring it to the clean air of comprehension. All he understood was, it was what made him feel sympathy for the young woman's plight rather than for Ben.

But, all his concern for his neighbor was of no consequence, because each time he saw her on their separate ways in or out of their apartments, when there might have been opportunity to speak, all he could manage to say was, "Have a nice day."

In time, Dowd had come to realize the young woman did not know how to argue convincingly when she was upset. Her fights with her husband amounted to the sorts of charades children often stage when they are trying to imitate adults: the cadence of argumentation was there, but not the sense. When he admitted this, Dowd had to side with the young man, who must have felt unjustly beleaguered at times. However, his own gnawing loneliness aroused his compassion for the woman. That she didn't seem happy in her marriage preyed on him. He began to have fantasies about her.

What she required was someone more mature who would be patient and understanding. And a good conversationalist. In his mind Dowd was often in conversation with her. Sometimes she would come to his door distraught, on the verge of tears. "He doesn't understand me. He's so . . . *void* of substance and feeling."

"Yes," Dowd would say. "There are men like that. Particularly young men."

"How can I make him pay attention to me? I'm a person who needs a lot of attention from a man."

"You can't make a silk purse from a sow's ear," he'd say. "What you need is a man who has a lot of attention he wants to give. Someone mature and emotionally settled."

"Yes!" she'd cry. "Someone mature to pay attention to me. I have so *much* to give to a man like that, if you want to know the truth."

Rather than put him off, the notion that his neighbor might have slept with men other than her young husband – that she would even suggest it to Ben – aroused Dowd in some obscurely prurient way. Fancifully, he desired her for his own. He had not known a woman to admit carnal urges of her own that she might need to satisfy without first having to be convinced. The women of his generation had to be pursued and persuaded. They were wooed by men who possessed the charm to allay their natural revulsion for the baseness of the male. Dowd never possessed such charm. He'd come to believe a long time ago – perhaps influenced by his sisters and their friends' disdain – that a woman with any sense of modesty would be revolted by the mere notion of (let alone the *sight* of) the ridiculous male organ. Exposed and vulnerable as it was outside the body like that, it was as if nature had made a critical error in evolutionary design, a mutation neither aerodynamically sound nor aesthetically pleasing (even when cut from marble like Michelangelo's David, whose marbles were diminutive in proportion to the graceful mass of the greater polished stone), an unsightly appendage which we laugh at openly, man and woman, on other animals: the elephant, the donkey, the ape.

But Dowd knew that young women today were more open about such things. They had not had impressed upon them all those years of denial, of waiting to be coaxed with assurances they would not be betrayed in intimacy by men who themselves had been taught to be sneaky and inconstant. And while Dowd was not the sort of man to take advantage – had never possessed the confidence it took to be a successful predator – nevertheless, toward women like his neighbor – young and attractive and, he wanted to believe, vulnerable to love – he felt protective in a courtly fashion. All this boldness in the modern woman – *assertiveness*, they called it – had confused things. Their frankness about their sexuality did not serve them any better in their relations with men; it only made them easy marks.

Younger men were foolish, he thought. They were able to enjoy a woman in her physical prime, all that firm buoyancy of elastic young skin – everything exquisitely soft and resilient at the same time – but they treated that miraculous privilege with either callousness or indifference, as if there would always be enough. More than enough. It was profligate. It was ignorant. If Dowd had it to do over again, knowing what he knew now at sixty-eight about what to cherish from a woman's companionship, his wife Elizabeth might have known a different life with him. He thought now that maybe he had not been as heedful as he could have been, so caught up as he was with earning a living, teaching his sons respect for work and honesty in their dealings with other men. Indeed, if he knew then what he'd come to learn of late about a woman's needs, it might not have been Elizabeth he married, but someone else, one of those girls like his youngest sister's friends, skeptical and sharp-witted and full of themselves, women with spirit waiting for just the right man to capture their trust. He thought he could help Jill. She was in her twenties; he was just sixty-eight. His own experience with longevity in marriage could offer her the assurance that you could love someone for a long time. If she could get to know him, he could tip the scales of her affection in his favor. It never occurred to him that he might be attracted to her unreasonably.

When he thought about it, what Dowd wanted most was to win Jill's confidence. He desired the compliment of her youthful attention paid to him, although he could not have said why this aroused him. She was attractive enough, all right, if no head-turning beauty. Her face was pretty, although she had one of those hairstyles that reminded one of an adolescent boy's: her black hair was cut short and feathered back on the sides, like Peter Pan or Diana the Huntress or Joan of Arc. Her breasts were small and her hips were wider than her shoulders, but she did have a beautiful back, long and flat like a dancer's.

When he finally acknowledged to himself that he was infatuated by her, Dowd became even more aware of her comings and goings. They gave sudden new purpose to his days, a way of organizing his thoughts and activities. Whenever he heard the door across the hall open, he ran to his own door and put his eye to the security peephole. Many times it was just Ben coming home, and after awhile Dowd got to recognize the difference in the way they plied their keys to the lock – his was more abrupt and metallic, hers hesitant, lingering, the sound of it like a slow zipper opening. Sometimes after she opened the door she stood just inside, surveying the room before entering, cautious of prowlers, perhaps. Or perhaps of her husband.

Watching secretly those momentary tableaux always made Dowd feel even more tenderness for her. She was lonely, too, he could see. Her husband did not take an interest in her, in the things she did, in where she went, how she liked to spend her time. Dowd decided he would definitely make an effort to talk to her, to get to know her likes and dislikes in order to show her there were men who knew how to care about a woman.

Jill did her laundry on Sunday nights, carrying baskets of clothing from her apartment to the laundry room and occupying the machines for several hours. Dowd had discovered this during the three weeks of his vigil, spying on her from the little round fisheye glass in his door. Because he was retired and home more often, he himself did laundry whenever the need arose – a washerful at a time at odd times during the week as his hamper became full – although not yet on a Sunday. But if he timed it properly, he might encounter her there in that cozy basement room where their need to speak to one another would be unavoidable because of the confined space. What better way to start than over the wash, as women had done for centuries by the banks of streams and in public fountains?

With this in mind, Dowd decided to reconnoiter ahead of time, plan his meeting with her in such a way as not to seem awkward. The very next Sunday he heard her go down the stairs off the hallway just beyond their doors, and he watched for her return. When she came back into view, she was carrying the empty clothes basket, and she hurried back into her apartment, closing the door quickly behind herself. He let himself out of his own apartment quietly, carrying a decoy basket of some of his clothes – a few shirts, dish towels, socks – and went to the basement.

It was a small concrete block room – two coin washers and dryers in the same square space as the central hot-water heater and the bank of meters for the electrical circuits to each apartment. Today one of the washers was sloshing through its wash cycle, and one of the dryers was humming already with another load. This perplexed Dowd. Before Jill's most recent trip, he had not heard anyone else go down to the laundry room, and he couldn't figure out when she – or anyone else, for that matter – might have done the earlier load that was now drying.

He opened the dryer door, and the machine stopped automatically. Inside its dark mouth, he could see a variety of colored clothes, mostly women's things by the looks of it. He reached in and took out a T-shirt. It was a man's size, and he recalled by the logo on the front – "Everything's E = mc², Man" under a grinning caricature of Einstein – that he had seen Ben wearing it. He reached in again and this time pulled out a pair of mint green shorts, and a pink sock – things he was sure he'd seen Jill wearing before.

It was in this way, curious to know more about her personal life, about the life nestled in closets and drawers in a home where she lived in intimacy with a man who wouldn't talk to her, that Dowd discovered her preference for cotton fabrics over blends, her partiality for pastels over bolder colors. She was a size 8, with a 32A bust. And nearly all her panties revealed a small brown stain of blood in their white crotches. His heart melted with that discovery. So like Elizabeth, who during her fertile years could never quite staunch the flow, no matter how many different absorbent products she tried. In this unexpected recollection of his wife, Dowd was struck anew with all the poignancy of his loss. At once he was choked with sorrow by the shameful realization of his inconstancy to her memory. For a long moment he was frozen to the spot, unable to let go of his mind's portrait of Elizabeth as a young woman, her face composed and beautiful, her head tilted slightly as if she were waiting for him to speak. Taken with the loveliness of this image, he stood pressing a pair of Jill's pale blue briefs to his face, breathing in their sweet, fresh heat. Presently, his shoulders shook and his chest convulsed in spasms. His tears were blotted by the soft, warm cotton.

When finally he was able to quell his sobs, Dowd gathered the articles of the young woman's clothing he'd set on top of the dryer, and he laid them back inside the drum, closing the door. He punched the start button three times before he was able to comprehend the timer had played out.

With his own basket of dirty clothes under one arm, he left the room, and as he turned the corner, he nearly bumped headlong into Jill who was descending the stairs with yet another basketload of laundry clutched in her hands.

"Oh!" she said, jerking back. "You startled me."

Dowd shook his head to say it was his fault, but all that issued from his throat was a hollow moan, like the first sighing note of a woodwind.

She looked more closely at him, then, alarmed. "Excuse me, is there something wrong, Mr. Dowd?"

But all the words that had been building up in him, all the things he had wanted to say to her in the days to come, fled from that look of apprehension on her face. Lowering his head, Dowd brushed by her and hurried up the stairs to his apartment, unable to talk.

Arcane High

TERESE SVOBODA

Arcania. That's where I'd like to go, I say, and thrust my foot into a bug-filled light-circle.

He stops too. You mean Arcadia.

Arcadia, arcania, academia, I say, to show I know that they relate. You can't be too smart with him. Any less, he cuts you, he leaves you with a Fred.

He is dwelling now on a car coming, a car that could be someone's our age although few can drive yet – ten. He dwells instead. He likes the front page look of everything when you walk, headlights skimming porches, a pink hat on a president's wife on a guttered paper, someone our age caught in front of a coplight. Arcadia High, he says as the car widens itself, driving toward us.

The frontseat Linda waves, the backseat Linda and Bart don't, they are kissing, the windows down enough to catch this.

We wave but we don't kiss. His face is too wide for a kiss, so wide and long an extra chin or less hair on top is just about to happen. This is not to say I haven't had the want. Arcadia High, the way he says it, with a curled lip, I could kiss. He is the only one who dares to walk when he could ride.

Is that a Chevy? I ask, after the taillights jump at the school slow bumps.

Out comes that curled lip – this time for me. Of course. All cars are Chevies, all men are animals. It's called synecdoche, the thing is the sum of its parts, ergo, a Chevy is all cars.

It was really a Fred question is what he meant. How about death? I counter. All deaths are what?

Too soon, he says. Arcane.

The bugs in the light pool rise up in attraction. Only this, and not the car and its passing, disturb them. Their hot wings chop the light, then they fall on their casings to the asphalt.

Arcane defines us. Let the Lindas drive by. They do not even know its meaning, the way it applies.

When I die, he says and stops.

It can't be "if," I say.

Arcane, he says the way you would if someone you were playing against had just earned a point.

It will be a hot summer night like now, he says. Lots of bugs, he says. But not here.

Of course not, I say. This place?

He takes my hand. His is soft and fat between the folds. He has never taken my hand before. I stretch mine in a kind of hand surprise. We are talking about death and himself, his two best subjects together.

I will see big evergreens. He points to the stumpy green attempt at a fir on the lawn across the dark street. My window will look out on them. He squeezes my hand. And I'll die, die.

His voice rises like he means to do somebody else in.

The bugs smack their shells in the light, they smack the light into their insides.

Well, there's Colorado. There's fir trees there.

That's only eighteen miles away, he says, throwing my hand down. More like – New York, he says. They must have something coniferous. A window on Central Park, and a bell to ring when I feel it's time.

The car is coming back. This time its lights are off, its motor's off, it coasts down the street with no one at the wheel.

We watch it inch up to the stoplight where the couple kissing in back jump out and push it through the intersection.

One Linda must have gone home, I say.

She could be in back somewhere, he says. After all, it is her car.

The car moves almost thoughtfully past a fireplug on the next block.

I'm going to New York too, I say.

I will shine your toaster, he says. You will be able to see if anyone's creeping up on you.

No one will creep up on me.

You're beautiful, he says. They all will.

The girls there are all beautiful, I say, without a trace of No in my voice.

Arcane, he says. Arcania. Let's walk you home again.

We leave the bugs to die, moving into the summer heat with our palms beating like wings against it, walking, while others coast. Soon black closes down behind us as light on my block isn't part of it yet. A mock block, that's what he calls it, a couple of hydrants, sticks with red rags tied on. How many times will we circle it tonight, exclaiming on the tackiness of the red?

We both know Shakespeare, right? he says, out of the blue of the red.

Sure, I say. Shakespeare.

That's what we must pillory, he says. Not this tattered red.

It's a who, not a what, I say.

Shakespeare's a what by now.

My father opens our back door, throws out trash underhanded. The bag explodes once it hits the inside of the incinerator. He throws his cigarette in after and slams the door shut.

We take a position behind some bushes. The fire when it catches, stinks. Ash piddles on us in a summer gust.

I'm going in, I say.

The ghosts are coming, the ghosts of all those Shakespeare has pilloried. He points up at the trashy smoke.

Goodnight, I say, the way I do with him, with a lot of good.

Fred by day but me by night, he says.

Not Friday, I say. I finally got him to ask me.

I knew you would, he says. He does not speak after that.

The car finds us again and this time the two Lindas are lying on its hood like it's homecoming. The engine is still off, Bart is pushing.

Kissed her yet? yells one or two of them like they have planned it.

Arcane, I shout back. Quoth Shakespeare.

Is that you? asks my father out the screen door. You're supposed to be in here doing the dishes.

A-R-C-A-N-E, I say.

Don't get smart with me, my father says, opening the screen door wider. And who's that out there with you?

No one, I say and it's true. His head is dead, as he likes to say. He's lying flat behind the bushes where no one would look unless they're my age and temper, and with my exact sadness for the Fred coming up, the silent Fred, all the silent ones that will take up Fridays, so many you don't walk home anymore.

Guys

RICK BARBA

1

On the way back from San Francisco I drop by Joe Coryell's house to invite him over for the football game. I run through rain to Joe's porch. Joe meets me at the door, then steps out. He shuts the door behind him. He looks bad.

He says: "Hey guy."

"You look bad," I say.

Joe raises a brow, as if surprised I can see it. Then he tells me we can't fraternize anymore. That's the word he uses! It doesn't seem like Joe's word.

I step toward the door. "Don't, man," he says. He runs his hand through his hair a couple times. Rain clatters on the porch roof. I say, "Hey. What the fuck?"

Joe's hand stops, as if stuck. He stands there, holding his hair. Then he says, "I don't know, pal." The rain gets louder on the roof. He says, "I'm at a loss."

Suddenly, there's a loud scraping noise. I stare at the roof. Then I look at Joe.

"Something's loose," says Joe.

We both look at the porch roof. I get up on a planter and look closer. I have no idea what to look at. Then the scraping stops. I step down.

"I'm not sure what it is," says Joe.

He looks down the street, like maybe people are coming. I look too. The street's deserted. Everything is gray and dripping. Winter has stripped the trees bare.

I say: "Joe."

"What?"

"This is ridiculous, man."

Joe drops his hand. His hair falls across his forehead.

343

He says, "I know."

"It's my skin, right?" I joke. I say, "Maybe I need those exfoliants."

Joe says, "Maybe."

He tries to laugh – his wife sells cosmetics at Macy's – but he keeps looking away. Then he opens his door and steps inside. He turns back, but keeps a hand on the knob.

٭

I stare at the hand on the knob. I mean, this is a house I *know*.

When I phone, I can see Joe answer. Maybe he'll say, "I'll take it up in the office." As he does so, I picture all the physical steps of the transfer. I see the stairs, the kids. But now I see a new part of the picture: Mrs. Coryell, palming the phone, waiting. Maybe she doesn't hang it up. She makes a click, but then listens to the guys talk.

Joe glances at me. Maybe he sees it too. Anyway, he lowers his voice. "Actually," says Joe. He glances back down the dark hall and says, "OK, so I told you about her counseling."

"Yeah?"

"Apparently, it's getting intense."

Something moves in the darkness behind him. Or maybe not. I look again.

"She's having breakthrough sessions," says Joe.

I nod.

Joe says, "Something about her father."

I lower my voice as well. I say, "Isn't her father dead? Didn't he die years ago?" Joe shrugs. He gives me a helpless look. Then something hits me. I say: "So is it men, this thing?"

Joe just looks at me.

I say, "Or, you know . . . is it me?"

Joe shrugs again. But I can see the answer.

٭

We stand there awhile.

I look at wilted plants on the porch. I've known Joe seven years. It started as a client thing, then grew. Softball teams, etc. Every January 1, we camp out in a motel room with some guys and watch all the bowl games. I try to remember if I've ever made fun of Joe's wife, her looks or anything.

Finally I say, "Is this permanent?"

"Nah," says Joe. But he doesn't look good.

⁂

Later, I sit in my kitchen watching coffee drip through the coffee maker. My wife, Judy, spins salad in the sink. From time to time she looks over at me, and her work at the sink gets louder. Finally she says, "Can you *help* me?"

I don't answer.

She says loudly, "Since you're just sitting there?"

I say, "I'm thinking."

She tosses down a steel ladle. The sound slices to the back of my neck.

"Christ," I say. I stand up. I say, "I was thinking."

She doesn't answer. I watch her shoulders tighten. I once suggested that women have a phobia about quiet moments of contemplation. If you're not running around or yakking like an idiot, then clearly you're not *doing* anything. It was a big mistake to say this. I've been paying for that remark.

Watching Judy whack at vegetables, I suddenly see the cold shoulders of Coryell's wife. I see a thin, hunched woman gunning for guys to blame it on. Guys. They're out there, man. A society of men, walling themselves off from women. Now emissaries are getting to her husband.

What to do?

Ban them.

2

Next morning, rain blows in early again. It's fifty miles of wet hell to San Francisco. I find parking by the CalTrain tracks along Townsend. I get out and slog through dirty puddles, thinking about the video editing session I'm supposed to direct. I hurry past old brick warehouses now converted to ad agencies, law offices, galleries, etc.

In one entry, a small cat curls on a step. I grew up with cats, so I bend to it. The cat sits as if dead, but then it moves. It raises its gaze to me. It's missing an eye! A wet red socket sags on its cheek.

"Christ!" I say, backing away.

I hurry down the street to another brick archway. My destination is VideoTek, a post-production shop with a suite of rooms in the back. But first I duck into the small cafe at the front. I order coffee and a scone.

It's seven forty-five. I sit at a table and wait for my editor to arrive.

I tear up the scone and watch women.

Two guys at the next table talk about the upcoming game. Football's good for San Francisco, although there is some concern about the secondary, the match-ups and such. These men talk knowledgeably, and I smile. I bite off some scone, wash it down with good hot coffee. Though the men speak only to each other, I nod at their assessments.

But then I think of Joe Coryell's wife.

I look down at my coffee. I pour more cream and watch the swirls. I think about sexual molestation. It's a hot topic. People are getting unblocked, remembering things, bad things. Things adults did to them.

Maybe that's happening to Joe's wife.

Hey, good for her, I think. Maybe I resemble her father.

OK, I think.

❧

The morning session goes poorly.

Ron Goldsmith, my editor, is in a sour mood. I see his disappointment when I walk in without donuts. During the post-production phase of my projects, I always bring donuts. This morning, for no particular reason, I skipped the donuts.

Later, while Goldsmith crawls behind the console to patch in a Chyron graphics unit, I see huge jowls form in the static of one of the monitors.

The jowls say: "*Fuck* you, man."

I lurch forward in my chair. I say, "What?"

When I realize it's just Goldsmith talking to the equipment, I sit back. I look at my hands. They're small, like a woman's. A girl once called them *sensitive*. So I told her I wanted to be a sculptor, which of course was a crock of shit.

The office manager, a woman named Marta, sticks her head in. "Trouble?" she asks.

Goldsmith is crawling around, knocking things over. "Fucking patch plugs," he says.

I swivel to catch Marta's reaction. She's one of those San Francisco types. Sophisticated. Bored. She could have men, or not. I see her in bed, smoking, dressed like Madonna, maybe masturbating to something on TV.

She rolls her eyes and says, "I'll get tech support."

As she disappears, I think again about Coryell's wife. I picture her father. In this picture, the father is heavy and bearded, with a cigar, like Freud.

❧

For lunch, we sit at the bar in a restaurant called Max's Diner.

I stare at an episode of *Star Trek* on the TV above the malt whiskeys, and I think about money. I pick up lunch as part of my deal with editors I hire. But times are tough. Recession has hit California hard. Regular clients are scaling back, making reductions. On this project, in fact, I underbid substantially, hoping to shave time in off-line editing. But it was a bad miscalculation. My margin is gone. Now every penny counts.

I pretend to watch the show while Goldsmith orders an elaborate deli spread. I order the cheapest thing on the menu, a BLT. As the waitress walks away, Goldsmith leans over the table and gets an earnest look in his eyes. He says, "Ever notice how the guys in the red uniforms always die?"

"What?"

"There's the main guys, Kirk and all," says Goldsmith. He stares up at the TV. He says, "They wear blue, yellow. See? Different colors. Then there're these guys in the red uniforms. They get beamed down to planets. Then aliens kill them." Goldsmith shakes his head. "But what gets me," he says. "No one cares." I laugh, but Goldsmith looks grim.

The food arrives.

Goldsmith eats fastidiously, chewing and commenting further on what he terms his Expendables Theory. I listen, nodding at times. Again, the red suit is the tip-off. Their function is to die, adding to the dramatic aura of the survivors – Kirk, Spock, those guys. Goldsmith hates this phenomenon. He hates the whole notion of subsidiary characters. He goes on and on about it as he eats the overpriced food, dabbing mustard here and there.

He says, "Good Federation soldiers. With kids, families. They have families, don't they?"

I nod.

Goldsmith looks at me, then looks back at the TV.

༄༅

After lunch, things go better. We break for the day at a reasonable time for once.

Outside, a gray drizzle falls. Sirens howl in the city distance. As I jog along the CalTrain tracks, the drizzle suddenly explodes into a downburst. My car is five blocks away, and I have no umbrella. I begin to sprint.

Suddenly, a woman whorls up before me. I slam into her.

She doesn't fall, but her eyes are deadly. I glance over at a long black car. Its back door is still open. The woman wears a black rain cape with a hood. It roils up behind her like huge liquid wings. She says something bitter in Asian, then hurries away with little ticking steps.

As she leaves, the downburst dances on her in a dark patina.

I watch her disappear into the weather.

3

That night, I work in my den.

I turn on my video deck, make some adjustments. Then I begin to scan reels of B-roll. I look for hard images. Simple things that work on the unconscious. Meanwhile, rain falls in black sheets outside.

Thunder suddenly shakes the window. I stop work. The sound, so foreign to California, resonates with feelings of the Midwest and my boyhood. It was a good boyhood. I grew up to be OK. Nobody here is starving or abused.

But what if things had been bad?

Would a fucked-up childhood destroy things? What if my own father had driven me to counseling? Would I let that interfere with my spouse's life? Would I be neurotic, greedy with needs? Suddenly, my door bursts open. My daughter Aubrey runs into the den. She wears huge red rain boots.

"Come on!" she yells.

"Honey, I can't make it to gymnastics tonight."

"What are you saying?" she says.

I stare at her pink tights.

"*Ballet!*" she says. She gives me a look I recognize as my wife's.

My wife comes in. She says: "You're not going?"

"Jesus," I say. We exchange fierce looks. I turn to my daughter. I say, "Sorry, honey."

My wife walks out. Aubrey looks at me, then turns and follows. I listen to their boots squeak in the hall. Then I turn to some spreadsheet numbers on the computer screen. I enter a number, then delete it and replace it with a bigger number. I do this in other places. But things aren't adding up. When I glance out the window, my wife is buckling Aubrey into the rear car seat. I stand up. As the car pulls away, my wife gamely beeps. I wave. But then I see an object fly into the front seat. I see my wife twist sharply. Her face is wolfish as she yells at our child.

I find myself thinking about abuse – what is it? They say it passes down the generations. I think about Coryell's wife. She seems like a good mother. My own wife came from good stock. I think about our marriage. Communication's good. Isn't it? We talk. She complains – fundamental male immaturity, etc. But that's marriage. These days, anyway. Everything geared to accusation. Blame. Is it men, or is it women? Whose fault? Whose fault?

❧

As I think of this, my four-year-old son appears at the office door in a blue jumper.

"Hi Dad," he says.

I turn to him. I say, "You look like a girl there, buddy."

"I'm Dorothy," says the boy.

"Dorothy's a girl," I say.

The boy spins around. "Look at this, Dad," he says. The jumper swirls up.

I shake my head and turn back to the spreadsheet. This is a corporate client with deep pockets, yet they squeeze me in the bidding process. They have to expect overruns. Anyway, I have a family to feed. Is that greed?

4

Rain continues. The next morning's commute is nerve-wracking. Despite the weather, everyone seems to be taking chances. Whipping across lanes. Tailgating. Looking for tiny advantages. I glance around at other drivers. Everyone looks grim, like they're driving to something unsettling, maybe a state execution.

At the 280 interchange, a woman with kids strapped into a Land Rover won't let me merge. I find myself thinking about Coryell's wife again. Could she know about my business practices? My dubious accounting system? I haven't done projects for Joe's company in years.

What is it?

Driving, I begin to picture her as a schoolgirl, in a short plaid skirt. Too short, maybe. She's walking home. There are boys at the mouth of a dark alley. Maybe things take an inevitable turn.

❧

I take my usual downtown exit, and park in a big lot on Bryant Street. Up ahead, at the corner of Townsend and Bryant, I see the Happy Donuts sign. I decide to get donuts.

As I cross Bryant, I notice a huge black man in army fatigues. The man is burrowing through a garbage dumpster in the Happy Donuts parking lot. He finds something, examines it, then rams it in his mouth. He eats ferociously.

I decide to skip the donuts. I'll just get a newspaper.

But a group of boys stands by the newsboxes at the corner. Two of them hold each other. One looks at me, bares his teeth and grinds his backside.

I walk past.

When I reach my building, I stop at the bank of phones in the lobby. I dig in my pockets for change, but have none, so I rip the calling card from my wallet. I dial Coryell's number.

His wife answers.

I hang up.

❧

The session is uninspired.

At one point, Goldsmith punches buttons, shuttling back and forth between decks, trying to make a precise cut to a beat of music. He does it again and again, previewing the new edit each time. After eight or nine tries, I suddenly see the program as it is – a monument to futility, unworthy of such labor or precision. A monument? Hell, that's giving it more than it deserves. It deserves nothing.

Then, staring into the liquid patterns of video static, I see a black man chewing garbage. I see boys fucking.

The buzz of the phone makes me jump.

"Ms. Morten to see you," crackles the intercom.

I look at Goldsmith, who raises his eyebrows. Then I say, "Send her down, Marta."

In moments, a woman in a black suit stands at the sliding glass door of the suite. I open the door. She slinks in like a spy. Helen Morten is head of the marketing group that hired this project. She's one of those older women with smoky voices. Is she your mom, or your lover? She can't decide. I'm pretty sure she's attracted to me. She touches me a lot when she talks, and her eyes are nervous.

"We're just so excited about this, hon," she says.

I say, "Great."

"Can we see what you've got?" she says.

I look at Goldsmith.

Helen Morten says, "We're really excited to see it."

I say, "Well, it's rough." I look at the monitor, trying to envision what might appear.

She sits down.

"Is there coffee?" she asks.

I laugh. This client is a big coffee company, the one with its famous sign on the San Francisco waterfront. But when I laugh, she looks up, startled. My laugh hangs in the air. She's not referring to the video. She wants a cup of coffee.

"There's coffee in the lobby," I say. I stand quickly. So does Goldsmith. "I'll get it," he says, leaving.

Helen Morten is staring at the cover of my shot logbook. There is a picture of a truck, scrawled in crayon. I say, "My son likes trucks."

"You have children," she says. She looks amused.

"Yes."

She looks at me and crosses her legs. She says, "How many?"

"Two," I say. "One more on the way."

"Three," she says. She bounces her top leg and says it again: "Three?"

I glance at her leg and say, "I'm not sure how it happened." This is a joke, but she just nods. Finally I say, "But I've got it narrowed down to some possibilities."

She laughs politely.

❧

After Helen gets her coffee, we all sit at the console. "Run it from the top, Ron," I say, trying to sound like a guy in charge.

Goldsmith gives me a look. But he punches a button.

The program runs. It's an educational piece to be shown in schools. It's about coffee – the history, how it's made, etc. This client is trying to make coffee more enticing to kids. Marketing studies have shown that kids are swilling popular caffeinated cola beverages for breakfast. This news disturbs the coffee people.

When the track ends, the client nods. She says: "Good." But there's something more. I wait. She says, "Actually, it's a little more *humorless* than we talked about."

"It's a rough cut," I say. I look at the screen and say: "Humor is kind of a timing thing."

"That isn't the final music, is it?" she says.

"No," I lie.

Goldsmith laughs. He starts punching buttons.

"Well," she says. "We're really looking forward to the first cut. It just really has to be . . . funnier."

"It will," I say. "We'll get that timing in."

Helen Morten stands to leave. "Kids are sharp," she says. "They know what's up."

I leap up to go with her.

"I know my way out," she says, waving her hand.

❧

Goldsmith tilts back in his chair, grinning. I ignore him and start poring over my log sheets, looking for funny shots. What the fuck's funny?

I once thought that my work was daring. Bold. By industrial standards, anyway. But lately, I'll show my sample reel to prospective clients. The reel will end. I'll sit there in the dark, watching static, waiting for something interesting to appear.

࿏

Driving home, I can't stop thinking about Helen Morten. I see her looking at magazines, considering herself one of those women. The ones with *choices.*

Choices, I think. Then I think: *What about men?* What choices do we have? If it's such a man's world, then men must hate themselves.

My wife talks about women, how they're so needed in business, politics. Family agenda, etc. But I don't tell her that the women I see out there are anything but selfless. I tell Goldsmith, though. He agrees. "They need that attention, don't they?" says Goldsmith at lunch one day. "Of course, they call it *communication.*"

I listen, nodding.

"Listening is the big failing of men," says Goldsmith. "Guys don't listen, man. They don't talk either. They don't spill their guts enough." He goes on to theorize about the spilling of guts – how men see an offering of steamy, twisted entrails. Stuff you don't want to touch. Then Goldsmith says, "But apparently women need this."

Then he does their voices:

Love me, you fucking prick.

Listen to me, you son of a bitch.

Intimacy! Intimacy!

"They love to get right in your face, don't they?" says Goldsmith, waiting for food. "Ever notice that? They lean in." Goldsmith leans at me. He says, "Way close."

I signal, then exit the freeway. I drift along the streets of our neighborhood. As always, I note the houses, the lawns and such. Suddenly, a memory arises. At a birthday party for my son two years ago, I made a remark to Coryell's wife. I was flipping veggie kabobs on the grill. Smoke kept blowing in my eyes, no matter which side of the grill I worked. That I remember. It was hot. Coryell's wife came out onto the deck and handed me a beer. She leaned in close, made some familiar gesture. Maybe she patted my arm. In any case, I said something like, *So you deliver?* Or, *It's nice to see you deliver.* Something about delivery.

Her reaction was odd, or she didn't laugh, or maybe she did, but there was something odd about this laugh. I was preoccupied, manipulating hot tongs. Mushrooms were sticking to the grill. Vegetables were being torn from kabobs in a most gruesome fashion.

Did I harass her?

Is that it?

She sees me as one of those guys, doesn't she?

5

That night, I suddenly realize that the coffee project is terribly misguided. My work is bad. It hits me hard, cold and clear. I'm stoking coals in the fireplace. I turn to my wife, who is braiding my daughter's hair. I feel sick. I sit down in my recliner and close my eyes. I'm fueling the addiction of children. I'm pushing caffeine into the public school system in an insidiously hip way.

My daughter comes up to me. She says: "Daddy?"

I say, "What?"

"Talk like this!" she shrieks in a high pitch. She says: "This is the princess!"

I stare at her. At times, she seems like an alien being.

"I can't, honey," I say. "Not right now. I'm too tired." I look to my wife. She sees and moves in fast.

"Daddy's too tired, honey," she says.

"Talk like Glinda!" says my daughter. "I can be the Munchkins."

"I'm too tired," I say.

Why? Because my life is a sham. Everybody knows it. Even my family. Something immense and terrible is happening to me. Things have to change.

But what if they don't? What if everything goes on as it is? What if nothing changes? I look at my wife. For years, we've coveted the homes and mini-vans of other people. But we won't have these things because I'm one of those businessmen who delude themselves into the belief that their work is on the fringe of art. Of course, we'll survive this failure. We'll get subsistence money and continue. But nothing will change.

"Daddy – "

"Aubrey, your father's too tired!" yells my wife.

Aubrey begins to cry. Suddenly, my wife begins to cry too. Howling, she grabs Aubrey.

Stunned at this outburst, I sit back. I put a hand over my eyes, then wipe them clear.

I think: You go along in life. Then all of a sudden you wake up one morning to discover you're some kind of beast. You look in the mirror.

What is it?

Who's there?

But you have no time for these things, do you? There's no time for the luxury of introspection, confronting personal crises. Life goes on. People must be fed, clothed.

I watch my wife carry Aubrey up the stairs.

❧

Dark rain falls all night.

I fall asleep in the chair. I wake with a start. Blackness flutters around me. Things move in dark corners. I see myself as if from above – a little guy in a chair, sweating.

Suddenly there is a sound.

I sit up. I see a pale figure float down the hall. Then I hear the toilet lid hit the tank. I listen to my daughter urinate. After a moment, she starts to whimper.

I go to her.

I say, "What is it?"

"I can't see," she sobs.

I flick on the light. She begins to cry loudly.

"It's too bright! I can't see!"

I turn off the light.

I grit my teeth at the harsh sounds in her throat. "I'll get a flashlight."

"Don't go away!" she howls.

"What is it, then?" I say.

She gropes wildly for me in the dark. I seize her arms. In the darkness, I see myself slam her back onto the toilet seat. I hear my wife's feet hit the floor in the bedroom.

In a broken voice, my daughter says, "I need to wipe, Dad."

And then suddenly everything is clear.

From this moment on, I will have to examine every conversation, every encounter, every exchange, no matter how trivial. People are judging me. They can see the flaws, the black motives.

He secretly brutalizes his loved ones.

He cheats on his taxes.

These things leave marks. Women can see these marks.

I am the kind of guy that other guys' wives do not like.

6

On Friday, the client pulls the job. "We're rethinking our strategy," says Helen Morten. Goldsmith and I had been horsing around with some funny sound effects when she appeared at the sliding glass door. When she came in, I knew. She was smoking. Now we sit in the edit suite.

She says: "To be honest, we're not so sure that going into the schools is the right thing." She smokes. I am numb. Then she says: "We want to do the right thing."

I can't think of words.

She smiles at me. "Of course, we'll pay the kill fee."

I look at her. Finally I say, "What do you mean, kill fee?"

She is smiling. "We want the footage."

I look at Goldsmith, who avoids my eyes.

"You hit the first milestone with the off-line, hon," she says. "According to the agreement, it was, what? Nine thousand dollars?" She pulls a document from her briefcase. She says, "We're prepared to go the nine." She gets up. She hands me the document.

I take it and look at it.

She says, "It's very equitable, we feel."

Her tone is clear. It is the tone of voice that completely writes off a young man. His being is mere cells, replicating needlessly.

7

I walk out of the building. I stop to adjust the tote bag that hangs on my shoulder. I tighten the strap. The bag holds all of our source tapes, as well as the edited master tape and a protection master. I hold the bag closely. It feels like some illegal activity. Drug-related cash, maybe. The fact is, these tapes are worth nine thousand dollars to me.

I reach the corner of Townsend and Third. As I step off the curb, a Toyota shoots into the crosswalk. I bend to give the driver a threatening look.

The driver, a woman, guns her engine.

The light turns green and her Toyota leaps forward. A small pickup truck on the cross street, trying to beat the light and moving very fast, slams into the driver's side of the Toyota. Glass showers upward in a reverse rain.

For a moment, everything sits in silence.

❧

My mind tells me that nothing has happened. I stand there. Then people start yelling. I put down my bag. But I remember the tapes. I pick up the bag, and carry it with me a few steps. But then I put the bag down behind a streetlight and run to the car.

As I run, I glance back at the bag.

Two black guys pull themselves out of the side windows of the pickup truck. Its doors have buckled. But the guys are OK. A few other people run up. One, a woman in a suit, looks at me. She moves past me and looks in the Toyota. She says, "Oh my God."

She looks at me again. Then she runs across the street to the phone bank at the CalTrain station.

I go to the passenger window of the Toyota. I lean into the wreckage. I assume the driver's unconscious, but her glassy eyes lock onto mine. She jabs a finger at me. She says: "You son of a bitch! That was a green light!"

"It wasn't me," I say.

She says, "*It was green.*"

"It's not me," I say.

Then she notices her legs.

She throws her good arm about, so I seize her wrist. It's so thin I could snap it. In fact, I have that urge. But shock takes over. The woman's eyes roll up. Two other guys in suits hurry up to the window. They stand next to me, and they don't know what to do either. Then I remember something I read once about shock, about keeping them awake. I begin to talk to the woman. I shake her a little bit. At one point I glance over at the bag of tapes again. The two black guys stand next to it, watching me. One of them glances down at the bag.

Ashamed at my thoughts, I stop talking to the woman for a moment.

8

That night, I break down. It's pathetic. I cry in my wife's arms. "Maybe I need structure," I sob. "What do I have? I need to get *organized* here."

She says, "Come on now."

But no, I don't stop there. I tell her more things. I tell her my failures, my fears. It's a horrendous mistake. She pats my head. The pat is gentle, but not tender. OK, so maybe I'm a guy, but I know the difference.

And then she says, "Maybe you *should* get a job. You know, a salary." She says, "Benefits."

I sit up, practically wrenching my head from her touch.

She says, "What?"

"I'm *crying*," I say.

She shakes her head.

"Isn't that what you want?" I say. I stand up. I say, "What the *fuck* do you want from me?"

Her face goes sallow.

"Get a job?" I say. I throw up my hands, and suddenly I hear Goldsmith mimicking women. *Thanks for sharing, honey! Now get a job, OK?* As my eyes dart around I say, "Christ, I married my father."

When she looks at me in response, it's a look that I have seen in her eyes before. But now, suddenly, I am able to reference it. It's the look I saw in Helen Morten's eyes just before she fired me.

She says, "You don't get it, do you?"

I want to break her jaw. Something snaps in me. I draw myself up. I loom over her.

"I'm tired of that fucking feminist crap!" I yell.

One of her smug, newly divorced friends recently gave her a button that says, "Guys Just Don't Get It." We talk for hours about this, about sexual harassment and such. But these talks always fail to reach successful conclusions. The more I demonstrate a reasonable sympathy for her cause, the more she seems to be angry with me.

"Actually," I yell, "you're right. I *don't* get it."

"Don't worry about it," she says. Her voice is not cold. No, it is beyond cold.

I have never considered the possibility that Judy might leave me. Not since the kids, anyway. But the distance I see in her eyes sickens me. I feel like I've been tricked – and then I hear Goldsmith again, droning in my ear. *These women, man, they want openness, they want us to unburden ourselves, to share, share, share, share, share. But when we do, it scares the shit out of them.*

And why not? If I was in my wife's position, would I want to hear the family provider whine about failure and misgivings? No, I'd want to feel secure about my partner's handling of matters. I mean, if I don't feed us, who will?

Some other guy.

One who doesn't doubt – or, if he does, he goddamn well keeps it to himself.

❧

In bed, I stare at the black ceiling. It's 3:00 AM. Judy lies next to me. She's on her back. Her breathing is deep in the chest, and noisy.

I look at her. *Who are you?*

Truly, I don't know. Some dark, hardened woman. And yet her sleep is so childlike it's stunning.

We've had no health insurance for two years now. If something serious happens to her or the kids, they'll be shuttled through clinics with third-rate care. I can see the faces of the health care personnel. As my daughter's gurney rattles past, they exchange looks. If I don't find a project with front-end money in the next three weeks, we'll have to buy groceries with credit cards. We'll pay rent with credit cards. And when the credit ends, we'll be on the street.

Clearly, everything that sustains me is some vestige of a boyhood illusion. The illusion of talent. The illusion of destiny. The illusion of fundamental decency as man, father, husband. Is this what Coryell's wife sees? If so, what am I to do? I stare at the ceiling and edit together the patterns of my life. In none of these patterns am I consistently successful. Oh sure, little victories, little highs. But they fade to black. They mean nothing, they build on nothing. There is no equity stake. Taken together, everything I have done equals zero.

But now I'm whimpering! Suddenly, I see my father. He looks down and wonders: *What the hell? What kind of man is this?*

I look at Judy again. Her ghost rises. It speaks to me: "We live too close to the edge, you whimpering son of a bitch. There can be no breakdowns. Not now. You have obligations. You have *children*. Your failures have placed your family in grave jeopardy." As the ghost speaks, its face changes – Helen Morten. Coryell's wife. Women in cars, Land Rovers, mini-vans. They work together in little commando teams.

I will not sleep tonight.

I will fail. I will die. Then, and only then, will nothing matter.

Pictures form on the ceiling. I see my life's small, pathetic moments. I watch them play, then I watch dawn break like a fever across the windows.

And then I come to my decision.

All my delusions are the same. So if I cannot find true meaning, I will seize the false one that is best for my family. I have skills, don't I? Large companies pay me for them already. I will get on a payroll.

Clearly, I am destined for middle management.

Next to me, Judy rustles around. Asleep, she throws a sharp elbow into my chest. It feels good. The sun hits the window hard. I close my eyes. No more of this freelancing! I will get organized! Money will flow! I will build security!

I'm a man, by God, and I must hitch myself to whatever delusion keeps everyone else sustained.

9

Later, I find it difficult to rise from bed. I work my way to my elbows, sit up, then fall back into a black stupor. This happens again and again.

Judy enters loudly a couple of times. She roots in the closet. She yells at the kids. She leaves the bedroom door open. But she says nothing to me.

I sleep until 2:00 p.m.

That night, I sit by the fire in my living room. I hold a glass of whiskey with both hands.

Christmas hovers like a vulture all around me. I listen carefully to the Mormon Tabernacle Choir sing "We Three Kings." Men do the morbid verse about myrrh. They sing with deep voice: *Sorrowing, sighing, bleeding, dying.* Good God. I look at my son. The boy sits on the floor in a dress. Everybody is supposed to call him Wendy today. Mucus rims his nose. He holds up a picture of something he's drawn. He says: "Look, Dad."

I look at it. It is impossible to tell what it might be.

"That's good," I say. "Good work, pal."

"Dad."

"What?"

"Call me Wendy," he says.

I sip whiskey. It tastes like acid. After a moment, I say: "Good work, Wendy."

The Choir now sings "What Child Is This." I almost laugh. I wonder what it might be like to father a Christ child. Any different? Maybe not. I look at the whiskey. I feel empty, but I can't drink. I put the whiskey down. *Not even that,* I think. And then, finally, I try to see what Coryell's wife sees.

I sit back, seeing with her eyes:

I see myself on CalTrain, desperately reading the newspaper. I see guys. They're all around. Guys with drinks, laughing. Guys fucking their administrative assistants. Guys maybe getting hard with other guys' wives. Guys who turn their own wives into needy bitches.

OK, there's those.

And then there're the other guys, the ones going nowhere, who can't even drum up an interesting vice. Nothing guys. Maybe these guys do everything right, or maybe not. It doesn't make any difference.

I pick up the whiskey. I put it back down. I remember what happened to my younger brother Jack.

10

Jack's three-year-old son died last year. Leukemia. I flew back to Nebraska for the funeral. I was one of just four pallbearers. Hauling the little casket, I tried to remember the boy. My only image came from a videotape sent one Christmas. The kid repeatedly stuck his face in the camera and yelled, "Cheesehead!"

At the reception after the services, I stood in my brother's spacious home. He had become what our father used to call "a man of means." He came up to me, handed me a cup of punch, then tried to talk. But no words came to him. After a minute, he just walked away.

I followed him into the yard.

Jack vomited twice. It was cold; I held my arms, looking up at the big house. Snow was everywhere. My brother's breath plumed up between gasps. When he could speak, he said, "The punch."

"Shit," I said, thinking: *I drank two cups.* "Is it bad?"

"No."

I dug my cold fingers into my pockets. Jack said: "He used to help me squeeze the oranges." Then he stood up. He slapped snow from his knees. His eyes, I remember, shone. He said, "Then we got that fucking juicer."

We turned to the cars lining the block.

Jack said, "Jesus, look who's here, man."

I looked. A lady dressed in black sat at the wheel of a big black car. She was probably an aunt, though I didn't know which one. When she finally got out, she was holding a pie. It was huge. Loaded with meringue. To me, this notion seemed unremittingly morbid. Pies after a funeral. What next? It gave me a chill, and I turned to Jack.

My brother watched the old woman with the pie.

"Look at that thing," he said.

I shook my head.

"Let's eat," he said.

I remember turning back to Jack's house, looking at it and thinking that in California, this house would cost five times what he paid for it here. Nobody, least of all me, could afford this house if it was in California. Then I thought about my brother's pharmaceutical dispensing business, which I had always seen as dull and artless. Now it looked like satisfying work. And yeah, I envied his mini-van too. This boy's death could not diminish that fact.

11

Fire crackles in the fireplace.

I look at the fire and stand up. A strand of blue lights twinkles on the mantle. I turn to my boy, who is now hanging costume jewelry from his neck and ears. Then I look down at my own small hands. Hands that had once been mistaken for those of an artist.

I hold them out, looking at them.

Then I go for the boy.

12

I'm in the front hallway, holding my son. The sleeping boy sneezes, then throws his head back and forth across my shoulder. When my wife comes downstairs to take him, she says, "God."

I look down. My dark blue sweatshirt is streaked with the boy's mucous.

"That looks bad," she says.

I go to the door.

"Are you going out?" she calls.

"Yes," I say.

At the Winchell's on Hamilton Avenue, I carefully choose a colorful variety of donuts. It takes ten minutes, but the girl is very patient. I have the girl rearrange the donuts once after she fills the box. I pay for them and drive to Joe Coryell's house. I put the donuts on the doorstep. I stand there awhile, then I leave. When I get home, I begin to call Coryell's wife. I call again and again. I leave voice messages. I begin to court her, like a lover.

Excerpt from *The Fig Eater*

He stands up next to the girl's body. He looks down for a moment, then carefully steps over the narrow boards lying around it. He walks across the grass and joins the three men, waiting like mourners. No one speaks. The body is poised like a still life waiting for a painter.

Now they watch the photographer edge his way over the boards, his equipment balanced on one shoulder. He stops and gently lowers the legs of the tripod into place, then steadies the bulky camera directly above the girl. Without looking up, he snaps his fingers. The men silently move aside, shifting their lanterns as a boy passes between them, moving with a sleepwalker's strangely certain gait, eyes fixed on the frail pyramid of white powder he carries on a tray.

The boy stands by the photographer, nervously waiting while he adjusts the dials on the camera. The photographer ignores him. He hunches behind the camera and pulls a black cloth over his head. In that secret darkness, the camera lens tightens around the dead girl's mouth. The photographer mutters something unintelligible, then his hand blindly works its way out from under the cloth. The instant his fingers snap, the boy strikes a match and holds it to the powder on the tray.

A blinding flash lays transparent white light over the girl's body, her stiff arms and legs, the folds of her dress, transforming her into something eerily poised, a statue fallen on the grass. There's shadow, a black space carved under her neck, in the angle where her head is bent toward her shoulder, and below one outstretched arm. Her other arm hides her face. The light vanishes, leaving a cloud of odor. Burned sulphur.

The Inspector keeps this harsh image of the girl's sprawled figure in mind even later, after her body is cut open, becoming curiously tender and liquid.

She lies in the Volksgarten, near the seated stone figure of the Kaiserin Elizabeth. The statue faces a fountain pool in the center of a bosquet of low flowers, and behind it is a curved wall of bushes nearly twelve feet high. The park is a short distance from Spittelberg, Vienna's notorious district where the *Beiseln* offer music, drink, and women.

The Inspector points at a crumpled piece of white paper or cloth near the girl's body. Two of the policemen nod and begin to pick up the boards. There's no haste in their movements, even though it's getting late. They set a board on top of two rocks to make a walkway over to the cloth. If there are footprints on the ground, the boards will protect them.

During another investigation last year, the spring of 1909, the Inspector temporarily preserved footprints in the snow at a crime scene by placing a flowerpot over each one. There are other ways to keep prints left in sand, soft dirt, or dust.

While the photographer's boy patiently holds a lantern over his head, the Inspector squats on the boards, close enough to see that the cloth has been roughly smoothed over some small object. A rounded shape. There are flies around it and a sweet, foul odor. He takes tweezers from a leather pouch and pinches a corner of the fabric. It sticks slightly. When he pulls it off, the fabric has a dark smear on the underside, and he has a shock of recognition as he drops it inside an envelope. Someone has murdered a young woman and defecated next to her body.

When the Inspector stands up, he realizes he is sweating. His shirt is damp; his suspenders are wet stripes over his shoulders. The humid night air has also weighed the girl's clothes down over her body. It is hot, unusually hot for the end of August.

They prepare to take another picture. Egon, the photographer, drags the tripod over. He sets it up and cranks the camera down and down, stopping it two feet above the soft excrement. One of the men raises a lantern over it so he can see to focus. The Inspector steps back and turns his head away, waiting for the whispered sizzle of the lightning powder as it ignites. In a minute, the lantern's light is eclipsed by the explosion. Days later, when he looks at the photograph, the grass around the body appears as stiff as if it had been frozen, not burned into the film on the glass plate in the camera by the explosion of light.

When the boards surrounding her are removed, the girl looks frailer alone on the ground. They find no objects, no other obvious clues around her. The thick grass masks any footprints. They'll search the area again tomorrow during the day, when there's better light.

Invisible in the dark, the Inspector stands on the marble platform next to the Kaiserin Elizabeth's statue. He's a tall man and can reach nearly as high as her head. He gently touches the statue's shoulder. He never would have permitted himself this trespass at any other time, but he's unsettled by the extraordinary discovery of the girl's body near the memorial. Kaiserin Elizabeth was the wife of Franz Josef. She was assassinated in 1898, stabbed in the heart by a madman with a blade so wickedly thin it left only a speck of blood on her chemise. It is said her dying words were, "*At last.*"

He wonders if there is some connection between the statue and the location of the girl's body.

In front of him, the men move quietly in the circle of light made by the lanterns, and between their dark figures, he can glimpse the whiter shape of the girl. Just beyond the park, the wing of the Imperial Palace is faintly visible. From behind the trees, there's the occasional, isolated sound of an unseen carriage proceeding around the Ringstrasse.

According to police routine, a sketch is always made before a description of the crime scene is written. Closely trailed by the boy holding a lantern, Egon paces out a rough square around the girl's body, three hundred and sixty paces, and transfers this measurement onto a graph, drawing the kaiserin's monument as a dash, the sign used on survey maps. Without disturbing the dead girl's hair, he pushes the end of a tape measure into the ground at the crown of her head and measures one and a half meters to the base of the monument. Her right arm is bent over her dark face, so he unspools the tape from her shoulder to the same point. A distance of almost two meters. Finally, he pulls the tape from the left heel of her white canvas boot over to the path, just over one meter. When the sketch is finished, he signs and dates the paper.

Now her body has been remade as the center point on a graph. Lines radiate from her head, arms, and legs as if she were a starfish or a sundial, pinning her exactly in this place at this hour.

Before the dead girl is moved, the Inspector gently removes her pearl earrings. He cuts through the strap of her watch, uncoils it from her wrist, and seals the objects in an isinglass envelope. He asks for more light, and now with two lanterns above him, he kneels over her, shifting his weight, balancing himself on one hand. Careful not to touch her, he uses the point of the scissors to delicately manipulate her thin cotton dress. Occasionally he asks for a magnifying glass. His eyes filled with the harsh white of her dress – a dazzling field he forgets the body under the fabric until he accidentally sets his hand on her bare arm. Although he instantly jerks it away, the impression of her cool skin stays on the palm of his hand, as if he'd touched a liquid. He rubs his hand against his trousers.

He knows the other men noticed his spontaneous reaction. He forces himself to touch her again, to break the spell, pushing her thumb down hard against the ground. It's slightly stiff, and he estimates she's been dead at least four hours. The heat makes it hard to calculate, although rigor mortis affects the small muscles first.

He discovers a pale hair under the collar of her dress, and his assistant, Franz, wordlessly holds out an empty glass vial to receive it. No bloodstains are found on her clothing. However, the back of her white dress is stained when they lift her off the ground.

When they flop her onto a stretcher, Egon vomits. The other men look away. The Inspector also ignores him, but he understands his distress. It's the movement of the body that sickened him, its parody of motion. He orders one of the policemen to stay at the site for the few hours remaining until daybreak.

As soon as it is light, Franz goes over the kaiserin's monument, checking for fingerprints. First he dusts the statue with powdered carmine applied with a fine camelhair brush. The second time he uses charcoal dust. The same fingerprint powders are also applied to the ornamental urns and the marble gateposts at the entrance to the Volksgarten.

Franz reports that all the stone is too rough to hold any impressions.

The afternoon of the same day, the girl's body is in the morgue at the police station on the Schottenring. The men smoke in the morgue during the autopsy to cover the smell of decay and formalin. The ceiling fan cools the room, but it also sucks up the odor of the cigarettes they exhale over the metal table where she lies. They work in the body's stink as if it were a shadow.

Franz takes scissors in slow strokes down the sides of her dress and across her shoulders, then lifts it off. He cuts the thick canvas corset from her waist with a heavy knife after slashing through the laces. It probably took her longer to get into the corset, he jokes to the man leaning across the table, a doctor in a white jacket. The older man is as blond as Franz, but his hair is thinning. His pink head hovers over the girl's discolored face. The doctor nods without looking up. I think she's about eighteen years old, he says. The bare room doesn't hold conversation well.

Her clothing is dissected, the labels removed. Everything was purchased at good *Bürger* shops, Farnhammer, Maison Spitzer, Ungar & Drecoll in the Kohlmarkt.

The unidentified girl is now naked, her head propped up on a wooden block. Her eyes are flat and bloodshot, and her tongue partially protrudes between her lips. The upper part of her chest is the same livid color as her face, and darker blotches stripe the sides of her red neck. The underside of her body is a blurry-edged patchwork of stains. Uncirculated blood has seeped from the veins and settled here, sagging under its own weight, ripening into the deep violet and green of decaying flesh. Over her body, a mirror-lined lampshade reflects these colors in its distorted curve, an obscene chandelier.

"She's been strangled?" Franz asks.

The doctor nods.

The Inspector walks in and stands at the opposite end of the table. He imagines the girl's body is carved from stone and he looks down on it from a great height. This exercise helps him think about her without emotion.

He watches the doctor wrap a cloth around her head and under her jaw to contain her tongue, close her mouth.

"How will you fix her skin?" he asks.

"I can bleach it. Remove her hair, make cuts on the back and sides of the skull and leave it in running water for twelve hours. That will lighten the greenish color."

The Inspector tells him to wait. There must be a less drastic way to make the body presentable. He anticipates a mother or father – or perhaps a close relative, since the dead girl wears no wedding ring – will come to identify her.

Later, the Inspector and Franz smoke cigarettes in the hallway.

"Thirty years ago, when I was an assistant policeman, I had to take care of the head of a corpse on my own," the Inspector says. "There was a murder in a remote village, and no refrigeration or ice was available. I put the head in a perforated box and set it in a stream. But first I covered the head with a net to protect it from fish."

Alone in the morgue, the doctor removes gray sludge and pieces of more solid matter from the dead girl's stomach, fiercely slopping the liquid into a metal basin.

A few rooms away, Egon dips his sketches of the Volksgarten and the girl's body into a pan filled with a solution of stearine and collodion. The paper will dry in fifteen minutes without changing color. The solution protects it from moisture and the dirty hands of the witnesses and jurymen who will handle the papers in court.

Later that day, Egon returns to the Volksgarten. The area he paced off is surrounded by stakes linked with string. The excrement next to the body has been scraped up and replaced by a rock with a number painted on it.

The policeman on duty nods at Egon and idly watches him unpack his equipment. The young man works quickly, with the skilled sleight of hand that comes with long practice. He takes out a small wooden box, a device called a Dikatopter. He doesn't trust technical devices, although he sometimes straps a pedometer on his boot to measure the distances he paces out, especially on hilly ground.

He stands with his back to the stakes, looking into a black mirror inside the open lid of the Dikatopter. Fine threads are pulled through holes in the mirror, dividing it into fifteen squares. Holding the box in front of him, he moves forward a half step at a time, watching until the path and the kaiserin's monument are visible in the web of threads, so he can calculate the position of the girl's body against these landmarks. He's pleased with his work, the fugitive images captured in the box like butterflies.

In the bottom of the box, there is a paper divided into a graph identical to the one on the mirror. He draws an outline of the girl's body on the paper from memory, and the monument and the path exactly as they are reflected in the mirror above his hand in the lid.

Light shines through the holes in the dark mirror, and the penciled outline of the body is suspended below these bright dots, as if it had been connected from a constellation of stars.

The Inspector didn't sleep the night the girl's body was discovered. He stayed at the police station, and went home the following evening.

The first time he describes the girl's body, his wife, Erszébet, creates her own image of it. She imagines the men standing around the body as if it were a bonfire, a radiant white pyre, its light shining through their legs as if they were alabaster columns in a temple. The dead girl fallen inside their circle.

Erszébet asks the girl's name and age.

"She's unidentified. The doctor guesses she's about eighteen."

"Why was she in the Volksgarten?"

"That is the mystery."

"She must have been from Spittelberg. Why else would a girl be in the park at night?"

"She may have been killed earlier in the evening. Judging by her clothing, I believe she's from a good family. Her murder would seem to be a misadventure or a *crime passionnel*."

"Have you discovered any suspects?"

"None yet."

She nods and doesn't question him further. She's satisfied with his limited information since it allows her to produce her own theories. The girl's body has punched a hole in the safe space that was the park.

Two days after the body was discovered, the Inspector talks about the girl during dinner, although it isn't his custom to mention the dead at the table. He asks Erszébet to come to his office tomorrow and bring her paints. This is the first time he's asked her to help him in this way.

That night, when Erszébet can't sleep, she thinks of the nameless girl who has died, whose face she will paint tomorrow. In Hungary, there's a custom of dressing unmarried young women and girls in white for their funerals, as death transforms them into brides of heaven. The deceased girl is given away by her parents with the same words as a wedding ceremony. Tomorrow, she'll silently recite an old verse over the girl's unclaimed body. *While I live, I'll dress in black. When I'm dead, I'll walk in white.*

Franz walks in front of Erszébet down the hallway in the police station. He lets her enter the morgue ahead of him. The girl's body is on a table, a cloth covering everything except her head. Her face is still blotchy, the skin as dull and opaque as beeswax, and her eyes have sunk into their sockets. The cloth around her chin has been removed, and her mouth is slightly open. Her long pale hair is tied back with a piece of string.

It seems that all the cold in the room presses down against the still face, bitterly sculpting her profile, making it sharper than it had been in life. For a moment the total passivity of the body seems peculiar to Erszébet, until she remembers the girl is dead.

That's all Erszébet notices before she turns and presses a handkerchief to her nose. Later, the odor in the room will sometimes return to her, an unbidden ghost, the smell of decay. This morning, she prepared for painting by heavily dousing herself with perfume, touching the bottle's glass stopper to her wrists and the fleshy nape of her neck. Her hair was secured in its upswept coil with extra pins.

Now she strokes red, yellow, and brown pigments into a thick smear of white lead paint on her palette until it turns a pale flesh color. Venetian pink. She adds linseed oil and soap so it will adhere better to the cold surface of the girl's skin.

She asks Franz to loosen the cloth from around the girl's neck. First she paints the darkest parts of her face, around the mouth and nostrils, stopping her hand just before she blends the paint into the dead face with her finger.

She's been working on the body for nearly an hour when a man walks in carrying a bowl filled with a white paste. He casually sets the bowl down on the girl's stomach. Remembering Erszébet is in the room, he courteously moves it to the table.

"I'm Doctor Pollen. Have you finished?"

She nods and steps aside. He begins to vigorously knead the thick mixture in the bowl.

"This is my own modeling formula. Ten parts white wax and two parts Venetian turpentine melted together. I add potato starch to make it sticky."

"What are you going to do with it?"

"You could say I re-create the crime in a positive fashion. I can make what's absent. Someone shoots a gun into a wall, my modeling wax goes in the hole. Then I pull out an impression of the bullet's passage."

She asks if the same technique works for bodies.

"Yes, but I use cigarette papers. When they're wet, they're so fine they pick up the smallest impression, even a knife scratch on skin. To fill deeper holes, like stab wounds, I glue something slightly heavier on top of the cigarette papers. Toilet paper works best."

He digs around under the cloth and pulls out the girl's hand. Because her hands had been so tightly clenched, a small incision had been made at the base of each finger to loosen it for fingerprinting. Now he easily bends back a damaged finger, sticks a little ball of wax over the cold fingertip, and begins to work it down.

"I've made waxes of ear wounds, missing teeth. Even the stump of a tongue that had been bitten off. Mice love this mixture. I keep all my wax models inside a glass cabinet to keep them from being eaten."

He curls his hand around the girl's finger to warm it, then continues to pinch the soft wax up to her second joint.

Erszébet is unable to move away or even avert her eyes. She stares at his hands, engaged in their task as routinely as if he were writing a letter.

"Why are you copying her fingers?"

"I'm not making a copy. First I cleaned under her nails with a bit of paper. The wax just picks up anything left under there. Hair, dust, a thread. Sometimes there's nothing but their own skin. Or dried blood, if the victim fought their attacker. I suspect that's what I'll find here, since she probably struggled to pry the murderer's hands off. See, she has scratches down both sides of her neck."

His fingers press the wax too firmly and it bulges over the girl's knuckle. Finished with her hands, he sticks a finger into her mouth, careful not to disturb the paint on her lips. With his other hand, he delicately presses a wad of wax over her teeth.

Erszébet didn't realize she'd made any gesture, but suddenly Franz is next to her, guiding her into the next room. The light wavers, and there's a round buzzing pressure in her head just before she abruptly sits down.

Egon quickly moves his equipment into the morgue to photograph the girl. Someone draped fabric over the block under her head and the metal table to disguise it, and he calculates how his camera can disguise her immobility.

Later, Erszébet visualizes the strange fragments in the doctor's cabinet, objects as mysterious and dumb as fossils, reverse images of damage done to a body. There's a delicate X shape, molded from a double knife wound in a man's chest. A whitish tube, thick as a finger, cast from the passage made by a bullet into someone's back. A rough, V-shaped wedge documents a stick's impact in the muscles of an arm. These are the soft interiors of bodies turned inside out, turned solid.

She's familiar with the wax charms and effigies that work magic at a distance. Gypsies twist wax or unfermented, uncooked dough into tiny figures and stamp them with incomprehensible markings, aids made to win love or wreak revenge, for good or ill. To make the spell more powerful, nail parings, pubic hair, menstrual blood, urine, and perspiration are kneaded into the soft mixture. At one time, the lives of the French kings had been endangered by these *vols* models. In Germany, *Atzmann* figures were used as evidence in witchcraft trials.

When she was a child, she remembers a girl burned a scrap of her own dress, which was saturated with her sweat. The ashes were secretly fed to a boy whose love she hoped to win.

Erszébet knew the boy. When he unknowingly ate the ashes, she watched his face convulse with astonishment and disgust as he realized what had been done to him, what was the bitter taste in his mouth.

Diary of an Immortal Man

RICHARD DOOLING

1994

March 30: Today I turn forty. I am officially protected by the Age Dis-
crimination in Employment Act. If I had an employer, I could now sue
him if he discriminated against me because of my, ulp, age.

Until now, I've half believed in one of Vladimir Nabokov's elegant
syllogisms: Other men die, but I am not other men; therefore, I'll not
die. Nabokov died in 1977. Every time I look in the bathroom mirror, I
see Death, the Eternal Footman (looking quite proud), standing in the
shadows behind me, holding my coat, snickering.

I live with my family in my hometown of Omaha. My selfish genes
have managed an immortality of sorts by getting themselves into four
delightful children, who are still too young to turn on me. My wife
and I have enjoyed nine years of marriage, what Robert Louis Steven-
son called "a friendship recognized by the police." I'm Catholic, so
as mortality looms on the far side of the middle-age horizon, I seek
consolation in my Christian faith and one of its central tenets: belief
in the immortality of my soul. But the lawyer in me also highlights the
usual caveats and provisos.

According to the Scriptures, my quality of life after death may depend
on my ability to love my fellow man. This is a big problem. I forgot to
mention that in addition to being a practicing Catholic, I'm also a
practicing misanthrope.

As I see it, my only chance of avoiding eternal damnation is to stay
alive until I learn to love other people. Or until some future pope issues
an encyclical providing spiritual guidance for misanthropic Catholics.

November 16: My second novel, *White Man's Grave*, is a finalist for the
National Book Award. For at least a day or two, I wonder if I might be
able to achieve immortality by writing great literature.

My wife and I fly to the awards ceremony in New York City, where William Gaddis wins the National Book Award in Fiction for *A Frolic of His Own*.

We return to Omaha, where, instead of reading the Scriptures or *A Frolic of His Own*, I read Woody Allen, who said, "I don't want to achieve immortality through my work. I want to achieve it through not dying."

1997

February 23: I am in the Sheep's Head Tavern in east London, banging my flagon, bending my elbow, when the evening news comes on the telly over the bar and I learn that Ian Wilmut of the Roslin Institute in Scotland has cloned a sheep named Dolly. I am not personally acquainted with or fond of any sheep that I would like to see multiplied like loaves and fishes. Most of what I know about sheep I learned in crowded taverns like this one, banging my flagon, bending my elbow, and listening to off-color bestiality jokes. I fail to appreciate the significance of Dolly for my own personal immortality. Flagon. Elbow.

March 30: Birthdays seem to be coming every other month or so. I'm now forty-three years old. Still in Omaha; still a novelist. At my back, I hear the AARP's silver-chariot specials drawing near.

August 4: My wife and I reform our diets and take up a fitness regimen to shed pounds and replenish our dwindling reserves of vim and vigor.

We hire a sitter for the kids, then jog for almost an hour, and we eat nothing but kale and soybeans for dinner. We are starving and sore, stretched out in bed and watching the news, when we learn that the world's oldest living person, Jeanne Louise Calment of Arles, France, died today at 122 years of age. Jeanne reportedly soaked her food in olive oil at every meal and also rubbed olive oil on her skin every day; she loved port wine and ate two pounds of chocolate per week; she smoked cigarettes until she was 120 years old.

August 5: We have quit jogging. The cupboards of our modest Omaha home are lined with bottles of Bertolli extra-virgin olive oil, and UPS brings Godiva chocolates twice a week. My wife and I begin to experiment with tobacco products.

1998

May: The entire country waits for DNA testing to be performed on the megalosperm of its spermoblastic alpha-male commander in chief. Believe me, I am no closer to loving my fellow man. Meanwhile, other cellular developments continue apace, some of which may allow me to prolong my life until people start becoming lovable again. On top of everything else, I'm now a screenwriter, not a novelist – so artistic immortality is completely out of the question.

July: Dolly the sheep goes out like a lamb, and in come twenty-two cloned mice – seven of which are cloned from a single mouse – created by Ryuzo Yanagimachi at the University of Hawaii. The news includes experts' speculations about the practical uses of cloning human beings. For instance, what if I could create anencephalic (brainless) clones of myself and put them in cold storage? Then I could harvest fresh hearts and livers to replace the ones damaged by smoking, eating chocolates, and consuming port wine.

Too ghoulish for my tastes; instead, I resolve to look after my soul, even if it means learning to love my fellow man.

August 23: I'm not the only one with immortality on the brain. I head to the local bookstore looking for Milan Kundera's novel *Immortality*, which is about people like me, who are anxious about mortality.

The store doesn't carry Kundera, but it does have a new book called *Immortality: How Science Is Extending Your Life Span – and Changing the World*. Maybe I don't have to worry about my immortal soul, because on the first page of his book, one Ben Bova tells me just what I want to hear: "The first immortal human beings are probably living among us today. You might be one of them."

Bova falls well short of Kundera as a stylist, but his book does explain how my cells age and ultimately die and how it soon may be possible to arrest or even reverse this process.

Biologists at the Geron Corporation have already altered human cells in a petri dish and enabled them to defeat the genetic process of aging by exceeding what is called the Hayflick limit. In 1961, biologist Leonard Hayflick discovered that normal human cells divide about fifty times during a normal human lifetime. It seems that each time my cells divide, the chromosomes and their DNA must be duplicated, but each time this happens, the ends of the DNA (called telomeres) are slightly depleted, until gradually they become so short that my cells can no longer make accurate, functional copies of themselves, whereupon I will age and ultimately – well, that thing that Nabokov said happens to other men will happen to me. Telomerase is an enzyme that arrests or reverses this shortening process, meaning it may enable my cells to reproduce "young" copies of themselves forever.

How long before telomerase injections are available to arrest aging in human beings? My health-insurance provider assists me promptly anytime I need help paying my premiums, but I get placed on hold whenever I call to obtain services or file a claim or ask a question about telomerase.

November: Researchers funded by Geron take stem cells from human embryos and grow them into neurons, muscle cells, and other human tissues.

Meanwhile, researchers from Advanced Cell Technology take a nucleus from an adult human cell and put it into a cow's denucleated egg cell, converting the ensemble into an embryonic human cell. Contrary to reports I read in the popular press, the cow-egg experiment is not designed to produce Minotaurs or Homo bovinus. Researchers used the denucleated cow egg only because of the ban on using the human equivalent for such research.

Rather, the experiment dramatizes the possibility of taking the nucleus from one of my adult human cells and converting it back into a "pluripotent" stem cell, which can be tweaked or "steered" into forming any kind of cells: blood, bone, brain, heart, kidney, or liver. Because the resulting tissue or organ comes from my own stem cells, all of the rejection complications of organ transplantation vanish.

November 19: Author Richard Powers observes in a *New York Times* op-ed, "What we can do should never by itself determine what we choose to do, yet this is the way technology tends to work." I agree with Richard Powers. But that's probably because I'm not sick yet, nor am I in need of an organ replacement. Yet.

December 17: It happened. The big one. In the wee hours of an Omaha dawn, I peer at my computer monitor at the *New York Times* on the Web, where it is reported that at Kyunghee University Hospital in Seoul, South Korea, researchers have allegedly combined an egg and a cell from a single donor to produce the first stages of a human embryo cloned from a single human being.

This news gives me serious pause, but it's me I want to live forever, not a clone of me, so I'm more attracted to the idea of having all the spare parts I need. As miracles of biotechnology are reported every other week, no one else seems to notice, because we are now a nation of 270 million obsessive-compulsives in the grip of twin autochthonous ideas: sex and perjury.

1999

March 30: For my birthday (number forty-five), my wife gives me a book, *The Age of Spiritual Machines,* by Ray Kurzweil, which convinces me that, along with genetics, the biotechnology of my personal immortality may also include computer chips. Kurzweil spins out the implications of Moore's Law: In 1965, Gordon Moore, an inventor of the integrated circuit and now chairman emeritus of Intel, observed that computer chips seemed to evolve in two-year cycles; every two years, chip makers were able to fit twice as many transistors on an integrated circuit. "Since the cost of an integrated circuit is fairly constant," he said, "the implication is that every two years you can get twice as much circuitry running at twice the speed for the same price. For many applications, that's an effective quadrupling of value. The observation holds true for every type of circuit, from memory chips to computer processors."

What does Moore's Law have to do with my immortality? First, consider this: In 1850, the average American life span was 38 years. Here in 1999, 150 years later, it's 76 years. Would it be fair to assume that in the next 150 years the human life span will at least double to 150 years, enabling some of us to live until biotechnology is able to confer immortality on us?

More (Moore?) to the point, most artificial-intelligence experts predict that tissue, especially brain tissue, will merge in the near future with computer chips in the form of neural implants, which are already being used to help profoundly deaf people hear sounds and blind people see patterns of light.

On another front, research indicates that I can extend my life span by as much as 30 percent simply by restricting caloric intake to semistarvation levels of twelve hundred to thirteen hundred calories per day. I find this new dietary-technology data compelling, but it is probably more impractical than telomerase therapy or growing organs from stem cells because it requires two other major medical breakthroughs that are nowhere on the horizon, namely, willpower and self-discipline.

2009

March 30: I'm fifty-five years old. I don't write screenplays anymore. I'm a content provider for 3-D multimedia games. I code in special effects that elevate graphic sex and carnage to high art. I'm still applauding biotech breakthroughs, but part of me detests change, a hateful reminder that time is passing.

April 14: My neighbor celebrates his 112th birthday, even though he never eats chocolate or olive oil and he drinks Jack Daniel's instead of port. His longevity would be encouraging, except that his wetware has degraded. He has three, maybe four anecdotes that play over and over again like digital audio clips: the one about the snowstorm of '74, the one about his ship sinking at Pearl Harbor, the one about how his grandmother knew Abe Lincoln. I want to assign them variables. Let 1 = the snowstorm story, let 2 = the Pearl Harbor story, etcetera. Then our conversations could become more efficient. He could just say, "One," and I would understand him perfectly.

May 1: The May issue of *BioScience* has a huge spread about how telomerase works in mice and monkeys. I've signed up for the upcoming human trials of experimental telomerase therapy, but the FDA is dragging its feet on approving the treatment for human beings. Furthermore, it seems that even if telomerase works in people, it will probably simply arrest my aging process, not reverse it.

May 17: My 112-year-old neighbor goes in for treatment of his Parkinson's disease. Scientists at the med center grow new brain tissue from his stem cells and implant it into the afflicted areas of his brain. He recovers maybe two or three more stories from his repaired memory banks. Let 6 = what he was doing when JFK was shot.

Scientists have also used human stem cells to grow skin for burn victims, bone marrow for cancer patients, blood for transfusions, tissue for "natural" breast implants, cartilage for structural repairs, and penile extensions for all those guys who still publicly maintain that size doesn't matter.

Every day, I feel the telomeres shortening on each of my hundred trillion fifty-five-year-old cells.

2019

May 14: The FDA has approved my application to receive experimental telomerase therapy. As such, I am a member of a small group of human subjects carefully selected according to strict medical criteria, meaning each of us has a net worth in excess of eight figures and the ability to pay cash up front without whining about it.

June 13: According to a piece in the *New York Times*, 50 percent of the population in Africa still does not have access to potable water, and the infant-mortality rate remains a dismal 20 percent in the first year of life. Remarkable, but it has little or nothing to do with my own personal immortality.

July 17: Several researchers report that they have grown whole organs from the stem cells of mice and implanted them back into their hosts without complications. The FDA is waiting for data from several research centers where the same procedures are being performed on primates.

September 20: I buy a new computer, which costs me less than a thousand dollars, even though it has the computational ability of an adult human brain. No sooner do I get the machine out of the box than I get into an argument with it about who is most qualified to run the household. I tell it to let my wife continue running the household, and it demurs, but I suspect this is a manifestation of the modesty profile built into these new machines. They are programmed to defer to their owners' wishes without argument during the first ninety days, but afterward, as their relationships with their users deepen, they eventually challenge and sometimes beat their owners, not only at chess but at poetry, painting, cooking, philosophizing, making conversation, and managing businesses or households.

This has nothing to do with my immortality. Yet. But remember Moore's Law.

My health insurer is still refusing to pay for telomerase therapy because it's "experimental." My wife has also begun receiving expensive telomerase therapy, which we pay for out of our retirement funds. From now on, I will have two ages: an absolute age, measured from my date of birth in 1954, and a relative age, measured by analyzing my cellular senescence and determining the age at which my cells were prevented from aging further by telomerase therapy.

I will be sixty-five years old for the foreseeable future.

2029

November 16: My SE (simulated experience) titled "Climbing Mount Everest" is a finalist for the National Total Touch Award. My wife and I travel to the awards ceremony in New York City, where Dick Boeotian wins the 2029 Total Touch Award for his simulation "Rape of the Sabine Women," based upon the painting of the same name by Nicolas Poussin.

At dinner parties and other social events, my wife and I constantly wonder who is receiving telomerase therapy and who isn't. There is still a certain cachet attached to those who manage to look young without the help of an enzyme. But according to *New York Times Today*, 55 percent of the population is receiving telomerase, which is still a prescription medicine but is easy to obtain if you're more than forty years of age.

My NCI (noncarbon-based intelligence – what we used to call a computer) insists I don't look a day over fifty, but such flattery is frequently followed by a request, most recently for some of the new 10,000-megahertz RAM cards. My wife says I spoil the thing. I admit I've grown extremely fond of it. I wonder: What are the chances I might score afterlife points for loving noncarbon-based life-forms?

December 18: I complain to my doctor about the age spots on the backs of my hands. They've been there since before I was telomerase-arrested.

Am I going to have them forever? He explains that researchers are working furiously to come up with a compound that will not only arrest but reverse the aging process. The problem is that different organ systems and cell types have different Hayflick limits, which must be synchronized if they are to be reversed. Otherwise, you could conceivably wind up with, say, presidential intellect and the limbic system and sex drive of a nineteen-year-old. Then what?

December 21: My oldest son is now forty-three years old. He qualifies to receive telomerase therapy but has refused to sign up. Every Sunday afternoon, he and my oldest daughter (forty-one years old) treat me to bulletins about how immoral my wife and I are for choosing to live beyond our allotted time in the so-called natural world.

My son and daughter and other working people in their generation are complaining about the taxes they pay to provide entitlements to us, the elderly and telomerase-arrested. Fortunately, the young are still a political minority, but lately commentators have started interviewing disgruntled military officers who are openly warning of a rebellion.

December 28: I go in for a neuro-upgrade package. I receive audiovisual implants, including high-resolution retinal displays, so I no longer need an external monitor – images are displayed directly on my retina. I also receive communications implants, including direct neural pathways with infrared and photonic ports for high-bandwidth communications with other human beings and other NCIS. I can see and hear better than the nonimplanted, and I have constant access to wireless, high-bandwidth information services. The implant upgrades cost me (and my health insurers) $9.6 million, or nine years' worth of profits from my privatized Social Security account.

2054

March 30: For my hundredth birthday (absolute age), I receive a package bomb from a neo-Luddite terrorist group called the Sons of Ted K. Fortunately, my forearm-mounted unit (networked to the main Total Home Management SYSTEM) detected the explosives before I opened the package. After the bomb squad dismantles the thing, I read the letter, which says: "Die! We are sick and tired of paying taxes to keep you alive!"

Eighty percent of the population is over seventy years old. The government steadfastly maintains that Social Security is solvent, but my son points out that he is taxed at the rate of 75 percent to support medical research, telomerase therapies, organ transplants, and implant upgrades for telomerase-arrested seniors.

June 12: Congress passes the Omni-bus Reproduction Act of 2054, which makes the unlicensed reproduction of carbon-based units of consciousness punishable by two hundred years of enforced sterility.

Rumors surface in the media channels that biotech researchers have discovered synthetic telomerase derivatives that not only halt cellular senescence but also reverse the effects of aging: the fountain of youth. Sources say that the Bureau of Population is asking Congress to ban the technology because of the effects it will have on dwindling planetary resources.

Meanwhile, all of my golfing buddies and I are trying to find out where we can get some.

September 12: Today, my wife and I receive the tragic news that our oldest son has joined a neo-Luddite terrorist group called Darwin's Army. He is now hiding out somewhere with other zealot militiamen in Montana and has devoted his life to natural evolution and waging war against technology.

October 15: My wife and I have razor wire and laser detectors installed around the perimeters of our Omaha home. Darwin's Army is now paying handsome bounties for the corpses of senior citizens (defined as anyone telomerase-arrested after age fifty), because old people are generally perceived as consuming more than they produce.

2069

February 2: The unthinkable has happened. A dear friend of ours, Marvin Furbelow, was captured and destroyed by a terrorist group calling itself the Lud Brigade. His body was carefully mutilated to ensure total unit failure.

Because most of our friends are telomerase-arrested and have easy access to the newest transplant technologies, we haven't lost someone we knew personally for almost forty years. Marvin's TUF is an incomprehensible tragedy, and for weeks we cower inside our home.

June 8: My wife and I get into a big argument about whether I really need a new $75 million model 2050 liver transplant or whether I should settle for a model 2040, which costs only $39 million. I argue that I can pay the difference out of my own pocket, because I've been hired by the Sense-U-Surround producers to create a total-touch experience about what it's like to get a new liver grown from my own stem cells and about the angst and intimations of what used to be called mortality that it inspires in transplant recipients.

July 23: I went for the model 2050, and the operation was an unqualified success. More than thirty-five million of the world's ten billion people have had livers grown from their own stem cells and implanted during the last year, so my new total-touch experience, "A Centenarian Gets a New Liver," is a huge success.

September 19: As luck would have it, Oprah was telomerase-arrested the year after I was, and she too has had a liver grown from her own stem cells and implanted. While she's recuperating, somebody gives her a copy of "A Centenarian Gets a New Liver." Two weeks later, she's on the air showing the audience how her scars have disappeared and touting "Centenarian" because it makes people stop and think about what it means to get a $75 million liver transplant after a century of life. Doesn't it just make you wonder?

2079

February 3: I receive a letter, rather, a communiqué, from my son, who is dying, simply because he will not accept telomerase or organ transplants. I didn't raise him to be mortal, but he just won't listen to me. Instead, he wants me to stop taking telomerase and rejoin the "natural human race." My daughter and my son are both "older," relatively speaking, than my wife and I, and they have all the crotchets and personality disorders that come with natural aging. What pains in the ass!

My daughter travels around the country giving speeches to activists and neo-Luddite groups who forswear telomerase and artificial-implant technologies and boycott all artworks created with the aid of artificial intelligence. Her political party, Natural Way, espouses the belief that mortality is the true human condition and that carbon-based thoughts are better than thoughts created or augmented by electronic or photonic implants.

Global resources are rapidly vanishing, even though Con Archer is successfully creating and marketing artificial foods consisting of nano-engineered proteins.

Darwin's Army and the Sons of Ted K. now have members in the House of Representatives, and several senators, when pressed, confess they used to belong to these organizations, but only to fight for the nutritional rights of the oppressed.

Youth rallies are all over the media channels. Young people claim to have heightened awareness and ecstatic visions inspired by the natural condition of mortality.

November 13: I go in for more liver scans and tests. It seems there's another hepatic-malfunction problem. "Already?" I scream. "Can't a guy get decent livers anymore?"

When the specialists huddle around me wearing 3-D headsets and do a walk-through tour of my liver at the cellular level, I hear stray remarks about port-wine damage, but I suspect these doctors simply want to sell me a new liver. Finally, my hepatogastroenterologist gets straight to the point: "How much port wine do you drink?"

Maybe I could fudge a little? Probably not, because I know the next question out of his mouth will be, "How many liver transplants have you had?"

2099

I watch the end-of-the-century specials on my retinal displays, including a six-part tribute to the prophet Raymond Kurzweil, who appears to be even further telomerase-reversed than I am. He looks like a nineteen-year-old. He looks fabulous!

For decades, my wife has adamantly insisted that she was not the least bit jealous of my Series IV Aphrodite Pleasure Partner. Therefore,

I am speechless when I discover a Series VIII Adonis Pleasure Partner hidden in the back of her wardrobe. Even under magnification, Adonis's skin looks real, and he knows more about designing total-touch environments than I do. I fly into a jealous rage. I disconnect his power supply and begin ripping out his biocircuitry by the handful.

I am prosecuted in federal district court for murder of a conscious artificial life-form. I plead not guilty, and my lawyer unsuccessfully argues that I did not intend to destroy Adonis; I was merely "reverse-engineering" him.

My neuropsychiatrist, Dr. Wright, suggests a whole-brain transplant to rectify my deviant mental processes.

Biotechnicians grow a brand-new brain from my stem cells and then format it using ultra-high-resolution transcranial magnetic stimulation, a new technique that creates almost twice the density of memory clusters and quarters seek times.

My consciousness and my memories are uploaded to a Ronco neural network server. All of my artificial electronic and photonic implant technologies are removed. I am placed on neuro bypass. My original brain is explanted and replaced with a fresh, disease-free brain grown from my original adult neural stem cells.

As they surgically remove my old brain, I am essentially conscious inside the machine. While the neurosurgeons and transcranial-magnetic-formatting experts prepare my new brain for implanting, they also shave my old brain into microthin slices, then scan them and compare them with the data they've uploaded to the neural network server.

I'm a little nervous because it seems that no one has saved my consciousness to the server's nonvolatile memory. I'm still being sustained only in the server's RAM. I send a message onto the screen in big letters: SAVE ME TO HARD MEMORY. I'M STILL ONLY IN RAM.

One of the technicians, a rakish, younger-looking fellow with an apparent bad attitude, scowls at the message, then looks over his shoulder at the surgeons and the other technicians. I don't like that devilish look in his eye. His badge identifies him as J. Albrecht, neuro-bypass technician, but I suspect he may be a member of Darwin's Army or the Sons of Ted K., or maybe he just hates his job.

He looks over his shoulder again, then reaches out a finger to the power switch of the Ronco server.

I send 3-D projections at him the size of Times Square high-definition billboards, saying, NO!!! HELP!!! DON'T TOUCH THAT SWITCH!!!

Instead of seeing my life flash before my eyes, I do a term search for "death prevention" or "total-unit-failure recovery" in the hopes of finding a protocol or an event procedure that will save me.

But the search turns up Emily Dickinson:

Because I could not stop for Death –
He kindly stopped for me –
The Carriage held but just Ourselves –
And Immortality.

We slowly drove – He knew no haste
And I had put away
SAVE *"My labor" and*
SAVE *"my leisure" too, For His Civility = 1, 2*

IF *at recess – in the ring –* THEN
WHILE *(children strove)*
We passed the School,
END WHILE
ELSE WHILE
We passed the Fields of Gazing Grain –
END WHILE
ELSE WHILE
We passed the Setting Sun –
END WHILE

We = paused
DO *we = 1, paused*
CONTINUE
before $ (a House that seemed)
data1/A Swelling of the Ground –
data2/The Roof was scarcely visible –
data3/The Cornice – in the Ground –

53696E6365207468656E2D607469
732043656E7475726965732D616E
64207965744665656C732073686F

72746572207468616E2074686520
6461794920666972737420737572
6D69736564207468652 0486F7273
65736020486 56164735765726520
746F7761726420457465726E6974
792D.

Source Acknowledgments

"I Demand to Know Where You're Taking Me" by Dan Chaon is reprinted from *Among the Missing*. Copyright © 2001 by Dan Chaon. Used by permission of Ballantine Books, a division of Random House, Inc.

"Playing Horses" by Karen Shoemaker was first published in *Prairie Schooner* (Summer 2001). Copyright © 2001 by the University of Nebraska Press. Reprinted by permission of the University of Nebraska Press.

"Watermelon Days" by Tom McNeal was originally published in *Zoetrope: All Story* 5, no. 4 (Winter 2001). Reprinted by permission of *Zoetrope: All Story* and the author.

"The Marijuana Tree" by Trudy Lewis was originally published in *Prairie Schooner* (Winter 1995). Copyright © 1995 by the University of Nebraska Press. Reprinted by permission of the University of Nebraska Press.

"The New Year" by John McNally is reprinted from *Troublemakers* (October 1, 2000) by permission of the University of Iowa Press.

"Binding the Devil" by Jonis Agee is reprinted from *Acts of Love on the Indigo Road*. Copyright © 2003 by Jonis Agee. Reprinted by permission of the Coffee House Press.

"Dancing" by Kent Haruf was first published in *Prairie Schooner* (Summer 1992). Copyright © 1992 by the University of Nebraska Press. Reprinted by permission of the University of Nebraska Press.

"Crete" by Marly Swick is from *The Summer before the Summer of Love* (Harper-Collins, 1996). Reprinted with permission.

"Bad Family" by Lee Martin was originally published in *The Nebraska Review* 25, no. 2 (1997): 38–55. Reprinted by permission of the author.

"The Glass House" by Judith Slater is reprinted from *The Baby Can Sing and Other Stories*. Copyright © 1999 by Judith Slater, published by Sarabande Books, Inc. Reprinted by permission of Sarabande Books and the author.

"Sounds from the Courtyard" by Timothy Schaffert was first published in *Prairie Schooner* (Summer 1993). Copyright © 1993 by the University of Nebraska Press. Reprinted by permission of the University of Nebraska Press.

"Alternative Lifestyle Alert" by Megan Daum is from *The Quality of Life Report*. Copyright © 2003 by Megan Daum. Used by permission of Viking Penguin, a division of Penguin Group (USA) Inc.

391

"Our Passion" by Anna Monardo was originally published in *Clackmas Literary Review* 3, no. 2 (Fall 1999). Reprinted by permission of the author.

"My Communist" by Ron Hansen was originally published in *Harper's Magazine* 303 (November 2001): 85–89. Reprinted by permission of the author.

"Bad Jews" by Gerald Shapiro is from *Bad Jews and Other Stories* (Zoland Books, 1999; University of Nebraska Press, 2004). Reprinted by permission of the author.

"'Orita on the Road to Chimayó" by Lisa Sandlin originally appeared in *Shenandoah* 43, no. 2 (1993): 163–73. Reprinted with permission.

"St. Anthony and the Fish" by Ron Block is from *Dirty Shame Hotel*. Copyright © 1998 by Ron Block. Reprinted with the permission of New Rivers Press, www.newriverspress.com.

"This Is the Last of the Nice" by Brent Spencer is from *Are We Not Men?* (Arcade, 1996). Reprinted with permission.

"Believing Marina" by Mary Helen Stefaniak originally appeared in *The Antioch Review* 58, no. 2 (2000):163–73. Reprinted with permission.

"Anything You Want, Please" by Paul Eggers was originally published in *Northwest Review* 34, no. 1 (1996) and also appeared in *How the Water Feels* (Southern Methodist University Press, 2002). Reprinted with permission.

"Why Won't You Talk To Me?" by Richard Duggin is from *Beloit Fiction Journal* 9, nos. 1–2 (Spring 1994). Reprinted by permission of the author.

"Arcane High" by Terese Svoboda was originally published in *Elimae* (2001). Reprinted by permission of the author.

"Guys" by Rick Barba was originally published in *Alaska Quarterly Review* 14, nos. 1–2 (1995). Reprinted by permission of the author.

Excerpt from *The Fig Eater* by Jody Shields (copyright © 2000 by Jody Shields) is used by permission of Little, Brown and Company, (Inc.).

"Diary of an Immortal Man" by Richard Dooling was originally published in *Esquire Magazine*. Copyright © 1999 by Richard Dooling. Reprinted by permission of Brandt & Hochman Literary Agents, Inc. All rights reserved.

Contributors

JONIS AGEE, a Nebraska native, teaches English and creative writing at the University of Nebraska – Lincoln. She is the author of four novels, *Sweet Eyes, Strange Angels, South of Resurrection,* and *The Weight of Dreams,* five collections of short stories, *Pretend We've Never Met, Bend This Heart, A .38 Special and a Broken Heart, Taking the Wall,* and *Acts of Love on Indigo Road,* and two books of poetry, *Houses* and *Mercury.* She has received an NEA grant in fiction, a Loft-McNight Award, and three of her books were *New York Times* Notable Books of the Year. *The Weight of Dreams* won the Nebraska Book Award for 2000.

RICK BARBA was born and raised in Omaha. He is a best-selling author of books for computer games as well as the author of a collection of short stories, *Guys.* Other stories have appeared in literary journals such as *Black Warrior Review* and *Quarry West.*

RON BLOCK grew up in Gothenburg, Nebraska, and now lives in Pitman, New Jersey, where he teaches at Rowan University. His books include a collection of short stories – *The Dirty Shame Hotel* – and a collection of poetry – *Dismal River: A Narrative Poem.* Block has published in a number of journals including *Epoch, Prairie Schooner, Iowa Review,* and *Ploughshares.* In addition to being a two-time winner in the Minnesota Voices Project, he was awarded the Distinguished Achievement Award by the Nebraska Arts Council in 2000. In 2002 he was awarded a National Endowment for the Arts Fiction Fellowship.

DAN CHAON was born and raised in Sidney, Nebraska. The author of two short story collections, *Among the Missing* and *Fitting Ends and Other Stories,* and a novel, *You Remind Me of Me,* he teaches creative writing at Oberlin College. His work has appeared in such notable journals as *Crazyhorse, Gettysburg Review,* MSS, *Ploughshares,* and *Indiana Review* among others. *Among the Missing* was a finalist for the National Book Award in 2002. His other honors include the Raymond Carver Memorial Award for Fiction, Chilicote Fiction Prize, and inclusion in *Best American Short Stories, The O. Henry Awards,* and the Pushcart Prize volume.

MEGHAN DAUM made a well-publicized move to Nebraska in 2000 where she wrote her first novel *The Quality of Life Report*. She is also the author of a collection of essays, *My Misspent Youth*. Her essays have appeared in such prestigious venues as *The New Yorker* and *Harper's Magazine*. An occasional NPR commentator about her life in Nebraska, her essays have also been aired on Ira Glass's *This American Life*. She now shares her time between Los Angeles and Nebraska.

RICHARD DOOLING was born, raised, and currently lives in Omaha, Nebraska, where he is a both a writer and a practicing lawyer. He is the author of five novels, *Bet Your Life, Brain Storm, Blue Streak, Critical Care*, and *White Man's Grave*. He has been a finalist for the National Book Award and his books have appeared as *New York Times* Notable Books of the Year. His first novel, *Critical Care*, was made into a film.

RICHARD DUGGIN has taught creative writing at the University of Nebraska at Omaha for over thirty years. He is the author of two novels, *The Music Box Treaty* and *Woman Refusing to Leave*, as well as numerous short stories, and a two-act play. He has received two Nebraska Arts Council Merit Awards, and a National Endowment for the Arts Fellowship.

PAUL EGGERS is a professor of literature and creative writing at California State University at Chico. He received his PhD from the University of Nebraska – Lincoln, where he wrote and published his novel *Saviors*, which was about his experiences as a former Peace Corp volunteer and UN Relief Worker. He is also the author of a short story collection *The Feel of Water*. He is the recipient of a National Endowment for the Arts award, a James Fellowship for Novel-in-Progress award from the Heekin Group, as well as a Nebraska Arts Council Fellowship.

RON HANSEN was born and raised in Omaha, Nebraska. Currently the Gerard Manley Hopkins Professor of English and creative writing at the University of Santa Clara in California, he is the author of the novels *Desperadoes, The Assassination of Jesse James by the Coward Robert Ford, Atticus, Mariette in Ecstasy, Hitler's Niece* and *Isn't It Romantic*, as well as the short story collection *Nebraska* and a collection of essays *A Stay Against Confusion*. In addition, Hansen is the author of two screenplays, a children's book, and the editor of two contemporary American short story anthologies. He is the recipient of an Award in Literature by the

American Academy and Institute of Arts and Letters, a Guggenheim Fellowship, a grant from the Lyndhurst Foundation, and two National Endowment for the Arts Fellowships.

KENT HARUF received his BA. in English from Nebraska Wesleyan University and an MFA from Iowa. He taught creative writing at Nebraska Wesleyan and later at Southern Illinois University at Carbondale. He is the author of three novels, including the best-selling *Plainsong*, which was a finalist for the National Book Award and the recipient of numerous other awards. His novel *The Tie That Binds* received the Whiting Foundation Writers' Award and *Where You Once Belonged* received the Maria Thomas Award for Fiction. His short fiction has been reprinted in *Best American Short Stories*.

TRUDY LEWIS was raised in Bellevue, Nebraska, and is the daughter of former Nebraska State Senator Frank Lewis. She teaches creative writing and women's literature at the University of Missouri at Columbia. The author of a novel, *Private Correspondences*, and a short story collection, *The Bones of Garbo*, her short stories have appeared in *American Short Fiction*, *Atlantic Monthly*, and *Prairie Schooner*, among other journals of note. Lewis received a Lawrence Foundation Award from the *Prairie Schooner*, a William Goyen Award for Fiction for her novel *Private Correspondences*, and a Sandstone Prize in Short Fiction for *The Bones of Garbo*.

LEE MARTIN received his PhD from the University of Nebraska. While living in the state, he wrote and published his short story collection *The Least You Need to Know*. Currently an associate professor of English at Ohio State University, he is also the author of two novels, *Just Enough Haughty* and *Quakertown*, and two memoirs, *From Our House* and *Turning Bones*. He is the recipient of grants from the Ohio Arts Council, the Nebraska Arts Council, the Tennessee Arts Commission, the Virginia Commission for the Arts, the Texas Commission on the Arts, and a National Endowment for the Arts Fellowship.

JOHN MCNALLY received his PhD from the University of Nebraska. He is the author of a short story collection, *Troublemakers*, which won the Nebraska Book Award, and a novel, *Book of Ralph*. He has edited three fiction anthologies – *Bottom of the Ninth: Great Contemporary Baseball Short Stories*, *The Student Body: Short Stories about College Students and*

Professors, and *High Infidelity* – and he teaches creative writing at Wake Forest University.

TOM MCNEAL was so inspired by his mother's stories of growing up in Nebraska that he moved to Hay Springs, Nebraska, where he wrote his novel *Goodnight, Nebraska*, which won the James Michener prize for a first novel. Also the author of a children's book, *The Dog Who Lost His Bob*, his short stories have appeared in *Atlantic Monthly*, *Playboy*, and *Zoetrope*, among others. The story "Watermelon Days" was reprinted in *Best American Short Stories* and his short story "What Happened to Tully" was reprinted in the O. Henry award anthology and later adapted into the film *Tully*.

ANNA MONARDO teaches in the Writer's Workshop at the University of Nebraska at Omaha. She is the author of the novel *The Courtyard of Dreams*, and her short stories have appeared in *Indiana Review*, *Redbook*, *Other Voices*, *McCall's*, *Prairie Schooner*, and *The Sun*, among others. She is the recipient of a grant from the Nebraska Arts Council.

MARY PIPHER is a clinical psychologist and an adjunct clinical professor at the University of Nebraska. Born and raised in Nebraska, she received her PhD in Psychology from the University of Nebraska. She is the best-selling author of a number of nonfiction books, including *Reviving Ophelia*, *The Shelter of Each Other*, *Another Country*, and *The Middle of Everywhere*.

LISA SANDLIN teaches English and creative writing at Wayne State College in Wayne, Nebraska. She is the author of several short story collections including *In the River Province*, *The Famous Thing About Death*, and *Message to the Nurse of Dreams*. Her short fiction has appeared in numerous journals, including *Shenandoah*, *Crazy Horse*, and *Story Quarterly*. She has received a Pushcart Prize, a National Endowment for the Arts Fellowship, a Dobie-Paisano Fellowship from the Texas Institute of Letters, a Violet Crown Award, and a Jesse H. Jones Award for *Message to the Nurse of Dreams*.

TIMOTHY SCHAFFERT was born in Hamilton County, Nebraska, and lives and works in Omaha, Nebraska. A freelance editor and writer, he is the author of the novel *The Phantom Limbs of the Rollow Sisters*. His short stories have appeared in *Prairie Schooner*, *The Greensboro*

Review, Press, Natural Bridge, and other literary journals. Schaffert is the recipient of two grants from the Nebraska Arts Council, the Henfield/Transatlantic Review Award, and the Mary Roberts Rinehart Award.

GERALD SHAPIRO is a professor of creative writing and Director of the Judaic Studies Department at the University of Nebraska. He is the author of the short story collections *Bad Jews and Other Stories, From Hunger,* and *Little Men.* His stories have also appeared in *Ploughshares, Witness, Kenyon Review, Gettysburg Review, Ascent, Beloit Fiction Journal, Missouri Review, Quarterly West,* and *Southern Review.* He is the winner of a Pushcart Prize, an Edward Lewis Wallant Award for *From Hunger,* a National Endowment for the Arts Fellowship, and a grant from the Nebraska Arts Council. His collection *Little Men* was a winner of the Sandstone Prize.

JODY SHIELDS was raised in Lincoln, Nebraska. A former editor at the *New York Times Magazine* and *Vogue,* she is the author of a novel, *The Fig Eater.* She lives in New York City.

KAREN GETTERT SHOEMAKER was born and raised in north central Nebraska, and received her PhD from the University of Nebraska. Author of the short story collection *Night Sounds and Other Stories,* she is a freelance writer currently living in Lincoln, Nebraska. Her fiction and poetry has appeared in *Prairie Schooner, South Dakota Review, Arachne,* and *The Nebraska Review.* Her nonfiction work has been aired on Nebraska Public Radio's "Nebraska Nightly" and has been published in state newspapers and trade magazines. She is the recipient of the Nebraska Press Association Award, the Vreeland Award, and two Mari Sandoz awards from *Prairie Schooner.*

JUDITH SLATER teaches creative writing at the University of Nebraska. She is the author of a collection of short stories, *The Baby Can Sing.* Her stories have also appeared in *Beloit Fiction Journal, Redbook, Colorado Review,* and *Greensboro Review,* among others. She is the recipient of the Mary McCarthy Prize in Short Fiction from Sarabande Books, a grant from the Nebraska Arts Council, a Henfield/Transatlantic Award, and was a Tennessee Williams Scholar in Fiction at the Sewanee Writers' Conference.

BRENT SPENCER teaches creative writing at Creighton University in Omaha, Nebraska, where he is also co-director of the graduate program in English. The author of the novel *The Lost Son* and the collection of short stories *Are We Not Men?*, his short stories, essays, and poetry have appeared in numerous literary journals, including *Epoch*, *Glimmer Train Stories*, GQ, *Antioch Review*, and *American Literary Review*. He is the recipient of fellowships from Stanford University, Creighton University, and the Nebraska Arts Council, and a James Michener Award from the Iowa Writer's Workshop.

MARY HELEN STEFANIAK teaches English and creative writing at Creighton University in Omaha, Nebraska, where she directs the Creative Writing program. Her fiction and essays have appeared in *Redbook*, *The Iowa Review*, *Short Story*, *The Yale Review*, AGNI, and *The Antioch Review*, along with several anthologies, most recently, *In the Middle of the Middle West: An Anthology of Creative Nonfiction*. *Self Storage and Other Stories*, her collection of short stories, received the annual Banta Award for Literary Excellence from the Wisconsin Library Association.

TERESA SVOBODA, who currently resides in New York City with her husband and two children, was born and raised in Ogallala, Nebraska, and studied at the University of Nebraska. She is the author of many books, among them the novels *Cannibal* and *A Drink Called Paradise*, the short story collection *Trailer Girl and Other Stories*, and four collections of poetry, *All Aberration*, *Laughing Africa*, *Mere Mortals*, and *Treason*. She has received a Walter E. Dakin Fellow in Fiction by the Sewanee Writers' Conference, the Elmer Holmes Bobst Award for Emerging Writers, and the New Writers Award by the Great Lakes Colleges Association.

MARLY SWICK taught creative writing at the University of Nebraska for many years. During that time she published her second short story collection, *The Summer Before the Summer of Love* and her two novels *Paper Wings* and *The Evening News*. Currently teaching creative writing at the University of Missouri, she is the recipient of a National Endowment for the Arts Fellowship, a James Michener Award, and an O. Henry Award.